’TIS THE SEASON

REGENCY YULETIDE SHORT STORIES

JENNIFER ASHLEY GRACE BURROWES
CHRISTI CALDWELL LOUISA CORNELL
EVA DEVON JANNA MACGREGOR
JESS MICHAELS

'Tis the Season: Regency Yuletide Short Stories

The characters and events portrayed in this book are fictitious. Any similarity to real persons, living or dead, is purely coincidental and not intended by the author.

CONTENTS

A FIRST-FOOTER FOR LADY JANE

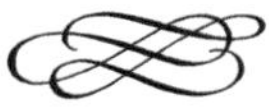

JENNIFER ASHLEY

CHAPTER 1

Berkshire, December 31, 1810

"You know precisely whom I will marry, Grandfather. You tease me to enjoy yourself, but all the games in the world will not change that Major Barnett will someday be my husband."

As she spoke, Lady Jane Randolph regarded her grandfather in half amusement, half exasperation. Grandfather MacDonald sprawled in his chair by the fire in the small drawing room in Jane's father's manor house, his blankets in disarray. Grandfather always occupied the warmest place in a room, in deference to his old bones, but he was not one for sitting still.

His lined face held its usual mirth, his blue eyes twinkling. Grandfather MacDonald liked to hint and joke, pretending a connection to the Scottish witches from Macbeth, who, he said, had given him second sight.

"What I say is true, lass." Grandfather fluttered his hands, broad and blunt, which her grandmother, rest her soul, had claimed could brandish a strong sword and then pick out a tune on the harpsichord with such liveliness one could not help but dance. Indeed,

Grandfather often sat of an evening at the pianoforte, coaxing rollicking music from it.

Grandfather had been quite a dancer as well, Grandmother had said, and every young woman had vied for a chance to stand up with the swain. When Hamish MacDonald had first cast his eyes upon her, Grandmother had wanted to swoon, but of course she'd never, ever admitted this to him.

"Mark my words," Grandfather went on. "At Hogmanay, the First-Footer over the threshold will marry the most eligible daughter of the house. Hogmanay begins at midnight, and the most eligible young lady in *this* house is you."

"Perhaps." Jane returned to her embroidery, a task she was not fond of. "But you know I already have an agreement with John. No First-Footer need bother with me. There will be other young ladies —Mama and Papa have invited all their acquaintance."

"But you are not yet engaged." Grandfather's eyes sparkled with a wicked light seventy years hadn't dimmed. "No announcement in the newspapers, no date for the happy event, no ring on your finger."

"There is the small matter of war with France." Jane had marred the pattern in her embroidery, she noticed, an inch back. Sighing in annoyance, she picked out the thread. "Major Barnett is a bit busy on the Peninsula just now. When Bonaparte is defeated, there will be plenty of time for happy events."

Silence met her. Jane looked up from repairing her mistake to find her grandfather glaring at her, his joviality gone.

"Am I hearing ye right?" he demanded. "Ye're discussing your nuptials like ye would decide which field to plant out in the spring. In my day, lassie, we seized the hand of the one who struck our fancy and made sure we hung on to them for life. Didn't matter how many wars we were fighting at the time, and when I was a lad, Highland Scots were being hunted down if we so much as picked up a plaid or spoke our native tongue. Didn't stop Maggie and me running off together, did it?"

Grandfather adored going on about his wild days in the heather, how he and Grandmother never let anything stand in the way of their great passion.

Times had changed, Jane reflected with regret. The war with Napoleon dragged on, the constant worry that France would invade these shores hovering like a distant and evil thunderstorm. She and John must wait until things were resolved—when John came home for good, there would be time enough to make plans for their life together.

The thought that John might never return, that a French artillery shell might end his life, or a bayonet pierce his heart, sent a sudden chill through her.

Jane shuddered and drew a veil over the images. There was no sense in worrying.

She missed another stitch and set the embroidery firmly aside. Grandfather could be most distracting.

"John is in Portugal," she reminded him. "Not likely to be our First-Footer tonight. But someday, perhaps."

"Course he's not likely to be the First-Footer." Grandfather scowled at Jane as though she'd gone simple. "He's a fair-haired man, ain't he? First-Footer needs to be dark. Everyone knows that."

"YOUR BETROTHED LIVES *HERE*?" CAPTAIN SPENCER INGRAM SHOOK snow from his hat as he climbed from the chaise and gazed at the gabled, rambling, half-timbered monstrosity before him, a holdover from the dark days of knights and bloodthirsty kings.

"Not betrothed," Barnett said quickly. "A childhood understanding. Will lead to an engagement in due time. Probably. Always been that way."

Barnett did not sound as enthusiastic as a man coming home to visit his childhood sweetheart might. Spencer studied his friend, but Barnett's ingenuous face was unconcerned.

Though it was near midnight, every window in the house was lit, and a bonfire leapt high in the night in the fields beyond. Spencer would have preferred wandering to the bonfire, sharing a dram or tankard with villagers no doubt having a dance and a fine time.

The house looked cozy enough, despite its ancient architecture. Lights glowed behind the thick glass windows, welcoming on the frigid evening. The snow was dry and dusty, the night so frozen that no cloud marred the sky. Every star was visible, the carpet of them stretching to infinity. Even better than the bonfire would be a place on the roof and a spyglass through which to gaze at the heavens.

A pair of footmen darted out to seize bags from the compartment in the back of the chaise. Both valises were small, in keeping with soldiers who'd learned to travel with little.

The chaise rattled off toward the stable yard, the driver ready for warmth and a drink. The footmen scurried into the house and disappeared, the front door swinging shut behind them.

Spencer leapt forward to grab the door, but it clanged closed before he reached it.

"What the devil?" Spencer rattled the handle, but the door was now locked. "I call this a poor welcome."

To his surprise, Barnett chuckled. "Lady Jane's family keeps Scots traditions. A visitor arriving after midnight on New Year's—no, we must call it Hogmanay to follow their quaint customs. A visitor arriving after midnight on Hogmanay needs to beg admission, and must bring gifts. I have them here." He held up a canvas sack. "Salt, coal, whisky, shortbread, and black bun."

"Black what?"

"Black bun. A cake of fruit soaked in whisky. It is not bad fare. I obtained the cake from a Scotswoman—the landlord's wife at our accommodations when we first landed."

Spencer had wondered why Barnett insisted on traveling to that inn, well out of the way, the venture taking precious time.

Barnett grinned. "The whole rigmarole is to prove we aren't Norsemen come to pillage the family. 'Tis greatly entertaining, is it not?"

Spencer had other ideas of entertainment. "We stand shivering outside while they decide whether to admit us? There is a good bonfire yonder." He gestured to the fire leaping high in the fields, shadows of revelers around it.

"They'll be waiting just inside. You will see."

Barnett stepped up to the door the footmen had all but slammed in their faces and hammered on it.

"Open, good neighbors. Give us succor." Barnett shot Spencer a merry look. "We must enter into the spirit of the thing."

Spencer heard the bolts rattling, and then the door opened a sliver. "Who is there?" a creaky, elderly man's voice intoned.

"Admit us, good sir." Barnett held the sack aloft. "We bear gifts."

The door opened wider to show a wizened, bent man wrapped in what looked like a long shawl. Spencer sensed several people hovering behind him.

"Then come in, come in. Out of the cold." The man added something in the Scots language Spencer didn't understand and swung the door open.

Barnett started forward, then stopped himself. "No, indeed. You must lead, Spence. A tall, dark-haired man brings the best luck."

He stepped out of the way and more or less shoved Spencer toward the door. Spencer removed his hat and stepped deferentially into the foyer.

Warmth surrounded him, and light. In the silence, he heard a sharp intake of breath.

Beyond the old Scotsman in his plaid shawl, in the doorway to a room beyond, stood a young woman. She was rather tall, but curved, not willowy. Her hair was so dark it was almost black, her eyes, in contrast, a startling blue, like lapis lazuli. They matched the eyes of the old man, but Spencer could no longer see him.

The vision of beauty, in a silk and net gown of shimmering silver, regarded him in alarm but also in wonder.

"Well met, all 'round," Barnett was saying. "Spence, let me introduce you to Lord and Lady Merrickson—the house you are standing in is theirs. Mr. MacDonald, Lady Merrickson's father, and of course, this angel of perfection is Lady Jane Randolph, Lord Merrickson's only daughter and the correspondent that keeps me at ease during the chaos of army life. Lady Jane, may I present Captain Spencer Ingram, the dearest friend a chap could imagine. He saved my life once, you know."

Lady Jane came forward, gliding like a ghost on the wind. Spencer took her hand. Her eyes never left his as he bowed to her, and her lips remained parted with her initial gasp.

Spencer looked at her, and was lost.

CHAPTER 2

Captain Ingram fixed Jane with eyes as gray as winter and as cool, and she couldn't catch her breath. A spark lay deep within those eyes, gleaming like a sunbeam on a flow of ice.

He was not a cold man, though, she knew at once. He was containing his warmth, his animation, being polite. Of course he was—he'd been dragged here by John, likely expecting an ordinary English family at Christmas, only to be thrust into the midst of eccentric Randolphs and MacDonalds.

Jane forced her limbs into a curtsey. "Good evening, Captain Ingram," she said woodenly.

Captain Ingram jerked his gaze to her hand, which he still held, Jane's fingers swallowed by his large gloved ones. Ingram abruptly released her, a bit rudely, she thought, but Jane was too agitated to be annoyed.

"Greet him properly, Jane," Grandfather said. He pushed his way forward, leaning on his stout ash stick, and gave Captain Ingram a nod. "You know how."

Jane swallowed, her jaw tight, and repeated the words Grandfather had taught her years ago. "Welcome, First-Footer. Please partake of our hospitality."

Why was she so unnerved? Grandfather couldn't possibly have predicted that John would step back and let his friend enter the house first, in spite of their conversation earlier today. Grandfather didn't truly have second sight—he only pretended.

Captain Ingram's presence meant nothing, absolutely nothing. After the war, John would propose to Jane, as expected, and life would carry on.

Then why had her heart leapt when she'd beheld Captain Ingram's tall form, why had a sense of gladness and even relief flowed over her? For one instant, she'd believed Grandfather's prediction, and she'd been ... *happy?*

A mad streak ran in Jane's mother's family—or so people said. It was why Grandfather MacDonald spouted the odd things he did, why her mother, a genteel but poor Scotswoman, had been able to ensnare the wealthy Earl of Merrickson, a sought-after bachelor in his younger days. Jane's mother had enchanted him, people said, with her dark hair and intense blue eyes of the inhabitants of the Western Isles. So far, her daughter and son had not yet exhibited the madness of the MacDonald side of the family, thankfully.

Only because Jane, for her part, had learned to hide it, she realized. Given the chance, she'd happily race through the heather in a plaid or dance around a bonfire like the ones the villagers had built tonight. And feel strange glee at the thought she might not marry John after all.

John, oblivious to all tension, hefted a cloth sack. "I've brought the things you told me to, Mr. MacDonald."

"Excellent," Grandfather said. "Jane, take the bag and lay out the treasures in the dining room."

Jane's cousins surged to her. They were the carefree Randolph boys, from her father's side of the family. The three lads, ranging from sixteen to twenty-two, fancied themselves men about town and Corinthians, well pleased that Jane's brother, who was spending New Year's with his wife's family, stood between themselves and the responsibility of the earldom. In truth, they were harmless, though mischievous.

"Come, come, come, Cousin Jane," the youngest, Thomas, sang as they led the way to the dining room.

Jane took the bag from John, trying to pay no attention to Captain Ingram, who had not stepped away from her. "How are you, John? How very astonishing to see you."

John winked at her. He had blue eyes and light blond hair, the very picture of an English gentleman. "Amazing to me when we got leave, wasn't it, Spence? Thought I'd surprise you, Janie. Worked, didn't it? You look pole-axed."

Jane clutched the bag to her chest, finding it difficult to form words. "I beg your pardon. I am shocked, is all. Did not expect you."

John sent Captain Ingram a grin. "*I beg your pardon,* she says, all prim and proper. She didn't used to be so. You ought to have seen her running bare-legged through the meadows, screaming like a savage with me, her brother, and her cousins."

Jane went hot. "When I was seven."

"And eight, and nine, and ten ... until you were seventeen, I imagine. How old are you now, Janie? I've forgotten."

"Twenty," Jane said with dignity.

"Mind your tongue, Barnett," Captain Ingram broke in with a scowl. "Lady Jane might forgive your ill-mannered question, as our journey was long and arduous, but I would not blame her if she did not. Allow me to carry that for you, my lady."

He reached for the bag, which Jane relinquished, it being rather heavy, and strode with it into the dining room where the rest of the family had streamed.

"He's gallant that way," John said without rancor. "I knew you'd approve of him. You've grown very pretty, Jane."

"Thank you," Jane said, awkward. "You've grown very frank."

"That's the army for you. You enter a stiff and callow youth and emerge a hot-blooded and crude man. I crave pardon for my jokes. Have I upset you?"

"No, indeed," she said quickly.

In truth, Jane wasn't certain. John was changed—he had been, as he said, stiff and overly polite when he'd come out of university and taken a commission in the army. This grinning buffoon was more like the boy she'd known in her youth.

John offered her his arm. "Shall we?"

Jane acquiesced, and John propelled her into the dining room. The cousins had already emptied the sack and now sifted through its contents with much hilarity.

"A lump of coal—that's for you, Thomas." His oldest brother threw it at him, and Thomas caught it good-naturedly.

"Excellent fielding," John said. "Do you all still play cricket?"

"We do," Thomas said, and the cousins went off on a long aside about cricket games past and present.

Lord Merrickson roared at them to cease, though without rancor. Lady Merrickson greeted John and Captain Ingram with a warm smile. John took on the cross-eyed, smitten look he always wore in front of Jane's mother. Jane did not believe him in love with her mother, exactly, but awed by her. Many gentlemen were.

Captain Ingram, on the other hand, was deferential and polite to Lady Merrickson, as was her due, but nothing more.

As Ingram moved back to Jane, she noted that his greatcoat was gone—taken by one of the footmen. His uniform beneath, the deep blue of a cavalryman, held the warmth of his body.

He leaned to her. "Do they ever let you insert a word?" he asked quietly.

Jane tried not to shiver at his voice's low rumble. "On occasion," she said. "I play a fine game of cricket myself. Or used to. As John said, I am much too prim and proper now."

"No, she ain't," the middle Randolph cousin, Marcus, proclaimed. "Just this summer she hiked up her petticoats and took up the bat."

"A pity I missed it," John said loudly. "We ought to scare up a team of ladies at camp, Ingram. Officers wives versus …"

Marcus and Thomas burst out laughing, and the oldest cousin, Digby, looked aghast. "I say, old chap. Not in front of Jane."

"Your pardon, Jane." John looked anything but sorry. He was unusually merry tonight. Perhaps he'd imbibed a quantity of brandy to stave off the cold of the journey.

"I am not offended," Jane answered. "But my mother might be."

Lady Merrickson was not at all, Jane knew, but the admonition made John flush. "Er ..." he spluttered.

"Whisky!" Digby snatched up the bottle and held it high. "Thank you, John. All is forgiven. Marcus, fetch the glasses. Mr. MacDonald, the black bun is for you, I think."

Grandfather snatched up the cake wrapped in muslin and held it to his nose. "A fine one. Like me old mum used to bake."

Grandfather's "old mum" had a cook to do her baking, so Jane had been told. His family had lived well in the Highlands before the '45.

Outside, the piper Grandfather had hired began to drone, the noise of the pipes wrapping around the house.

"What the devil is *that*?" John demanded.

"I believe they are bagpipes," Captain Ingram said. His mild tone made Jane want to laugh. "You have heard them in the Highland regiments."

"Not like that. Phew, what a racket."

Grandfather scowled at him. "Ye wouldn't know good piping from a frog croaking, lad. There are fiddlers and drummers waiting in the ballroom. Off we go."

The cousins, with whisky and glasses, pounded out of the dining room and along the hall to the ballroom in the back of the house. John escorted Jane, hurrying her to the entertainment, while Captain Ingram politely walked with Grandfather. The terrace windows in the ballroom framed the bonfires burning merrily a mile or so away.

Three musicians waited, two with fiddles, one with a drum. They struck up a Scottish tune as the family entered, blending with the piper outside.

Guest who'd been staying at the house and those arriving now that the First-Footer ritual was done swarmed around them. They were neighbors and old friends of the family, and soon laughter and chatter filled the room.

Grandfather spoke a few moments with Captain Ingram, then he threw off his shawl and cane and jigged to the drums and fiddles, cheered on by Jane's cousins and John. Ingram, politely accepting a whisky Digby had thrust at him, watched with interest.

"I am not certain this was the welcome you expected," Jane said when she drifted near him again.

"It will do." Ingram looked down at her, his gray eyes holding fire. "Is every New Year like this for you?"

"I am afraid so," Jane answered. "Grandfather insists."

"He enjoys it, I'd say."

Grandfather kicked up his heels, a move that made him totter, but young Thomas caught him, and the two locked arms and whirled away.

"He does indeed." Some considered Jane's grandfather a foolish old man, but he had more life in him than many insipid young aristocrats she met during the London Season.

The music changed to that of a country dance, and couples formed into lines, ladies facing gentlemen. John immediately went to a young lady who was the daughter of Jane's family's oldest friends and led her out.

"Lady Jane?" Ingram offered his arm. "I am an indifferent dancer, but I will make the attempt."

Jane did not like the way her heart fluttered at the sight of Captain Ingram's hard arm, outlined by the tight sleeve of his coat. Jane was as good as betrothed—she should not have to worry about her heart fluttering again.

Out of nowhere, Jane felt cheated. Grandfather's stories of his courtship with her grandmother, filled with passion and romance, flitted through her mind. The two had been very much in love, had run away together to the dismay of both families, and then defied them all and lived happily ever after. For one intense moment, Jane wanted that.

Such a foolish idea. Better to marry the son of a neighbor everyone approved of. Prudence and wisdom lined the path to true happiness.

Jane gazed at Captain Ingram, inwardly shaking more than she had the first time she'd fallen from a horse. Flying through the air, not knowing where she'd land, had both terrified and exhilarated her.

"I do not wish to dance," she said. Captain Ingram's expression turned to disappointment, but Jane put her hand on his sleeve. "Shall we walk out to the bonfires instead?"

The longing in his eyes was unmistakable. The captain had no wish to be shut up in a hot ballroom with people he didn't know. Jane had no wish to be here either.

Freedom beckoned.

Captain Ingram studied Jane a moment, then he nodded in resolve. "I would enjoy that, yes."

Jane led him from the ballroom, her heart pounding, wondering, as she had that day she'd been flung from her mare's back, if her landing would be rough or splendid.

CHAPTER 3

As much as he wished to, Spencer could not simply rush into the night alone with Lady Jane. Such a thing was not done. Lady Jane bade two footmen, who fetched Jane's and Spencer's wraps, to bundle up and accompany them with lanterns. The lads, eager to be out, set forth, guiding the way into the darkness.

Five people actually tramped to the bonfires, because the youngest of the cousins, Thomas, joined them at the last minute.

"You're saving me," Thomas told Spencer as he fell into step with them. "Aunt Isobel wants me standing up with debutantes, as though I'd propose to one tomorrow. I ain't marrying for a long while, never fear. I want to join the army, like you."

"Army life is harsh, Mr. Randolph," Spencer said. "Unmerciful hours, drilling in all weather, not to mention French soldiers shooting at you."

"Not afraid of the Frenchies," Thomas proclaimed. "Tell him, Janie. I want to be off. I'll volunteer if Uncle won't buy me a commission."

"He does speak of it day and night," Lady Jane said. She walked along briskly but not hurriedly, as though the cold did not trouble her at all. "Do not paint too romantic a picture of army life, please, Captain, or you might find him in your baggage when you go."

"Perhaps Major Barnett should speak to him as a friend of the family," Spencer said, trying to make his tone diffident.

Jane laughed, a sound like music. "It is Major Barnett's fault Thomas wants to be a soldier in the first place. John writes letters full of his bravado. Also of the fine meals he has with his commanding officers, and the balls he attends, which are full of elegant ladies."

Spencer hid his irritation. Lady Jane held a beauty that had struck him to the bone from the moment he'd beheld her—her dark hair and azure eyes more suited to a faery creature floating in the mists of a loch than a young miss dwelling on a country farm in the middle of England.

If Spencer had been fortunate enough to have such a lady waiting for him, he'd write letters describing how he pined for her, not ones about meals with his colonel and wife. As far as Spencer knew, Barnett did not have a mistress, but he did enjoy dancing and chattering with the officers' wives and daughters. Man was an ingrate.

Barnett had mentioned the daughter of his father's closest neighbor on occasion, but not often. Never rejoiced in receiving her letters, never treasured them or read bits out. Nor hinted, with a blush, that he couldn't *possibly* read them out loud.

He'd only spoken the name Lady Jane Randolph that Spencer could remember a few weeks ago, when he'd announced he'd be returning to England for New Year's. He'd obtained leave and had for Spencer as well.

Spencer had been ready to go. Melancholia commanded him much of late, as he saw his future stretching before him, bleak and grim. If he did not end up dead on a battlefield with French bullets inside him, he would continue life as a junior officer without many prospects. Bonaparte was tough to wedge from the Peninsula—he'd already taken over most of the Italian states and much of the Continent, and had his relatives ruling corners of his empire for him.

Only England and Portugal held out, and there was nothing to say Portugal would not fall.

Even if Napoleon was defeated, there was noise of coming war in America. Spencer would either continue the slog in the heat and rain of Portugal or be shipped off to the heat and rain of the New World.

Even if Spencer sold his commission in a few years, as he planned, what then? He itched to see the world—not in an army tent or charging his horse across a battlefield, but properly, on the Grand Tour he'd missed because of war. But Bonaparte was everywhere.

More likely, Spencer would go home and learn to run the estate he'd eventually inherit. He didn't like to think of *that* day either, because it would mean his beloved father had died.

John Barnett, rising quickly through the ranks, courtesy of familial influence, had this beautiful woman to return to whenever he chose, one with a large and friendly family in the soft Berkshire countryside.

And the idiot rarely spoke of her, preferring to flirt with the colorless daughters of his colonels and generals.

If Bonaparte's soldiers didn't shoot Barnett, Spencer might.

The village was a mile from the house down a straight road, easy to navigate on a fine night, but Spencer shivered.

"Are you well, Captain Ingram?" Lady Jane asked in concern. "Perhaps we shouldn't have come out. You must be tired from your travels. Holidays are not pleasant when one has a cold."

"I am quite well," Spencer answered, trying to sound cheerful. "I was reflecting how peaceful it all is. Safe." No sharpshooters waiting to take out stragglers, no pockets of French soldiers to capture and torture one. Only starlight, a quiet if icy breeze, a thin blanket of white snow, a lovely woman walking beside him, and warm firelight to beckon them on.

"Yes, it is. Safe." Lady Jane sounded discontented.

"Janie longs for adventure," Thomas confided. "Like me."

"I, on the other hand, believe this a perfect night," Spencer said, his spirits rising. "Companionship, conversation. Beauty."

Thomas snorted with laughter, but Spencer saw Jane's polite smile fade.

At that moment, village children ran to envelope them and drag them to the bonfire.

The footmen eagerly joined friends and family around the blazes. A stoneware jug made its rounds to men and women alike, and voices rose in song.

Jane released Spence's arm, the cold of her absence disheartening. She beamed in true gladness as village women greeted her and pulled her into their circle.

Spencer watched Lady Jane come alive, the primness she'd exhibited in her family home dropping away. Her face blossomed in the firelight, a midnight curl dropped to her shoulder, and her eyes sparkled like starlight—his faery creature in a fur-lined redingote and bonnet.

Barnett has a lot to answer for, he thought in disgust. *She deserves so much more.*

But who was Spencer to interfere with his friend's intentions? Perhaps Barnett loved her dearly and was too bashful to say so.

The devil he was. When Barnett had greeted Jane tonight, he'd betrayed no joy of at last being with her, no need for her presence. He was as obtuse as a brick. Barnett had Jane safely in his sights, and took for granted she'd always be there.

Man needed to be taught a lesson. Spencer decided then and there to be the teacher.

JANE HAD FORGOTTEN HOW MUCH SHE ENJOYED THE BONFIRES AT NEW Year's. The villagers had always had a New Year's celebration, and when Grandfather came to live with Jane's family after Grandmother's death, he'd taught them all about Hogmanay. None of the villagers were Scots, and in fact, had ancestors who'd fought Bonnie

Prince Charlie, but the lads and lasses of Shefford St. Mary were always keen for a knees-up.

Jane had come to the bonfires every year as a child with her brother and cousins, and tonight, she was welcomed by the village women with smiles, curtseys, and even embraces.

The villagers linked hands to form a ring around one of the fires. Jane found her hand enclosed in Captain Ingram's large, warm one, his grip firm under his glove. Thomas clasped her other hand and nearly dragged Jane off her feet as they began to circle the fire at a rapid pace.

She glanced at Captain Ingram, to find his gray eyes fixed on her, his smile broad and genuine. His reserve evaporated as the circle continued, faster and faster. He'd claimed to be an indifferent dancer, but in wild abandon, he excelled.

Jane found she did too. Before long, she was laughing out loud, kicking up her feet as giddily as Grandfather had, as the villagers snaked back and forth. This was true country dancing, not the orchestrated, rather stiff parading in the ballroom.

The church clocks in this village and the next struck two, the notes shimmering in the cold. Village men seized their sweethearts, their wives, swung them around, and kissed them.

Strong hands landed on Jane's waist. Captain Ingram pulled her in a tight circle, out of the firelight. A warm red glow brushed his face as he dragged Jane impossibly close. Then he kissed her.

The world spun, silence taking the place of laughter, shouting, the crackle of the fire, the dying peal of the bells.

Spencer Ingram's heat washed over Jane, dissolving anything stiff, until she flowed against him, her lips seeking his.

The kiss was tender, a brief moment of longing, of desire simmering below the surface. Jane wanted that moment to stretch forever, through Hogmanay night to welcoming dawn, and for the rest of her life.

Revelers bumped them, and Spencer broke the kiss. Jane hung in his arms, he holding her steady against the crush.

She saw no remorse in his eyes, no shame that he'd kissed

another man's intended. Jane felt no remorse either. She was a free woman, not officially betrothed, not yet belonging to John, and she knew this with all her being.

Spencer set her on her feet and gently released her. They continued to study each other, no words between them, only acknowledgment that they had kissed, and that it had meant something.

Thomas came toward them. "We should go back, Janie," he said with regret. "Auntie will be looking for us."

He seemed to have noticed nothing, not the kiss, not the way Jane and Spencer regarded each other in charged silence.

The moment broke. Jane turned swiftly to Thomas and held out her hand. "Yes, indeed. It is high time we went home."

"A BONE TO PICK." SPENCER CLOSED THE DOOR OF THE LARGE ROOM where Barnett amused himself alone at a billiards table in midmorning sunlight. His eyes were red-rimmed from last night's revelry, but he greeted Spencer with a cheerful nod.

"Only if you procure a cue and join me."

Spencer chose a stout but slender stick from the cabinet and moved to the table as Barnett positioned a red ball on its surface and rolled a white toward Spencer.

Spencer closed his hand over the ball and spun it toward the other end of the table at the same time Barnett did his. Both balls bounced off the cushions and rolled back toward them, Spencer's coming to rest closer to its starting point than Barnett's. Therefore, Spencer's choice as to who went first.

He spread his hands and took a step back. "By all means."

Spencer was not being kind—the second player often had the advantage.

He remained politely silent as Barnett began taking his shots. He was a good player, his white ball kissing the red before the white dropped into a pocket, often clacking against Spencer's white ball as well. Spencer obligingly fished out balls each time so Barnett could continue racking up points.

Only when Barnett fouled out by his white ball missing the red by a hair and coming to rest in the middle of the table did Spencer speak.

"I must tell you, Barnett, that I find your treatment of Lady Jane appalling."

Barnett blinked and straightened from grimacing at his now-motionless ball. "I beg your pardon? I wasn't aware I'd been appalling to the dear gel."

"You've barely spoken to her at all. I thought this was the lady you wanted to marry."

Barnett nodded. "Suppose I do."

"You *suppose*? She is a beautiful woman, full of fire, with the finest eyes I've ever seen, and you *suppose* you wish to marry her?"

"Well, it's never been settled one way or another. We are of an age, grew up together. Really we are the only two eligible people for miles. We all used to play together—Jane, her brother, her cousins, me." Barnett laughed. "I remember once when we dared her to climb the face of Blackbird Hill, a steep, rough rock, and she did it. And once—"

Spencer cut him off with a sweep of his hand. "A spirited girl, yes. And now a spirited woman fading while she waits for you to say a word. She's halting her life because everyone expects you to propose. It's cruel to her to hesitate. Criminal even."

"Jove, you are in a state." Barnett idly took up chalk and rubbed it on the tip of his cue. He leaned to take a shot, remembered he'd lost his turn, and rose again. "What do you wish me to do? Propose to her, today?" He looked as though this were the last thing on earth he'd wish to do.

"No, I believe you should let her go. If you don't wish to marry her, tell her so. End her uncertainty."

"Hang on. Are you saying Jane is pining for me?" Barnett grinned. "How delicious."

Spencer slammed his cue to the table. "I am saying you've

trapped her. She feels obligated to you because of family expectations, while you go your merry way. Your flirtations at camp border on courtship, and I assumed your intended was a dull wallflower you were avoiding. Now that I've met her ... You're an idiot, Barnett."

"Now, look here, Ingram. *Captain*."

"You outrank me in the field, *sir*. In civilian life, no. Lady Jane is a fine young woman who does not need to be tied to you. Release her, let her find a suitor in London this Season, let her make her own choice."

Barnett's mouth hung open during Spence's speech, and now he closed it with a snap. "Her own choice—do you mean someone like *you*?"

Spencer scowled at him. "First of all, your tone is insulting. Second, when I say her own choice, I mean it. Cease forcing her to wait for you to come home, to speak. Let her begin her life."

Barnett laid down his cue with exaggerated care. "Very well. I suppose you pulling me away from that Frenchie's bayonet gives you some leave to speak to me so. Happen I might propose to her this very day. Will that gain your approval?"

Not at all. Spencer had hoped to make Barnett realize he didn't care for Lady Jane, never had, not as anything more than a childhood friend.

The man who proposed to Jane should be wildly in love with her, ready to do anything to make her life perfect and happy. She should have no less.

When Spencer had kissed her—

The frivolous, New Year's kiss had instantly changed to one of intense desire. Need had struck Spencer so hard he'd barely been able to remain standing. He'd wanted to hold on to Jane and run with her to Scotland, to jump the broomstick with her before anyone could stop them.

She never would. Spencer already understood that Jane had a deep sense of obligation, which she'd thrown off to dance in the firelight last night, like the wild thing she truly was. But today, she'd be back to responsibility. He hadn't seen her this morning, not at breakfast, which he'd rushed to anxiously, nor moving about the house, and he feared she'd decided to remain in her rooms and avoid him.

Spencer did not know what he'd say to her when she appeared. But he refused to put the kiss behind him, to pretend it never happened.

He didn't want Jane to pretend it hadn't happened either. He'd seen in her eyes the yearnings he felt—for love, for life, for something beyond what each of them had.

Spencer faced Barnett squarely. "Do not propose to her," he said. "Do not force her to plunge further into obligation. She won't refuse you. She'll feel it her duty to accept."

"It is her duty, damn you. What am I to do? Leave her for you?" When Spencer didn't answer, Barnett's eyes widened. "I see. Devil take you, man. I brought you home as a friend."

Spencer held him with a gaze that made Barnett's color rise. "That is true. Are you going to call me out?"

Barnett hesitated, then shook his head. "I'll not sully our friendship by falling out over a woman."

Spencer fought down disgust. "If you loved her, truly loved her, you'd strike me down for even daring to suggest I wanted her, and then you'd leap over my body and rush to her. You don't love her, do you? Not with all your heart."

Barnett shrugged. "Well, I'm fond of the gel, naturally."

"*Fond* is not what I'd feel, deep inside my soul, for the woman I wanted to spend the rest of my life with." Spencer slapped his palm to his chest. "Release her, Barnett. Or love her, madly, passionately. She merits no less than that."

Spencer seized his white ball and spun it across the table. It caromed off one edge, two, three, and then struck the red ball with a crack like a gunshot and plunged into a pocket.

"Add up my points," Spencer said. "If you will not tell Lady Jane what is truly in your heart, *I* will."

He strode from the room, his heart pounding, his blood hot. *The captain is a volatile man,* he'd heard his commanders say of him, *Once he sets his mind on a thing, step out of his way.*

Behind him, Barnett called plaintively, "What about the game? I'll have to consider it a forfeit, you know."

A forfeit, indeed.

Spencer went down the stairs to the main hall and asked the nearest footman to direct him to Lady Jane.

CHAPTER 4

The gardens were covered with snow, the fountains empty and silent, but they suited Jane's mood. She ought to be in the house entertaining guests, or helping her mother, or looking after Grandfather, but she could not behave as though nothing had shaken her life to its foundations.

She should be glad John was home, feel tender happiness as the reward for waiting for his return.

All she could think of was Spencer Ingram's gray eyes sparkling in the firelight after he'd kissed her. Could think only of the heat of his lips on hers, the fiery touch of his tongue. It was as though John Barnett did not exist.

Was she so fickle? So featherheaded that the moment another man crossed her path, she eagerly turned to follow him?

Or was there more than that? John had more or less ignored her since he'd arrived. Instead of resenting his indifference, Jane had been relieved.

Relieved. What was the matter with her?

A pair of statues at the far end of the garden marked the edge of her father's park. Both statues were of Hercules—the one the right battling the Nemean lion; on the left, the hydra. Beyond these guardians lay pastureland rolling to far hills, today covered with a few inches of snow.

Jane contemplated the uneven land beyond the statues and reluctantly turned to tramp back.

A man in a blue uniform with greatcoat and black boots strode around the fountains and empty flower beds toward her. He was alone, and his trajectory would make him intersect Jane's path. No one else wandered the garden, few bold enough to risk the ice-cold January morning.

Running would look foolish, not to mention Jane had nowhere to go. The fields, cut by a frozen brook, offered hazardous footing. Plus she was cold and ready to return to the house. Why should she flee her own father's garden?

Jane continued resolutely toward Captain Ingram, nodding at him as they neared each other. "Good morning," she said neutrally.

"Good morning," he echoed, halting before her. "Is it good?"

Jane curled her fingers inside her fur muff. "The weather is fair, the sun shining. The guests are enjoying themselves. The New Year's holiday is always pleasant."

Ingram's eyes narrowed. "Pleasant. Enjoying themselves." His voice held a bite of anger. "What about you, Lady Jane? Are you enjoying yourself?"

"Of course. I like to see everyone home. If my brother and his wife could come, that would be even more splendid."

"Liar."

Jane started, her heart beating faster, but she kept her tone light. "I beg your pardon? I truly do long to see my brother."

"You are miserable and cannot wait for the morning Major Barnett and I ride away."

Jane lost her forced smile. "You are rude."

"I am. Many say this of me. But I am a plain speaker and truthful." His gray eyes glinted as he fixed an unrelenting gaze on her. "Tell me why the devil you are tying yourself to Barnett."

Why? There was every reason why—Jane simply had never

thought the reasons through. "I have known him a very long time …"

Spencer stepped closer to her. "If you were madly in love with him, you'd have slapped me silly when I tried to kiss you, last night. Instead you joined me."

Jane rested her muff against her chest, as though it would shield her. "Are you casting my folly up to me? Not very gentlemanly of you."

To her surprise, Spencer smiled, his anger transforming to heat. It was a feral smile, the fierceness in his eyes making her tremble.

"*I* am the fool for kissing you," he said in a hard voice. "I couldn't help myself. I think no less of you for kissing me back. In fact, I have been rejoicing all night and morning that you did. Haven't slept a bloody wink."

Jane swallowed. "Neither have I, as a matter of fact."

"Then you give me hope. Much hope."

He took another step to her, and Jane feared he would kiss her again.

Feared? Or desired it?

She pulled back, but not because he frightened her. She stepped away because she wanted very much to kiss him, properly this time. She'd fling her arms around him and drag him close, enjoying the warmth of him against her.

She touched the muff to her lips, the fur tickling.

Spencer laughed. "You are beautiful, Lady Jane. And enchanting. A wild spirit barely tamed by a respectable dress and winter coat."

"Hardly a wild spirit." Jane moved the muff to speak. "I embroider—not well, I admit—paint watercolors rather better, and help my mother keep house."

"Your grandfather told me stories of himself and your grandmother last night. You are much like her."

Jane wanted to think so. Maggie MacDonald, what Jane remembered of her, had been a laughing, happy woman, given to telling frightening stories of ghosts that haunted the Highlands or playing games with her grandchildren. She also loved to dance. Jane had a memory of her donning a man's kilt and performing a sword dance as gracefully and adeptly as any warrior. Grandfather had watched her with love in his eyes.

"She was a grand woman," Jane said softly. "I can't begin to compare to her."

"She is in your blood." Spencer took another step, pushing the muff downward. "I saw that when we were at the fire. You were free, happy. I will stand here until you admit it."

"I was." Jane could not lie, even to herself. "Last night, I was happy."

"But this morning, you have convinced yourself you must be this other Jane. Dutiful. Tethered. *Un*happy."

Jane ducked from him and started toward the statues at the end of the garden. She had no idea why she did not rush to the house instead—Hercules was far too busy with his own struggles to help her.

Unhappy. Yes, she was. But that was hardly his business.

She heard Spencer's boots on the snow-covered gravel behind her and swung to face him. "Why do you follow me, sir? If I am miserable, perhaps I wish to console myself in solitude."

"Because I want to be with you." Spencer halted a foot from her. "There, I have declared myself. I want to be with you, and no other. I do not care one whit that you and Barnett have an understanding. He is not in love with you—I can see that. Such news might hurt you, but you must know the truth."

It did hurt. Jane had grown complacent about her friendship with John, pleased she could live without worry for her future, thankful she had no need to chase gentlemen during her Season and could simply enjoy London's many entertainments. She assisted other ladies to find husbands instead of considering them rivals.

Spencer's arrival had shattered her complacency, and now its shards lay around her.

She fought to maintain her composure. "Are you suggesting I throw over Major Barnett and declare myself for you?"

"Nothing would make me happier."

Spencer leaned close, and again, Jane thought he'd kiss her. Anything sensible spun out of her head as she anticipated the brush of his lips, the warmth of his touch. He came closer still, his gaze darting to her mouth, his chest rising sharply. Jane's very breath hurt.

When he straightened, disappointment slapped her.

"Nothing would make me happier," Spencer repeated. "But I'm not a blackguard. If you have no regard for me, if you cannot imagine yourself loving me, then I will not press you. I won't press you at all. What I want, my dear lady, is your happiness. I know in my heart it does not lie for you with Major Barnett."

Jane shook her head. "The world is convinced it does."

"Then the world is a fool. I would be the happiest man alive if you chose me. But I won't ask you to, won't coerce you." His dark brows came down. "I want you to be free, Jane. Free to choose. Go to London. Have your Season—laugh, dance, *live*. If you find a better man than I there, then I'll … well, I'll sink into despondency for a long while, but that despondency will have a bright note. I'll know you are happy. Find that man, and I will dance at your wedding. I promise."

Her breath came fast. "You amaze me, sir."

"Why?" Again a smile, bright and hot. "I admire you. I hate to see you pressed into a box, your nature stifled, all because of an ass like Major Barnett."

Jane attempted a frown. "Should I throw off my friends the moment they displease me? Is this freedom?" Her voice shook, because in her heart, his words made her sing.

"You know Barnett has been displeasing you for years," Spencer said. "Else you'd have looked happier to see him."

Truth again. Was this man an oracle?

"How dare you?" Jane tried to draw herself up, but her question lacked conviction. Spencer unnerved her, turned her inside out, made her want to laugh and cry. "This is none of your affair, sir."

She ought to threaten to call her father, have Captain Ingram ejected from the house, even arrested for accosting her. Or she could simply slap him, as he'd told her she should have done last night.

Spencer's gaze held her, and Jane could do nothing.

"It is my affair because I care about you," he said. "But *I* do not matter. You do. Please, Jane, be happy."

Blast him. Before he'd arrived, Jane's life had been tranquil. At ease. Now confusion pounded at her, and shame.

Because she knew good and well she hadn't been tranquil at all. She'd been impatient, angry. Stifled, as he said.

Spencer's eyes held anguish, rage, and need. Jane knew somehow that Spencer Ingram would always speak truth to her, whether she liked it or not.

And she knew she wanted to kiss him again.

The house was far away, and high yew hedges edged the path on which they stood. No one was about, not even a gardener taking a turn around the empty beds. Most of the servants had been given a holiday.

Jane took the last step toward Spencer. As he regarded her in both trepidation and simmering need, Jane wrapped her arms around his neck and kissed him.

His lips were parted, his breath heating hers an instant before he hauled her against him, his answering kiss hard, savage.

The world melted away. All Jane knew was Spencer's solid, strong body, his hands holding her steady, his mouth on hers.

He pulled her closer, the tall length of him hard against her softness. His lips opened hers, mouth seeking, whiskers scratching her cheek. He filled up everything empty inside her, and Jane learned warmth, joy, longing.

We never let anything stand in the way of us, Grandfather always said about himself and his beloved Maggie.

That was long ago, Jane would reason.

But *this* was now.

Jane abruptly broke the kiss. Spencer gazed at her, desire plain in his eyes. He traced her cheek, and her heart shattered.

Jane drew away from him, and ran. She snatched up the freedom he offered her and sprinted down the main path, her arms open, muff hanging from one hand, and let the cold air come.

"John, may I have a word?"

Jane was surprised she had breath left after her mad dash through the garden. She'd taken time to shed her outdoor things and compose herself before she sought John.

She found him in the library, book in hand, but he wasn't reading. John gazed rather wistfully out the window to the park in front of the house, the book dangling idly.

When he heard Jane, he rose to his feet and pasted on a polite smile. "Good morning, Jane. Did you have a nice walk?"

Jane halted, her cheeks scalding. Had he seen the kiss? Or been told about it?

John's face, however, held the bland curiosity of a man who had been thinking of everything but Jane, only recalled to her existence by her presence.

"The walk was agreeable," Jane said hastily. She glanced behind her to make certain the few servants who'd agreed to stay and help today did not linger in the hall. She dared not close the door in case a guest insisted that Jane shut into a room with her old friend meant either her ruin or their engagement.

She had no idea how to begin, so she jumped to the point, bypassing politeness.

"John, I would take it kindly if you did not propose to me."

John stared at her as though he didn't understand her words, then his brows climbed, his mouth forming a half smile. "I beg your pardon?"

Jane balled her hands and plunged on. "Please do not propose marriage to me. It will be easier for both of us if I do not have to refuse you."

CHAPTER 5

"Oh." John gaped at her. His features were still very like those he'd had as a child—round cheeks, soft chin, bewildered brown eyes. "Damn and blast—Ingram has got at you, has he? Viper to my bosom."

"Captain Ingram?" Good heavens, had Spencer discussed this with John? "Captain Ingram has nothing to do with this," Jane said heatedly. "Or, if he does, it is that he made me see keeping silent is hurting you as well as myself. We do not care for each other—not in the 'til-death-do-us-part fashion, in any case. Of course I have affection for you as a friend, and always will. We grew up together. But that does not mean we should continue as man and wife, no matter how many members of our family and friends believe so."

John's astonishment grew as Jane rambled, and she trailed off, her face unbearably hot.

John lifted his chin. "I cannot believe you so flighty, Jane, that you could allow a man, who pretends to be a gentleman, change your thoughts so swiftly."

"He did not." Jane shook her head, her heart squeezing. "I've had these thoughts a long time, even if I did not admit them to myself.

But I did not want to hurt you, my dear old friend. I believe now that *not* speaking will do even more harm. What happens if, in a year or two, you meet a lady you truly love? One who could be your helpmeet, your friend, the mother of your children? And you were already betrothed or married to me? Let us prevent that tragedy here and now."

John scowled. "Or is it that *you* wish to fall in love with another and not be tied to *me*?"

"Nonsense," Jane said. "I have no intention of marrying anyone."

She flushed even as she spoke. Spencer tempted her, yes, but she barely knew him. She would not fly from an understanding with John to an elopement with Spencer in the space of a day.

Would she?

"I believe you," John said in a hard voice. "Your nose held so high, your frosty demeanor in place. You've grown cold, Jane. If I haven't spoken to you about sharing a stall for life, it is because you are quite disagreeable these days. Your letters to me are so formal, about what calves were born and who danced with whom at the village ball. Enthralling."

Jane's coolness evaporated in a flash. "These in answer to the very few letters you have sent *me*. I've not heard from you since summer, in fact. Do not bother to use the excuse of battles, because your mother has had plenty of letters from you, as has my brother, and I know that the sister of a man in your regiment has heard plenty from *him*—the letters arrive in England on the same ship. But none from you to me."

John reddened. "Hardly seemly, is it, writing to a lady to whom I am not engaged?"

"It did not stop you the first year you were gone, nor has it stopped you scolding me for not writing scintillating letters to you."

John attempted a lofty tone. "You are such a child, Jane."

"No, I am not. I am twenty, as I reminded you last night, older than several ladies of my acquaintance who are already married. Old enough to be on the shelf, as you know. But I will not tie us to a marriage neither of us wants to avoid that fate."

"Ah, so that is why you were always sweet to me, eh, Janie? So you'd never be an ape-leader?" John's mouth pinched. "I'll have you know that I planned to speak to you this week, my dear, but not to propose. To tell you there is the sister of an officer who has caught my eye, and as you have become so cool, and she is quite warm, that we should agree to part."

Jane's heart stung, and she regarded him in remorse. She hadn't wanted to anger John, but how could he not be angry? His stabs at her came from his bafflement and hurt, but Jane sensed that he was more insulted at her refusal than deeply wounded.

John would return to his regiment and happily court the officer's sister, and forget he ever had feelings for Jane. In fact, John had behaved, since his arrival, as though he'd forgotten those feelings already.

Hopefully, in time, John would forgive her, and they'd continue as friends, as they had been all their lives. But friends with no obligation attached.

"Good-bye, John," Jane said, and quietly walked out of the room.

Spencer did not see Jane the rest of the day. He walked through the gardens, the park, the woods, then took a horse and went on a long ride. It was snowing by the time he returned, and dark.

He did not see Barnett either, which was a mercy. Spencer then realized he'd seen no one at all as he returned to his chamber. He washed and changed and descended in search of supper, but the residents of the house were elusive. Where had they all gone?

"Hurry up, lad," a voice with a Scottish lilt said to him. "You're the last."

"The last for what, sir?" Spencer asked Lady Jane's grandfather as the elderly man tottered to him.

"The hunt, of course. Here's your list. You're with Thomas and my daughter. Off you go."

Spencer gazed down at a paper with a jumble of items written on it: A flat iron, a locket, a horseshoe, a thimble, and a dozen more bizarre things that did not match.

"What is this?" he asked in bewilderment.

"A scavenger hunt, slow-top. The first team to gather the things wins a prize. Go on with ye."

Spencer hesitated. "Where is Jane? Lady Jane, that is."

"With the older cousins and a friend from down the lane. Why are you still standing here?"

"The thing is, sir, I ... I'm not sure who to speak to ..."

The old Scotsman waved him away, his plaids swinging. "Aye, I know all about it. Give the lass time to settle, and she'll come 'round. She only gave Major Barnett the elbow a few hours ago."

Spencer's heart leapt. "She did?"

"Yes. Thank the Lord. Now, hurry away. Enjoy yourself while you're still young."

Spencer grinned in sudden hope. "Yes, sir. Of course, sir."

As he dashed away, he heard Grandfather MacDonald muttering behind him. "In my day, I'd have already put the girl over my shoulder and run off with her. Otherwise, she'd not think I was sincere."

JANE HANDED HER SPOILS—A BLUE BEADED SLIPPER, A QUIZZING GLASS, and a small rolling pin—to her cousin Digby, and slipped into the chamber she'd spied her grandfather ducking into. The small anteroom was covered with paintings her father's father had collected. A strange place for Grandfather MacDonald to hide—he believed Van Dyke and Rubens over-praised. Only Scottish painters like Allan Ramsay and Henry Raeburn had ever been any good.

"Grandfather."

Grandfather looked up from a settee, where he'd been nodding off, but his eyes were bright, alert. He came to his feet.

"Yes, my dear? Are you well?"

"No." Jane sank down to a painted silk chair. "Everything is turned upside-down, Grandfather. I need your advice."

"Do you?" Grandfather plopped back onto the settee, smile in place. "Why come to me, lass? Not your mum?"

"Because when things are topsy-turvy, you seem to know what to do."

"True. But so do you."

Jane shivered. "No, I do not. I was perfectly happy with my life as it was. Then John began to change, and Captain Ingram—"

"A fine young man is Ingram," Grandfather said brightly. "My advice is to run off with him. You like kissing him well enough."

Jane's face flamed. "Grandfather!"

"I do not know why you are so ashamed. I saw you kissing him in the garden, and young Thomas says you kissed him at the bonfire." Grandfather shook his head in impatience. "Latch on to him, Janie, and kiss him for life."

Jane's face grew hotter, her mortification complete. "You ought to have made yourself known instead of lurking in the shrubbery."

"Tut, girl. I was out for a walk, a good stride through the yew hedges. Not lurking anywhere. You were standing plain as day by those ridiculous statues. Which is why I don't understand your shame. You did not kick Ingram in the dangles and run away. You embraced him. With enthusiasm."

"Even so." Jane's embarrassment warred with elation as she thought of the kiss. "I cannot disappoint my family and uproot my life on a whim."

"Why not?"

"Because …" Jane waved her hands. "What a fool I'd be. I barely know Captain Ingram. He might be the basest scoundrel on land, ready to abandon me at a moment's notice. The real world is not a fairy tale, Grandfather."

"Thank heavens for that. Fairy tales are horrible—the fae ain't the nice little people painted in books for maiden ladies. Trust me. I'm descended from witches, and I know all about the fae."

"Of course, Grandfather." If not stopped, Grandfather could go on for some time about how Shakespeare based Macbeth's witches on the women in his mother's family. "What I mean is I can't simply change everything because a handsome gentleman kissed me," she said.

"You can, you know. This is why you came to me for advice, young lady, and not your mum. Isobel is my pride and joy, she is, but she's the practical sort. The airiness of your grandmother and the wickedness of my side of the family didn't manifest in her. Isobel's more like me dad, a stolid Scotsman who never put a foot wrong in his life. Didn't stop the Hanoverians taking all he had." Grandfather's gaze held the remote rage of long ago, then he shook his head and refocused on the present.

"Janie, you are unhappy because you believe life should be simple. You long for it to be. You fancied yourself willing to marry Barnett because it was the easy choice. He's familiar to your family, you know what to expect from him, and you'd congratulated yourself for not having to chase down a husband to look after you the rest of your life. But you'd be disappointed in him. He might be the simplest choice for a husband, but you'd end up looking after *him*, and you know it."

"Why is such a thing so bad?" Jane asked, heart heavy. "Grandmother looked after *you*."

Grandfather shook his head. "She and I looked after each other. And we did not have a peaceful life at first—our families were furious with us, and we had to weather that, and find a way to live, *and* raise our children. It weren't no easy matter, my girl, but that is the point. Life is complicated. It's hard, hard work. So many try to find a path around that, but though that path might look clear, it can be full of misery. You sit helplessly while things happen around you instead of grabbing your life by the horns and shaking it about. Happiness is worth the trouble, the difficult choices, the path full of brambles. Do not sit and let things flow by you, Jane. You deserve much more than that. Take your happiness, my love. Do not let this moment pass."

Jane sat silently. She felt limp, drained—had since she'd told John they could never be married. She thought she'd feel freedom once she'd been truthful with John, as Spencer had told her she would, but at present, Jane only wanted to curl up and weep.

"But I could misstep," she said. "I could charge down the difficult path and take a brutal tumble."

"That you could. And then you rise up and try again. Or you could huddle by the wayside and let happiness slip past. If you don't grab joy while you can, you might not have another chance."

Jane's heart began to beat more strongly. "I am a woman. I must be prudent. A man who falls can be helped up by his friends. A woman who falls is ostracized by hers."

Grandfather shook his head. "Only if those friends are scoundrels. I imagine your family would stand by you no matter what happened. I know *I* would." He raised his hands, palms facing her. "But you are worrying because you've been taught to worry. Do you truly believe Ingram is a hardened roué? With a string of broken hearts and ruined women behind him? We'd have heard about such things. Barnett would have told us—you know how much he loves to gossip. And he wouldn't have brought Captain Ingram home to you and your mum and dad if he thought the man a bad 'un, would he?"

Jane had to concede. "I suppose not ..."

"Your dad knows everyone in England, and he's no fool. He'd have heard of Ingram's reputation if the man had a foul one, and he'd have never let him inside. It's harder than you'd think to be a secret rake in this country. *Someone* will know, and feel no remorse spreading the tale."

Jane didn't answer. Everything Grandfather said was reasonable. Still, she'd seen what happened when a woman married badly—she found herself saddled with an insipid, feckless man who did nothing but disgrace his family and distress his friends.

The man John could so easily become ...

"Spencer Ingram seems a fine enough lad to me," Grandfather went on. "Family's respectable too, from what I hear. Besides, Ingram is a good Scottish name."

"Of course." Jane gave a shaky laugh. "That is why you like him."

"One of the reasons. There are many others." Grandfather jumped to his feet. "What are you waiting for, Janie? Your happiness walked in the door last night. Go to it—go to *him*."

"I don't regret telling John I will never marry him," Jane said with conviction. "And I suppose you're right. I won't send Captain Ingram away, or push him aside because I'm mortified. He will be visiting a while longer. We can get to know each other, and perhaps ..."

Her words faded as Grandfather snorted. "*Get to know each other*? *Perhaps*? Have you heard nothing I've said?" His eyes flashed. "You are trying to make things comfortable again, which means pushing aside decisions, waiting for things to transpire instead of forcing them to."

He pointed imperiously at the door. "Out you go, Jane. Now. Find Captain Ingram. Tell him you will marry him. No thinking it over, or lying awake pondering choices, or waiting to see what happens. Go to him this instant."

Jane rose, her heart pounding. "I can't tell him I'll marry him, Grandfather. He hasn't asked me."

"Then ask *him*. Your grandmother did me. She tired of me shillyshallying. So she stepped up and told me I either married her, or she walked away and looked for someone else."

Jane covered her fears with a laugh. She could picture Maggie MacDonald doing just that. "But I am not Grandmother."

Grandfather's eyes softened. "Oh, yes, you are. You are so like her, Janie, you don't realize. Her spitting image when she was young, and you have her spirit. She knew it too." Tears beaded on his lashes. "I miss her so."

"Oh, Grandfather." Janie launched herself at him, enfolding him into her arms. Grandfather rested his head on her shoulder, a fragile old man, his bones too light.

After a time, they pushed away from each other, both trying to smile.

"Go to him, Janie," Grandfather said. "For her sake."

Jane kissed his faded cheek and spun for the door. As she turned to close it behind her, she saw Grandfather's tears flow unchecked down his face, he wiping them away with a fold of his plaid.

CHAPTER 6

Spencer observed that Barnett did not seem too morose that Lady Jane had thrown him over. He watched Barnett fling himself into the hunt, crowing over the things he'd found for his group, all the while glancing raptly at the daughter of guests from Kent. His behavior was not so much of a man bereaved as one reprieved.

Spencer knew that if Jane had given *him* the push, he'd be miserable, tearing at his hair and beating his breast like the best operatic hero.

He feared Jane had dismissal in mind when she gazed down from the upper gallery and caught his eye. She gave him a long look before she skimmed down the stairs and disappeared into the library.

Spencer, who'd found none of the items on his list, his heart not in the game, handed his paper to Thomas and told the lad to carry on.

"Jane?" Spencer whispered as he entered the library. It was dark, a few candles burning for the sake of the gamers, the fire half-hearted against the cold. The chill was why no one lingered here—the room was quite empty.

Spencer shut the door. "Jane?"

She turned from the shadows beside the fireplace. Spencer approached her, one reluctant pace at a time.

When he was a few strides away, Jane smiled at him. That smile blazed like sunshine, lighting the room to its darkest corners.

"Captain Ingram," Lady Jane said. "Will you marry me?"

Spencer ceased breathing. He knew his heart continued to beat, because it pounded blood through him in hot washes. But he felt nothing, as though he'd been wound in bandages, like the time a French saber had pierced his shoulder and the surgeon had swaddled his upper body like a babe's.

That shoulder throbbed, the old pain resurfacing, and Spencer's breath rushed back into his lungs.

"Jane ..."

"I am sincere, I assure you," Jane said, as though she supposed he'd argue with her. "I know I am doing this topsy-turvy, but—"

Spencer laid shaking hands on her shoulders, the blue silk of her gown warmed by her body. "Which is the right way 'round for you, my beautiful, beautiful fae."

"Grandfather would faint if he heard you say so," Jane said with merriment. "I believe he's rather afraid of the fae. Even if he married one."

Spencer tightened his clasp on her. He never remembered how Jane ended up in his arms, but in the next instant he was kissing her, deeply, possessively, and she responded with the mad passion he'd seen in her eyes.

That kiss ended, but they scarcely had time to draw a breath before the next kiss began. And the next.

They ended up in the wing chair that reposed before the fire, placed so a reader might keep his or her feet warm. Spencer's large frame took up most of it, but there was room for Jane on his lap.

They kissed again, Spencer cradling her.

How much time sped by, Spencer had no idea, but at last he drew Jane to rest on his shoulder.

"Shall we adjourn to Gretna Green?" he asked in a low voice.

Jane raised her head, her blue eyes bright in the darkened room. "No, indeed. I wish my family and friends to be present. But soon."

"How fortunate that my leave is for a month. Time enough to have the banns read in your parish church. And then what? Follow me and the drum? It can be a hard life."

Jane brushed his cheek. "I do want to go with you. I am willing to face the challenge, to forsake the safer path." She spoke the words forcefully, as though waiting for Spencer to dissuade her.

He had no intention of it. With Jane by his side, camp life would cease to be bleak. "I plan to sell my commission a few years from now, in any case. I do not see myself as a career army man, though I am fond of travel."

"I long to travel."

The words were adamant. With Jane's restlessness and fire, Spencer believed her. "After that, I will have a house waiting for me," he said. "One of my father's minor estates."

Her smile beamed. "Excellent."

"Not really—it needs much work. Again, I am not promising you softness."

"I do not want it." Jane kissed his chin. "I am resilient. And resourceful. I like to be doing things, and I do not mean embroidery. Come to think of it, my grandmother never did embroidery in her life."

"I know." Spencer nuzzled her hair. "Your grandfather spoke much about her when I met him in London."

Jane stilled. Very slowly, she lifted her head. "You met my grandfather in London?"

Spencer nodded. "Last spring. I was on another leave-taking, much shorter, to visit my family. I spent a night in London, and at the tavern near my lodgings, I met an amusing old Scotsman who was pleased to sit up with me telling stories. I mentioned my friendship with Barnett, and your grandfather was delighted."

"He was, was he?" Jane's tone turned ominous.

"Indeed. But when I arrived last night, he asked me not to speak of our previous meeting to anyone. I have no idea why, but I saw no reason not to indulge him."

He leaned to kiss her again, to enjoy the taste of her fire, but Jane put her hand on his chest.

"Will you excuse me for one moment, Spencer?"

Spencer skimmed his fingertips across her cheek. "When you speak my name, I cannot refuse you, love."

Her eyes softened, but she scrambled from his lap. Spencer rose with her, a steadying hand on her waist. "I won't be long," she promised.

Jane strode from the room, her head high. Spencer watched her go, then chuckled to himself and followed her.

"Grandfather."

She found he'd moved to a smaller, warmer sitting room, only this time he'd truly nodded off. The old man jumped awake and then to his feet, the whisky flask he'd been holding clanging to the floor.

"What the devil? Janie, what is it?"

Jane pointed an accusing finger at his face. "You met Captain Ingram in London this past spring."

"Did I?" Grandfather frowned, then stroked his jaw in contemplation. "Now that you call it to my mind, I believe I did. My memory ain't what it used to be."

"I cry foul." Jane planted her hands on her hips. "You knew he was John's friend. *You* put the idea into John's head to bring Captain Ingram here for Hogmanay, didn't you? Do not prevaricate with me, please."

"Hmm. I might have mentioned our meeting in a letter to young Barnett."

"And you told John to send Captain Ingram into the house first."

"Well, he is dark-haired. And tall. And what ladies believe is handsome." Grandfather spread his hands. "My prediction came true, you see? You will marry this year's First-Footer. I see by your blush that he has accepted your proposal."

Jane's cheeks indeed were hot. "Prediction, my eye. You planned this from the beginning, you old fraud."

Grandfather drew himself up. "And if I did? And if I met Ingram's family and determined that they were worthy of you? Captain Ingram is a far better match for you than Barnett. My lady ancestors were witches, yes, but they always had contingencies to make certain the spell worked."

Deep, rumbling laughter made Jane spin around. Spencer leaned on the doorframe, gray eyes sparkling in mirth.

"Bless you that you did," he said. He came to Jane and put a strong hand on her arm. "You and your ancestors will always have my gratitude, sir. Jane and I will be married by the end of the month."

Grandfather gave Jane a hopeful look. "All's well, that end's well?"

Jane dashed forward in a burst of love and caught her grandfather in an exuberant embrace. "Yes, Grandfather. Thank you. Thank you. I love you so much."

"Go on with you now." Grandfather struggled away, but the tears in his eyes touched her heart. "The pair of ye, be off. Ye have much more kissing to do. It's Hogmanay still."

Spencer twined his hand through Jane's. "An excellent suggestion."

"And don't either of you worry about Barnett. I've already caught him kissing Miss Pembroke."

Jane blinked. Miss Pembroke was the daughter of her parents' friends from Kent. "He is quick off the mark. The wretch."

"Then he can toast us at our wedding," Spencer said. He pulled Jane firmly to the door. "I believe I'd like to adjourn to the library again, to continue our ... planning."

Jane melted to him, her anger and exasperation dissolving. She needed this man, who'd come to her so unexpectedly to lift her out of her dreary life. "A fine idea."

In the cool of the hall, Spencer bent to Jane and whispered in her ear. "You are beauty and light. I love you, Janie. This I already know."

"I already know I love you too."

They sealed their declaration with a kiss that burned with a wildness Jane had been longing for, the fierce freedom of her youth released once more.

Left alone in the sitting room, Hamish MacDonald raised his flask to the painting of a beautiful woman whose flowing hair spilled from under a wide-brimmed hat. She smiled at him over a basket of flowers, her bodice sliding to bare one seductive shoulder. Her eyes were deep blue, her hair black as night.

"I did it, Maggie," he said, his voice scratchy. "I've seen to it that our girl will be happy. Bless you, love."

He toasted the portrait, done by the great Ramsay, and drank deeply of malt whisky.

He swore that Maggie, his beloved wife, heart of his heart, forever in his thoughts, winked at him.

ABOUT THE AUTHOR

Jennifer Ashley is the *New York Times* bestselling author of more than 100 novels and novellas. Readers who wish to try her popular historical romance series, The Mackenzies, should start with *The Madness of Lord Ian Mackenzie*. The series is ongoing, with book 10, *The Devilish Lord Will*, out in November of 2018.

Jennifer also writes historical mysteries with a touch of romance. *Death Below Stairs* begins her Victorian mystery series featuring Kat Holloway, a cook to the wealthy; and *The Hanover Square Affair* leads off the Captain Lacey Regency mysteries she writes as Ashley Gardner.

More information on all her series can be found at

www.jenniferashley.com
www.gardnermysteries.com
www.katholloway.com

ALSO BY JENNIFER ASHLEY

The Mackenzies / McBrides Series

The Madness of Lord Ian Mackenzie

Lady Isabella's Scandalous Marriage

The Many Sins of Lord Cameron

The Duke's Perfect Wife

A Mackenzie Family Christmas: The Perfect Gift

The Seduction of Elliot McBride

The Untamed Mackenzie

The Wicked Deeds of Daniel Mackenzie

Scandal and the Duchess

Rules for a Proper Governess

The Stolen Mackenzie Bride

A Mackenzie Clan Gathering

Alec Mackenzie's Art of Seduction

The Devilish Lord Will

Below Stairs Mysteries

A Soupçon of Poison

Death Below Stairs

Scandal Above Stairs

Death in Kew Gardens

Captain Lacey Regency Mysteries

(w/a Ashley Gardner)

The Hanover Square Affair

A Regimental Murder

The Glass House

The Sudbury School Murders

The Necklace Affair (and Other Stories)

A Body In Berkeley Square

A Covent Garden Mystery

A Death in Norfolk

A Disappearance in Drury Lane

Murder in Grosvenor Square

The Thames River Murders

The Alexandria Affair

A Mystery at Carlton House

Murder in St. Giles

Death at Brighton Pavilion

A KNIGHT BEFORE CHRISTMAS

GRACE BURROWES

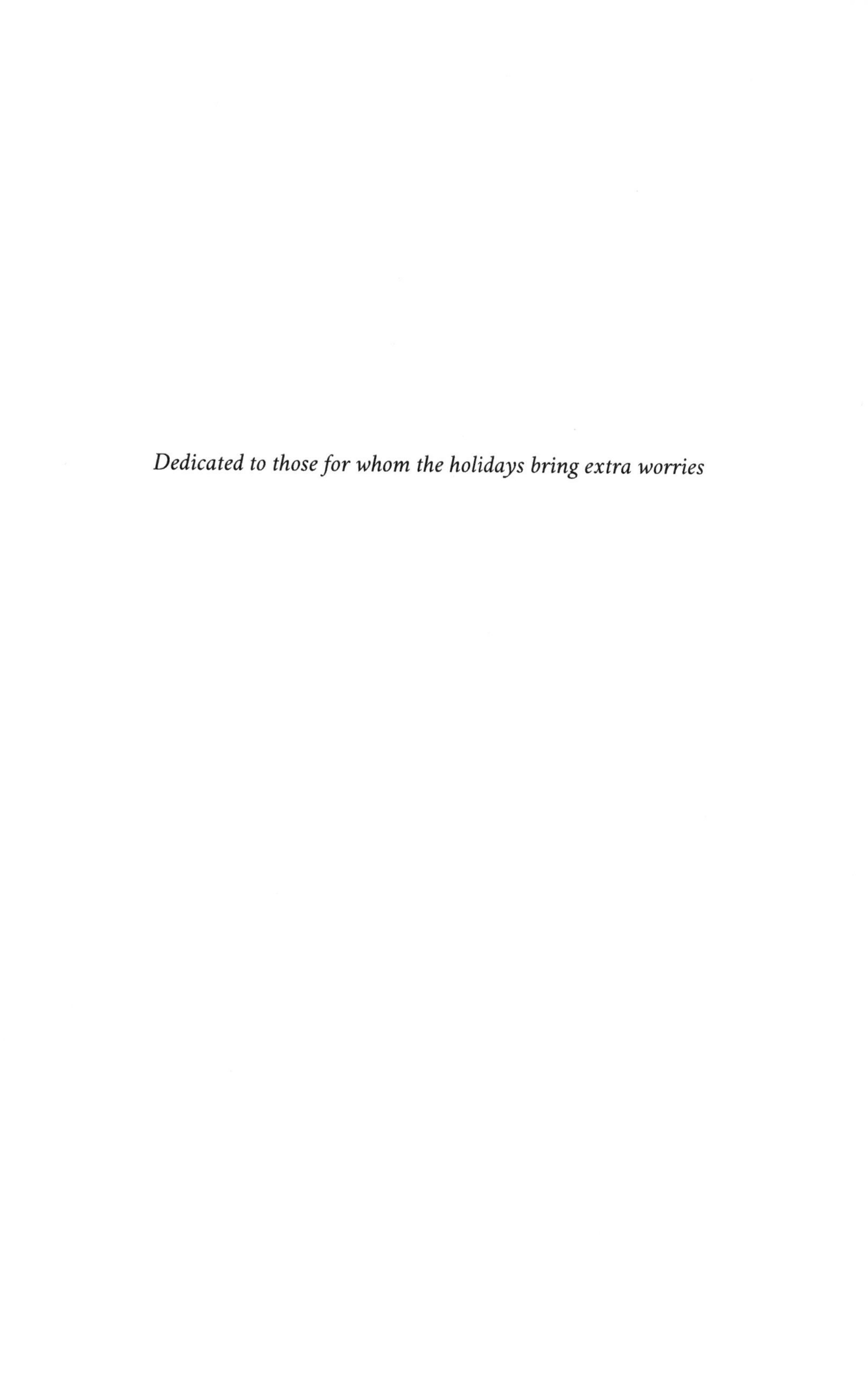

Dedicated to those for whom the holidays bring extra worries

CHAPTER 1

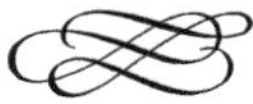

"Mr. Farris is back again," Faith whispered as she reshelved biographies. "He's lurking among Mrs. Radcliffe's offerings."

"Leave the man in peace, sister," Chloe replied, adding four more volumes to the stack in Faith's arms. "Many a man enjoys Mrs. Radcliffe's novels, all the while protesting that his purchase is for a wife, mother, or sister."

"But Mr. Farris already owns everything Mrs. Radcliffe has ever written."

"True enough." Mr. Aidan Farris was a loyal customer, though lately he must have been spending all of his free time reading.

Chloe crossed to the bookshop's front counter rather than indulge in idle speculation. "Mr. Nelson, have you made your selection?"

Faith sidled away, for Mr. Nelson was a prodigious ditherer. He spent good coin for his books, though, so Chloe came around the counter, patience at the ready.

From the corner of her eye, she watched as Mr. Farris paged through a bound version of *The Romance of the Forest*. He'd taken Mrs. Radcliffe's tale to the shop's front window, where the light was best. Reading glasses sat on a fine blade of a nose, and winter sunlight found red highlights in sable hair. He was gray-eyed, tallish without approaching awkward height, and more sober in his demeanor than Vicar Waites's holding forth on the topic of irresponsible wagering.

Mr. Farris maintained that serious demeanor while he read a rollicking tale of thwarted passion, undeserved penury, and misplaced heroism. What sort of story would provoke a man like that to smiling?

"I'll take this one for my missus," Mr. Nelson said, using the counter to assemble a stack of loose chapters into a neat pile. "She does love when I read to her of a long, dark evening."

"We have bound copies," Chloe replied. "Mrs. Nelson might like one of those. Some of them are very handsome, Mr. Nelson." And a bound copy would be a more profitable sale for the shop, at a time when every ha'penny was desperately needed.

"Bound copies come dear," he said, looking uncertain. "Perhaps I'd best buy the first few chapters, and if Missus enjoys them.... But then I'll have to either buy the rest, or pay for the whole book *and* the first few chapters."

Chloe mentally kicked herself. This equivocation could go on for an hour, during which she'd not be assisting other patrons as the day drew to a close and buying on impulse became more likely. The result might be no sale at all, which was exactly what she deserved for trying to inspire Mr. Nelson to make the larger purchase when he'd already come to a decision.

"Or I could buy just the one chapter," Mr. Nelson went on, "and see what she thinks of that. Missus is particular, not like me, and woe to the man who offers her a tale she doesn't care for. Hard to tell much from one chapter though. Perhaps the lending library—"

"The lending library is three streets over, and might not have such a popular tale," Chloe said. "I'd hate to see you travel that far in the cold for nothing."

Chloe frequently patronized the lending library, reading their inventory to judge what she ought to stock in the shop. Soon, she wouldn't be able to afford the membership there, but what would that matter if she and Faith lost their home and their livelihood?

"Activity is good for us," Mr. Nelson countered, sending the chapters in his hand a dubious look. "One should not pay for milk without first making sure it's fresh."

Mrs. Draper was standing at the opposite end of the counter, a pamphlet on flower arranging in her hand. A small purchase, but she was an impatient woman. She'd happily leave the pamphlet, the better to get to the cookshop just as the day's roast was carved.

The light changed and a man came up on Chloe's right. "Ah, but a rousing tale is not a pitcher of milk, is it?" Mr. Farris peered at the chapters Mr. Nelson held. "Excellent choice. I have the bound version of all six of her novels, and read them frequently. Alas we shall have no more stories from Miss Austen's pen."

Mr. Nelson peered up at Mr. Farris. "Did she get married?"

Mrs. Radcliffe had written *all* of her novels while married. Chloe kept that observation behind her teeth while she caught a whiff of Mr. Farris's fragrance. Either he'd recently loitered in a bakeshop, or he liked the scent of cinnamon.

"Miss Austen went to her reward before her last novel was published," Chloe said. "She never married."

"The poor creature," Mr. Nelson murmured. "You say you've read all six of her novels, young man?"

"I have a handsome set of bound volumes, which I expect will become collector's items. When an author is no longer extant, one never knows how much longer her works will be available, and her books are some of my favorite stories."

Mr. Nelson's bushy white brows drew down. "But one should not buy from the dairymaid without first sampling…"

"Come," Mr. Farris said, "I'll show you where the bound volumes are. Milk is for cooling our tea. Stories are for lightening the heart and enriching the mind. The thrill of discovering a tale page by page is more important than saving a few pence, don't you think? And heaven help a fellow if his lady becomes enthralled with a story and he can't get his hands on the next installments. Do you prefer red leather or brown?"

Bless you, Mr. Farris. Chloe got back to the counter just as Mrs. Draper had set the pamphlet down.

"Flowers are so cheering this time of year, aren't they?" Chloe asked. "The illustrations in that pamphlet are worth framing according to Mrs. Dash."

"Myra Dash said that?"

Mrs. Dash's son was an aspiring painter, while Mrs. Draper's daughter was fast approaching spinsterhood. The two held rousing arguments in the print shop across the street, but neither one was of a literary bent.

"I did hear something to that effect," Chloe replied as Mrs. Draper passed over two small coins. "And Mrs. Dash has such good taste where the visual arts are concerned. I wonder if she's solicited her son's opinion of the illustrations?"

Mrs. Draper tucked the pamphlet into a voluminous beaded reticule. "Lord knows the boy has opinions on everything else."

"Perhaps if he were invited over for a cup of holiday punch and some fresh biscuits, he might share those opinions with you and Miss Draper. Have a pleasant day, ma'am, and enjoy your pamphlet."

Chloe dropped the pennies into the drawer beneath the counter, where they joined a precious small collection of coins and a few worn notes.

"I was so sorry to hear about Mr. Thatcher," Mrs. Draper said, leaning nearer as she drew her reticule closed. "I hope you young ladies can manage."

So do I. "Thank you for your condolences, ma'am. Grandfather is at peace, and we are doing all we can to protect his legacy." Chloe said those words at least a dozen times a day, but like the coins in the drawer, they weren't enough.

A few platitudes did not convey the grief she and Faith endured, or the sheer terror they'd faced as the extent of Grandfather's indebtedness had become plain. They kept the shop heated, they didn't dare burn so much as a lump of coal in the upstairs rooms where they lived.

For their customers, they wore smiles and made cheerful small talk. Upstairs, they wore three shawls and dropped exhausted into bed without saying much of anything except prayers that by some miracle they'd be able to prevent Mr. Barnstable from foreclosing on Grandfather's shop.

"WHERE HAS OUR MR. FARRIS GO OFF TO?" JOSHUA PENROSE ASKED.

Joshua Penrose paced when he was thinking, a singularly bothersome habit in Quinn Wentworth's opinion, because Joshua was so very prone to cogitation. Worse, he did much of his thinking in the partner's conference room, the largest private space at the Wentworth and Penrose bank.

Quinn finished tallying the column of figures before him, which balanced to the penny with the sum he'd totaled across the page. No matter how wealthy he became—and he was very wealthy—he'd always take pleasure in figures that behaved as they ought.

"I sent Farris to inspect the premises at the corner of Willoughby and St. Jean's," Quinn said.

"We've had this discussion," Joshua replied, taking the high-backed, cushioned chair on the other side of the polished mahogany table. "A second location for the bank to do business makes no sense."

"Smart bankers have been establishing operations at locations convenient to their customers for centuries. The Italian banks did business in France 500 years ago, and earned a tidy profit from their neighbor's trade. Consider a branch location an experiment."

Quinn should not have used that word. Joshua was suspicious all of things speculative, which is why he and Quinn made a strong, if contentious, partnership. They were opposites in appearance too, with Quinn being dark-haired, blue-eyed, and quick to foreclose on a delinquent account. Joshua insisted the bank's contractual terms always include a thirty-day grace period, and relied on charm while Quinn cited contract wording.

"You simply want Farris to have a project so he won't leave us," Joshua said. "He's been with us since you found him picking pockets in Covent Garden, and we've promoted him from messenger to teller to supervisor to bank solicitor. If he's smart, he'll take a post with a rival institution because we have nowhere to promote him."

Quinn capped the ink and laid his pen in the tray, for once Joshua embarked on a difference of opinion, he was like a rat with an apple core. Then too, Joshua's arguments tended to have an annoying grain of truth about them.

"Farris was not picking pockets. He was trying to pick pockets and failing." A signal distinction. "He will never willingly leave Wentworth and Penrose and you know it."

Joshua propped his boots on the corner of the table and tipped the chair back. "Instead of sending Farris to spy on Barnstable's property, why don't you for once leave the ledgers and do some Christmas shopping for your siblings? Stephen loves all books, Constance would enjoy a volume on French portraiture, and Althea…."

Quinn took off his spectacles and gave them an unneeded polishing. "Althea can buy whatever silly stories she pleases to read," he said. "I have no use for books, and don't see a need to bring any more into my home."

He had a library full of books—his siblings did enjoy them—but hadn't read a single novel. Contracts, mortgages, deeds of trust, bills of lading, memoranda of agreement—those were the tales that had fascinated him enough to inspire him to sit through Cousin Duncan's reading lessons.

"If you aren't looking for a means to keep Farris in our employ," Joshua said, "and you know Barnstable is eager to foreclose on that bookshop property, then why involve yourself in that situation at all? Shop owners die, their estates are liquidated, and the family either establishes a business elsewhere or goes into service."

Simon Thatcher's demise was more complicated than Joshua knew, or let on that he knew.

"Smart banks hold with tradition while looking to the future," Quinn said, sprinkling sand over the initials he'd written at the bottom of the page. "If we don't establish a branch closer to the better shopping areas, then Barnstable will. Once he's taken that step—and increased his profit as a result—other banks will flock to do the same and commercial rents will rise as a result of increased demand. Wentworth and Penrose will be behind the trend instead of leading it. I don't care to fall behind, Joshua. Do you?"

Joshua tipped his head back, as if consulting the cherubs cavorting amid the clouds painted onto the ceiling. "Not fair, Quinn."

Joshua was competitive, Quinn was calculating. The two qualities were often complementary, though in this case, they would not be, not if all went according to Quinn's plan.

"I will continue to send Farris around to monitor the situation at Thatcher's Bookshop," Quinn said. "He thinks I'm simply keeping an eye on Barnstable's activities."

"Because you also send him around to monitor everything else our competitors get up to. What are you really up to?"

Not even Joshua could be trusted with that information. "Farris alerted me to Thatcher's failing health several months ago. Farris knows we're looking for a branch location."

Joshua laced his hand behind his head. "*You* are looking for a branch location."

"That I am." The plain truth, but not the entire truth. "It makes sense for Farris to follow up on acquisition of the bookshop. If Barnstable's greed renders that prospect unprofitable, I will simply look elsewhere. Barnstable is merely the mortgagor, though. He must make the building available at a public sale, and when he does, I intend to buy it."

"You are forgetting one thing, Quinn."

"So please enlighten me before the New Year. I'm expected home for dinner."

"Every cit and merchant in the London will likely bid against our man Farris at a public sale. The corner of St. Jean's and Willoughby sees more foot traffic than probably any other location in London, and that building is both handsome and well constructed."

Quinn rose and rolled down his shirt sleeves. "Dear me, you mean there might be—one shudders to say the very word—*competition*? A few *obstacles* between me and my objective? Never say I shall have to *work* at establishing our first branch at the ideal location for that venture. Work is so *common*."

He slipped gold sleeve buttons into his cuffs and maneuvered into a jacket that wrapped his frame like long-lost lover.

"You are up to something," Joshua said. "I don't know what, I don't know why, but you are up to something."

Quinn fastened the onyx buttons closing his jacket. "Haven't you heard? I dine on the bones of orphans, and entertain myself by sending widows to the poor house. Christmas approaches, when my cold heart delights in tossing beggars into the Thames, though I usually call upon Lucifer first to use a little hellfire to melt the river ice for me."

These and other stories were gleefully circulated by Quinn's competitors, and—to his consternation—even repeated in gentlemen's clubs.

"When will you remember to despoil a few virgins?" Joshua drawled. "You're growing soft in your dotage."

The virgins were safe around Quinn, as were the orphans, widows, and beggars. Thatcher's bookshop was another matter entirely.

"Farris should have returned by now," Quinn said. "I expect he'll have news to relate in the morning. We can discuss this project in more detail then, if you're so inclined."

Quinn checked his appearance in the pier glass that hung between the bay windows. A tall, sober, dark-haired man stared back at him, one with cold blue eyes, wearing morning attire as stitch-perfect as Bond Street's best could make it. Appearances mattered, and he'd never allow the employees or customers see in him any hint of the shivering, starving boy he'd once been.

"What is the point of argument?" Joshua said, coming to his feet. "You've made up your mind, and that bookshop is as good as ours. Happy Christmas, one and all."

CHAPTER 2

Mr. Nelson bustled up to the counter as Mrs. Draper left the shop. "I'll take both," he said, rapping his knuckles on a pair of leather-bound volumes. "That Mr. Farris is quite knowledgeable. You should hire somebody like him to take Mr. Thatcher's place."

Nobody could ever take Grandpapa's place in Chloe's heart or in the bookshop. His knowledge of literature had been encyclopedic, and his knowledge of the customers greater still.

"Perhaps after the holidays," Chloe said, "we'll be in a position to take on a clerk. Shall I wrap these for you, Mr. Nelson?"

"No need. I'm just trotting 'round the corner." He passed over enough money to pay for both books. "Missus will be very pleased with me. Mr. Farris assures me of that, and he's a young fellow who knows what he's about."

Aidan Farris was something of a mystery for all he made frequent purchases. According to Mrs. Draper, he was a solicitor in the employ of the Wentworth and Penrose bank, an establishment located much closer to the City. A Mr. Stephen Wentworth occasionally ordered books from the shop—always bound volumes, bless the man—but Chloe had never met him.

She surveyed the shop floor, and spotted Mrs. O'Neill browsing the biographies. She was Chloe's favorite kind of customer—a fast reader with a half-empty library and a full coin purse.

Mr. Farris stepped up to the counter. "I'd like to purchase this one, if you'd wrap it up for me, please." He'd chosen a tale by Mrs. More, *Coelebs in Search of Wife*.

"Have you read it?" Chloe asked.

"My sister recommends it, though she says not much occurs, other than the hero coming across one person after another on the way to London. She claims the author writes well and raises worthy philosophical questions in an entertaining style."

Chloe examined the volume, which was bound in pristine brown leather, the title embossed on the front in gold lettering. "Charles takes a wife and is happy, Mr. Farris, as is the lady. Is that your version of not much occurring?"

He'd extracted a purse from an inner pocket and begun rummaging for coins, but looked up as Chloe posed her question. She at first thought she'd given offense, because his expression went blank, and then...

He grinned. "To the contrary, Miss Thatcher. I account the union of man and wife a very significant occurrence indeed, one which I hope someday might be mine to experience."

Those wintry gray eyes could dance with humor, that solemn mouth could curve to reveal abundant white teeth and—Lord, have mercy—a dimple in his left cheek.

"We've hung a sprig of mistletoe near the door," Chloe said, taking the money he passed over. "Perhaps if you lingered amid the cookery books, you might begin your quest for a wife under the guise of respect for holiday tradition."

"Very clever, to hang the mistletoe where the ladies congregate." The smile dimmed and his gaze softened. "How are you and Miss Faith getting on, if I might inquire? Losing family is difficult any time of year, but to part with a beloved elder as the holidays approach would be particularly trying."

How had he known of Grandfather's passing? Mr. Farris was a gentleman, not of the merchant or working classes, and yet, he was also a frequent customer. The shop had been closed for a week in early October, all the time Chloe and Faith could spare for mourning. They'd not hung crepe or otherwise indulged in the rituals observed by their betters.

"The holidays are a comfort, actually," Chloe said. "We keep busy, and customers in a merry mood are never a trial." Then the customers left, the money in the drawer was never enough, and Mr. Phineas Barnstable made his daily inspection of the premises, peering through the shop window, swinging his cane at Grandfather's sign.

"I cannot envision Mr. Nelson in a merry mood," Mr. Farris said, "but I would not argue with a lady. As it happens, I am looking for a cookery book to gift my sister."

He was… flirting? Teasing? No matter, he'd already purchased one book and inspired the sale of two others. Perhaps Mr. Farris was an angel in disguise, one who'd bring the shop enough custom to keep Mr. Barnstable from selling the place.

"We have many, many books for the kitchen," Chloe said, coming out from behind the counter. "Does your sister prefer French or English?"

Chloe chattered on about various choices, and some of the other customers joined in the discussion. Mr. Farris subtly and politely inspired them to extolling the virtues of various volumes to one another, with the result that several ladies made purchases, while he remained undecided.

And positioned directly under the mistletoe, though only Chloe seemed to notice that detail.

"Have you any ambition to run a bookshop?" Chloe asked, as Faith collected payment at the counter. "You've sold more literature in the past hour than I've sold all afternoon."

"Your grandfather did not leave you comfortable, did he?" Mr. Farris had lowered his voice on that question, though the women gabbling with Faith at the counter were paying him no mind now. Darkness would soon fall, and they were doubtless eager to hurry home with their purchases.

"We might have managed," Chloe said. "Except that all of Grandpapa's creditors demanded payment immediately after his passing, which means we had not the holiday revenue in hand at the time."

"They refused to wait until the end of the year? I find that odd. Accepted practice is to pay up on accounts due at the end of each year."

A light snow had begun to fall, turning the candlelit windows across the street magical in the later afternoon gloom. Perhaps Mr. Farris's visit had been meant as a sign of hope, a reminder that good fortune could follow bad.

"You are a man of business. Would you extend credit to two young females trying to maintain a modest shop while carrying significant debts?"

"But the location of your establishment is excellent, your clientele loyal. I've had occasion to study on the matter, and you should be able to sell this place for—"

Chloe's attention was caught by a dark shape outside the window. Mr. Barnstable, making his rounds earlier than usual.

"If we sell this business we have nothing, Mr. Farris. Grandfather took out a mortgage on the property, and as his health declined, he became lax about making payments. Penalties for late payment, interest on the penalties, fees, and interest on the unpaid fees has made the situation very difficult. The shop can support us, and we could easily have made the regular payments, but we do not own this establishment. It belongs to Grandfather's estate, and our solicitor has advised us to plan accordingly."

More honest than that, she could not be with a near stranger.

"I'm… sorry," Mr. Farris said, reshelving the French dessert book he'd been examining. "I'm very sorry. Is there nothing to be done? No relatives who might step in?"

Barnstable made another pass, like a vulture circling a carcass. He carried his walking stick propped against his shoulder, and his hat sat at a jaunty angle.

"Grandfather was estranged from his only brother," Chloe said. "Great-uncle lives in Northumbria and we wrote to him of Grandfather's passing, but we rely on our great-uncle at our peril. The books will fetch something, and we're permitted to keep the proceeds of the sales we're making now as our wages. The solicitors were able to win that much of a concession from the mortgagor."

The last of the other customers had filed out the door, and the bell had ceased its intermittent jingling.

"I'll lock the drawer upstairs," Faith said. "Take your time, Mr. Farris. We'll need at least another hour to tidy the shelves for tomorrow and add up the day's sales."

Chloe and Faith usually lingered down in the shop as long as possible rather than face the chill upstairs. Chloe also did not trust Barnstable to merely patrol the walkway. As mortgagor, he likely had a key, and what he might do with it was the stuff of her nightmares.

"Is there nobody else who can aid you?" Mr. Farris asked, gaze very serious. "No friends, no suitors, nobody?"

The whole matter was none of his business, and yet, Chloe was tired of keeping the worry to herself, tired of reassuring Faith, tired of exuding good cheer in the face of unrelenting dread.

"We will have some funds by the time the holiday season concludes. We are willing to work hard. I've applied at the agencies, and Faith has done likewise. We'll manage." The agencies had not contacted either sister for so much as a single interview, for their only references were from the vicar, whose praise had been more vague than profuse.

Mr. Farris looked around the shop, which was well lit, because customers could not read what they could not see.

"Who said that those who can afford to buy books do not read them, and those who read them do not buy them?"

"You're paraphrasing Mr. Southey," Chloe said, as Mr. Barnstable came to a halt outside the window. She moved away from the cookery books and the mistletoe the better to keep Barnstable in view. "Mr. Barnstable could afford to give us a few months grace, but it's as you say: The property is worth a great deal, and Grandfather's mortgage-holder knows that."

"What's *he* doing here?" Mr. Farris posed the question with obvious distaste.

"You know Mr. Barnstable?"

"I am employed by a bank, and Barnstable owns a bank. I'd rather say I know of him, but our paths occasionally cross."

Barnstable removed some sort of document from within his greatcoat and unrolled it against the outside wall between the large front window and the shop's door.

"This cannot bode well," Chloe muttered, for Barnstable could be up to no good.

A rhythmic pounding followed as he rapped against the side of the building, affixing his document to the wood framing beside the front door.

"I don't like this," Mr. Farris said. "I don't care for this at all."

The pounding put Chloe in mind of the sound made when Grandfather had been laid in his coffin, and the lid secured for the last time. Slow, heavy blows like the beat of a sorrowing heart.

"Come along," Mr. Farris said, taking Chloe by the hand. "This is still your place of business, and he has no right—"

Chloe twisted free. "He has every right. We are in default of our mortgage, and he need not allow us any opportunity to catch up. We must pay the whole sum owing or face—"

Mr. Farris had wrenched open the door as Barnstable stepped back to admire a document affixed to the building.

"Miss Thatcher, good evening." Barnstable tipped his hat and nodded. He was balding, paunchy, and wearing enough expensive wool to keep Chloe and Faith warm until spring. "Mr. Farris, how fortuitous that you're here just as I'm posting the notice of sale. I'm sure Mr. Wentworth will be interested in the news. Happy Christmas to you both."

Chloe whirled to read the notice, which advertised a sale by auction of the entire building one week hence.

"One week! You aren't even giving us until Christmas?"

"Business is business," Barnstable replied. "I am in business to make a profit, in fact, I am duty-bound to do no less. Mr. Farris can explain it to you. Have a pleasant week until next we meet."

He strolled off into the deepening gloom, while Chloe's heart broke—broke right in half, the pain even greater than grief.

"I can't believe he'd do this," she said. "We thought we'd at least have until the New Year. So many people make last-minute holiday purchases…" She wiped a tear from her cheek and drew her shawl more tightly around her.

"You knew this was likely to happen?" Mr. Farris asked, peering at the notice.

"We feared it, but Barnstable led us to believe he'd not pounce until the holidays were concluded. One week… we'll be without a home days before Christmas."

Mr. Farris stared after Barnstable as he disappeared around the corner in the direction of the bakeshop.

"I fear I am to blame for this, Miss Thatcher. I very much fear I am the author of your difficulties."

He sprinted off into the darkness, leaving Chloe shivering in the cold.

"Barnstable is holding a public auction," Aidan said. "A bedamned public auction days before Christmas. How can he do such a thing to two young women who have nowhere to go and are still grieving the death of their grandfather?"

Aidan paced his employer's office, grateful for its deep carpets and thick walls. No sound escaped from Mr. Wentworth's private chamber, not to the conference room next door, not to the bank lobby one floor below. Mr. Wentworth was nothing, if not fanatical regarding privacy.

Like everything else about Aidan's employer, that emphasis on confidentiality was expressed most often in disapproving silence or the occasional raised eyebrow. Quinn Wentworth did not engage in overt displays of sentiment, and Aidan usually admired him for that. The bank, as Mr. Wentworth often remarked, was not a theater.

"Barnstable is in business to make a profit," Mr. Wentworth replied turning a page of the document he studied. "As are we. When you alerted me to Thatcher's passing, I assumed you did so in order that the bank might acquire his property. Was I in error, Farris?"

Nothing rattled Quinn Wentworth. He sat at his massive desk, as calm as an undertaker and dressed with nearly the same lack of ostentation. Aidan felt a rare frisson of resentment toward the person who'd plucked him from the street, given him a safe place to sleep, a job, and then an education.

"You have encouraged me to keep an eye on the merchant community, Mr. Wentworth, and I do that. I chat up the butcher's boy when he makes his deliveries, I inquire into the dairymaid's health when she brings the milk around of a morning. I drop into this or that shop, and report to you what I find. I had no idea Thatcher's granddaughters were nearly destitute."

"Why should you? Their situation is no concern of ours." Wentworth penciled a note into the margin of the document. "Thatcher was getting on in years, and ought to have made better provision for his dependents. You knew the bank was looking for a property to house a branch office and that Thatcher's location was ideal for that purpose. What did you think I'd do with the information that the bookshop owner had gone to his reward?"

Aidan had passed along news of Thatcher's death two months ago, amid the usual gossip: A prominent mercer had sued a newspaper for libel. A theater troupe had been laid low on opening night by bad eel pie. The vicar at St. Euphonia's had been posted to a village outside Leeds amid rumors of mishandled funds.

"I quite honestly forgot I'd told you, sir, and now that we know the young ladies will be rendered homeless by the sale, we can look elsewhere for a better branch location."

Another note scribbled onto the margin. "Can the young ladies bid on the property themselves?" He didn't even look up to pose that question.

"My understanding is that they have very limited means. What coin they can earn from holiday shoppers might be all they have to show for years of minding that shop."

Look at me. At least have the decency to look me in the eye when you decide to ruin two innocent lives.

Silence stretched, one of Quinn Wentworth's favorite negotiating tools. Aidan had worked for the banker too long to be drawn out by that tactic though. For once, Quinn Wentworth would explain himself.

He turned another page. Aidan waited until Mr. Wentworth sat back and removed his spectacles.

"Here's where we are, Farris. The community of merchants, mindful that one of their own has died leaving two dependents destitute, will bid vigorously on that property because that is their version of charity. The season of the year works to the advantage of the seller, meaning Barnstable. He will at the very least collect all of his trumped up fees, penalties, and interest in addition to the principle owed."

"You're saying the merchants will bid generously, knowing that the young ladies face penury?"

This theory, like all of Mr. Wentworth's theories, had merit. If mercantile London was ever generous and decent, it was at Yuletide and to one of their own.

"Wait until January, though," Wentworth continued, "and the merchants quickly resume business as usual. Your young ladies will see more coin from the sale if it's held before Christmas. They will present a pathetic spectacle, orphans turned out into the frigid night, and their performance will be rewarded."

This was what Quinn Wentworth did. He applied logic with unflinching disregard for emotion, as a director of a stage play considered how gestures or lines of dialogue would affect the audience. Usually, Aidan was impressed with the workings of such an orderly, sensible mind.

Not this time. "You are wrong, sir." *It won't be a performance.*

One dark brow lifted to a merely curious height. "I am in error? How novel. Do enlighten me, Mr. Farris."

"The holidays are when most commercial establishments are busiest, and the week between Boxing Day and New Year's is typically when a bookshop sees the most sales. People return one book and buy two to replace it. Boxing Day social calls mean all of London is out and about, and yet, the longest weeks of winter are still ahead. If ever we buy books, we do it as the holidays are passing, and January looms before us in all its dreary interminability."

Aidan knew the habits of book purchasers both from discussions with old Mr. Thatcher and from years of being a devoted reader.

"Not all of us, Farris, have the leisure time to waste with Sir Walter's maunderings."

That comment bordered on unfair, and Quinn Wentworth was never unfair. He did, on rare occasion, benefit from hearing another's viewpoint.

"Not all of us, sir, are so lacking in imagination that we can think of aught else to do the livelong day besides work, cipher, and think about work and ciphering."

The eyebrow of eternal damnation lofted a tad higher, into the did-I-hear-you-correctly range, though Aidan would not take back his words. Mr. Penrose had once indicated that Mr. Wentworth had come to reading later than most, but so had Aidan, and he'd loved books ever since.

"Are you discontent with your post at the bank, Mr. Farris?"

The question was polite, the threat clear, but again, Aidan knew his employer, and knew better than to show how this discussion upset him.

"I owe my employer my loyalty, Mr. Wentworth, therefore, I must be discontent when the bank proposes an action that will unnecessarily redound to its discredit. If you purchase that shop at auction and turn the young ladies out as the holidays approach, Barnstable will be made whole.

"We both know," Aidan went on, "Barnstable will twist and misrepresent the sums owed by the estate so that he makes much profit on the sale while leaving nothing for the young ladies to inherit. You and this bank, however, will have paid an inflated price for the property in your eagerness to gain possession of that building. Worse yet, the bank's reputation—turning helpless women out into the cold at Yuletide—will suffer as well."

Mr. Wentworth rose, and though he was only two inches taller than Aidan, he carried the height in a manner that made other men feel lesser. Perhaps the problem was that Mr. Wentworth moved as quietly as he spoke, or perhaps the stretch of fine tailoring across broad shoulders hinted at the bully boy Wentworth had once been.

"Redounding, are we?" he asked with mock dismay. "Polishing my image as Bad Fortune's personal errand boy? I treasure that image, Farris. Knowing that I mean what I say and never go back on a contract once signed saves all and sundry a great deal of heartache and drama."

He strolled around the massive desk, hands linked behind his back. He might have been a tutor preparing to wax eloquent about the Shakespearean tragedies, except that the tragedy for the Thatcher sisters would be all too real.

"You do raise an interesting point," Wentworth said. "Putting unearned profit into Barnstable's greedy hands is a logical outcome of an expeditious sale. Suppose we can't have that. Not when Phineas has been such a naughty fellow the live-long year. I'll have a word with him, and suggest the sale be moved back until after Christmas."

He collected the document on the desk and passed it to Aidan. "Direct the clerks to make three copies of this contract as annotated, please, and keep an eye on that bookshop. I want daily reports, Mr. Farris. How much custom, of what variety, purchasing which titles."

"Yes, sir." Aidan accepted the thick sheaf of pages and left his employer to his ciphering.

Something about the interview didn't sit well, as if Aidan had arrived at a conclusion Mr. Wentworth had intended for him to arrive at, but no matter. Aidan had earned the Thatcher sisters another week at least in which to collect revenue from brisk sales, and himself another week to pray they'd find a miracle, before Quinn Wentworth saw them cast out into the cold.

CHAPTER 3

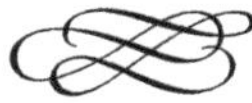

"A nip to ward off the chill, Mr. Wentworth?" Phineas Barnstable lifted a crystal decanter from a mahogany sideboard as he made that offer. "My selection includes very fine brandies, but perhaps your tastes run to rum or,"—he paused, his smile becoming insolent—"*gin*."

Gin, the drink that had ruined Quinn's father. "I prefer not to take spirits during business hours, thank you just the same. I'd like to discuss the Thatcher sale."

He ambled the perimeter of Barnstable's office rather than take a seat. The paintings hanging on the walls were good quality, but nudes every one. Put those images in a Seven Dials pub, and they'd be lewd. Here, they were art.

"The Thatcher *auction*," Barnstable countered, pouring himself a drink. "I am merely the mortgagor, liquidating an asset on behalf of the old man's estate. To your health." He lifted his glass and made a little performance of sampling the contents, holding the drink beneath his chin, then beneath his nose, then audibly swishing the first taste about in his mouth.

Quinn knew how to consume brandy. That skill was necessary

for moving in gentlemanly circles, so he'd learned it. He'd learned how to dress in the first stare of fashion, even how to damned waltz.

He'd never learned how to cheat at business, but Barnstable could have taught university courses on the subject.

"Will you entertain a private sale of the property?" Quinn asked. The mantel held a thin coating of gray coal dust. As warm as Barnstable kept this room, the whole office likely needed dusting three times a day.

"My dear Mr. Wentworth, I have already advertised the auction to the commercial public. If they learned I'd instead transferred the property to you without benefit of full and open competition, how could I prove to the courts that I'd got the best price for the place? An estate must be rendered solvent if possible, and a public auction means I've done my part to make that happen."

He spoke genially, as if instructing a clerk. He was also misrepresenting the law, which he did well and frequently.

"If what you seek is full and open competition, you'll wait until after Christmas," Quinn said. "But perhaps Barnstable's is a bit short of coin, and must liquidate assets hastily? The banking business is such a fraught undertaking."

Quinn turned his back on his host as if to admire the view of the street below, a deliberate rudeness in exchange for deliberate insults, plural.

Barnstable's bay window was fogged with grime, as every London windows was in winter, but Quinn could make out the crossing sweeper at the intersection, a child shivering in ragged clothes. The boy darted out into traffic to collect horse droppings while they were still warm, and shoveled them into a barrel. The lad huddled next to the barrel, gaze riveted on passing vehicles.

Quinn knew firsthand the ache in those small knees, the focus that blotted out almost all awareness of the cold. He'd graduated from crossing sweeper to groom at a livery, and still found a stable a place of peace, warmth, and refuge.

This stuffy, ostentatious office had, by contrast, authored much undeserved hardship. Quinn's good deed for the year—he permitted himself one charitable undertaking each Yuletide—would be to serve Barnstable a portion of justice.

Barnstable set his drink on the ornate reading table in the center of the room. "Mr. Wentworth, do you imply that my establishment is insolvent?"

"Several hypotheses come to mind to explain the undue haste with which you put the Thatcher property up for auction," Quinn said, wandering away from the window. "First, your bank needs ready coin. Banks fail all the time, and the present economy is a tribulation to all in the financial business."

Barnstable gestured with his glass. "One cannot take offense at platitudes, but I assure you, Barnstable's quite sound and you imply otherwise at peril to my civility."

Quinn did not give one frozen horse dropping for Phineas Barnstable's civility. "Second, you have failed to take into account the nature of the parties likely to bid on the Thatcher property."

"Now you do insult me, Wentworth. You come to my office, begging me for special consideration, insinuating—"

Quinn picked up Barnstable's drink and held it beneath his chin, the raised it to his nose, then set it down. Not first quality. A slight hint of wet dog about the nose, a faint note of boar-in-rut below that.

"I beg for nothing, Barnstable. I felt it incumbent upon me as a fellow banker to discuss with you the folly of a precipitous sale, of which the courts would naturally take notice. The merchants eager to get their hands on that property are themselves short of cash prior to Christmas Day itself. Accounts owing are typically not paid until Boxing Day, and thus far more ready money will be in their pockets after Christmas than before. Perhaps this signal fact slipped your mind."

Barnstable's brows drew down, suggesting that this obvious fact had escaped his notice. "One doesn't want to involve the courts, Wentworth. I had merely hoped to see the matter tidied up sooner rather than later. The merchants are not hard-hearted toward their own, and the Thatcher girls face the proverbial *plight*, you see. They will be penniless and homeless unless the sale is very successful. I've put that word about, and the reception has been most encouraging."

Quinn pretended to study the painting over the mantel, a much-darkened rendering of Artemis with her loyal stag, and without much clothing.

"You are using the Thatcher sisters' situation to play upon the sympathies of the bidders, then?"

"Why not? Nothing like a little holiday generosity to make Yuletide feel complete. The Thatcher sisters will benefit, I'll benefit, the estate's other creditors will benefit."

The estate had no other creditors. Quinn had established that much several weeks ago. The Thatcher sisters had nearly beggared themselves paying off every sum due, and of course, Barnstable had ensured that those bills had been delivered almost before the old man's funeral.

Barnstable was thus free to manipulate his accountings without any fear of oversight or interference from other creditors.

And—Quinn was certain of this—Barnstable's institution was perilously short of cash.

"Holiday generosity does not disappear on Christmas night," Quinn said. "We both know Boxing Day ushers in at least a week of brisk commercial activity as accounts are paid and calls are made. If you have the sale immediately after Christmas, you will see much higher bids, and you'll still be able to play upon the sympathies of the merchants. You will also have less to fear from the courts, who take a dim view of unnecessary haste where orphaned females are concerned."

Regardless of the timing of the sale, Barnstable would keep every ha' penny for himself, and allow the Thatcher sisters a pittance by way of an inheritance. Their grandfather's solicitor would be only too happy that his own outstanding invoice was settled, and the hardworking young ladies would end up on the parish or worse.

Quinn knew that tragedy line by line.

"Your reputation for shrewdness is well earned, Mr. Wentworth," Barnstable said. "May I ask what you would have offered for the place?"

"You may ask, I'd be a fool to share that information. I might, however, be persuaded to send a representative to your little auction."

Barnstable's smile would have been a credit to Father Christmas. "Your Mr. Farris has been seen on the premises at least twice a week since old Thatcher's death. You doubtless sent your loyal hound to reconnoiter, which is how I knew you were interested in the property. You are welcome to bid as high as you please at my *little auction*."

"If you hold that auction before Christmas, don't expect me to bother. I can't have the courts meddling in the transaction, particularly not when I'll likely end up paying a premium price for the place."

The courts did meddle occasionally, and when they did, an estate could languish for years. Barnstable did not have years. If Quinn's information was correct—and it was—Barnstable barely had weeks.

Barnstable sloshed more liquor into his glass. "I'll hold that auction whenever I please, Mr. Wentworth."

"And I," Quinn said, "employ enough idealistic young solicitors to make you regret any precipitous behavior. The Thatcher sisters grew up in that shop, I'm told, and they know their trade well. You might have allowed them to catch up the mortgage after their grandfather's illness, but you chose not to. The courts will be interested to know that, I'm sure, and will examine your records very closely if prompted to do so."

Barnstable's smile winked out like a snuffed candle. "You don't care one whit for those girls and neither do I, Wentworth. The working classes are resilient, and if those young women know their trade so well, they can ply it in somebody else's bookshop. Why do you need an extra week? Is Wentworth and Penrose short of funds, is that it?"

The next part was delicate, for Quinn would not lie. "Wentworth and Penrose has enemies, which is no secret. The old, established banks regard us as an upstart aberration, unworthy to transact business in their backyards. If I do purchase the Thatcher property, it will be to open a branch close to where the better families like to shop. I anticipate resistance to that endeavor, and a precipitous auction is a perfect excuse to involve the courts."

Every word of that recitation was the truth, and Barnstable appeared to accept it as such.

"Why not wait a month, then?"

A month during which Barnstable would tack more principle, interest, fees, and penalties onto what the Thatchers supposedly owed him.

"Because by tradition, commercial accounts are settled in the next week or so, Barnstable. How many times must I remind you? Even the courts have to acknowledge a custom that's been centuries in the making. Longer than that, I do not care to wait. If the sisters close up shop and leave Town, there's no telling what condition the property will be in after London's vagrants have made free with it."

Barnstable studied the rug, a plush Axminster that stretched from wall to wall. Somebody swept this carpet regularly, for the red, green, and cream pattern of leaves and blossoms was brightly visible.

"Very well," Barnstable said, "I'll hold the auction after Christmas, and regardless of who the successful bidder is, I will anticipate no interference from the courts. You are reputed to be shrewd to a fault, but honest, so I will look forward to seeing one of your idealistic solicitors at the sale. Do we have an agreement, Mr. Wentworth?"

"We have had a productive discussion," Quinn said, declining to offer a handshake. He did not rely on the word of cheats or liars. Barnstable cared not who ended up with the property, he simply wanted Quinn's bid to drive up the final price.

Which it would do, if all went according to plan.

"Then I'll wish you good day, Mr. Wentworth."'

Quinn strode for the door, the discussion having gone as well as could be expected. Not everything he'd hoped for, but—

"There is one other consideration," Barnstable said.

Quinn turned slowly, lest his anticipation show in his eyes. "Do enlighten me."

"If I'm to wait another week for the sale, then I'll want to ensure the bidding is as brisk as possible. I'll hold the sale without reserve, Mr. Wentworth. You will have competition for that property, and I will have a good price for it. A very good price."

A sale without reserve attracted the widest possible array of bidders, because the terms of the auction guaranteed that *somebody* would end the day in possession of the property. The bidding began where it began and ended who knew where, but the property was guaranteed to change hands.

"Barnstable, is that wise? You'll attract every cit and nabob from one end of London to the other."

"That's the point, isn't it? To show the courts that I'm acting in good faith, doing my bit for a pair of orphaned females?"

"Your notice does not specify that this is a sale without reserve." Quinn had read the notice word for word, several times.

"I'll put up new notices specifying the later date, and clarifying that the auction will be without reserve. Then neither you, the merchants, nor the courts can complain." He held the door open, and Quinn sent him a scowl that would have intimidated even the stalwart Mr. Farris.

Only when Quinn was once again out in the brisk winter air tossing a half-sovereign to the crossing sweeper did he permit himself the smallest, pleased smile.

"I don't understand," Chloe said. "You work for Mr. Wenthworth's bank, but it's Mr. Barnstable who holds Grandpapa's mortgage."

The afternoon lull had started, the hour after luncheon when people paid social calls. A stop by the bookshop might follow such a call, but rarely preceded it.

"I work for Wentworth and Penrose," Mr. Farris said, pacing the shop's worn carpets. "I am a solicitor and banks have much need of legal services. Mr. Wentworth has long admonished me that a man of business pays attention to his community. I'm to notice when the farmers bringing produce to Covent Garden begin to complain of drought, for example, or the modistes start experimenting with new fabrics."

He circled the shop as he made this explanation, his boots thumping against the floorboards. His steps were measured, his tone even, but Chloe had the sense he was upset.

She was upset. Barnstable's damned notice had been tacked to Grandfather's very building, right by the front door where all must see it. The morning's sales had been ominously light, though many people had stopped to read the auction notice.

"What has this to do with an auction six days from now, Mr. Farris?"

He paused by the biographies. "My employer, Mr. Wentworth, wants to buy this shop."

"I expect half of London wants to buy this shop. Great-grandfather chose the location well." And yet, Chloe was certain that no matter how handsome the sale price, she and Faith would nonetheless be paupers by New Year's.

"Mr. Wentworth only learned of your grandfather's illness through me," Mr. Farris said, turning his hat in his hands. "I report what I find, like an intelligence officer, whether it's an altercation between dandies in the park, a new hotel opening up, or a play closing after less than a fortnight."

"So you gossip with your co-workers. How is that related to Mr. Barnstable's infernal sale?"

He circled on the braided rug near the storybooks, where Chloe had arranged a few small nursery chairs not too far from—and not too near—the parlor stove.

"I alerted Mr. Wentworth to your grandfather's passing, and Barnstable well knows who my employer is. He's doubtless seen me here on many occasions."

Tuesdays and Fridays, most weeks. Chloe looked forward to

those days, and Aidan Farris was the reason. Why must she only now grasp that connection?

"You are a loyal customer and an avid reader, Mr. Farris. That you frequent our shop is not unusual."

Faith had hung a cluster of red and green silk bows from the chandelier, and red bunting adorned the mantel. The store was as festive as last year's decorations could make it, but standing amid the children's tales, Mr. Farris looked miserable.

"I am also loyal to my employer. Years ago, Mr. Wentworth found me searching the Covent Garden middens for scraps of food, and gave me a job as a bank messenger. The other lads at the bank and I ran all over London on bank business and reported back what we'd seen. We had food, a place to sleep, and work that didn't keep us cooped up in some mill or foundry—or worse."

A fine, handsome boy loose on London's streets could come to a very bad pass. Mr. Farris was grateful to his employer, in other words. Was his employer appreciative in return?

"Mr. Wentworth is daily confronted with urchins beyond number," Chloe said. "That is simply the nature of London. If he offered you a job, he saw something worthy in you."

"I hope so, for like you, I was raised by my grandparents. They succumbed to influenza, and overnight, I was cast out to make my way as best I could. I cannot bear—" He looked around the shop, a humble space, but Chloe's home and the focus of all of her dreams. "I cannot bear that Quinn Wentworth's ambitions, and my support of them, are why you will lose this legacy."

Aidan Farris was such a decent man. "This Wentworth fellow apparently had designs on the shop before he knew of your fondness for books. You need not torment yourself on our account."

Mr. Farris wandered to the cookery books, which had sold so briskly the day before thanks to him.

"I am more than fond of books. Books became my family, my comfort. The junior clerks at the bank were expected to teach the messengers to read and cipher. I did well at that, and I can manage accounts competently, but the words, the magical, mysterious words… My grandmother had given me a start, and when I got to the bank I read everything I could find. Labels on patent remedies, pamphlets, contracts, discarded newspapers. Mr. Wentworth noticed, and eventually sent me off to read law."

"Now you read Mrs. More."

His gaze swiveled from the books to Chloe. "What's-his-name in search of a wife?"

Why must he ask that question while standing beneath the mistletoe?

"One of many fine tales." Chloe smiled, despite the impending sale, despite the now-empty shop, despite all, because Mr. Farris was smiling at her. She'd not seen that exact expression from him before, had not known how breathtakingly attractive he could be with that light of masculine devilment in his eyes.

He was really quite handsome, which was just too bad considering that in a week—

"He's back," Mr. Farris said, marching to the window. "What could Barnstable possibly want now, and why is he…?"

Chloe stood side by side with Mr. Farris while Barnstable ripped down the notice he'd put up the evening before. In its place, he tacked another paper of the same size. He tipped his hat to Chloe and sauntered on his way, while Chloe's dread sank to new depths.

"He's likely moved the sale to this week," she said. "He cannot turn Faith and me out fast enough, and we've yet to hear from our great-uncle in Northumberland that we even have leave to visit him."

"Let's read the notice," Mr. Farris said, taking Chloe by the hand. "Barnstable will not have as many bidders if he moves the auction up, and that would mean a lower price for the property."

Chloe let herself be towed into the bright winter sunshine, for she did not want to read the notice at all, much less alone.

"Tell me what it says."

"The sale has been moved back until after Christmas. An auction without reserve will be held December 27 at this location, the property to change hands January 2. All interested parties are to apply to P. Barnstable's Bank for details."

"Why is he doing this?" And why did holding Mr. Farris's hand bring such unaccountable comfort?

"Because Mr. Wentworth had a private discussion with him. We have a little time, Miss Thatcher, to gather up a sum for you to bid on this property or to take with you when you leave." He held the door for her and Chloe hurried back into the shop's warmth.

"Your employer had the sale set back until after Christmas? For what reason?"

Mr. Farris resumed his pacing by the cook books. "I told him to, though Wentworth never does anything contrary to his own interests. I used to admire that about him."

Chloe positioned herself between Mr. Farris and the books. "Why did you tell him to, Mr. Farris? A few days one way or another can't make much difference. Faith and I are reconciled to enduring some difficulties. We've put our names in with the agencies, we've contacted every bookshop in Bloomsbury, and we're prepared—"

He toucher her lips with a single finger. "I feel responsible, but that's not the whole of it."

She had one moment to read the intent in his eyes, one moment to smile at him in response, and then he kissed her.

"WHERE HAVE YOU BEEN?" JOSHUA ASKED.

Quinn laid his hat on the sideboard, and hung his greatcoat on the hook by the conference room door. "Shopping for holiday tokens."

Joshua set aside the ledger he'd been reading. "It's not like you to spend part of the work day wandering from shop to shop, Quinn. Also not like you to lie."

"I called upon a butcher, a baker, and a candlestick maker, and my intent was commercial." Quinn hadn't wandered, he pursued a well planned itinerary, chosen for how inclined to gossip each shop's proprietor was—and how successful. "Why are my comings goings any of your business?"

Joshua rose. He'd affixed a sprig of holly to his lapel, which ought to have looked ridiculous. "Because you have embarked upon some convoluted scheme. We are partners, and occasionally, your machinations benefit from thoughtful discussion."

"I truly was out visiting the shops."

"On reconnaissance, then. Farris hasn't been much in evidence lately either."

This apparently bothered Joshua, who took a particular interest in the bank's stable of messenger boys and how they progressed in life.

"Farris is growing restless," Quinn said. "He needs to be kept busy."

"If you want to set up that branch location so he can manage it, you might tell him that."

Quinn peered at the figures Joshua had been studying. "Is that what I want?"

"You and I both know Farris will never go to work for a competitor, never establish his own practice as a solicitor. He feels beholden to the bank, and he would never betray our best interests. He's a perfect candidate to open our first branch office, but right now, he's not very happy with you."

Few people were happy with Quinn. He preferred it that way. "Has Farris grumbled to you?"

Joshua drew out his watch, shiny gold affectation that every banker was supposed to carry. Quinn did as well, but like every poor child in London, he still told time by the bells of St. Paul's.

"Farris would never grumble to me, but he practically grew up at this bank. He's not happy with you, and if he understood that he's to manage the new branch, he'd be less discontent."

"Counting chickens before they've hatched, Joshua? I haven't mentioned a possible promotion for Farris to anybody, and I'd certainly discuss it with you before I broached it with him."

Joshua sauntered toward the door. "No, you'd patiently allow me to air my opinions, then do as you originally intended to anyway. I wish you *had* been out holiday shopping, Quinn. There is more to life than this damned bank."

A popular sentiment lately. "Where are you off to?"

"None of your business, but in the spirit of respect for holiday traditions, I'll refrain from rendering any orphans homeless. I'll try to catch Mrs. Hatfield beneath the mistletoe instead, and provide entertainment for the clerks."

Mrs. Hatfield was the bank's auditor. Quinn gave her a wide berth and a generous paycheck. Nobody would catch her within ten feet of the mistletoe unless she wanted to be caught there.

"If you're planning to flirt with our Mrs. Hatfield, I hope your affairs are in order, Penrose."

Joshua paused by the door, and looked like he wanted to say more. He merely shook his head and left Quinn alone with the ledger.

CHAPTER 4

"You kissed me," Miss Thatcher said.

Aidan had kissed her, gently, respectfully, and not nearly as much as he'd wanted to. "We're alone, and not visible through the front window. You haven't slapped me." Miss Thatcher was in fact smiling, *at him*, else he would never have been so bold.

"It was a lovely kiss, Mr. Farris."

If she thought that chaste peck on the lips was lovely… Oh, the kisses he wanted to share with her. "My name is Aidan, and I'm arguably the author of your misfortunes. I should be whipped at the cart's tail for presuming."

"We're beneath the mistletoe," Miss Thatcher said, pointing upward. "Holiday tradition is the farthest thing from presumption."

"The mistle—?" Aidan looked up, at pale green leaves and small white berries. "So we are." He plucked a berry and put it in his pocket.

"That wasn't a holiday kiss?"

The moment became something more as quiet spread over the shop. The fire in the parlor stove crackled softly, harness bells jingled merrily outside the door.

"Miss Thatcher, you must know that as much as I esteem a good book, I esteem you far more. You are never too busy to assist an elderly customer, you are patient with the children. I adore that about you. You read to them on Tuesday afternoons—I nearly worship you for that—and you have biscuits for them, just for them, fresh from the bakeshop. You work hard here, and clearly, you have the vocation to put the right books into the right hands. I envy you that calling."

She regarded him as if trying to decide between suggesting one of Sir Walter's rousing Scottish adventures or Miss Austen's witty social allegories.

"I thought you liked books, Mr. Farris."

"I love books, but there are many bookshops in London. There is only one Chloe Thatcher." Who would soon leave for Northumberland if he could not find a means to save her shop.

She took a step back, her smile dimming. "And you have only one employer, to whom you are loyal, and he apparently wants to close my shop. I'd best get my reshelving done."

And there, in a few honest sentences, lay the difficulty. "Mr. Wentworth saved my life."

She picked up a stack of bound volumes. "Does that give him the right to ruin mine? Or Faith's? She's fifteen, Mr. Farris, and pretty and innocent. Does her fate trouble Mr. Wentworth of a night?"

Chloe Thatcher was pretty too, also angry, and justifiably so.

"I'll have another talk with Mr. Wentworth," Aidan said. "A very pointed discussion. Perhaps he'd like to own a bookshop."

Maybe—when pigs circled the dome of St. Paul's. Quinn Wentworth had an abacus where his heart should have been. He might not loathe books outright, but he had no use for them. Books, he'd often opined, were written by those with too much idle time on their hands, and read by those with the same affliction.

Fat lot he knew. The thought was disloyal and liberating.

"I would like to own a bookshop," Miss Thatcher said. "I suspect you would as well, but apparently that's not to be."

Aidan took a look around at the rows of shelves, each one holding undiscovered treasure. Truth be told, he liked even the scent of a bookshop—faintly vanilla, with a tang of leather and learning.

"I cannot leave the bank, Miss Thatcher. The employees are like family to me, and gave me a chance when I was just another dirty boy living on the streets."

She shoved a book between the other bound volumes. "This situation is not your fault, Mr. Farris, I know that. I respect you, I like you, and were the circumstances different..." Her gaze went to the mistletoe, probably the saddest glance ever directed at holiday greenery, then she resumed her work.

Faith came in carrying a sack redolent of cinnamon. "I've brought the biscuits," she said over the jingle of the doorbell. "Hello, Mr. Farris. Care for a biscuit?"

Aidan wanted much more than a biscuit, and for the first time in years, his ambitions did not lie in the direction of advancement at the bank.

"I'm afraid I cannot stay, Miss Faith. I must return to my office."

Though inspiring Quinn Wentworth to extravagant generosity was a doomed undertaking. Still, if Aidan cared for Miss Thatcher—for both of the misses Thatchers—he had to try.

THE DAYS MARCHED FORTH FOR CHLOE IN A CHILLY SUCCESSION OF forced smiles, anxious hours, and sales that were brisk, but not brisk enough. Because she and Faith were hoarding every spare groat, they had agreed that Christmas dinner would be cheese toast and apple tort with a fresh pot of tea. Faith had splurged to the extent that the tea would have a dash of sugar and a dollop of milk, luxuries Chloe had taken for granted three short months ago.

"Two copies of Fordyce's Sermons," Faith said, flipping the sign on the door from *open* to *closed*. "What a thrill it must be for a young lady to unwrap her own copy of a lot of preaching and scolding on Christmas morning."

She twisted the lock on the door and leaned her back against the jamb. "We're about to lose this place, and if nothing else, I finally realize how dear it is to me."

Chloe had no need to count the money in the drawer. Remaining open on Christmas had resulted in little more than the two sales Faith mentioned. She and Faith had passed the time playing whist and pretending to enjoy the quiet.

"We can cook our feast down here," Chloe said. "No need to freeze our toes on Christmas night."

"You want to celebrate the holidays where we've been so happy," Faith said, setting the kettle on the parlor stove. "So do I. I feel as if we're letting Grandpapa down by losing the store, but some things cannot be helped."

Mr. Farris must have reached the same conclusion, for he'd not graced the bookshop since he'd kissed Chloe beneath the mistletoe. She'd pondered that kiss often, and wondered if Mr. Farris would attend the auction on Wednesday.

"We have much to be grateful for," Chloe said. "We will arrive at Great-uncle's with some coin in our pocket, a willingness to work hard, and many happy memories. Others have far less."

She thought of Mr. Farris, and the dirty boy he'd been. If his employer had rescued him from that fate, then of course he must be loyal to the bank. Still…

A pounding on the door interrupted her wishful thinking.

"Somebody has forgotten to purchase a Christmas token and cannot wait until tomorrow to make their choice," Faith said, unlocking the door and opening it. "Mr. Farris. Good evening."

He stood in the doorway, hatless for once, snow dusting his dark locks. "Ladies, may I come in?"

He held several parcels, his boots were damp about the toes, and his complexion was ruddy.

"You've been out in the elements," Chloe said. "Of course you may come in.

"Something smells good," Faith murmured. "Good and hot."

Mr. Farris put his packages on the counter. "I wish I could say I bring tidings of great joy, but all I have is some roast goose, fresh bread, a potato and cheddar casserole, some—"

"You brought a feast," Chloe said, taking the largest package from him. "A holiday feast."

"And plum pudding," Faith added, holding up a small blue crock. "You brought hot plum pudding. You must stay and join us."

Mr. Farris stared at his toes, he brushed melting snow from his sleeves, he looked anywhere but at Chloe. "One doesn't want to intrude, especially not on an occasion typically reserved for family gatherings, but I know how lonely the holidays can be when a loved one has recently passed."

Chloe unwrapped his scarf from his neck. "I suspect, ten years from now, we will still miss Grandpapa at the holidays. You must stay, Mr. Farris. We can't possibly finish all this food ourselves, and we would appreciate the company."

"The food will get cold if you stand about and argue," Faith added. "Please do stay."

He stayed, he partook of the feast, and he even had a small helping of the plum pudding. He read to them from the Gospel of Luke, as Grandpapa had always done, the story of the lowly baby and the young parents far from home. He helped carry the leftover food upstairs, where the cold ensured it would keep well.

Then he escorted Chloe downstairs, and much to her surprise, she realized her Christmas had been happy after all.

"Do you go home to a chilly garret, Mr. Farris?" She blew out the candles on the mantel as Mr. Farris lowered the chandelier.

"Not a garret, but chilly enough. I have rooms near the bank. I strive to be economical with my coal expenditures so I have more money for books."

Why must he mention the dratted, almighty bank? Some of the evening's warmth faded as Chloe passed Mr. Farris the candle snuffer.

"Will you be at the auction the day after tomorrow?"

He lifted the glass chimneys with his handkerchief and put out the candles one by one. "I have been wanting to tell you something, but haven't found the words."

Oh, please not now. Not a declaration of sentiments that could go nowhere.

"We have privacy," Chloe said, for Faith had remained abovestairs. "If you are bidding on the property for Mr. Wentworth, you need not apologize. But for him, you'd likely have starved. I know that."

Mr. Farris passed her the snuffer and raised the chandelier back to the cross beam. "Mr. Wentworth would be the first to tell you that he doesn't believe in charity. He found a likely lad, willing to work hard for a fair wage, and that's the extent of it, to hear him tell it."

"Have all of his likely lads become solicitors, Mr. Farris?"

He closed the curtain over the shop's front window, casting the interior in shadows Chloe had been able to navigate before she'd put up her hair. This was her home, her livelihood, her everything, and yet, come the new year, it would all be taken away.

That reality was too awful to grasp, and too sad to ignore, much like Grandpapa's final illness.

"I am one of several solicitors in Mr. Wentworth's employ," Mr. Farris said, "which is partly why turning in my resignation without notice earlier today bothered me much less than I thought it would. The bank does not need me."

Chloe set aside the broom she'd been using to tidy up around the parlor stove. "He *sacked* you? That rotten, presuming, hard-hearted, miserable—he *sacked* you? On Christmas Day?"

"You haven't even met the man, and he'd apparently do well to avoid your notice. Mr. Wentworth did not sack me. I quit. We had a difference of opinion."

She took Mr. Farris by the hand and led him to the worn sofa at the back of the biographies. "I argued with Grandpapa all the time. If Mr. Wentworth is so delicate that he cannot tolerate some honesty from a subordinate, he doesn't deserve you."

"I told him that if he cared at all for the bank's reputation, he'd simply take over the mortgage on the bookshop, and let you and Faith carry on with your grandfather's legacy."

"Banks will not lend to a pair of young women, Mr. Farris."

He covered her hand with both of his. "I know that, but Mr. Wentworth has sisters, he knows what it is to be poor. I thought he'd make an exception, but he never makes exceptions. He contends that Barnstable would never have agreed to simply transfer the mortgage in any case."

To sit side by side with Mr. Farris, holding hands in the darkened bookshop was comforting, though the topic was not comforting at all.

"I suspect Mr. Wentworth was correct. Perhaps he'll give you your job back if you apologize, Mr. Farris."

"I don't want my job back, and please call me Aidan."

"Aidan." Saying his name should not be a guilty pleasure, much less sad, but it was both. "Pride goeth, and all that. Faith and I will present ourselves on our great-uncle's doorstep as pattern cards of humility, you may be sure of that."

"I quarreled with Mr. Wentworth, Chloe. He seemed to think that if Barnstable wouldn't let anybody else take over your mortgage, that was an end to the discussion. Mr. Wentworth is still focused on buying this property. He's been letting the other merchants know of his interest, which means they won't bid against him. He'll get the property for a song, and you and Miss Faith will be left with nothing."

"He'd do that? Give employment to a pack of wild boys then turn around and leave Faith and me destitute?"

Aidan brought her hand to his lips. "I don't know. Mr. Wentworth asked me what token I'd like for Christmas, if I could name any gift worth any sum. I told him that for Christmas, I'd like a clear conscience, and if I could not enjoy that boon while in his employ, then I considered myself free to pursue other opportunities."

Grandpapa had always liked Mr. Farris. "That was courageous of you. I hope you haven't made a very powerful enemy for nothing."

Aidan tucked an arm around her shoulders as if they'd sat like this often, cozied up at the end of a day tending the shop.

"He's not like that. He's fair, he always keeps his word, and he cannot abide gratuitous drama. I, on the other hand, love a good tale, the more exciting the better."

The conversation drifted to books then, about which Aidan was nearly as enthusiastic as Chloe.

"You must come by and help tomorrow," Chloe said. "Boxing Day is always terribly busy, and I'd like the company."

He rose. "Until tomorrow then, and I won't let you face that damned auction without an ally, Chloe. Had I known…"

He fell silent, as he helped Chloe to get to her feet. She kept his hand in hers. "Had you known that Mr. Wentworth would bid on the shop, it would have changed nothing, Aidan. A messenger, a clerk, somebody would have told him of grandfather's passing. Barnstable would be just as greedy, Grandfather would still have let the accounting fall into disarray. You can go to bed tonight with a clear conscience."

Which was… something. That he'd parted ways with his employer troubled Chloe, but a man who'd nearly memorized *Waverly* deserved more than contracts and ledgers to fill his day.

"You mean that, don't you?" he said. "You hold none of this against me. You're not even angry with Wentworth."

"I am very angry with Phineas Barnstable. Grandpapa regretted borrowing from him, and I wish we weren't losing the shop. Sometimes though, a fresh start, whether we want one or not, is a boon. Goodnight, Aidan."

The mistletoe was a good eight feet away, but Chloe kissed him anyway. She kissed him in gratitude for a lovely and unlooked for Christmas feast, for an evening spent in good company, and for the wonderful gift of his friendship.

And then she kissed him because she wanted to, and because in less than two weeks, she might well be kissing him good-bye forever.

When Aidan left the shop a good hour later, the streets were empty, darkness had fallen, and a falling snow had brought a peaceful hush to Christmas night. Chloe watched him go, until his footsteps had filled with fresh snow, and even the shop grew chilly.

Aidan had expected that delivering an ultimatum to Mr. Wentworth would have resulted in all manner of misgivings and self-doubt. Instead, he'd spent Boxing Day at the bookshop, reading to small children, discussing poetry with Mr. Nelson, and getting ambushed by Mrs. Draper under the mistletoe. The mood in the shop had been jolly despite the sale scheduled for the next day, though the shadows in Chloe's eyes tore at his heart.

Were they truly to have only one day together before the dratted bankers wrecked everything with their ambition and greed? Aidan had some money saved, true, but not enough to outbid Quinn Wentworth. Not nearly enough.

Aidan went back to his rooms near the bank after an evening meal of leftovers with the Thatchers. The sale was tomorrow morning, and the ladies had simply tidied up the shop as if cleaning up their store after any other busy day. Their good cheer, their courage, broke his heart, and thus he didn't notice Quinn Wentworth until he'd nearly plowed him into the snow.

"Mr. Farris, good evening. Did you enjoy your day at the bookshop?"

Of course, Wentworth would know that. "I did, sir. I am surprised to admit I enjoyed my day as a bookseller very much."

Mr. Wentworth fell in step beside him, as if they were off to the club for a hand of cards, though Wentworth only belonged to clubs for form's sake.

"Why would that surprise you?" Wentworth asked. "You've had your nose in a book more or less since you came to work for me. One marvels at such devotion to a lot of printed words. I've never understood it myself."

"Books aren't simply printed words, sir. They are companionship for the lonely, enlightenment for the curious mind, diversion from life's hardships. Books are wisdom and inspiration and how we ensure each generation can learn from the previous ones, and each nation from others."

They came to an intersection where a crossing sweeper shivered in the gathering shadows. The poor lad looked to be about nine years old and three-quarters frozen.

"In all your years at the bank," Wentworth said, "have you ever waxed as eloquent about commerce as you just did about a musty old lot of books, Mr. Farris? Has the law ever inspired you to such panegyrics? Watching the customers and tellers in the bank lobby, are you ever as fascinated as you have been with Sheridan's plays?"

A week ago, Aidan would have measured his answer, but he was free now, of the bank and of the need to gauge every word for its impact on his former employer.

"Commerce and finance are important, sir, but unlike you I have no passion for them. I had more joy from one day in the book shop than I did from ten years at the bank. I apologize if that sounds ungrateful, because I am very grateful to you and Mr. Penrose for all you've done for me."

Wentworth's path would take him one direction, Aidan's another.

"Never apologize for being honest," Mr. Wentworth said. "And don't you dare bid against me tomorrow."

So much for pleasantries with a former employee. "I'll bid against you if I jolly well please to, sir, and there's nothing you can say to it."

Was that a smile? Whatever it was, Mr. Wentworth's expression was too fleeting for Aidan to parse.

"You truly do have a passion for books, Mr. Farris. Do not bid against me, *please,* lest it be perceived that I'm bidding against myself. I've kept news of our recent discord to myself. I want no hint of irregularity about tomorrow's proceedings lest the courts interfere or Barnstable cry foul. Have the young ladies speak for themselves at the auction."

What was he up to? "The young ladies?"

"The Misses Thatcher. Comely, bookish, hardworking. I believe you've made their acquaintance. If they seek to thwart me at the auction tomorrow, let them bid against me openly. I won't take it amiss. Just the opposite."

The crossing sweeper looked up from where he was hunched against a steaming barrel. "Evenin', Mr. Wentworth."

The boy's face was grimy, he had neither gloves nor scarf, and his boots were soaked.

"Any news, Leonidas?" Mr. Wentworth asked.

"Just busy people today, sir. Everybody paying calls, dashing about. A sleigh overturned on Oxford Street, and Mr. Pritchard-the-curate fell on his arse because the Gazette didn't get its walkway shoveled clear. My barrel's almost full."

Mr. Wentworth passed the boy a coin. "Go home, lad, and thanks for the report."

"Happy Christmas, Mr. Wentworth!" The boy darted off, coin clutched in his little fist.

"You expect him to loiter about in this cold simply to bring you gossip?" Aidan asked.

Mr. Wentworth adjusted his scarf, a purple cashmere that wound several times about his neck. "His uncle beats him if he abandons the intersection before dark. I merely provide the lad some discreet supplemental income. I've suggested he quietly pass that money directly to his mother after the uncle has taken all of the child's other vales. I'll see you tomorrow, Mr. Farris—you and the young ladies."

Aidan walked the rest of the way home in solitude. On the one hand, Chloe and Faith should not have to watch as their livelihood was sold out from under them. On the other hand, the bidders would assemble on the bookshop's very steps, and Chloe would want to look Barnstable in the eye as he wrecked two innocent lives.

Then too, Aidan had seen the coin Mr. Wentworth had passed to that shivering little boy.

Half a crown. A man who gave a poor child that much money

believed in charity, compassion, and doing unto others, despite a lot of braying and posturing to the contrary.

Aidan would stand with Chloe and Faith tomorrow, and hope for the best.

CHAPTER 5

"For a man who claims to eschew drama," Joshua Penrose said, "you are going to great lengths to make an entrance."

"The shoppers have turned the streets into a filthy quagmire," Quinn replied as the carriage rolled along. "Of course I'd take the town coach to a business appointment."

"An auction is not an appointment."

Perhaps not, but Quinn was determined to transact some business on the bookshop's steps. The town coach made a statement of sober luxury, being finished in black lacquer with red trim. He'd taken this coach in payment for a debt incurred by an impecunious viscount, and regarded it as a reminder to one and all that Quinn Wentworth was no respecter of titles.

A debt was a debt.

When the coach came to a halt, Quinn waited while the liveried footman set down the steps and opened the door.

"Shall I bid for you?" Joshua asked.

"You shall not. The merchants are expecting me to participate in this farce personally, so participate, I shall."

He climbed from the coach and let all the gawkers have a good look. He was attired no differently than most men who engaged in commerce for a living, but he was taller than most, and clad a prize fighter's physique in Bond Street finery.

"Mr. Wentworth," Barnstable called above the murmuring of the crowd. "So glad you could join us. The auction will start in"—he flashed his pocket watch—"five minutes."

The merchants had turned out in quantity, which was gratifying. If the sale was well attended, that made the results harder to attack from any legal angle.

Quinn ignored Barnstable, and ignored the whispers circulating through the bidders. "Damned Wentworth," and "rich as Old Scratch," figured prominently, as usual. To the pair of young ladies standing off to the side with Aidan Farris, Quinn tipped his hat.

The young ladies glowered at him, which was entirely appropriate. Farris's expression was admirably devoid of emotion.

At least the fellow had learned that much.

"Are you sure you want to do this?" Joshua murmured. "All of London will see you render those young women homeless. We can put the damned branch on some other street corner."

"I am very certain I want to do this. One must be willing to pay a cost when pursuing a worthwhile objective."

The bells from St. Paul's tolled the hour, and the crowd grew quiet.

Barnstable climbed the shop's front steps and held up his hand. The usual patter ensued, about how fine the structure was, how many rooms it featured, how well respected Mr. Thatcher had been, and what a conscientious owner.

Barnstable was stalling, hoping for an even greater crowd, until somebody bellowed from the back of the group.

"Get on w' it, man. Can't ye see the young misses are cold?"

The younger girl looked a bit chilly. The older of the two was in a white hot fury, though she'd cloaked her rage in dignity. Quinn looked her straight in the eye, and—unlike many a man twice her age—she stared right back at him.

"Very well," Barnstable said, holding up a wooden gavel. "Hear ye, hear ye! This is an auction without reserve for the property before which we are gathered. The bidding will now open. Who shall start us off, gentlemen?"

He smiled at the crowd, they did not smile back. Quinn had spent the past week making sure every merchant in London—and their wives—knew exactly what Barnstable was about.

"Oh, come now, friends," Barnstable said. "Let's not be shy. Mr. Wentworth has joined us, true, but even he isn't made entirely of gold. What am I bid for this fine property?"

Another silence, as a cold wind blew down the street.

"One pound," Quinn said, which caused a ripple through the crowd. One pound was an insultingly, outrageously low opening bid, and Barnstable's smiled slipped.

"I have one pound," he said, "and that will do for a start. Who can top one pound? Surely with the holidays upon us, somebody has more than one pound to spend on this beautiful edifice? Gentleman, you cannot allow Mr. Wentworth to steal this building for a single pound. T'wouldn't be sporting!"

"What the hell is going on?" Joshua muttered.

"Quiet," Quinn replied, once again giving Miss Chloe Thatcher a direct stare.

She held up a gloved hand. "Two pounds."

"Miss Thatcher bids two pounds," Barnstable said, "and she well knows that's a mere pittance compared to what this building is worth. Come, gentlemen. You know old Thatcher's heirs stand to benefit from your generosity today. A bid of two pounds, when Quinn Wentworth is in our midst, is nothing short of bad form."

The crowd shifted restlessly. A man standing near the shop window raised a hand as if to bid. The person beside him, a printer, batted the man's hand down.

"Do I have another bid?" Barnstable called out. "Sir, are you entering the affray? Don't be shy, now. Some lucky bidder will end this day in possession of an enviably well placed commercial establishment. Let's make sure it's not Mr. Wentworth. What do you bid, my good fellow?"

"His nose itched," the printer yelled.

Another man farther up the walk way looked as he was thinking of bidding. The man beside him whispered in his ear.

"Will nobody give me a bid?" Barnstable bellowed. "I cannot consider this an auction if there's no bidding, my friends."

"You said it yourself," the printer retorted. "An auction without reserve. Mr. Wentworth put in his bid, and Miss Thatcher topped him."

"That's an auction, Barnstable," a burly young fellow called. "For once you don't get to cheat anybody."

Barnstable was losing control of the crowd, and Quinn wasn't quite ready for that to happen. He lifted his walking stick as if to examine the handle.

"Ah, Mr. Wentworth!" Barnstable cried. "I see you're ready to resume bidding. You've had your little moment, but now let's get down to business, shall we?"

Well, yes. The young ladies—and Mr. Farris—must not be made to stand about in the frigid air any longer than necessary.

Quinn took off his hat and bowed very correctly to the Misses Thatcher. "Ladies, congratulations on placing the winning bid. I wish you Happy Christmas. Mr. Barnstable, conclude your auction."

A beat of silence went by before Joshua spoke over the crowd. "You heard him, Barnstable. Conclude the auction."

Barnstable held his little wooden hammer, while the merchants murmured and shuffled.

"Say it, man," the printer called, "or we'll make you wish you had."

The silence stretched while the crowd shifted restlessly. Quinn merely waited, for this group knew what it was to work hard, knew the fury of having been cheated by a crooked banker. For once, that banker was not going to win.

"You heard Mr. Wentworth," a prominent butcher called. "Conclude the auction, Barnstable."

"Conclude the auction now," another voice added, "or you'll get worse than a lump of coal for your reward, Barnstable."

Barnstable looked about, his gaze the fearful disbelief of cornered prey.

"Now, Barnstable," Joshua said again. "Or there will be consequences."

Three more heartbeats went by, during which Mr. Farris, in a shocking lapse of decorum that pleased Quinn no end, slipped his hand around Miss Thatcher's.

"Going once," Barnstable croaked. "Going twice. Sold to Miss Thatcher for two pounds."

A loud cheer went up as Quinn returned to the coach and gave his driver leave to trot off. On the steps of the bookshop, Mr. Farris was looking ordinately pleased for a man who'd turned his back on a lucrative career in finance, but then, Miss Thatcher was in his arms, laughing, crying, and kissing Farris's cheek.

While Barnstable looked to be entirely, absolutely ruined.

"Happy Christmas?" Joshua asked, as the horses trotted on.

"One might say so," Quinn replied. "Alas for all my scheming, we won't be opening up our branch at the corner of Willoughby and St. Jean's."

Joshua peered out the window. "But?"

"But the printer across the way is ready to retire. He tells me bookstores generate a tremendous amount of foot traffic, and that benefits the entire neighborhood. I'd be a fool to close down a thriving bookshop when I'm thinking of opening up a branch in the area. Particularly when I can keep that shop open and in the right hands without spending sixpence."

Joshua's smile was patient. "And banks generate a lot of foot traffic, making it more likely the bookshop will thrive."

"Particularly if a highly trained man of business is assisting with the bookshop's management." A nice thought, though Quinn still had no idea why anybody would want to spend their entire day around a lot of dull old books.

No idea at all.

Joshua sat back, his expression amused. "You are a good man, Quinn Wentworth, though your secret is safe with me."

"Don't be ridiculous. I am competent at commerce and fair in my dealings. That is all I shall ever aspire to be." He was also proud of Aidan Farris, who'd demonstrated a sound sense of honor when honor was needed. No need to go bleating to Joshua about that.

Joshua's smile became a grin as the coach pulled up at the corner nearest the bank. "Perhaps your sisters might have some idea what sort of gift to send along when Mr. Farris and Miss Thatcher's nuptials are announced."

Quinn climbed down from the coach. "I have no skill choosing gifts. I'll leave that task to those better suited to it."

Joshua joined him on the walkway. "Oh, I agree. You are not skilled at choosing gifts, you have no patience with sentiment, and drama has no place in commerce. Right."

"Stop trying to annoy me. We have a full day of bank business to tend to. Let's be about it." Quinn jaunted off in the direction of the bank, pausing only long enough to flip an entire crown in the crossing sweeper's direction.

"Happy Christmas, Mr. Wentwort," the boy called back, slipping the coin in to his pocket.

"Go on," Joshua muttered. "Say the words, Quinn. You've earned them."

Quinn turned and tipped his hat to the boy, also to every generous-hearted merchant in London, and to every person who'd ever patronized the Thatcher's bookshop. "Happy Christmas, indeed!" he called, a bit too loudly.

Then he jaunted up the bank's steps and settled in for a full day of work minding the bank's business.

AUTHOR'S NOTE

To My Dear Readers,

Is not Yuletide perfectly suited to romance? I love how our hearts seem to grow to the size of "ten men plus two" around this time of year, and I hope this story has added a touch of warmth to your holiday anticipation.

Quinn Wentworth cannot be left ciphering and banking to his heart's content, though. That would be much too easy. His story, ***My One and Only Duke,*** comes out November 6. If you're in the US, please vote and *then* dive into Quinn and Jane's HEA, 'kay? Their tale kicks off my **Rogues to Riches** series, and I've included a short excerpt below. If you'd rather not wait for Nov. 6, ***A Truly Perfect Gentleman***, my latest Regency romance, came out on September 25.

Grey Birch Dorning, Earl of Casriel, is a bit too mannerly, and a bit too fixated on marrying well to solve all of his family's problems. Beatitude, Lady Canmore, has news for him. Excerpt below.

I will be writing and publishing up a storm in the months to come, both novels and novellas. If you'd like to get a short email notice of new releases, pre-orders, and deals, the best way to make that happen is simply to follow me on **Bookbub** (https://www.-bookbub.com/authors/grace-burrowes). If you'd also like to get the kitten pictures and coming attractions reel, please do sign up for **my newsletter** (https://graceburrowes.com/contact/). I'm having great fun lately on **Instagram** (https://www.instagram.com/grace-burrowesauthor/?hl=en) too (more kitten pictures!).

Happy holidays, and happy reading!

Grace Burrowes

EXCERPT: MY ONE AND ONLY DUKE

BY GRACE BURROWES

On sale November 6, 2018

When Quinn Wentworth and Jane Winston spoke their wedding vows in Newgate prison, neither expected the result would be a lasting union. But here they are, a month later, no longer in Newgate, very much in love, and not at all sure what to do about it...

Having no alternative, Quinn went about removing his clothes, handing them to Jane who hung up his shirt and folded his cravat as if they'd spent the last twenty years chatting while the bath water cooled.

Quinn was down to his underlinen, hoping for a miracle, when Jane went to the door to get the dinner tray. He used her absence to shed the last of his clothing and slip into the steaming tub. She returned bearing the food, which she set on the counterpane.

"Shall I wash your hair, Quinn?"

"I'll scrub off first. Tell me how you occupied yourself while I was gone."

She held a sandwich out for him to take a bite. "This and that.

The staff has a schedule, the carpets have all been taken up and beaten, Constance's cats are separated by two floors until Persephone is no longer feeling amorous."

Quinn was feeling amorous. He'd traveled to York and back, endured Mrs. Daugherty's gushing, and Ned's endless questions, and pondered possibilities and plots—who had put him Newgate and why?—but neither time nor distance had dampened his interest in his new wife one iota.

Jane's fingers massaging his scalp and neck didn't help his cause, and when she leaned down to scrub his chest, and her breasts pressed against Quinn's shoulders, his interest became an ache.

The water cooled, Jane fed him sandwiches, and Quinn accepted that the time had come to make love with his wife. He rose from the tub, water sluicing away, as Jane held out a bath sheet. Her gaze wandered over him in frank, marital assessment, then caught, held, and ignited a smile he hadn't seen from her before.

"Why Mr. Wentworth, you did miss me after all." She passed him the bath sheet, and locked the parlor door and the bedroom door, while Quinn stood before the fire and dried off.

"I missed you too," Jane said, taking the towel from him and tossing it over a chair. "Rather a lot."

Quinn made one last attempt to dodge the intimacy Jane was owed, one last try for honesty. "Jane, we have matters to discuss. Matters that relate to my travels." And to his past, for that past was putting a claim in his future, and Jane deserved to know the truth.

"We'll talk later all you like, Quinn. For now, please take me to bed."

She kissed him, and he was lost.

EXCERPT: A TRULY PERFECT GENTLEMAN

BY GRACE BURROWES

Beatitude, Lady Canmore, has no intention of marrying again. Grey Birch Dorning, Earl of Casriel, must marry well and soon. Alas the course of true love sometimes does go stumbling down a woodland path to end up with unlikely declarations from unsuitable parties...

The sun shone through the trees at the same angle as it had a moment ago, the water on the lake rippled beneath the same breeze, and yet, Grey's world had endured a seismic shock.

"You would like to have an affair with me," he said slowly. Then, to make sure he hadn't indulged in wishful hearing, "An intimate affair?"

Lady Canmore glowered up at him. "Is there another kind?"

"I would not know."

She stalked along at his side. "You've *never* enjoyed the company of a woman outside the bounds of wedlock?"

"By London standards, I am retiring when it comes to those activities. I have reason to be."

Lady Canmore took him by the hand and dragged him down a barely visible side trail. For a small woman, she was strong.

"The hermit's folly is this way," she said. "What do you mean, you have reason to be? To be a monk? I have been a monk for the past several years. Monkdom loses its charms. If you think that makes me fast or vulgar or unladylike, then I think such an opinion makes you a hypocrite. There's not a man in Mayfair who doesn't indulge his appetites to the limit of his means, and a few beyond their means. Roger told me swiving is all many men think about."

"I most assuredly think about it." That admission was not polite. Not gentlemanly. Not… what Grey had intended to say.

Her ladyship came to an abrupt halt in the middle of the trail. "You do? You think about it with *me*?"

Oh, how that smile became her, how that light of mischief transformed her gaze. "You have broached this topic, my lady, but are you certain you want to pursue it in present company?" A gentleman had to ask, for the discussion would soon pass the point where her overture could be dismissed as a jest or flirtation.

"You haunt me," Lady Canmore replied, clearly not a disclosure that pleased her. "Men I've been dancing with for the past eight years now strike me as lacking stature, though I myself am short. When I arrive at a gathering, I look for you, even though all the way to the venue, I tell myself I must not do exactly that. You and I are engaged in a semblance of a friendship, I tell myself, only a friendship."

Lady Canmore took a turn off the path that Grey would have missed. She knew where she was going, while he was increasingly lost.

"I don't want to be your mistress," she went on. "I want to be your lover."

Grey almost sagged against the nearest oak. "Do you frequently make such announcements in the same tone of voice most people reserve for discussing the Corsican, long may he rot in memory?"

The way ahead opened into a clearing that held a small three-sided stone edifice on a slight rise. The surrounding woods had been carefully manicured to give the folly three views. One looked out over the lake, another toward Brantmore House. The third faced the woods sloping away to the east.

A circular portico framed the interior of the folly, where benches provided a private place to rest.

"I am not happy with myself for becoming interested in you," Lady Canmore said. "But there it is. You are kind, gentlemanly, and a fine male specimen. Your flirtation is original without being prurient or presumptuous. You dance well. You humor Aunt Freddy. You love your siblings. You are not afraid of hard, physical work. In fact, I think you need it to thrive."

She paced before the folly, listing attributes that made Grey's heart ache. She *saw* him, saw him clearly, and appreciated who and what she saw.

"You are the comfort of your aunt's declining years," Grey said, "a ferociously loyal friend, a minister's daughter who has learned how to manage polite society without being seen to do more than smile and chat. If I had to choose one word to describe you, that word would be courageous. I can't help but watch you, even when you dance with others, because you have such inherent grace. I see you walking away, and I know I have nothing to offer you, but I want to call you back, every damned time."

She came to a halt before him. "My lord, what are we to do?"

"My name is Grey, and as for what to do… I would like to kiss you."

HOME FOR THE HOLIDAYS

THE BRETHREN STORY

CHRISTI CALDWELL

PROLOGUE

Kent, England
Winter, 1821

One might say Caroline Whitworth, the Duchess of Sutton, knew her husband, Samuel Whitworth, the Duke of Sutton, better than anyone.

Nor was it an exaggeration. Betrothed as a babe to the then future duke, there hadn't been a time when she *hadn't* been near Samuel.

As such, many times she teased that she knew his nuances and mannerisms and thoughts better than Samuel himself did.

It was why she knew precisely how he would respond to the news she brought.

It was also why she'd asked her son, Heath, the ducal heir and oftentimes a calming influence, to be present.

Folding the note she'd just read to him along its pointed crease, she neatly rested it on her husband's immaculate desk. "Married." She repeated the most important contents of the missive. "Our son is married."

"Say it's the Aberdeen girl," he gritted out.

"Oh, come, Samuel. That does not make sense. Lady Emilia arrived earlier this afternoon with her parents and occupied the second chair from yours not even five hours ago. It could hardly be Emilia."

Her husband whipped up the page and slashed it around the air. "Are you making light of… of… this?"

Heath shifted in his chair, and the leather groaned under the uneasy movement. He cast a quick glance over his shoulder, contemplating escape.

Another time, Caroline might have felt some compunction at placing her son in the unenviable role of witness, and participant, in a debate between her and her husband. Not this time.

She was all out of patience with the three equally obstinate males in her family. "Hardly, Samuel. I'd never dare jest about Emilia's unwed state or our son's recently wedded one."

The familiar vein bulged at the corner of his right eye. His cheeks had flushed with angry color. Oh, yes, he *wanted* to bellow. He wanted to shout down the residence, filled with now slumbering guests.

Heath shoved back his chair. "I'm not entirely certain my being here—"

"Sit," Caroline ordered, ending any such hope of flight.

Her son settled back in his chair.

"Now," she went on in more modulated tones, smoothing her skirts, "this requires attention from *each* of us. Whether you approve or not, Samuel, your son has married by special license."

A garbled groan and growl stuck in her husband's chest. Oh, yes, this was dire indeed.

"And the world is already abuzz with that news."

"How can the world be abuzz?" Samuel waved the fast-wrinkling scrap about. "By the accounts of this, he's been married just three days."

Caroline forced a serene smile. "Because he took out a proper announcement, as he should."

She braced for it. One, two—

"He did what?" her husband bellowed, slamming the page down.

Well, that was quicker than she'd expected. Yes, dire, indeed.

Heath winced and made yet another attempt at escape. "Perhaps I should allow you both—"

Husband and wife spoke in unison. "Sit."

Yanking at his cravat, Heath fell back in his seat and muttered something under his breath that sounded very much like a curse aimed at his younger brother.

Caroline abandoned all attempts at her usual affable demeanor. "I beg your pardon?" She turned a frown on first her son and then her husband.

"He's gone and married a widow with a scandalous past," her husband needlessly reminded. "A..." He dropped his voice to a hushed whisper. "A... a... a..."

"Bigamist?" Heath supplied for him.

Both parents shot glares in his direction.

"Bloody hell. What? According to the digging your man-of-affairs did and turned up, that is precisely what she is. Or... rather, was...?" Heath puzzled his brow. "Which is the proper tense for a bigamist? I suspect the title is one that always follows a person... unless it is 'former bigamist'?"

Caroline swatted him with the other note—still undisclosed—in her hand. "Enough. You're upsetting your father."

"*I'm* upsetting him?" Heath arched an affronted brow. "I'm not the one who's come with the tidings of Sheldon's marriage to a big—"

"Enough," Caroline and Samuel spoke as one, interrupting the remainder of the factual statement.

"So this is the reason for a house party after I just rid my household of guests," her husband said flatly.

"*Our* household," she reminded him with a frown. "And yes, I'd thought throwing another house party at Christmas to welcome Graham and his new wife would help ease her way into Polite Society."

"His name is Sheldon," her son pointed out, deliberately needling.

She scowled. "He prefers Graham," she stated, before returning her attention to the matter at hand. "Furthermore, you enjoy entertaining. *Far* more than I do." She quite detested it. She simply put on a good show for her husband's sake.

"Bloody hell, Caroline," her husband blustered. "I—"

"Mm-mm," she cut him off with a shake of her head. "Try again, Samuel."

His color deepened. "My apologies... dear heart." Their son squirmed at the familiar endearment that his father directed to his mother. "I should not have cursed." He turned his ducal displeasure on their son. "Nor should you curse in the presence of your mother... or any lady."

"You've both gone bl—" Heath caught himself. "Mad," he finished. "You'd focus on propriety and manners in even *this*?"

They ignored him.

"*We*"—her husband gestured between himself and her—"were in agreement on protecting Sheldon from a mistake that could not be undone. *We* agreed to send Barclay, my man-of-affairs, to give her a sizable sum to leave Sheldon alone. We—"

"That is enough. I know the rest." Caroline brought her shoulders back. "*I* was of the belief that we should find out what sent our son running away for the holidays and making certain that he was happy." Nonetheless, guilt found its proper mark. It didn't matter that her husband had orchestrated the plan to free their son from the "tangles of a scheming woman." All that had mattered had been revealed the moment that same lady had thrown that offer in Barclay's face. Her refusal to take the money had said as much about Martha Donaldson's integrity as it had said about the Whitworth family. Caroline could have, at least *should* have, attempted to quash her husband's interference in their son's life... but she had not. With that failure, she'd only hurt her son. But she would put that error to rights.

Heath shot a hand up, and Caroline and Samuel looked over. "If I may redirect us back? I believe we were seeking clarity on the matter? Mother, it was your attempts to wed him off to Lady Emilia Aberdeen that resulted in Sheldon's flight and current circumstances and subsequently *our* current circumstances."

Guilt sent heat rushing to her cheeks. "I don't believe *that* is what sent him off to… to… Miss Donaldson's. Regardless, who or what was to blame"—herself included—"there is no lamenting on what has already come to pass. Instead, we need to look to the future. First…" And most important. Caroline stuck a finger up. "Graham is in love with his wife, which indicates he's happy, which is of utmost importance."

Samuel harrumphed. "Graham has known the woman less than a month. Given her economic situation, I trust desperation more than any true sentiments drove that love match."

"Yes, everyone knows based on your marital union that matches decided upon a child's birth are the only ones that breed any true success," Heath drawled, looping his ankle across his opposite knee.

Samuel pounded his desk. "Precisely!"

Heath's lips twitched, and he hid his grin behind his hand.

Caroline narrowed her eyes. Their son was enjoying all of this entirely too much. That was fine. She'd deal with him next…

Actually, she'd deal with all of them. For now, there was the more pressing matter to attend: Sheldon and his wife, Martha.

"Regardless of how you may feel, Graham is married, until death do they part. And though I've not"—yet—"met his wife, I've seen our son and can tell you without question that he is in love with her. Their marriage will, of course, be met with gossip."

"Of course it will," Samuel mumbled.

"But we are family, and as such, we should"—Caroline gave them each a pointed look—"and will do everything within our power to ease their way before Polite Society."

Samuel sat upright in his chair. "What have you done?"

She went on without missing a beat. "I've gone and invited Graham, Martha, and their children for the remainder of the house party."

Her husband's eyes slid closed. "Bloody hell. You've... you've..."

Heath cupped his hands around his mouth. "She's invited *Sheldon* for the holidays," he boomed.

With a frown, she favored her son with another thump on his arm. "First, your brother has long preferred being called by his second name—Graham. Nearly thirty now, it's only appropriate that we honor that wish. Now, secondly, hiding Graham and his wife away without acknowledging them would only create further scandal."

Which Caroline couldn't give a jot less about. The gossips could all go talk and then hang. She did, however, care as to how her children's happiness was directly impacted by that gossip.

"And has he accepted?" Heath asked, displaying that deep knowing of his younger brother.

Caroline caught the inside of her cheek between her teeth. "I've not received word back." Why should Graham come? Why should he wish to subject his new family to the family who'd threatened their happiness?

"He won't come," Samuel said, and Caroline searched for some hint of what he was thinking or feeling, and yet, he remained coolly implacable. As much as she loved him, that impassivity was the one trait of her husband's that she abhorred.

"I suspect he shall," she said with a confidence she did not feel.

"All of this conversation was a hypothetical?" Heath asked as if her assurance meant nothing.

"He's coming," she said firmly. That confidence came from one who knew her son, and the other men in this room, better than she knew herself.

But you do not know Graham's wife...

Releasing a sigh, Samuel abandoned the note and fell back, deflated, in his seat. "You're right."

I usually am. Caroline repressed her own smile.

"If they wish to come," he went on, "I'll allow her to visit, but I don't have to like her."

At that boylike bluster, Caroline resisted the urge to roll her eyes. "No," she corrected. "*I've* invited her, and as such, she was always coming. You don't allow or disallow anything in this marriage, Samuel. Second, to treat her with anything less than kindness and warmth will only stir the gossip."

The crimson circles splotched his chiseled cheeks again. "You want me to pretend to like her?"

"He's a duke," Heath piped in. "No one would think anything amiss if he was as cool and aloof with her as he is with everyone." His grin deepened. "Present company included."

"Precisely," Samuel said with a nod.

Caroline remained silent, all the while acknowledging that her son wasn't altogether far from the mark. The bluster, the anger, the ducal pomposity were nothing more than an act. A veneer of falsity that Caroline saw through and under… but her sons never could.

Nor should they have had to. Their father had owed them an unrestrained love and sincerity in his regard for them and their lives.

"Now, for the second reason behind this family meeting…"

Heath sighed. "Is any other reason truly needed?"

"There is the awkwardly uncomfortable matter of Lady Emilia Aberdeen."

Heath's dark brows snapped together. Yes, he'd always been clever. Alas, not clever enough to have gathered long before this moment the precise reason he was here.

"What about her?" Samuel asked impatiently.

"Well, all the guests have already suspected and whispered about our trying to coordinate a match between Emilia and Graham."

"You," Samuel clarified. "You were the one who is responsible for this… What are we calling it now?"

"The Reason for the Family Meeting," Heath put forward in careful tones devoid of all his earlier bravado and swagger.

"Either way, we've inadvertently made Emilia the gossip of the house party."

"Which will all be forgotten when Sheldon and his bride arrive," her son quickly added.

Tsk-tsk. Oh, Heath… How terribly predictable—and self-serving—he was.

"Nonetheless, it stands to reason that none should suspect that she was here intended to be matched with Graham. After all, she's already suffered a scandal no lady ought." Betrothed to the Duke of Renaud, a notorious rogue… The gentleman had broken it off and instead hopped a packet and sailed off, leaving Emilia as Society's favorite *on dit* of gossip in his literal and figurative wake. "I'd simply ask that you give Emilia some attention."

"Attention," her son echoed back.

"Some indication that mayhap it was you we'd intended for her to make a match with, and then…"

Heath choked, the strangled cough cutting off whatever reply he'd intended. Coming out of her seat, Caroline went over and thumped him between the shoulder blades.

"You want me to court her?"

"I want you to simply act as though she is… someone you want to be around. It's the least you can do."

Her son drew back. "What in blazes did *I* do?" he cried.

"Your best friend is, after all, the one who jilted her."

"*I* didn't jilt the lady." Heath spoke through gritted teeth. "I don't even know the lady."

"All this I-I-I, Heath. Really. Furthermore," she continued, "it speaks a good deal to your snobbishness. We've been family friends with the Duke of Gayle since before your birth. The least you can do is be friendly to the girl."

"The girl is nearly thirty."

"All I'm asking is that you be friendly with her. If she's alone… see that she has company. Take the gossip off of Graham's desertion and make Society question whether you, in fact, are the one with intentions towards her."

"Mad, Father. Tell her she's gone utterly insane."

It spoke volumes about her husband's frustration that he didn't correct that affront.

"You both have your instructions," Caroline said, giving her skirts a snap. "Kindness… towards your son and his new family," she directed at her husband. "And *you* towards Lady Emilia," she said to Heath.

"Where are you going?" Samuel called after her as she swept away.

"To see that rooms are prepared for our son's arrival."

As she exited, she drew the door closed behind her—and smiled.

Caroline was hosting a house party for the holidays, and she'd be damned if her family didn't have peace, love, and holiday cheer this season.

CHAPTER 1

London, England
Winter, 1821

After a miserable marriage to a man whose deception had left her children illegitimate, Martha Whitworth had despaired of knowing any true happiness for her and her three children.

Life, however, had proven there was happiness to be had for widowed women with fractured families.

Nay, *life* had not taught her as much… rather, her husband, Lord Graham Whitworth, had shown her that love was real and that she was deserving of it.

Her family, once divided, had been brought together by him. He'd married her. He'd given her and her children, at last, a name—an honorable one.

And much like the romantic tales she'd read as a girl, Martha might have said that hers was the happily-ever-after that young women dreamed of and most never attained.

For, everything was perfect.

Almost.

Hovering outside her husband's office, Martha lingered in the hall… uncertain in ways she'd not been with Graham since their first meeting. But that had been before, back when he was a stranger. Back when she was still jaded and hadn't trusted his motives for coming to her village.

And yet… in the middle of the boisterous din of the laughter and discourse between her children at the dining table, a note had arrived. Graham had read it. Pocketed it. And though he'd smiled and laughed in all the right places, attending whichever questions her daughters, Iris and Creda, had put to him, or taken part in whatever stable talk her son had for him, he'd been… different.

There had been a remoteness to his enthralling smile.

She brushed her fingertips over the brass door handle and then drew her hand back. Martha lifted her knuckles to knock.

"What are you doing?" she mouthed into the quiet. The long-familiar habit of speaking to herself had started after her late husband's death and her daughters' departure, still too recent to be vanquished. "This is Graham." Before she faltered once more, Martha gripped the handle and let herself in.

"I was wondering if you were going to enter," her husband said with his devilishly wicked half grin. Tossing his pen down, Graham unfurled all six feet, three inches of his towering, wiry frame.

Closing the door, Martha pressed her back against the oak panel. "Mr. Whitworth," she greeted, testing the name that was now her own and, after just two days of marriage, so very foreign still.

His grin deepened, meeting his eyes and making her heart flutter. "Mrs. Whitworth," he murmured, taking long, languid steps forward.

Let that be enough… Do not borrow trouble and concern where there is none.

And yet… she knew this man. As such, when Graham stopped several steps away, the earlier distance between them now erased, Martha identified the absence of the slightest dimple in his right cheek.

Fighting back the unease needling around her lower belly, she forced a smile of her own.

They spoke at the same time.

"Is everything—?"

"Are the children—?"

Martha and Graham both ceased talking. Bowing his head, Graham motioned for her to continue.

"The children are… fine." Though the girls they'd retrieved from Mrs. Munroe's Finishing School had become miniature versions of adults in the nearly two years Martha had been away from them. Strangers she barely recognized.

Of a sudden, she wanted to cry.

"What is it?" he murmured, cupping her cheek, and she leaned into that touch, strong, and yet, tender at the same time. "Are they… not happy?" he asked, and there was a hesitancy there from this man who'd only ever been more confident than God himself.

"No, they are happy. Very much so," she rushed to assure. As confident and fearless as Graham had proven to be, Martha appreciated how foreign it was for him to go from being a bachelor to being a stepfather with three children—two of whom had been strangers until just yesterday. "They are… excited to be here."

Some of the tension eased from his frame, and capturing her hand, Graham lifted it to his fingers. "I am glad," he said, pressing his lips to her knuckles.

A delicious shiver radiated from the lingering caress. Some of her fears melted away as he continued those sensual ministrations, caressing his lips along the inside of her wrist. "So there is… another reason you've come," he whispered between kisses, his breath tickling and tempting at the same time.

A breathless laugh escaped her. "You are distracting m-me, Graham."

"Distractions are good," he murmured, and his lips teased at the corner of her mouth.

Martha's head tipped back, rattling the door panel. "Th-they are," she agreed as his lips covered hers. The heat of the kiss brought her eyes closed, and she climbed her hands about his neck, turning herself over to his embrace. Meeting each slant of his mouth.

Allowing herself to feel. Letting herself forget that there'd been a reason he'd shut himself away from his offices, while she'd gone on to bed.

Reality intruded, cold, unwelcome, and the thief of joy it always was.

Reluctantly, Martha sank back on her heels.

Graham moved his attentions to her neck.

"Behave," she chided, giving his forearm a little pinch. "This isn't why I've c-come."

"You're certain?" he asked, lightly suckling the skin where her pulse pounded.

"Q-quite." Her voice was breathless and unconvincing to her own ears.

With a sigh, her husband straightened. "Very well, madam." He swept his arm out in invitation toward the broad, mahogany Chippendale desk. Ledgers and books lay open, along with several notes, on the usually immaculate surface.

Martha swept forward, taking the chair closest to his desk, closest to those documents.

"You are busy," she noted needlessly.

An agent for a secret division of the Crown, called the Brethren, her husband would always be… *busy*.

"Never too busy for you, love," he vowed. His silken baritone contained a promise within it that sent heat stealing to her heart.

That devotion should be enough. Mayhap it was selfishness. Nay… it was not that. Her coming here to speak with Graham was because the realization that she'd finally come to—with the help of this man before her—was that she was deserving of happiness. And so was he.

"You're…" She started to speak when her gaze snagged on a note on his desk.

My dearest son…

Martha's stomach muscles contracted as Graham deftly folded that missive and slid it under his diary.

His family. That was what this… detachment… was about.

"You're not yourself, Graham," she said quietly. Holding his stare, she dared him with her eyes to speak the truth. Demanded that he not require her to put questions to him, pulling forth the reason for his distractedness since dinner.

He scrubbed a hand down his sharp jawline, dark from a day's growth of beard. "My family… My mother wrote me."

There it was. He'd given her the truth when he could have prevaricated or sidestepped with false assurances. Her heart swelled with her love for this man. Perfect. Pure. And yet, that love was offset by his revelation. "Did she?" Martha managed the question in even tones.

Wordlessly, he slipped the note from its hiding place and came around the desk to sit beside her.

He held out the hated missive.

Martha stared between the note and Graham, before taking it with reluctant fingers, not wanting to know the words there, but at the same time needing to know. She unfolded the page, noting the officious gold wax seal. Even broken it revealed the stamp of power. And then she read the neat, elegant scrawl.

My dearest son…

I'm never too proud to recognize and admit my own flaws and mistakes, Sheldon. I'm a flawed being… and I can acknowledge openly to you, that I was wrong…

Her hands convulsed reflexively upon the page, crinkling it at the corners, and she forced herself to loosen her grip as she stared transfixed at those several lines. Ones she'd have wagered her very life that a duchess could never, and would never, cede to anyone.

And they painted Graham's mother… in an altogether different light. It had been far easier to resent his family when they'd been the ones who'd interfered and sought to keep Martha and Graham apart.

This, however? This very real woman who admitted that she'd made a mistake? And about Graham's relationship with Martha, no less? It didn't fit with what she'd come to believe or expect of his ducal parents.

She continued reading and then stumbled over the next paragraph.

It is my greatest hope that you and your family will join us this holiday season.

Oh, blast and damn. Her husband's family, the Duke and Duchess of Sutton, were inviting them to visit.

IN THE TIME GRAHAM HAD KNOWN HIS WIFE, HE'D COME TO appreciate that silence was not something Martha shied away from.

Where previous women of his acquaintance had prattled and trilled misplaced laughter before ever surrendering to any silence, Martha always comfortably owned it.

Being both pensive and measured had become two of the many qualities he appreciated and admired in his wife.

This stretch of quiet, however, was different, because he knew where this quiet came from—his family's treatment of her.

The familiar rage that had consumed him when he'd discovered his father had sent round his loyal man-of-affairs to pay off Martha had since receded, to be replaced with... a deep, aching hurt that nagged.

He'd expected such interference from his father. The Duke of Sutton had never had a high opinion of Graham and had little faith in his judgment. His brother hadn't given a jot what he did with his life. But Graham's mother? He'd expected more from her.

Martha finished reading before folding the note along the crease and turning it back over.

"We're not going," he said when his wife made no attempt to speak.

There was the slightest, most infinitesimal stiffening of her slender frame that, had he not been seated a pace away, he would have missed. "Beg pardon?"

"I've no intention of us journeying to visit," he repeated. Coming to his feet, he tossed the missive atop his notes from the Brethren.

"Not for the holidays?" she put forward hesitantly.

Not ever, if he had his way. "No." He perched his hip on the edge of his desk.

Except, there was no tangible hint of her joy at that announcement. "Your family wishes to see you, Graham."

"Correction. My *mother* wishes to see me." And by the contents of the note, she also wished to meet Martha and see Frederick again. Ever the peacemaker in the fractured Whitworth family, she'd not be content until Graham and his family were reunited. Alas, too much injury had been done. An affront against himself he could forgive—he'd been recipient enough through the years. An affront against Martha and her children he could not. "I have altogether different plans for us, love." Plans that did not include placing her before the ducal father who'd rip apart her worth.

"What manner of plans?"

Graham shoved lazily to his feet and strolled before her. "Curious, are you?"

A smile teased at her lips. "You don't have plans. You're inventing them as reasons why you can't, or won't, travel to your family for the holidays."

He slammed a hand to his chest, and in a mock display of outrage, Graham stumbled to his knees. "You've wounded me, love."

Martha laughed, those rich, husky tones wrapping around him, enveloping him in a warmth that had him joining her in laughter. "Very well, then," she said with a flick of her hand. "Let us hear of these grand plans preventing you from traveling."

"The grand plans I have that prevent us from traveling…" he murmured, leaning forward to take her lips in a too brief kiss. "Return to Hyde Park with you and Frederick, and this time bring your daughters, to skate together." The one and only time they'd journeyed to Hyde Park, that place his artist wife had longed to sketch, had been with Frederick… and—his throat moved—he'd not allow himself to think of how close he'd come to losing her that afternoon, just days ago.

Martha's lips parted on a breathless sigh. "Oh."

"Shall I continue?"

"Please."

"Then, I thought we should honor that peculiar, but fascinating tradition Frederick shared with me."

"The tree-cutting and decorating?"

He winked. "The very one. Fascinating stuff, and it all sounds like a very good time."

His wife rested her palms against his chest, and she smoothed her callused digits, stained with charcoal, along the front of his lapels. "It all sounds… perfect."

Graham leaned up to kiss her again, but she drew away. "But we'll have a lifetime to do those things as a family."

God, she was tenacious. She'd been so from their first meeting at the White Stag Inn. "And there will be a lifetime of miserable winter house parties."

His wife folded her hands on her lap and tipped her chin up at a defiant angle. "You need to go, Graham."

His brows came together.

"*We* need to g-go," she substituted, that slight telling tremble indicating she'd even less of a desire to visit his family—as she should.

"We do not need to do anything." And he'd certainly not do anything or take his new family any place where they'd be uncomfortable or treated poorly.

Her chin came up another notch. "Are you ashamed of us?"

He reeled. "That is what you believe?" Despite his training with the Home Office and the work he did, he was unable to mask his hurt. "You could think so ill of me?" Restless, Graham quit his place at her feet and strode over to the windows. Outside, snow had begun to fall, tiny flakes floating down to the quiet streets below. How could she doubt his love for her?

The leather groaned, and the floorboards creaked as she moved just beyond his shoulder. "No," she said quietly. "I-I…" Graham glanced over his shoulder. Martha sighed. "Very well… I… This is all still new."

"Us?" he supplied.

A sound of frustration escaped her. "This happiness, and I don't want it to end."

Graham caught her lightly by the shoulders. Drawing her close, he rested his forehead against hers. "This," he whispered, "will never end, Martha. Our life together—mine and yours, and Creda and Iris and Frederick—it is only beginning. Your happiness… you and your children… our children, that is what matters most to me. And so a summons from my family, after they tried to separate us? They don't merit a response or a visit."

Tears glazed her eyes, and he caught the first errant drop to fall with the pad of his thumb, stroking it away. "You'd sacrifice seeing your family for me?"

"In a heartbeat." Gathering her tightly balled fists, he brought them to his mouth and kissed them slowly. "There is no sacrifice in being with you and rejecting those who'd hurt you."

Martha stepped out of his arms. "But this isn't your mother and father hurting or rejecting me. This is them attempting to bring you back into their fold."

"This is my mother's usual effort following any row I've had with my father," he said dryly. Martha was making more of the missive than there was. "She doesn't appreciate any discord."

"You're wrong, Graham," she said with her usual confidence. Martha rushed over to his desk. The hint of lavender that clung to her skin wafted past, filling his senses. She brandished the duchess' note. "This is not a letter from a duchess. This is a letter from your mother."

He puzzled his brow. "Aren't they quite the same?"

"They are not at all the same. This is not a formal summons. This is simply her asking you to come home."

"I am home," he said automatically. "Where you are is home."

The heart-shaped planes of Martha's face melted. "Oh, Graham," she breathed, and walking over, Martha went up on tiptoes and kissed him once more.

Their mouths met in another tender meeting that ended too quickly.

Martha stepped away. "I love you, and I'm grateful that you'd make that sacrifice for me."

"It is no sacr—"

"But I'll not be the one that holds you… or us back from visiting your family." With that, she pressed the note into his fingers and swept off.

"Where are you going?" he called after her.

Martha continued on without so much as a glance back. "To see our belongings packed. We leave on the morn." She drew the door shut behind her.

Graham reread the already familiar lines in his mother's hand, seeing the words as Martha had indicated they'd been written.

This is them attempting to bring you back into their fold.

It had been settled. He and Martha would return to Graham's family's home and face the beasts of Polite Society who'd come for his parents' latest house party—whether he wished it or not.

CHAPTER 2

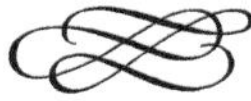

The prospect of meeting a duke would be daunting for any woman. It was even more so for a woman who'd gone and married a duke's son… after that same duke had attempted to pay her to leave his son alone.

As such, when they were forced to stop at a quiet inn because of snow, Martha could only feel secretly relieved that their journey to Graham's family was delayed.

"The sun is out!" Frederick piped in happily.

Or their journey *had been* delayed.

Martha's stomach muscles twisted in knots, vicious, unrelenting knots that made it impossible to break her fast at their corner table of the Fox and Hare Inn. Martha spared the dubious contents of her plate a glance. Though, in fairness, even if she hadn't sat there dreading her impending meeting with her in-laws and their host of societal guests, the ivory-colored slop atop what might or might not be charred potatoes was enough to give any person pause. Sighing, she set down her fork and abandoned all pretense of eating.

"I preferred the snow," her eldest twin daughter, Creda, was saying, long contrary to both her siblings. She spoke around an alarmingly large bite of the suspect morning meal.

Iris snorted.

Creda swallowed another spoonful down and then dabbed at her lips with her napkin. "What? I dooooo," she said for her younger-by-eight-minutes sister. "It's ever more interesting than the sun," she groused, leaning down and rubbing at her shin.

"I prefer the sun, too." Frederick glanced back and forth from between his bickering sisters. His smile stretched from ear to ear in a way it hadn't since his sisters had been sent away and he and Martha had remained on alone. "But I also like the snow." Nay, he'd smiled again. But it hadn't been because of Martha. It had been because of Graham. The man who'd slipped into her life, pretending to be a stable master, and stolen her heart, and given her and her children his name in the process.

Creda beamed. "See?" She preened. "There's nothing *wrong* with loving the snow."

"Graham enjoys it, too," Frederick chattered, excitement dripping from the words as they tumbled from his lips.

Iris rolled her eyes. "I didn't say there was anything wrooong with liking snow, just that we should be respectful that as long as it is snowing, Lord Whitworth will not be able to continue on to visit his family for the holidays."

"Just Graham," Frederick put forward. "He's married to Mother, and therefore, Graham will do."

"You're just excited about meeting a duke," Creda shot at her sister.

"Am not."

"Are too."

Frederick looked helplessly at Martha.

"That will be all," she said quietly, and apparently, despite the time apart, that cease-bickering-immediately-tone still had power behind it. Martha, who'd never allowed bickering to go on and always ended it with a hug, was, however, finding her way again.

Her three children looked to her. The girls were near-identical images of each other, their brother dark-haired while they were light.

Pushing aside her untouched plate, Martha drew in a slow breath. "I know… this… is unusual to each of you."

They stared back in silence, revealing nothing about what they were thinking in their usually expressive features.

"Creda and Iris, you've been… a-away." Emotion garbled the words, making a mess of them. Learning her husband had been married to another and her father responsible for coordinating the murder of the man who'd deceived her, Martha's entire family had been shattered. Of all she'd lost, these two more mature versions of the little girls she'd sent off to finishing school had been the greatest. "And so… this…" Martha made herself speak again and motioned around the table. "Behaving with one another, or acting with one another…"

Creda cocked her head. "What are you saying?" God love her eldest twin. She'd always been direct when Martha had herself only just discovered that skill.

"She's saying it's awkward to be around one another," Iris said flatly.

For the first time since Martha had shared with her son Graham's offer to marry her, the perpetual smile Frederick wore slipped. "It's not awkward." Anger flashed in his eyes. "We're family. We always are and always will be… Now, we have Graham, too."

They looked as one to the window where Graham stood outside, speaking to the drivers of the two carriages. All the while, the pair of footmen who'd accompanied them arranged the trunks atop the conveyances. He was saying something. Periodically, the drivers would nod.

Whatever Graham said just then earned laughter from both men.

As if he felt their collective stares, Graham looked over.

Martha's heart did a little somersault in her chest.

Graham smiled, a lazy half grin that had captivated her from the moment he'd turned it on her, before then shifting his attention to her daughters. Doffing his beaver-fur-lined top hat, he bowed his head for Creda and Iris.

Both girls giggled, and it was the first time the contrary twins had shown a like response to anyone or anything, ever.

Yes, Graham had that effect on… any woman of any age. He could charm a lady out of her good name if he so sought. And even with that magnetizing pull, he still was and had only ever been honorable. To her, when the world had called her "whore" and "bigamist" and her son a "bastard"… he'd defended them at every slight.

"I like him," Creda said when Graham had gone back to coordinating the details of their departure.

Iris pointed her eyes skyward. "You don't even know him."

Frederick surged to the edge of his seat, but Creda was already ticking off her defense on her fingers. "He answered four nonstop hours of questions from Frederick on how to care for horses in the snow—"

"Hey," Frederick exclaimed.

With her spare hand, Creda ruffled his dark curls and continued her enumeration.

"He did not so much as twitch a facial muscle when you, Iris, said you wanted to become the first female doctor so you could cut open dead bodies."

Martha buried a laugh in her hand. "Graham wouldn't." He was unflappable. That ease and calm didn't come with the rank he'd just recently taken on as an agent for the Home Office.

Iris bristled. "Graham being unfazed merits more of a reaction than the prospect of cutting open dead bodies?"

"Only because we all know you couldn't have changed that much since you were gone," Frederick supplied for her. "You can't even tolerate a worm in your hand."

The girl's cheeks went bright red. "There were fifty of them… in my bed."

Frederick thumped the table, commanding the pair to silence. "Creda has not finished her defense of Graham."

Martha's eldest twin gave a toss of her head, reveling in that defense. "More important, it bears stating and repeating that

Graham could have quite contentedly left us behind at Mrs. Munroe's."

"We wanted to be at Mrs. Munroe's," Iris pointed out.

That cut through the lightness the previous dialoguing had stirred in her chest. Martha frowned and sat upright. "What?" Her daughters had wanted to remain at Mrs. Munroe's?

Her daughters continued speaking over her query. "But he said he wished to meet us and introduce us to his family," Creda countered. "It doesn't matter that we want to remain at Mrs. Munroe's, but rather, that he wished to meet us. After all, most stepfathers are content without young children underfoot."

"Says who?" Frederick shot back, bristling with his ten-year-old's indignation.

Iris released a long sigh. "Everrrrybody knows it. But Lord... Graham was more interested in meeting us, and therefore, that speaks a good deal about him." A mischievous sparkle lit her eyes. "Furthermore, Graham is fine with you underfoot, so he has to be incredibly patient."

Frederick stuck his tongue out, and as the pair resumed their bickering, Martha's focus lingered not on that endearing and observant enumeration provided by her daughter, but rather, one statement. "You want to remain at Mrs. Munroe's?" she blurted.

That cut across the quarreling siblings. "Of course we do," Creda said for the pair.

"I... see." Martha clasped her fingers and stared at the interlocked digits. *What did you expect? You drove your daughters away. Did you think they should want to live with you?* Yes, it had been to protect them. And now she'd rushed headlong to Mrs. Munroe's to retrieve them... with a new husband... and stepfather.

"You're sad," Iris said hesitantly.

"I'm not." How did Martha manage that lie so easily? Since Graham had asked her to marry him and said he wanted to be a family with her three children, she'd been only happy. Until now.

Creda covered her hands with one of her own. "It is... not

because of you, Mama," she said gently, in the greatest of role reversals. "You do know that?"

No, she didn't.

"Why should she know that?" Frederick snapped. "When you don't even want to be with u-us." And the façade of anger gave way to a trembling syllable that conveyed the depth of his like sadness. "Is it because of Graham?" The fire was back in his eyes. "Because if it is, it's only because you don't know him. He's kind and wonderful, and he throws snowballs and—"

"You think that's what this is about?" Creda creased her eyebrows. "That we don't want to be with you, as a family?" Folding her arms at her chest, she passed an accusatory stare between her mother and brother. "That we don't like Lord… Graham?"

Martha wet her lips. "You… do?"

"Of course we do," Iris said with another of her usual eye rolls. "We're not so selfish that we don't want to see our own mother happy."

"What manner of ill opinion do you have of us?" Creda muttered.

"We are very happy to be reunited for the holidays," Iris went on, the eternal peace-keeper. "And come to know Graham."

"He smiles quite a lot, and it's hard not to like someone who smiles so much," Creda chimed in.

"We just have come to enjoy our lessons and instructors at Mrs. Munroe's."

Martha sank back in her chair. "Indeed?"

These almost two years apart, she'd imagined her daughters morose, missing their cottage in High Town, forlorn. Only to find that, all this time, they'd been—

"You're happy there?" Frederick asked the question for her, his incredulity her own.

Both girls nodded and spoke in unison.

"Quite so."

"Abundantly so."

The twin girls exchanged a look. There was another slight nod from Iris, who spoke on their behalf. "Now would be an apt time to ask that, after the holidays, we be permitted to return for the next semester."

"We're studying powerful women in England's history," Creda said excitedly. "Or we were... but we left and did not see the conclusion of the unit."

This was what this was about? Her daughters wanted to remain on as students?

"I daresay Frederick and I have the great honor of spending company in three women to rival those late figures."

Martha gasped, and she and her children swung their gazes to the tall figure towering over them.

Her heart did another quick leap, as it always did—as it always had—whenever her husband was near.

"Graham!" Frederick cried, jumping to his feet. He rushed headlong into Graham's arms, and her husband immediately folded the boy in an easy paternal embrace that Martha's own father, who'd loved her, had never managed. Nor the man who'd sired Frederick.

Dropping their chins atop their palms, the twin girls released matching sighs.

Over the top of Frederick's tousled curls, Graham held Martha's stare. "The carriage is readied."

She forced a smile, the muscles of her face strained so tight her cheeks ached.

It was time.

CHAPTER 3

Graham despised his mother and father's winter house parties.

To be fair, he'd abhorred them since he'd been a boy of three. It was, in fact, one of the oldest memories he carried. He'd been marched out in a neat little line with his two older brothers, presented like little ducks for the lords and ladies invited by his mother.

The guests had oohed and aahed over the ducal heir, spare, and... Graham, the third-born, less-useful spare.

Now, he'd subject his new family to that same misery.

"It is so very grand," Creda whispered.

Pulled from his musings, Graham looked to the little girl with her nose pressed to the carriage window.

"I can't see," Frederick grumbled from the opposite end of the bench the three siblings occupied.

Iris and Creda ignored him and vied for the better place at the lead pane to catch sight of the properties. The wooded hills and valleys lay covered in a smooth, untouched blanket of snow. The winding waters surrounding the sprawling manor had since frozen.

"It is... a castle," Iris breathed.

The monumental country house had been constructed just over

one hundred years earlier. "A palace," he replied, the rote familial ancestry lesson slipping out. The design by Sir John Vanbrugh had been commissioned by the current duke's great-grandfather. "The castle-constructing phase of English history had been completed by—"

"The year 1500," Iris interrupted.

Graham bowed his head in acknowledgment of that acumen. "Very impressive."

The young girl preened under his praise. "We've studied architecture of Great Britain," she explained. "I enjoyed the classes, but Creda fell asleep during the lectur—owww." She glared at her twin. "Don't kick me."

"I didn't fall asleep."

"Girls," Martha admonished, and as the pair continued their quarrel, Graham found his first smile of the day. This... normality was something his own family had been without.

He and his brothers had not expressed their discontent with words, but had instead settled disputes and fraternal discord with battles: swimming, racing, fencing, and ultimately the ride that had claimed his brother Lawrence's life.

The pain of that loss was always more acute... here, in the place where it had happened. The fateful race between Graham and Lawrence had seen his elder brother with a broken neck and then dead. It was, of course, why his family hated him...

Martha slid her fingers into his, and he clung to them, accepting the offering of support she gave, finding comfort when there'd been none all these years.

His driver knocked on the door.

"Are you ready?" she mouthed.

To suffer through the whispers and pointed looks? He'd become accustomed long ago to the gawking interest. His new family, however, had not. As such, he was tempted to order their trunks hefted atop the carriage once more and the conveyance turned back to London. "As ready as one can be prepared for my family," he muttered as Terry drew the door open.

The children clambered for the door, pushing and shoving against one another. "Hurry."

"Move."

"Won't you please get—"

Frederick's, Creda's, and Iris' frustrated commands all rolled together, until there was, at last, silence.

Neither Graham nor Martha made a move to climb down.

"I should… warn you before we enter, my father isn't a warm man." Graham clenched and unclenched his jaw.

Why can't you be more like Heath or Lawrence?

In the bereaved tones of his father, those words had been a lamentation nearly two decades ago. Now, they rang out as clear as they had then, that moment Graham had come to acknowledge that his father saw him as a failure and nothing more.

Martha touched two gloved fingertips to his jaw. "You've shared enough with me about your father to know he's not warm. No man should treat his son the way yours did you. But I'd still have you know peace with your family."

It was the fanciful wish of an optimist. "You're certain? It is not too late to return to London and skate at Hyde Park."

Martha laughed softly. "As tempting as it is, we will have to wait for Hyde Park. Now, go." She gave him a teasing shove.

Graham jumped out, the gravel crunching noisily under his boots. Reaching back, he held a hand inside, and Martha, without hesitation, placed her fingers in his.

Together, they made the trek down the remaining length of the drive and up the first tier of long limestone steps.

The wind gusted lightly, carrying the excited murmurings of the three children ahead. Their laughter came so freely. Even with the struggle they'd known at their tender years, they had somehow reclaimed—or, mayhap in the girls' case, retained—an innocence, an ability to laugh. Whereas Graham had been so guarded, building walls to keep everyone out early, early on.

"It's going to be all right, Graham," Martha said softly, lightly squeezing his hand.

He paused at the first patio, bringing them both to a stop. His wife gave him a questioning look. She sought to reassure… him? "There is no one like you," he whispered, brushing several crimson curls back behind her ear.

Her cheeks pinkened. "I've not done anything."

Graham lowered his brow to hers. "Any other woman would embrace her deserved resentment over my family's treatment and let my mother go hang for her interference. And yet, you insist on us being here."

"Because it is the right thing to do," she said so simply that he fell in love with her all over again.

"Mama? Graham?"

Standing at the top step, his little hands propped on his hips, Frederick stared impatiently down at them.

"He and his sisters are far braver than I," he said from the corner of his mouth as they started up the second tier of stone steps.

"They're children. And somehow still have an optimism that most would have lost had they experienced what they did." Martha's expression briefly darkened, but then that shadow lifted. "You helped him find that child's joy again, Graham. *You.*"

"No, together we did that," he murmured. How very different the little boy now skipping in an impatient line was from the surly one he'd met over a month ago. "You, me, and Frederick together." They'd all helped one another heal.

And for her talk of a child's innocence, Martha's resolve to be here at the holidays and her talk of peace with his family revealed more of her son's optimism than she credited to herself.

They reached the terrace, and Frederick abruptly stopped his pacing. "About time," he groused, trotting over to his sisters, who remained in a neat line at the arched entryway. The trio parted as Graham and Martha came forward.

Graham had reached for the door knocker, that regal winged figure he'd been intrigued by as a child, when Creda spoke.

"Zeus and… the Nike of Samothrace," she breathed, reaching past him.

"Who?" Frederick asked.

"She's just spouting off a tale one of the instructors regaled the younger girls with," Iris insisted, but her sister continued on, pausing only to glare at her twin.

"It's not a tale. The Greeks worshipped her because they believed she could prevent them from dying and help grant them the ability to be victorious in any task they undertook."

And there was the ode of his father, the reason he'd despised Graham, a child and then young man unable to properly focus in any task. Once, his father's shame had gutted him. He'd hardened himself to that rejection. It hadn't been until Martha, however, that he'd come to see his own worth, to realize that his weaknesses did not define him, but rather, were just part of him.

Graham held her gaze. "I love you," he said quietly.

Her eyes lit. "I love you, too."

With that, Graham found the courage to knock.

Before the metal even hit the oak panel, the doors were drawn open, yanking the bronze Nike from Graham's fingers.

Avril, his hair a stark white and a vivid contrast to the crimson livery he wore, greeted Graham with his usual smile, even as the family's loyal butler knew every secret and story of the nobleman he served. "Lord Whitworth." He swept aside, allowing them to enter.

Despite the tension and unease that had dogged him since his mother's letter had arrived, Graham felt himself grinning. "Avril, my good man," he returned as he allowed Martha, the twins, and Frederick to enter ahead of him. "May I present my wife, Lady Whit… worth," he finished as his stare caught on the regal duchess at the top of the curved marble staircase.

His mother wound her way down the crimson carpets that lined the center of the steps. "Graham," she called down, her voice bouncing off the forty-foot ceiling. Those crisp tones managed to at last silence the three children.

Graham? What… in *blazes*? None of his kin, not even his mother, had called him by that preferred name. It was a nonsensical detail to note as she made her deliberate march, slow step by slow step, toward his new family, the family she'd previously rejected, and yet, even with that, Graham's brow creased.

Martha stood with a regal bearing to rival the Duchess of Sutton's, her shoulders back, her spine straight, and her head up. If she was unnerved by her first meeting with Graham's mother, she gave no indication.

Aside from the handful of servants milling about, there was one notable absence for Graham's homecoming… or rather, two: the Duke of Sutton and Heath.

Anger simmered within him, safer and more welcome than any of the regret that his brother and father could never, nay, would never be the men he always expected them to be.

Quashing those useless sentiments, Graham slipped his hand into Martha's in a telltale showing of solidarity.

Her fingers curled reflexively in his, clenching and unclenching.

His mother stopped at the bottom step and surveyed the group assembled upon her white Italian marble foyer, before her gaze ultimately settled on Martha. Or, more specifically, on Graham's and Martha's joined palms.

His wife's chin came up a notch, and then she dipped a slow, deep curtsy. "Your Grace," she murmured.

Martha's daughters immediately followed suit.

Creda shoved a discreet elbow into Frederick's side.

With a grunt, the boy added a belated bow.

His mother drifted closer to Martha and then paused, stretching her palms out.

Confusion in her eyes, Martha looked at the duchess' hands before placing hers in them.

A watery smile curved his mother's lips. "I am so very happy to meet you, Martha."

As Martha's mouth parted with her shock, the duchess drew her close and folded her in her arms.

Martha's arms hung uselessly by her sides, and over the top of the smaller woman's head, his wife's gaze met his. Then, with a smile, she brought her arms up about Graham's mother.

CHAPTER 4

When she'd mentally braced herself for her first meeting with Graham's mother, Martha had anticipated an icy derision only a noblewoman could manage.

She'd suspected her new mother-in-law might ignore her.

Of all the expectations Martha had, a warm smile and a hug had not been among them.

No, that cool reception inevitably came… from the guests assembled at the duke and duchess' dining table.

This was the life her father had desired for her, seated amongst lords and ladies with the most venerated titles.

Coward that she was, Martha found herself counting down course after endless course and envying her children, who'd had the good fortune to be whisked away to the nurseries.

For this was a special kind of hell.

Her skin burned from the furtive and, in most cases, not-so-furtive glances sent her way by the thirty guests assembled.

The smallest of gratitude, however, came from being seated alongside an occasionally dozing white-haired nobleman, Lord Lisle.

Spear, slice, fork, eat.

Vastly different than the mantra *dunk, scrub, rinse, repeat* that had played through her head just weeks ago.

Ironically, she found herself preferring the grueling work of laundering, even with her callused hands and cracked knuckles, to this—being on display before Polite Society and Graham's family.

Graham's father, who occupied the seat at the head of the table, still couldn't be bothered with any pleasantries. *What did you expect of such a man who's been so cold and cruel to his own child?* She stole another peek at the Duke of Sutton, tall, broad-shouldered, and in possession of the same heavily chiseled features as Graham. He was his son in every way… physically. The aloof set to those same features marked him so very different from his son, different in the ways that most mattered.

She felt Graham's stare before she glanced across the table and found his gaze on her.

"I told you," he mouthed. "Horrid."

Her lips twitched, and she quickly gathered up her napkin and hid her smile.

Her husband winked, and the tension melted from her. With him at her side, she could face anyone and anything, pompous members of the peerage—his father—included. "I love you," she said, the vow noiseless.

"I love you, too."

Warmth blossomed in Martha's chest.

Just then, her dining partner jolted himself awake with a snorting cough. "Who… what… were you saying, gel?"

"I was just commenting on the delightful company," she answered, and pulling her attention away from the only man in the room who existed for her, Martha attended Lord Lisle's discourse on the upcoming desserts prepared by the Duchess of Sutton's French chef.

After a seemingly endless repast, the Duke and Duchess of Sutton's guests filed from the room… for… for whichever activities occupied Polite Society after they dined.

With the duke and duchess leading the way through the corridors, Martha forced her feet forward, wanting to turn in the opposite direction and flee. Searching... for her husband.

Where was he? She craned her neck, looking around the procession. He couldn't have simply... disappeared. Falling back, Martha allowed the handful of couples trailing behind her to pass.

A hand wound around her forearm, and she gasped as she was yanked down the intersecting hall. The shocked exhalation was quickly quashed by a gloved palm pressed against her lips—a familiar gloved palm.

Martha scowled at her own entirely too pleased grin. It was all too easy to forget that this man she'd fallen in love with and married was also an operative for the Crown, capable of losing himself in crowds of all sizes.

"Do I need to worry that if I draw my hand away you'll scream, madam?" he whispered against her ear. His breath, containing a trace of claret and honey, teased at the sensitive shell.

"You'd be wise to worry, Lord Whitworth," she returned in equally hushed tones.

Graham guided her against the wall, and propping his arms on either side of her head, he anchored her between him. Heat poured off his body in waves, his nearness, the feel of his body pressed close to hers headier than the wine that had flown so freely this night.

She raised her mouth close to his, wanting his kiss, even as it was scandalous to long for his embrace here of all places, in the hall where anyone might pass.

But then she registered the serious glint in his eyes.

"What?" she asked hesitantly, her smile fading.

"Has anyone offended you?" he asked evenly.

"They haven't, Graham," she promised, running her palms along the front of his black sapphire-trimmed jacket.

"Because if they have, I'll order the carriages readied now—"

"Graham," she murmured, touching an index finger to his lips. "No one has offended me."

"They're miserable affairs, though, aren't they?"

That she would concede to him. "Regardless, everyone has been only… polite."

Graham's body went taut, and he drew away from her.

"What is…?" Martha's question went unfinished as a young lady turned the corner.

Flawless, with golden curls upswept in a loose chignon studded with diamond haircombs, the olive-hued beauty was the embodiment of English perfection. An equally flawless blush filled her cheeks.

Martha's stomach knotted. Lady Emilia—the woman Graham's family had sought to marry him off to.

"Lady Emilia," Graham greeted, dropping a bow.

"Lord Whitworth, Lady Whitworth, forgive me," the young woman murmured, sinking into a curtsy. "I was… on my way to join the other ladies."

Had Martha not been studying the voluptuous Athena so closely, she'd have missed the ever-so-slight tightening of those bow-shaped lips. A grimace. The lady had… grimaced. At the prospect of joining the duchess' other guests? Or at having come upon Martha and Graham?

The lady quickly had a smile in place, and it was pearl white and as perfect as the lady herself, and Martha was besieged by the sudden need to cry. "Would you care to join me, Lady Whitworth?" she asked, extending an elbow.

Martha was so mired in the misery of meeting the woman Graham's family had handpicked for him to wed that it took a moment for the offer to register.

It was… an *unexpected* offer of support. An attempt to include Martha. For what end? For what purpose?

The other woman stared back patiently, and this time, Martha noted the details she'd failed to note moments ago—the sincerity and warmth in her heart-shaped face. "That would be… lovely," Martha said softly. Sliding her fingers upon the other woman's sleeve and resisting the urge to glance back at her husband, she allowed Lady Emilia to lead her off to join the other ladies.

CHAPTER 5

Any time he'd attended his mother and father's house parties, Graham had relished these moments of solitude.

In fact, he'd made it a point to seek out that blessed gift whenever and wherever he could.

Now, he found himself, as he'd been at so many of the previous parties before, alone—and wishing for the company of another.

More specifically… his wife.

"Psst, Graham."

He started.

"Over here, Graham."

Following the endearingly loud child's whisper to the opposite intersecting hall, he found Frederick lurking around the corner.

"I didn't hear you," he acknowledged, the words coming out for the praiseworthy ones they were. Frederick's furtive steps could one day see the boy with a role in the Brethren, if he so wished it. On the heels of that was the significance of finding Frederick lurking here and not in the nursery. "Is everything all right?"

"Yes. Fine, fine. My sisters went exploring to see the Portrait Rooms, and I was alone and bored."

"Well, we cannot have that." Graham threw an arm around the

boy's small shoulders. "Allow me to take you to my most favorite of places to sneak off to during these dull affairs."

"Oh, they aren't dull," Frederick contradicted. "There's so many people here, and the gentlemen were off taking drinks and laughing. All very exciting stuff."

The three children had been granted an anonymity that lent a level of intrigue to the duke and duchess' grand affair. Graham had never shared that joy. Unlike Frederick, Creda, and Iris, Graham had been perpetually on display and had hated it all. Not wanting to kill the boy's joy, he neatly directed them to the last room at the end of the corridor. "Now, this is very exciting stuff," he promised as he pressed the handle. "The bill…" His words trailed off at finding that he and Frederick were not the first to appropriate the room for the evening.

Heath.

Graham's brother was poised over the table as the world never saw him, sans jacket and his shirtsleeves rolled up. Graham hadn't seen such negligence in his attire since—he scoured his mind—he couldn't even remember.

"Billiards," Frederick whispered in reverent awe.

"Forgive me," Graham said stiffly. "I didn't realize the room was occupied." He gave Frederick's shoulder a light squeeze. "We should—"

"Please, won't you join me?" Heath directed the unexpected invitation not to Graham, but rather, the little boy at his side. He completed his shot.

Frederick raised a pleading gaze to Graham's.

As a rule, Graham made it a point to avoid his brother. In fairness, they both went out of their way to do so. Alas, working for the Brethren, Graham had received enough training that he could put on a false show for his son's benefit. "Of course."

Letting out an excited whoop, Frederick went racing over to the red-velvet-lined table and gripped the edges of the broad mahogany piece.

"Frederick, may I present… my brother, Lord Heath," he said as he closed the door behind them.

That brought the boy up short. "You're… *brothers?*" He scratched at his puckered brow. "You don't seem like you're brothers."

"Indeed, we are," Heath drawled. Wandering over to the cue shelf, Heath retrieved two additional sticks. "And come… we're of a ducal family, but I daresay my new nephew might call me Uncle," he offered, tossing one of the sticks across the table. Frederick scrambled to catch it. "Or, at least, Heath." He followed that with a wink for the boy's benefit.

Heath? Uncle? What in blazes…?

Collecting himself, Graham joined the pair at the table and accepted the cue. His brother didn't even bother looking at him, instead speaking to Frederick.

"Have you played before, Frederick?"

The boy gave a mighty shake of his head. "I haven't. I've always wanted to. My father once told me that I was too little to ever be good at it… or anything," he tacked on, almost as an afterthought.

That casual admission froze both Graham and his brother in their tracks. Even after a month of learning the cruelty and pain Frederick and his sisters and mother had suffered at the hands of the late viscount, the reality had the ability to cleave Graham in two every time.

Over the top of Frederick's head, Heath at last spared a look for Graham. And of all the wonders and shocks, it appeared that they, two brothers who'd been at odds the whole of their lives, could prove united in something, after all—a shared outrage for Frederick's revealing admission.

"Is…" Frederick cleared his throat. "Is it a problem that I don't kn-know how to play?" he asked, misinterpreting the reason for the silence blanketing the room.

Heath caught Frederick's shoulder in a like manner to how Graham had lightly gripped him in the hall and then patted his arm. "No, lessons are perfect." He dipped his voice to a conspiratorial whisper. "That way, you can learn from the best."

It was that usual cocksure arrogance that had been the most natural of skins for his brother to wear, and it had always grated. Only this time, as Frederick giggled, there was none of Graham's usual enmity toward his brother.

"First, both opponents' balls are white, but one of them"—Heath lifted it in display—"is marked with a black dot. We also require a red object ball. Each player"—he glanced to Frederick—"or team?"

Content to observe the pair, Graham waved Heath on.

"Each team or player use a different ball," his brother finished. Leaning over the table, Heath brought his cue into position. "The trick to striking a ball," he said to the boy hanging on his every word, "is to move your arm slowly back." He demonstrated the smooth movement. "And then forward in a pendulum motion." He urged Frederick into a like position.

The boy practiced, his movements slightly jerky.

"Keep the rest of your body still," Heath coached. "Now, when you're ready, strike whichever cue you decide."

Frederick continued shifting, testing the motions, and then he let his stick fly.

The balls cracked as he found his mark.

Frederick let out a triumphant shout. "Graham! Did you see…? I did it!"

With a grin, Graham brought his hands together, clapping. "Bravo. As Heath said, you've learned… from the best." And where that statement would have been uttered only with jaded mockery, this time… there was none.

All Graham's life he'd used his brother's successes as the bellwether for his own successes… and, more commonly, failures. Only to find in this moment that he didn't need to compete with Heath. What Heath accomplished or achieved wasn't a mark against Graham, or evidence of any flaw in Graham. It was simply… a skill his brother possessed, independent from Graham.

Graham went and made himself a drink at the rosewood-inlaid tantalus. As he sipped brandy, he studied the pair at play in the crystal windowpane. The full moon's glow cast a bright shine upon the glass, bringing Frederick and Heath into better focus. They moved about the table, conversing as easily as if they'd known each other the whole of the boy's life. All the while, they alternated between Heath's meticulous billiards lesson and some lighthearted remark made to the boy that earned one of Frederick's precious laughs.

Graham glanced into the amber contents of his snifter and let himself think about the last time he'd played billiards with his older brother.

"I don't want to play with you. You always beat me... and you're always mean about it, Heath."

"Fine. Don't play with me, Shelly. Father is right. You're a whiny baby who can't do anything anyway."

Frederick laughed, that snorting expression of mirth at odds with the memory Graham carried of the misery he'd endured during any game with the man who now got on so easily with Martha's son.

Shaking off the melancholy thought, he faced the pair. "I'm afraid that must be the end of the billiards lesson for the evening," Graham said. "Your mother will surely be stopping by your rooms." As he'd come to learn in the short time they'd lived together as husband and wife, Martha performed the nightly ritual with each of her children.

Frederick groaned. "Awww. Can't I just play five more minutes?"

Heath set his stick on the side of the table. "We can have another lesson tomorrow," he promised. He paused. "Or perhaps Graham might deliver your next one."

It was a veiled acknowledgment that Heath thought he might have overstepped and now graciously backed away from that interference.

Handing over his stick, Frederick dropped a bow. "I had a good time, Lord... Heath. Graham." He called out the parting greeting with a wave before he dashed off.

And Graham and his brother were left—alone.

Tension crackled like the roaring fire in the hearth.

"What did I ever do to you, Heath?"

His brother straightened. "I beg your—"

"Oh, come," he scoffed, cutting across the false protestation. "If you can muster honesty for a small child, you can certainly spare it for the brother you've known your whole life."

"I'm not here to fight with you," Heath gritted out. Stalking over to the enormous globe in the corner, he grabbed his sapphire jacket flung across the cylinder so quickly the object whirred in a fast counterclockwise circle.

Let him go. Whatever had come between them… it was too far gone to repair.

"I am your brother, Heath," he rasped, the glass shaking in his hand. Nay… "You are my older brother, and I adored you. I… loved you." That brought Heath to a jerky halt. "You are great at everything. Everything comes naturally to you." When Graham had struggled with every skill, scholarly or athletic. "And yet, you had to tear me down along with him?" He should have defended Graham. Protected him. Graham gave his head a disgusted shake and set his barely touched drink on the edge of the billiards table. "You hated me as much as he did."

"Do you think it was easy?" Heath whispered. His brother faced him. "Do you think that being the ducal heir spared me from Father's expectations? You… The expectations placed upon you, you think were great? What do you think they were for me?"

That knocked Graham back on his heels. For the truth was… he'd only ever seen his brother's life as a charmed one. The cherished heir, valued and appreciated for his strengths and for the rank he'd one day inherit. *What if… I too have been wrong all these years?* It was an unnerving realization to confront… and yet, all too easy to see the truth there.

"We should have both been there for one another," Graham said quietly.

"Yes. We should have." Heath flashed a sad smile. "And I never hated you, Sheldon. I just forgot how to be… around anyone." It was the closest his brother would ever come to an apology.

And yet… what would an apology do? It wouldn't make up for the time lost. There was only going forward. "We both shut one another out, Heath," he murmured. Graham was as much to blame. He knew that now.

His brother's throat moved. He opened his mouth as if to say more. But then the walls went up once more. His cheeks flushed with embarrassment, Heath coughed into his hand. "Good night… Graham."

With that, his brother left.

This time, Graham felt there might be something he'd believed impossible to find with his brother—peace.

CHAPTER 6

It took several long walks down three different hallways for Martha to realize the woman escorting her was either lost or had no intention of leading her to the parlor in this palatial household where the duchess currently entertained her guests.

Given Lady Emilia's connection to the Whitworths—the other woman and her family were close enough to have been visitors enough over the years—she should know her way about even this near castle.

Which left the only likely alternative—she was deliberately keeping Martha from the guests.

To what end?

"Here we are." Lady Emilia guided Martha into the last room in the hall.

They'd arrived—Martha's eyebrows drew together—in an empty room.

A…

"It is lovely, is it not?" Lady Emilia called out, her bell-like voice pinging off the frosted glass windows.

Martha took a reluctant step forward, touching her gaze on the space. The full moon's glow cast a bright light over the conservatory, dousing it with a brightness greater than any candles.

"It is… lovely," Martha finally said. And it was. The nine-bay symmetrical façade divided by composite pilasters bordered the duke's wooded properties.

"I've always preferred this room," Lady Emilia murmured, rubbing her gloved fingers back and forth, as if bringing warmth into chilled digits. Also serving to bring Martha's attention to the satin articles embroidered with gold metallic yarns and spangles. Not even a week earlier, Martha had had to her name but two pairs of gloves, both tattered. Lady Emilia's were fine enough that they likely cost more than all the garments she and her son had, combined, after her late husband's passing.

That observation, coupled with the woman's exquisite beauty, sent pain shooting to her chest. She was to have wed Graham. Had Graham's mother and father had their way of it, the pair would be married even now… in a match both the duke and duchess approved of. Unlike Martha. And what was more, Lady Emilia's honest admission just served as an unwanted reminder of the familiarity between Graham and this woman. Unable to meet the lady's lovely blue-eyed stare, Martha glanced around the conservatory; taking in the blooming trees and bright flowering plants so at odds with the winter-covered landscape beyond the glass panels.

Her chest tightened painfully. *Do not… You are stronger than that now.*

Graham had helped her to see her own worth. She was not lesser than this woman because of her station or appearance. "I trust you've not brought me here to speak about the duke and duchess' conservatory?" Martha noted as the lady drifted over.

"It is actually an orangery," Lady Emilia acknowledged in animated tones. "And… oh. Yes. Right. Our… meeting. I confess it was no coincidence that I… came upon you and Lord Whitworth in the corridor earlier." The lady's cheeks pinkened, a pretty blush and not like the usual splotches of color whenever Martha's went hot in a like manner. "I have been waiting to seek you out since you arrived. Since *before* you arrived."

Warning bells went off. No doubt she'd sought her out to speak about Graham. Martha curled her toes in her slippers. Refusing to give in to any questions, she waited.

As if they met in a parlor owned by the lady herself, Lady Emilia motioned to the two white wrought-iron chairs nearest to her. The other woman didn't continue speaking until both she and Martha sat. "There are rumors circulating among the guests about... about..."

"You and my husband?" she asked bluntly. Her days of carefully tiptoeing about what she really wished to say were at an end.

Lady Emilia's blush deepened. "There are those, thanks to my mother's loose tongue. But there are also thoughts about..." She gestured between them, the movement sending the crystals that dangled from her glove dancing. "Us. Polite Society expects that I dislike you and that you'll feel antipathy for me because of"—her face pulled—"circumstances that a pair of other women sought to orchestrate. Circumstances that never really had anything to do with you or I, or even Lord Whitworth." Her lips formed a hard line. "But the world as a rule generally doesn't care what a woman wants." The woman spoke with a staggering directness, about their relationship and Society and women's perceived place in the world, in ways Martha had never expected a lady of the *ton* might. Nay, she spoke... as a woman who knew all too well the injustices that faced all women—nor was that injustice reserved to one's station.

"Too often, family, Society, they care more about what they *believe* we want."

The lady's eyes glimmered. "Precisely. As such, I felt... a connection to you before you arrived." Lady Emilia smiled. And despite the reservations she'd felt for the woman, based on nothing more than her own unfounded jealousies, Martha found herself smiling. "And it is my hope that we might... be friends." Lady Emilia leaned closer. "And it is not just to confuse the duke and duchess' guests, though that will be a delicious by-product," she said in a loud whisper, startling a laugh from Martha.

Lady Emilia joined in.

When their amusement ebbed, the other woman held her fingers out.

Martha shook her hand, the limerick gloves Graham had given her exquisitely soft, and yet, understated against Lady Emilia's. Only… that difference didn't matter. She knew that now. "I should like very much to be friends."

Lady Emilia beamed. "Splendid. One always needs good friends about." Her smile faded on a sigh. "Alas, I've skirted the evening's festivities enough that everyone will be speaking. And though I don't give a jot for the duke's guests, I do worry about the lecture I'll have to suffer through from my mother," she said, coming to her feet. "Parlor games with the duchess' company is a small sacrifice compared to that."

Martha hopped up. "Lady Emilia, it was a pleasure," she murmured, meaning those words. How wrong she'd been about the other woman.

Lady Emilia's face pulled. "Oh, pishposh. There'll be none of that. Friends do not go about referring to one another by titles and such." She lifted a finger. "Or they shouldn't. Some do." Her cheeks dimpled from the breadth of her smile. "I would prefer not to. Alas…" She sighed. "I must rejoin the others. Martha," she said, bowing her head.

Martha followed the regal woman's retreat, the crystals adorning her skirts tinkling slightly. Until she was gone.

After she'd discovered her first husband's treachery, Martha had formed an opinion about Polite Society. Because of the treachery of that blackhearted monster and then the failures of the gentleman at the Home Office who'd promised to help her and her children after the viscount's death, Martha had come to believe all members of the peerage were ruthless devils.

Until Graham had entered her life. Oh, he'd entered her life initially on a lie. But in time, she had come to see the goodness in his soul.

And the kindness from his mother, who'd welcomed Martha this holiday season.

And now Lady Emilia.

They had all helped her to see how wrong she'd been to categorize an entire people because of their rank.

"Tsk-tsk. Hiding in the orangery, love."

With a gasp, she whipped her gaze to the entryway. Her heart did its familiar leap at the sight of him. Her husband lounged with one shoulder propped against the mahogany frame. Devastating. Not a single man on the whole of God's green earth should possess the dangerous beauty of Graham Whitworth. It wasn't fair for a woman's heart. "Are you spying on me, Graham Whitworth?"

He flashed a devilish half grin. "If I were spying, I wouldn't be caught," he said with a cocksure arrogance that raised a laugh.

"You're impossibly full of yourself, dear husband."

Graham waggled his dark brows. "Oh, undoubtedly so."

And then she noted that which had previously escaped her notice. Her husband was dressed in his cloak and top hat and heavy leather gloves, and over his arm hung her own recently purchased by him velvet-trimmed wool cloak. At his side, he dangled her boots by their laces. Her stomach pitched. They were leaving. It could only mean he'd come to blows with his father. "What happened?" No doubt the quarrel this time would have been over her.

"Ah, my pessimist of a wife," he gently reprimanded. Meeting her across the room in several long strides, he brought her cloak about her shoulders. "Who determined that anything has to be wrong?"

"Because of where we are. Because of your father's role in trying to separate us. Because—" He kissed the remainder of the list from her lips.

"Fair points. All of them," he conceded. "Here, sit." Graham urged her onto the wrought-iron bench she'd occupied earlier. "This time, there is no conflict. Or at least, not yet," he said with a wink.

"You are incorrigible and not funny."

He gave her a hurt look.

"Not in this instant anyway."

Graham dropped to a knee and lifted her skirts. "You wound me, love." The cooler air brushed her skin. "What..." He slid off one slipper and then set it down. The other followed. "What are you doing?"

Reaching for her gleaming brown leather boot, Graham loosened the laces, widening it so he could more easily slide her foot in. "I'm helping you into your boots." He quickly laced up the article and tied the laces into a neat bow.

A smile twitched at her lips. "I see that. I meant... for what purpose are you putting my boots on?"

"You'll see, love." His husky baritone wrapped her in a warmth, and as he drew her other boot on, Martha stared at his bent head, the thick tendrils of his dark hair.

"You met with Lady Emilia," he said suddenly, a statement more than anything.

When she didn't answer, he looked up from his task. Martha gave him a bemused smile. "Is there anything you don't know?"

"I observed Lady Emilia taking her leave down the opposite corridor."

It was an unneeded reminder that his work with the Home Office required him to be observant of every last detail. His life and the country's secrets were reliant upon it.

And I hate it...

She bit the inside of her cheek, staggered by the realization she'd not allowed herself to admit until now.

She hated the work he did. She hated that soon another assignment would come, and he'd be taken away from her. Each leaving would present the possibility that she'd never see him again. Tears pricked her lashes. "It was fine," she whispered, blinking them back.

His expression darkened. "What did she say?"

"Nothing." Nay, the other woman's words had not been "nothing." Martha stepped out of her husband's arms and made an angry swipe at her tears. "She was only kind and warm and offered me friendship."

He cocked his head. "That has you upset?" he asked in the tones of one trying to sort through a complex puzzle.

Martha let out a sound of frustration. "No. That has me happy. You..." Except... it wasn't Graham, but rather, his work.

"Martha," he said quietly. "What is it?"

I hate your work. I hate that soon you'll leave. I hate that every time you do might mark the last time I ever do see you...

Except... how did she bring herself to say as much? How, when he served the Home Office and took pride in the work he did?

"I'm simply wondering what you are up to, Graham Whitworth, that you've fetched my cloak and are now putting on my boots."

And mayhap he didn't want to walk the path of reality and the troubled questions between them either, for he finished tying her other boot. "Very well." Jumping up, he took her by the hand and guided her through the orangery until they reached a narrow hall that emptied out of the orangery. Drawing the door open, he motioned for her to exit, and Martha picked her way down the hall until she reached another pair of glass doors. He pressed the handle of one, and a gust of cold air whipped through the hall.

Her husband again took her by the hand and led her outside. "Wh-what are we... doing?" she asked, her teeth chattering in the cold.

A fresh dusting of snow covered the stone terrace, crunching under her boots as they continued out farther, toward the balustrade overlooking the duke's properties.

Then Graham stopped. "When I met you, Martha, I was captivated at first sight," he said into the winter still. Despite the small clouds of white formed by his breath as he spoke, Graham gave no indication that he either felt the cold or that it bothered him in any way. "You walked into that tavern and challenged the entire lot of small-minded villagers, and I was yours."

Her lips trembled. "And I was yours," she whispered. She just hadn't realized it. She'd fought the magnetic pull that had crackled between them from the start.

"And soon, all I knew," he went on, palming her cheek, and she leaned into that tender touch, "was that I wanted you to be happy. I wanted you to smile. Do you remember the first moment you laughed with me?"

She searched her mind. All the darkness of her past marriage and all that had come to pass, he'd replaced in a short time with love and happiness that muted those blackest of memories. "You were ou-outside with Frederick," she remembered, huddling deeper within the folds of her cloak.

"We were playing in the snow."

"Throwing snowballs." Their voices rolled together from the joy of that shared memory.

"And you joined in."

"I did," she said with a smile, when until that moment her whole life had been laundering tattered garments and attending the livestock and stables.

"But then you stopped laughing."

Because she'd believed she hadn't been deserving of that joy. She'd sent her daughters off to finishing school so they could be free of Martha and the scandal she'd inadvertently visited upon them. Graham had opened her eyes to the fact that she didn't have to punish herself for crimes that weren't her fault. He'd taught her that regardless of what came to pass, she and Creda and Iris and Frederick, with Graham at their side, were a family.

"You taught me to smile, Graham Whitworth. That is a gift you gave me." One of so many."

He wandered away, and then he stopped with his back to her, staring out at the snow-covered landscape.

And then he turned around.

Her gaze snagged on the snowball in his hands just as he launched it.

With a laugh, she darted sideways, and his shot found its mark on her right shoulder, splattering her cloak with snow. "You do not p-play fair," she called, in between breathless laughter.

He replied by hastily assembling another snowball.

Martha quickly built her own, and then with a battle cry to rival

Frederick's, she launched her snow-packed missile. It hit Graham square in the chest.

Both of them froze.

Her shoulders shaking with mirth, Martha stifled her laugh behind her palm. "I see my aim is better than yours, Lord Whitworth."

He slowly picked his head up until their gazes met. "War has been declared, love," he said on a silky whisper, and letting out a cry, Martha took off running.

As she darted around the Duke and Duchess of Sutton's terrace, fighting in the snow with her husband, Martha turned herself over to the beauty of laughing once more.

CHAPTER 7

He was not hiding.

Samuel Whitworth, the Duke of Sutton, was working.

All right, he was hiding… somewhat.

He'd rather turn over his title than admit as much. The world after all had certain expectations of him. And he had an image. And said image, under no circumstances, did not include the Duke of Sutton, in possession of one of the oldest titles, eight properties, and hundreds upon hundreds of acres, doing anything so plebian as… hiding.

In his own home, no less.

Seated at his desk, Samuel examined immaculate column after immaculate column. Such was the problem with the standards he'd held himself to over the years: There wasn't even a single error in his accounting to serve as a damned distraction.

And a distraction was what he needed… always at this time of the season. This particular year, however, the need was even greater.

Samuel made to toss down his pen.

You will one day be a duke. Hold your pen like one. Hold yourself like one… at all times.

His late father's brusque command ringing in his head, Samuel returned his pen to the crystal inkwell. That tray, centered on his desk, was perfectly framed by the floor-to-ceiling windows directly across from his desk.

This space over the years had proved to be one of his favorite places to be. At this vantage point within the Whitworth Palace, he was afforded a clear view of the expansive countryside. Situated upon the highest point of the property, his office overlooked rolling hills and thick forests, grounds that were blanketed in snow.

Now, this space looked out on the scene of the greatest mistake he'd made and the deepest regrets he carried—and would carry until he drew his last breath.

Closing his eyes, Samuel let the memory in.

"You summoned me, Father?"

"Your brother is struggling again, Lawrence. It is riding." This time. There was nothing Sheldon didn't struggle with. Why could nothing be easy for the boy? "One of the boys at Eton beat him badly in a race. Humiliated him for it." No one would mock his son. Any of them. The world would see them as the best... because they were. Even Sheldon with his struggles.

"But, Father..." Samuel glanced up from his work at the boy standing on the other side of his desk. With his build, strong jaw, and golden hair, he was a blend of both Samuel and Caroline. "I've not finished my reading. Can Heath not race him?"

"Heath's tried unsuccessfully to motivate him." Lawrence would be gentler with the boy. Gentler when Samuel himself could not be. Hadn't ever been. "You can finish after you help your brother. Go race."

Samuel forced his eyes open, staring blankly at the windows now lightly frosted.

Go race.

With that command, Samuel had glanced down and returned to his work, Lawrence forgotten.

Had his son sought to protest after that? Had he lingered? Samuel had dismissed him so quickly outright that he'd failed to miss the precious last details before his oldest son had done his bidding and gone off… to do a job that should have been Samuel's.

There was a light rap at his door. "En—" The command hadn't fully left his mouth before the panel swung wide, and his wife swept in.

His wife, the hostess of the house party, who by her appearance here had gone and left their guests unattended. Oh, bloody hell. This was indeed bad.

Caroline stalked over. "Well?" she demanded.

"I'll be along shortly to join the parlor games."

Narrowing her eyes, she pressed her palms on the edge of his desk and leaned down. "Is that what you think this is about?" she countered, a warning in her tone.

That absolute strength had made him fall in love with her as a young man.

It had both inspired and impressed.

Now it terrified.

Bloody impressive.

"Are you smiling, Samuel Whitworth?"

"I'd never dare dream of it," he said, smoothing his lips into an even line.

"Your display thus far? Has not been friendly."

Samuel scoffed. "I don't know what you mean." He grabbed his pen from the inkwell and tapped the tip against the edge, setting the crystal to tinkling.

"No," his wife said, as if speaking to a stubborn child. "I don't believe you do. *Friend-ly.*" She enunciated each of those two syllables. "Smiling. Happy. Kind. How you have been to our new daughter-in-law and our son?" She slapped her gloved palms on his desk. "That was not even polite, Samuel."

This slip of a woman, more than a foot shorter than his own height and slender as a wisp, managed to make him feel small.

Or mayhap you've made yourself feel small.

Samuel's ears went hot… with something unpleasant—shame.

Oh, it wasn't a foreign sentiment. It was, however, a sentiment he'd masked the world from seeing. He'd done such a convincing job, he'd even managed to convince himself. Most times.

"Well?" Caroline persisted. "What do you have to say for yourself, Samuel Sheldon Constantine?"

"I treated them no different than any other of your guests," he mumbled. Caroline, his wife, was the only person who could make him mutter, mumble, or blush.

"Precisely, Samuel," she said, her voice as chilled as the winter grounds below.

"I'll..." He struggled within himself and then tried again. "I'll..."

"Try?" she supplied for him.

"Precisely." Jumping to his feet, Samuel waved his hand at the air. "I'll *try*."

Her lovely golden brows dipped. "That is incorrect."

What? "But that was *your* answer, Caroline," he whined. How in blazes could it have been the wrong reply?

"Because you will do *better* than try." Ah, so he'd stepped into a trap. She stalked around the desk, and he retreated from that advance. "You *will* be kind to them. You *will* speak to Martha and Graham, and you'll do it all with a smile on your face." Samuel's legs knocked into the French walnut corner library, rattling the ledgers neatly lining the shelf. "Are we clear, dear husband?" she asked in deathly quiet tones, even as she had to go on tiptoe to hold his gaze.

How did he say to this woman who owned his heart that he didn't know how to be what he needed to be in this regard? He'd always sought to be the man she deserved. They'd been matched by their parents when she'd been a babe, and he'd once seen her only as a duty... an obligation, and then she turned out to be a woman so much greater than the man he could or ever would be. Where their children were concerned, he'd always failed her. Worse, he'd failed his children. "We are... clear."

Her lips softened into the alluring smile that always enthralled him. "Splendid, Samuel." Caroline ran her palms over his immaculate lapels, smoothing them. "That makes me very happy."

Samuel leaned down to claim her mouth in a kiss.

She turned her head, so that his lips missed their mark and found another. "Uh-uh, Your Grace. I'm still angry with you."

"You're certain?" He kissed the soft shell of her ear, rousing a breathless laugh.

"Quite certain," she said, less convincing than she'd been moments ago. Nonetheless, she stepped out of his arms. "Mayhap if we did not have a house full of guests no doubt wondering after me, I might consider your roguish advances."

"Might consider?" he whispered, reaching for her once more.

Caroline swatted at his hand. "Do behave," she said without inflection, the desire and tenderness in her pretty blue eyes belying that order.

Samuel sighed. "Oh, very well." He stared regretfully after her retreating figure, her hips lightly swaying in pale silver skirts that molded her body, her waist not as trim as it had been when she'd made her Come Out and her hips wider, but tenfold more beautiful with every passing year. "Caroline?" he called when she reached the door.

His wife cast a glance back.

"I love you, dearest," he said gruffly.

Her lips trembled. "I love you, too, Samuel." She blew a kiss from her fingertips, and Samuel made a show of catching it and pressing it to his heart. "Now, make it right with Martha and Graham, Samuel."

With that, she left.

Make it right. What in hell did that even mean? His damaged relationship with his youngest son went back to when Graham had been a young boy taking reading lessons, and the damned instructor, after noting Graham's inability to focus, had raised questions about a history of familial madness. Samuel had sacked the bastard and sought to find others who could teach his son, seeking to protect him from that dangerous charge leveled against him.

Or were you more worried about how it would reflect on you?

Shame brought his eyes closed.

For, at this point in his life, at nearly sixty years, he acknowledged that it had been… a bit of both—a need to protect his name, but also to protect his son.

When it should have only ever been about Graham.

Laughter reached his ears, juxtaposing his tortured musings. Drawn to the clear, unfettered mirth, he wandered to the window.

Squinting, he searched the grounds below for the owners of that merriment and found the pair. Graham… and his wife, Martha. Playing like children on the terrace. An interloper watching their joy, Samuel at the same time could not look away from it.

Were their guests to see the couple, they would be scandalized.

And a scandal was something he never tolerated.

Another peal of laughter echoed from below.

The sound sprang him into movement, and with a quickened pace, he started down toward the cacophony of noise.

CHAPTER 8

Graham had remembered how it felt to really laugh.

Not the affected, roguish chuckle he'd perfected for ladies who hadn't mattered, but rather, the pure, unadulterated sound that came from a place deep inside, born of joy and love.

And all because of the love of a young woman.

A young woman he now hunted around his father and mother's terrace.

He scanned the area, touching his gaze on the pillars and stone statues he'd hidden behind countless times as a boy while playing hide-and-seek with his brothers.

There was a faint scurry of footsteps, and he caught a flash of dark skirts from the corner of his eye as Martha went rushing off.

And then silence fell once more.

"Surrender, Lady Whitworth," Graham called. "You're caught. Come and face… your fate."

"Never," she cried, darting out just as a door creaked open behind him, distracting him.

He glanced back toward the tread belonging to a heavier footfall.

Martha's snowball found its mark at the back of his head, knocking his hat loose.

"Graham?" she called out, her voice ringing with a hesitancy.

"Playing child's games, I see." And just like that, the ducal tones, as austere and as cool as the winter landscape, slashed across the earlier merriment, stealing it away like the frigid winter breeze did the air from one's lungs.

Graham stiffened as his father stepped from the shadows. Except, the Duke of Sutton was not the only one who'd mastered such stony greetings. "Your Grace."

Martha slid close to Graham. Winding her fingers through his, she lightly squeezed, giving him strength, reminding him that, for the first time, he was not alone. Not as long as she and her children were in his life.

"You always did like to play games," his father noted, coming to a stop two paces away. He ran his aloof stare over Graham and his wife, his gaze lingering a moment on the interlinked hands. No doubt he disapproved of the show of affection and love. "And now I see you've found a woman who enjoys those same... pleasures." The clouds parted for the full moon at that moment, revealing the duke's slight wince.

After years of his father's indifference—and worse, loathing—Graham felt his patience snap. "By God, say what you would about me. I long ago grew accustomed to your coldness. I accepted that you hold me to blame for Lawrence's death, but I'll be damned if I'll allow you to speak ill of my wife," Graham gritted out.

Confusion glazed his father's eyes. "I don't..." The duke shook his head as if clearing it. "I was speaking the truth, Sheldon Graham Malin Whitworth," the duke shot back. "I—"

"You wish to speak about the truth?" Martha interjected, and both Graham and his father were knocked into silence. "Your son is a man of honor and courage and convictions. Is he also one who knows how to smile and laugh? Yes. He is." She took a step toward the duke. "But he's also wise enough to know that there is only joy to be had in those emotions. And only good to come from being kind and letting love rule his heart. Unlike you."

Graham's heart nearly burst with his love for her. She would go toe-to-toe with his father for him? Against the Duke of Sutton, when Graham hadn't even managed over the years to launch his own defense?

Red blotches of color slapped the duke's cheeks. "I—"

"I am not done with you, Your Grace." Martha seethed, breath-taking in her fury. "You are a father. Your son deserves kindness and love from you."

The duke recoiled.

"Martha," Graham said softly. "It is enough."

"It is not," she gritted, not taking her gaze from the duke, who for surely the first time in his life had been effectively silenced. "You are his father. He was and still is and will always be deserving of your support and not your disdain. Of your love and not your shame. Of—"

The duke's agonized whisper at last managed to cut through Martha's diatribe. "I never blamed you for Lawrence's death, Sheldon." Pain was an emotion Graham had seen only once before in his father's eyes, in the days after Lawrence's death. And he had not seen it since. "Is that what you believe?"

Emotion wadded in Graham's throat, and he forced words past it. "It is what I know. You blamed me, but no more than I blamed myself."

Martha's fingers found his once more, and he clung to them, taking the support she offered. She made him stronger.

His father searched his eyes over Graham's face. "Never, Sheldon. I *never* blamed you." His face crumpled. "I blamed myself."

The admission came so faintly that Graham struggled to make sense of it. He…? "What?" Graham whispered.

Martha glanced between father and son and then took a step aside, allowing them slight space, but standing close enough to Graham that he knew she was there at his shoulder.

The duke turned his wrinkled palms up, hands that showed his advancing years. "I was the one to blame, Graham. Never you. I was… always rot at being a father, but after Lawrence?" His face contorted into a paroxysm of grief. "I realized that I couldn't protect any of you. I failed Lawrence just as I failed to help you."

Just as I failed to help you.

"That is what you thought you were doing by setting me in competition against my brother?" he asked incredulously. "Helping me?"

"It's what I knew, Sheldon... Graham," his father amended, at last acknowledging and honoring the address Graham had sought. "My father and his father before taught me everything about how to conduct myself... in all matters. I didn't know any other way." He continued on a rush, "I am not seeking forgiveness, but rather, I'm trying to explain how a father fails so." Graham's father shifted his focus to his daughter-in-law. "You are right, Martha." He clarified. "In what you said earlier." He looked at his son once more. "I have not been the father you deserve. I didn't know how. I didn't know how to be with my children... or the world, but you, and Heath and Lawrence... You were the ones who mattered."

It took a moment for those words to penetrate Graham's mind. He shook his head dumbly.

"I hated that you struggled." His father moved closer. "I hated it because I saw how it tore you apart inside, and I didn't know how to make it better. It was the one thing beyond my control." A pained chuckle rumbled past the duke's lips. "Or, that is what I believed. In my old age, I've come to appreciate my fallibility. I love you, Graham. I have just never known how to show it."

The wind gusted around them, whipping Martha's and Graham's cloaks about, the only sound in the wake of those admissions.

All his life, he'd sought his father's approval. He'd wished his father was someone different—a loving father, a proud one.

Graham stared at his father. With his shoulders stooped and his head bent, the Duke of Sutton was reduced to a man Graham didn't recognize. The Duke of Sutton wasn't one who admitted any weakness or forgave vulnerability in others. And yet...

His mind in tumult, needing some distance, needing to try to make sense of *everything* his father had revealed, Graham wandered over to the balustrade. He gripped the snow-covered edge and gazed out unseeingly. How easy it had been to hate his father for how he'd treated him. Graham had taken his father's lectures and chastisements as an indictment against his own failings. Never before had he considered that buried within that gruff directness had been a father who'd just wanted to take away his son's suffering.

Now, having Martha's son in his life and loving the child as if he'd sired him, Graham understood what it was like to want to protect someone at all costs.

And his father had attempted to… in his own way.

He felt Martha's presence at his side. Borrowing from her strength, Graham faced his father.

"I spent my life resenting you," Graham said quietly, the wind carrying the admission around the terrace so that it echoed damningly in the winter quiet. "I wanted to know why you couldn't love me. All I wanted was your approval, all the while knowing those efforts were futile."

His father took long, lurching steps over to him. "I do love you, Graham. I—"

Graham held up a hand. "I know that now." His father loved him… He just hadn't known how to show it. "I love you, too." He loved him, and yet, he could not simply forgive him for interfering in Graham's relationship with Martha. "Martha is my wife."

"I know that," his father said.

"No, I'd have you hear this." He caught Martha's hand in his and drew her close. "You sought to separate us… not even knowing anything about her. Not even caring that I love her with all my heart. And I might forgive you for how you treated me as a child, but I cannot pardon what you did to my wife."

"I'm not asking for forgiveness, son."

Graham stiffened.

His father spoke on a rush. "Not because I don't believe I was right in my actions towards Martha, but rather, because I do not expect you or Martha to forgive me." Turning to Martha, the duke pressed a hand to his chest. "I will forever regret having attempted to separate you and my son. Just as I will be eternally grateful to you for bringing my son home to me this holiday season."

Martha's lips quivered. "I love your son. And it is my hope that all of us can begin again." She glanced quickly at Graham. "If my husband so wishes that."

All of this was foreign, and yet, what Martha spoke of, a new beginning, filled him with a lightness. "I would like that very much," he said hoarsely.

His father spread his arms and then let them fall immediately to his sides. He straightened an already flawlessly folded cravat. "As would I," he said in more composed tones. Of course, this expression of emotion would be new to all of them. "I will leave you both to your amusements. I trust the guests have already long wondered where I've gone off to. Before I do..."

Graham stared questioningly on as, with a hand that trembled, his father fished a small stack of notes from inside his jacket and held them out.

"Here," he said with his usual gruffness. "This is for you..." He glanced over at Martha. "For the both of you."

Not allowing so much as a question to be asked, Graham's father left.

Neither Martha nor Graham spoke a long while after. She was the first to break the silence.

"As parents, we do the best we can, Graham. We try to be the best for our children and give them the world. Until it's too late, and we realize we don't always know what is best. We realize mistakes were made and"—her gaze drifted beyond his shoulder—"there can be no undoing them." She spoke as one who commiserated with the duke.

Graham closed the handful of steps between them. "You'd forgive him, Martha?" She'd been wronged so many times by so many men. And how he despised that his father had been another one to hurt her.

Martha lifted her palms. "Graham, my daughters should by rights hate me for sending them away when I did," she said softly.

"And if it hadn't been for you, I would have never allowed myself to see them again. They'd even now be at Mrs. Munroe's for the holidays."

He palmed her right cheek. "You are a remarkable woman, Martha Whitworth. You make me a better man."

She matched his movement, cupping his cheek in her smaller hand. "We make one another better people, Graham."

"How I love you, Martha," he whispered against her lips. They kissed each other in an exchange that teased the promise of the new beginning they would embark on together.

After they parted, he held her close against his chest, his cheek resting against the satiny softness of her crimson curls. The packet given to him by his father crinkled, and they looked at it.

Tugging at the black velvet ribbon, Graham proceeded to read the pages, and then he went absolutely motionless.

MARTHA HAD COME TO APPRECIATE THAT ANY TIME A MISSIVE ARRIVED for Graham, it never portended anything good. The first time had been a letter written by his father in a bid to separate them. And then, there was the fear—the one that had prevented her from truly being happy these past days as a new wife—that an assignment had been sent for him.

That interruption of her and Graham's time was inevitable, and then he would go off and risk his life in the name of king and country.

As he read, his head bent, his gaze slowly and carefully running over the words there, her stomach muscles twisted with a sickening dread.

The dread robbed her of the joy she'd found in watching her husband find some semblance of peace with the father who'd so wronged him.

As the silence marched on, she was unable to keep the question from tumbling from her lips. "What does it say?" *How is my voice so steady?* How, when the next words he uttered would usher in a temporary parting that could possibly turn into forever?

Wordlessly, he held out the packet.

Martha stared at the hated pages his father had delivered. Not wanting to take it. Not wanting to know what was written there. She wanted instead to continue on as the coward she was.

"Read it," he urged, pressing it into her shaking hand.

Drawing in a silent breath, she reluctantly lowered her gaze. She frantically took in the elegant scrawl, bold slashes of black ink that could belong only to a duke.

Graham,

You were always more skilled than I credited. You have a love of horseflesh of the likes I've never witnessed in any man I've ever come across in my eight and fifty years. I should have lauded those talents.

I know the mistakes I made... There are too many to put to paper. But this is just some small attempt to recognize your capabilities.

Signed,

Your Father

Martha turned to the next page and gasped.

Dumbstruck, she lifted her gaze.

"He's gifted us a horse farm." The muscles of his throat jumped. "To establish my own business."

Nay, not a horse farm. "Three hundred acres," she whispered. Her heart lifted and soared. Three hundred acres of land that belonged to them, with stables of horseflesh for Graham to care for, along with Frederick. And her daughters, when they wished to leave their school, could run freely through the countryside, and—

Then her heart promptly sank to her toes numb from the cold. "Oh."

He frowned. "What is this, love?" he murmured, caressing the downturned corners of her mouth.

She shook her head and forced a smile she didn't feel. Except...

He is your husband now. Their relationship required honesty and communication, even if his answer might shatter her.

"Your work... with the Brethren." She would be forever grateful to the organization, for it had brought Graham into her life, but she would also forever hate it because it represented another who commanded his loyalty and devotion. "This"—she held the page aloft—"would require you to… not do the other."

Her husband sighed.

Martha bit the inside of her cheek, trying to make sense of that slight exhalation. Was it pity? Regret that he could not give her that which she truly wished—him and only him, with their children, never separated, not even for the good of the Crown? "You still don't know, do you, Martha?" he finally asked, his breath fanning her cheeks.

"Know?" she echoed.

He caught her hands in his, wrinkling the gift his father had given them. "Do you truly believe I want to live a life traveling the globe when everything"—he shook his head—"*everyone* I've ever been searching for is right here before me?"

A sob escaped her. "Wh-what are you saying?" she pleaded.

"I'm saying that if you would not mind living a life married to a man who breeds h—oomph." Graham stumbled and then quickly caught her as she threw herself into his arms.

"No," she rasped, drawing herself up on tiptoe so she could pepper his face with kisses.

"No, you do not want to be married to a man who breeds horses. Or—" Martha kissed the rest of the teasing retort from his lips.

"You silly man," she whispered between tears. "I don't care where we are, or what either one of us does in life, as long as we do it together."

He grinned. "Is that a promise, my love?"

"That is a promise," she vowed.

As the snow began to fall around them, Martha wrapped her arms about her husband and held tightly, eager for their future—together.

ALSO BY CHRISTI CALDWELL

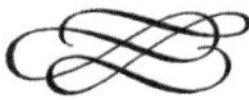

Enjoyed Martha and Graham's holiday story? Read their novel, *The Rogue Who Rescued Her*, along with the rest of The Brethren series now!

"The Rogue Who Rescued Her"
Book 3 in the "Brethren" Series by Christi Caldwell

MARTHA DONALDSON WENT FROM BEING A NOBLEMAN'S WIFE, AND respected young mother, to the scandal of her village. After learning the dark lie perpetuated against her by her 'husband', she knows better than to ever trust a man. Her children are her life and she'll protect them at all costs. When a stranger arrives seeking the post of stable master, everything says to turn him out. So why does she let him stay?

Lord Sheldon Graham Whitworth has lived with the constant reminders of his many failings. The third son of a duke, he's long been underestimated: that however, proves a valuable asset as he serves the Brethren, an illustrious division in the Home Office. When Graham's first mission sees him assigned the role of guard to a young widow and her son, he wants nothing more than to finish quickly and then move on to another, more meaningful assignment.

Except, as the secrets between them begin to unravel, Martha's trust is shattered, and Graham is left with the most vital mission he'll ever face—winning Martha's heart.

"The Lady Who Loved Him"
Book 2 in the "Brethren" Series by Christi Caldwell

In this passionate, emotional Regency romance by Christi Caldwell, society's most wicked rake meets his match in the clever Lady Chloe Edgerton! And nothing will ever be the same!

She doesn't believe in marriage....

The cruelty of men is something Lady Chloe Edgerton understands. Even in her quest to better her life and forget the past, men always seem determined to control her. Overhearing the latest plan to wed her to a proper gentleman, Chloe finally has enough...but one misstep lands her in the arms of the most notorious rake in London.

The Marquess of Tennyson doesn't believe in love....

Leopold Dunlop is a ruthless, coldhearted rake... a reputation he has cultivated. As a member of The Brethren, a secret spy network, he's committed his life to serving the Crown, but his rakish reputation threatens to overshadow that service. When he's caught in a compromising position with Chloe, it could be the last nail in the coffin of his career unless he's willing to enter into a marriage of convenience.

A necessary arrangement...

A loveless match from the start, it soon becomes something more. As Chloe and Leo endeavor to continue with the plans for their lives prior to their marriage, Leo finds himself not so immune to his wife – or to the prospect of losing her.

"The Spy Who Seduced Her"
Book 1 in the "Brethren" Series by Christi Caldwell

A WIDOW WITH A PAST... THE LAST THING VICTORIA BARRETT, THE Viscountess Waters, has any interest in is romance. When the only man she's ever loved was killed she endured an arranged marriage to a cruel man in order to survive. Now widowed, her only focus is on clearing her son's name from the charge of murder. That is until the love of her life returns from the grave.

A leader of a once great agency... Nathaniel Archer, the Earl of Exeter head of the Crown's elite organization, The Brethren, is back on British soil. Captured and tortured 20 years ago, he clung to memories of his first love until he could escape. Discovering she has married whilst he was captive, Nathaniel sets aside the distractions of love...until an unexpected case is thrust upon him—to solve the murder of the Viscount Waters. There is just one complication: the prime suspect's mother is none other than Victoria, the woman he once loved with his very soul.

Secrets will be uncovered and passions rekindled. Victoria and Nathaniel must trust one another if they hope to start anew—in love and life. But will duty destroy their last chance?

"Her Duke of Secrets"
Book 2 in the "Brethren of the Lords" Series

DEATH WAS PREFERABLE...

Since his wife was killed in an accident that stole his happiness and left him injured, William Helling, the Duke of Aubrey, is a broken man. Neither strong drink and loose women nor the power he wields as leader of the Brethren of Lords can free him from the nightmares that haunt him. He prefers to be left alone, and has no desire to heal the wound his life has become. Then one day Miss Elsie Allenby, rumored to be a skilled healer, enters his household.

He should send her away and yet he's enthralled by the mysterious stranger.

Healing was her life…

But not a day passes when Elsie Allenby doesn't miss her father nor remind herself where the blame for his death lies: The Brethren of Lords. Since that betrayal, she's made a life for herself on the fringe of society, caring for wounded animals. Her peaceful life is turned upside down when her help is requested by the Brethren, and she finds herself in the presence last person she ever thought she would aide: William Helling, the leader of the Brethren.

With every exchange, passion grows between Elsie and William. Soon the protective walls they've built, begin to crumble. But when danger threatens them both, they'll need to overcome the treachery around them. Will the past steal their passion or will love find a way?

"My Lady of Deception"
Book 1 in the "Brethren of the Lords" Series

****This dark, sweeping Regency novel was previously only offered as part of the limited edition box sets: "From the Ballroom and Beyond", "Romancing the Rogue", and "Dark Deceptions". Now, available for the first time on its own, exclusively through Amazon is "My Lady of Deception".*

Everybody has a secret. Some are more dangerous than others.

For Georgina Wilcox, only child of the notorious traitor known as "The Fox", there are too many secrets to count. However, after her interference results in great tragedy, she resolves to never help another… until she meets Adam Markham.

Lord Adam Markham is captured by The Fox. Imprisoned, Adam loses everything he holds dear. As his days in captivity grow, he finds himself fascinated by the young maid, Georgina, who cares for him.

When the carefully crafted lies she's built between them begin to crumble, Georgina realizes she will do anything to prove her love and loyalty to Adam—even it means at the expense of her own life.

And Coming Soon by Christi Caldwell:

The Governess
Book 3 in the Wicked Wallflowers series

RIVALRY, ROMANCE, AND SCANDAL RUN HOT IN THIS WICKED Wallflowers novel from *USA Today* bestselling author Christi Caldwell.

Regina (Reggie) Spark has loved Broderick Killoran, the resourceful and protective proprietor of the Devil's Den, ever since he saved her from the streets and made her his right hand at the notorious gaming hell. For just as long, Reggie has never admitted her true feelings for him. Nor has she revealed her spirited ambitions—to buck convention and expectations and open a music hall.

While Broderick built his gaming empire with ruthless cunning, his loyalty to his employees is boundless. So when he learns of Reggie's plan to leave his side and take charge of her own future, the betrayal cuts Broderick to the core. He responds as he would to any business rival...with swift retribution.

Instead of wilting, the savvy Reggie rebounds with a fury that shocks Broderick and stirs a desire he's been holding in reserve for only ladies of nobility. But as their seductive battle of wills ignites under the harsh spotlight of the London Season, secrets are exposed as well—ones that could be ruinous in decent society but invaluable for the heart.

STEALING CHRISTMAS

LOUISA CORNELL

STEALING CHRISTMAS

December, 1817
Hampshire

Slam!

Over the past six days Sebastian Brightworth had begun to hear it in his sleep—the indignant fury of his wife quitting a room upon discovering his presence in said room. Followed by the dainty storm of footsteps down the corridor and a litany of assessments of his character that would put a sailor to the blush. His sweet, proper, vicar's daughter of a wife had an inventive command of the English language, especially when in high dudgeon. A few more weeks of this and every door in the house would be off its hinges. At least the slamming would cease.

"Colonel Brightworth?"

Sebastian slid the book he'd pulled back onto the shelf. "Yes, Figgs."

"I've brought a fresh pot of tea and a cold collation," Figgs announced in a stage whisper as he closed the library doors and glanced over his shoulder as if in anticipation of an attack. The man fairly staggered under the weight of the tray he bore.

"Real food?" Sebastian steadied a teetering stack of books on the floor and fairly ran to the hearth where his butler placed the loaded tray onto a low fireside table. "Bless you, Figgs. I don't think I could stomach another bowl of porridge, runny eggs, and cold tea."

"Well, if you please, Colonel, not a word to Mrs. Figgs or we'll both be sleeping in cold beds." He blanched and ran a finger around the top of his neckcloth. "I do beg your pardon, sir, that was terribly—"

"Honest?" Sebastian mumbled around a bite of one of Cook's delicious lemon tarts. "Your secret is safe with me, Figgs. No sense in both of us suffering." He finished off the lemon tart and began to construct a sandwich of thick fresh bread, roast beef, and good Hampshire cheese. "How did you manage the tarts? I thought Cook had those under lock and key."

"I didn't," Figgs said, his hand outstretched, palm up. "Master Edward did."

At the mention of his industrious stepson's name, Sebastian laughed and fished half a crown out of his waistcoat pocket to drop into Figgs's hand. "Worth every penny. Make certain his mother does not see this or we will all be in the soup." He took a bite out of the sandwich and closed his eyes in silent appreciation. Since his quarrel with his wife, Sebastian had been restricted to the most unpalatable repasts imaginable by the women in his household. He was master here in name only. His wife, his housekeeper—Mrs. Figgs, and Cook ruled the house at Chesnick Wharton. Most days they allowed him command of the rest of the estate.

The matter was made all the worse by the fact Cook had started her Christmas baking, and the house was replete with the sweet aromas of holiday fare.

"Are you looking for one book in particular, Colonel?" Figgs stood in the middle of Chesnick Wharton's vast library and surveyed the carnage Sebastian had wrought. Shelves of books had been rearranged, some emptied completely. Books had been stacked on tables and on the floor. One of the reasons Sebastian had chosen the estate and house had been the size of the library. Minerva loved books. Minerva, who had not spoken a word to him in days.

"I was hoping to find a book on how to cope with an angry wife. My grandfather spent a great deal of time here, hiding from his. If ever a man needed a book on dealing with a wife, it was him." He shuddered at the mere thought of his paternal grandmother. "A thousand years of British literature, philosophy, science, history, and religion on these shelves, and not one man thought to write a book on the subject of difficult women."

"I have it on the best authority no man knows enough about women to write such a book, and women are forbidden to do so. It is against the code," Figgs said. His solemnity was belied by the unrepentant twinkle in his eye. He set about moving the books on the floor back onto the shelves.

"The best authority?"

"Mrs. Figgs."

"Ah. What code?" Sebastian emptied half the cup of tea he'd prepared in one long draught.

"The code whereby women make the rules, change the rules on a whim, and take those rules to the grave with them before ever revealing them to any man," an all too familiar voice replied. D. Harold Forsythe, Earl of Creighton, closed the library doors behind him and crossed the thick Persian carpets to shake Sebastian's hand.

"What are you doing here, Creighton?" Sebastian had a strange sensation along the back of his neck. He shook his best friend's hand, but had no idea what had brought him all the way from Kent in the middle of December. Something was most definitely afoot. Any hopes he'd held for a calm, cozy, first family Christmas with his wife and stepson faded like so much smoke. Creighton did nothing calm, nor cozy, and most emphatically did nothing to do with family, for most excellent reasons.

"I let you steal my bride, Brightworth, at the altar, no less. I never said I wouldn't visit her from time to time," Creighton said as he settled into the chair on the other side of the fireside table. "It is Christmastide, you know."

Of course, he knew it. This entire debacle had been caused by Christmas. "I didn't steal her. Minerva was always mine. Did she invite you here?"

"Not exactly. You may not have stolen my bride, but you did manage to filch my under-butler, my housekeeper's assistant, my cook's sister, and one of my best grooms. How are you faring, Figgs? Are you ready to come home yet?"

"We are all faring very well, my lord," Figgs assured him. "I am most glad to see you, but I have no desire to return to Creighton Hall."

"Neither do I," Creighton said. "But I have no choice."

"Stop trying to steal my staff, and why are you really here?" Sebastian knew his friend too well to give credence to a mere holiday visit as the earl's reason for sitting before his fire, drinking his tea, and eating his lemon tarts.

The library doors slammed open. "They're coming," Lord Xavier Fitzhugh announced as he burst into the room. "You said she'd be happy to see us, Creighton. Brightworth's wife looks ready to murder someone. Is that roast beef? Is there any mustard, Figgs?"

"Who is coming?" Sebastian asked as Fitzhugh shoved past him and reached for some bread. "The only person my wife wishes to murder is me, but that could change at any moment. Yes, that is roast beef and no, there is no mustard for you. Creighton did you not feed him between here and Kent?"

"You m'know he m'id not," Fitzhugh mumbled around a mouthful of roast beef sandwich, which he finally managed to swallow. "Lady Aphrodite received a letter from your wife, and nothing would do but we make all haste to see what sort of a mess you've made of your marriage. I thought it a grand idea until I saw your wife. Did we know she was with child? Very much with child?"

"I suspect Brightworth has known for a while," Creighton drawled. He took the cup of tea Figgs prepared for him with a nod and a murmured thanks.

Sebastian's head began to spin. A frequent occurrence in the presence of these two troublemakers. After the past week, however, he needed his wits about him. He *had* made a mess of his marriage, no sense in denying it. Apparently, those who'd helped him win Minerva intended to watch him try and win her all over again. Worse, they might feel the need to help him.

"Will you two, stop talking, stop eating my food, and tell me exactly why you are here?"

"That is an excellent question, Colonel Brightworth. I certainly had no need of their escort." Lady Aphrodite Forsythe, Creighton's younger sister, strolled into the library and stopped, arms akimbo, to glare at her brother and Lord Fitzhugh.

Sebastian barely noticed her. He only had eyes for the lady at her side. He'd loved Minerva since she was a girl of sixteen. Ten years apart—him at war and her married to another, and seven months of marriage had done nothing to dim the love and passion that coursed through his veins at the mere sound of her name. And now, her body rounded with his child, she was more beautiful than he'd ever thought possible.

"Minerva," Sebastian murmured.

She only met his eyes for a moment, long enough for him to see the hurt and anger there. Creighton rose and offered her a brief, but elegant bow. Fitzhugh stumbled to his feet and attempted to do the same. Difficult to do with a sandwich in one hand and a lemon tart in the other.

"You're looking in rude good health, Mrs. Brightworth," Fitzhugh said.

"Good God," Creighton said and rolled his eyes.

"What?" Fitzhugh gawked at them whilst Minerva favored him with an indulgent smile.

"Don't try to turn her up sweet, Fitzhugh," Aphrodite warned. "You and my interfering brother were *not* included in my invitation to spend Christmas here. I am arrived safely, you may toddle off back to Creighton Hall and spend Christmas with Mama."

"You are a cruel woman, Lady Aphrodite," Fitzhugh said. "I'd rather spend Christmas on a Thames prison hulk."

"That could be arranged."

Minerva laughed. "Now, Aphrodite," she chided. "I would not wish Christmas with your mother on my worst enemy."

Sebastian's heart did a little flip. He'd not heard his wife's laugh in quite some time. In fact, he couldn't remember the last time he'd heard her laugh.

"If we are imposing on your hospitality, Minerva, I will throw Fitzhugh back into my carriage and make for Kent within the hour," Creighton said quietly.

"Of course, you must stay, Harry, you and Lord Fitzhugh both," she assured him.

Minerva.

Harry.

Sebastian's jaw locked. Creighton, the fiend, had proposed to Minerva first, and the two of them had remained friends. He trusted the man. Most of the time. After all, she'd chosen Sebastian. If slamming doors and cold porridge counted for anything, a choice she was coming to regret.

"In fact, it is fortuitous you are here," Minerva continued as she gave Sebastian a wide berth and walked to the fireside table. She picked up the plate of lemon tarts and then rejoined Lady Aphrodite, who now stood with her arms folded across her chest and a disparaging look on her face. "Another guest will be arriving tomorrow, and as my husband has forbidden me to welcome him to Chesnick Wharton, perhaps you gentlemen will do so in my stead."

She walked to the library doors, still graceful in spite of her condition, Creighton's sister close on her heels. "Figgs, please arrange rooms for Lord Fitzhugh and Lord Creghton."

"Of course, Mrs. Brightworth," the butler replied. He eyed the plate of tarts and swallowed hard.

"And if you have secreted another half a crown in your pocket for my son, you will return it to Colonel Brightworth, if you please. Dinner is at seven, gentlemen." With that, the ladies swept out the doors. The slamming shook the windows.

"You forbade her?" Creighton raised an eyebrow at him.

"Why did she take the tarts?" Fitzhugh groused as he collapsed into a highbacked leather fireside chair.

"You *forbade* her," Creighton said once more.

Figgs handed Sebastian the half a crown and hurried out of the library. Sebastian subsided onto the large leather-button ottoman across from the fireplace, his head in his hands.

"*Tsk.* Even I know you don't *forbid* a woman," Fitzhugh said as he put together yet another sandwich, this one with mustard, which Figgs apparently carried about in his pocket. "No wonder she isn't speaking to you."

"How do you know she isn't speaking to me?"

"Aphrodite," Fitzhugh and Creighton said together.

Sebastian groaned. Creighton's sister wasn't a Christmas guest. She was reinforcements.

"Who did your wife, your wife very much in the family way—a different species of woman entirely—invite for Christmas to make you so foolish as to forbid her, Brightworth? Prinny? My mother? An old mistress?" Creighton asked.

"My brother," Sebastian mumbled without looking up.

"Your…"

"Anthony Chesnick Brightworth, Earl of Haddenfield. My half-brother. Minerva has been corresponding with him for months and invited him here as my Christmas gift from her. I told her he was the very last person on earth I wanted to see, I had no intention of welcoming him into my home, and I forbade her to do so."

"You're right," Fitzhugh said.

"I am?"

"The only person your wife wants to murder is you. Why did she take the lemon tarts?"

MINERVA LOWERED HERSELF INTO HER FAVORITE CHINTZ CHAIR AND toed off her slippers with a sigh of relief. It had been an incredibly long day and tomorrow loomed before her like the sound of drummers calling a soldier to arms. She took the cushion Aphrodite handed her and stuffed it behind her in an effort to soothe the bowstring tautness of her back. In the eight years since Edward's birth she'd nearly forgotten how uncomfortable this entire child-birth endeavor could be.

"Dinner was… delicious," Aphrodite said as she settled onto the wide arm of the chair opposite Minerva.

"Dinner was a pleasant disaster and you know it." Minerva heard footsteps in the dressing room she shared with her husband. He'd left the door into his chambers open. His voice and the voice of the young footman who served as his valet drifted against the door into her bedchamber, muffled but noticeable.

"It was certainly a disaster for Colonel Brightworth. What on earth did Cook serve him?"

Minerva laughed. "I am not certain, but I believe last week's leek soup and a cut of meat Cook declared *'Not fit for t'young master's dog.'* were involved. As to the rest…" She shuddered.

"Is it badly done of me to have enjoyed watching him try to eat it whilst you ignored him utterly, and Lord Fitzhugh described in exquisite detail how delicious each remove was as we ate it?"

"Not at all. I rather enjoyed it myself," Minerva replied. She hadn't, not truly. She loved Sebastian with all her heart and had spent the last seven months turning Chesnick Wharton into a comfortable home for him. After the sorrow and depravation of his childhood and his long years at war, her husband deserved a home —a place to lay his head and know he was loved and honored, a place where he belonged. Had she ruined it all by inviting his brother for Christmas?

"How long do you intend Cook to torture the poor colonel like this?" Aphrodite asked.

"Until he comes to his senses?"

"Good Lord, the man will starve to death long before that happens."

Minerva sighed.

Aphrodite stared at her intently, a sad little smile on her face. "He loves you, Minerva. I have never seen a man so much in love."

"I know he does. And I love him. Lord Haddonfield is his only blood relation. I don't count the horrid grandmother. Sebastian has fought so many demons for so long. I thought Christmas was the perfect opportunity to put some of those demons to rest."

"No one counts Lady Haddonfield. She makes Mama look the very model of motherhood."

"Lord Haddonfield gave us Chesnick Wharton because Sebastian asked him for it. For me and for Edward. But I don't think he is truly happy here. Something in this house haunts him, Ditey. Sebastian spent the first eight years of his life here. I don't know what happened between him and his brother, but it is time to lay it to rest."

Aphrodite stood and brushed out her skirts. "You make him happy, Minerva. More happy than the stubborn, addlepated *arse* deserves." She patted Minerva's shoulder as she walked past on the way to the chamber door. "Silence never works. I find men prefer it when we leave them alone. Talking to him is a much fitter punishment. It is almost as bad as a week-old leek soup."

Once the door had *snicked* closed behind her friend, Minerva hoisted herself to her feet and crept to the dressing room door. She pressed her ear to the door in time to hear a horrendous crash and a string of all too familiar swear words.

"Thomas did you move my travel desk?"

"No, Colonel, I never touched it," the beleaguered footman replied.

"Fell off that shelf and damn near killed me. Would have saved my wife the trouble."

"Yes, Colonel. I mean, no Colonel. I mean—"

Minerva opened the door and stepped into the dressing room. "He knows what you mean, Thomas. Might I have a moment with my husband?"

The footman bowed and scurried out of the dressing room, into the master's bedchamber, and out the chamber door, which he slammed on his way out. Sebastian started and Minerva tried not to laugh. He was such a handsome devil, drat him. In his quilted black velvet dressing gown, his black hair still wet from his bath, he was far more enticing than anything Cook had prepared for dinner.

"Ten years in Old Beaky's cavalry and now I'm in my dotage a slamming door frightens me," Sebastian groused. He stared at her, his dark brown eyes alight with the heat and intensity which never failed to make her shiver.

"You are far from your dotage, husband. My proof of it wakes me daily at three in the morning to make use of the chamber pot." Minerva rested her hand on her belly. "Might I speak with you?"

"I never asked you to stop."

Minerva rolled her eyes and brushed past him into his bedchamber. Sebastian followed. He tossed the travel desk onto the bed. She spotted several pieces of crumpled parchment next to a chair by the fire. Before he tried to stop her, she scooped one up and eased into the chair by the hearth to open and read it.

Dearest, Minerva

I

She held the parchment out to him.

"I have not been able to finish it," he said somewhat sheepishly.

"Finish it now, Sebastian. Make me understand."

"There is nothing to understand. I don't want Haddonfield here for Christmas. I don't want him here at all." He leaned against the thick oak bedpost and crossed his arms.

"Why? Can you make me understand why you want nothing to do with your last connection to your father? You loved your father, Sebastian. I know you did."

"Love is not a title. It is not passed on with a piece of paper and a royal decree. I wish you would leave this be, Minerva. You, and Edward, and the child your carry are enough for me. Why can you not believe that?"

"Because I see you when you think I am not watching." She struggled to her feet and padded across the carpets to him. "I know every line in your face, every expression, every sorrow in your eyes. Your brother gave you Chesnick Wharton because he believed you would be happy here."

"He gave me the estate out of guilt because I asked him."

"He was ten years old when your father died. What guilt could a ten-year-old boy possibly bear?"

"Leave it, Minerva. No good will come of this. He can live without my forgiveness. He has done so quite handily for the last fourteen years." Sebastian cupped her cheek. "We can have a good Christmas—you, Edward, and I—even if we must include our interfering friends." He pressed his lips to her hair and rested his cheek against the top of her head. "I am happy here. I am happy anywhere you are."

She wanted to give in. It would be so easy to do so. They were happy. Her past was behind her. She'd married the wrong man for the wrong reasons and both she and her first husband had suffered a miserable marriage for it. She'd forgiven herself for it. More important, she'd forgiven Edward's father.

Sebastian had given her that gift, had shown her and told her in a million little ways her mistakes were simply that, choices she had made of necessity and had survived with tenacity and grace. And Sebastian? He still blamed himself for so much. She saw it in the lightning flash moments of breath caught when he walked into the entrance hall. She heard it in his voice when he guided Edward and his pony around the paddock.

As beautiful as the house and estate were and as much as he loved working to be a good landlord and master, this place held some secret pain for him. And it was all tangled up with his hatred of his brother. She drew a steeling breath and stepped out of his arms.

"The forgiveness isn't only for your brother, my love. It is for you. I will not share you with ghosts, Sebastian. And your brother loves you. I wish you would find a way to love him too." She walked towards the dressing room door. Sebastian followed.

"Love him? I don't even like him, Minerva. He is a pompous, arrogant thief. He is stealing a perfectly peaceful and happy Christmas from us by coming here. And I am certain he knows it. I will *not* allow you to bring him into this house."

She put up a staying hand. "I may be speaking to you, sir, but I will not share a bed with a man so narrow-minded and unforgiving as to forbid me welcoming a guest into my own home."

He threw up his hands. "Be reasonable, Minerva."

She patted his chest. "For your information, I don't like you very much at the moment either, Sebastian Brightworth." She kissed his chin. "But I do love you."

He braced his arms in the doorway and leaned in to kiss her.

"Good night, husband. I wish you pleasant—"

"He-e-e-lp! For God's sake get it off me!"

Minerva ducked under Sebastian's arm and waddled across his bedchamber into the corridor.

"It's only Fitzhugh, Minerva. Come back here." Sebastian marched into the corridor after her.

"Precious, you let Lord Fitzhugh go this instant." Minerva grabbed the brown sausage-shaped dog attached to her husband's friend's arm and tugged. "Sebastian, make her release him."

"Me? She hates me even more than she hates Fitzhugh," he replied even as he pried Edward's pet off his friend.

"What in God's name is going on out here?" Creighton, dressed in a wine-colored banyan, entered the corridor from a door across the way.

"Brightworth's lunatic dog attacked me," Fitzhugh declared as he checked his shirt for damage.

"Precious?" Creighton took one look at the dog in Sebastian's arms and retreated into his room, slamming the door behind him.

Sebastian started and closed his eyes.

Fitzhugh grinned. "Good night, Brightworth. Mrs. Brightworth." He sauntered back in the direction of his room.

"You must call me Minerva, Lord Fitzhugh. Anyone who is attacked by Precious and lives is allowed to call me Minerva."

"Good night, Minerva."

A weariness suddenly hung on her limbs and began to cloud her thoughts. She wanted nothing more than to curl up in bed with Sebastian, but she simply must remain strong. She started towards her bedchamber door. And immediately turned when she sensed her husband's footsteps behind her.

"I meant what I said, Sebastian. I suggest you go to *your* bed and sleep on what we discussed."

"Minerva," he murmured as he stepped close and used his free hand to trace the contours of her lips. "That bed is cold and lonely. Surely you would not begrudge me a warm bed and some company."

"Of course not, my love." She opened her door. "Precious usually sleeps with Edward, but I am certain he can spare her for a few nights." She patted the dog's head and offered Sebastian her sweetest smile as she waved him down the corridor towards his chamber door.

"If she bites me I am tossing her out the window," Sebastian muttered as he walked away.

SEBASTIAN FINALLY SUCCUMBED TO CURIOSITY AND CHECKED HIS appearance in the peer glass in the corner of his chamber. He'd slept little last night and when he did sleep he was plagued with confusing dreams. He'd breakfasted with Creighton and they'd ridden out to view the estate before Fitzhugh or the ladies had stirred from their beds. Minerva, normally an early riser, had an excuse to lie in and take a tray in her rooms. He had no idea what Fitzhugh or Lady Aphrodite's excuses might be. Actually, Creighton's sister had likely joined Minerva for breakfast so they might plan their next move together. His painful demise, perhaps?

A knock on his chamber door interrupted his musings. He glanced at the bed and shook his head at the red dog happily ensconced under the counterpane with her head resting on his pillow.

"I am glad one of us is enjoying the bed." He strode into the corridor where Creighton and a sleepy-eyed Fitzhugh awaited him.

"You aren't wearing that, are you?" Fitzhugh looked him up and down and sniffed.

"I'm sorry, Fitzhugh, when did I hire you as my valet?" Sebastian strode down the corridor's green and primrose patterned Aubusson carpets towards the stairs.

"You didn't, not to put too fine a point on it, but you are sorely in need of one. I thought your lovely wife had divested you of your parsimonious ways."

"What is he on about?" Sebastian asked.

"I think he wants to know why you are wearing old buckskins and an even older hunting jacket to greet your brother," Creighton explained. "Especially as we both know how much you spent on a new wardrobe at Weston's when you and Minerva went to Town after you married."

"Precisely. You mentioned the sum in three separate letters to me, if I recall," Fitzhugh said and gripped Sebastian's arm at the top of the stairs. "Did you sleep in the kennels last night?" He picked several red hairs from Sebastian's jacket and proceeded to circle him brushing, plucking, and straightening as he went.

"And in four letters to me," Creighton added.

Sebastian snatched his arm away from Fitzhugh. "If you touch me one more time, I will toss you down these stairs."

"You truly have no Christmas spirit, do you, Brightworth? Threatening to throw me down the stairs because I know your wife will not be happy to see you dressed like someone's poor relation to greet your brother. Not in the Christmas spirit at all."

"Very well. Fitzhugh, if you say one more word about my clothing I will beat you to death with a branch of holly. Is that Christmas enough for you?" Sebastian asked as he reached the first-floor landing. "You need not worry about Minerva's opinion of my attire. She will not be here to see it."

"Are you certain of that, Brightworth?" Creighton asked as he peered over the bannister to the ground floor.

Standing in the entrance hall below them, Minerva consulted with the housekeeper, Mrs. Figgs, who hurried off to do her bidding. Lady Aphrodite came out of the formal parlor and joined Minerva at the bottom of the stairs. Both ladies were stylishly dressed—Lady Aphrodite in a gown of bright gold wool and Minerva in a gown of green velvet.

What the devil was she doing?

The sound of running feet drew their attention behind them. Edward Faircloth, Sebastian's stepson, pelted down the wide corridor, pausing only a moment to greet him, Creighton, and Fitzhugh.

"The coach is coming up the drive, Papa. It's very grand. And there are outriders," the boy called over his shoulder as he took the stairs two at the time. Once he reached his mother, Minerva settled him down and then glanced up towards the first-floor landing.

Amidst his anger, trepidation, and the thousand other things racing through his mind, Sebastian lost the ability to breathe at how incredibly beautiful Minerva was. The vivid green of the gown so complimented her glowing skin and golden bronzed hair she put him in mind of a Renaissance madonna. The drape and fall of the skirts softened the curves of her body. In less than two months' time, she would bring his child into the world—a child who, if it was in Sebastian's power, would never know want, or pain, or sorrow.

The clatter of horses' hooves announced the arrival of the Earl of Haddonfield's coach outside the front doors. Figgs moved into position. This was not what Sebastian had planned.

"Figgs, wait right there, if you please," Sebastian ordered and started down the stairs, Creighton matched him step for step.

"I must warn you, Brightworth," he said quietly enough that only Sebastian might hear. "If you embarrass Minerva I will be forced to draw your cork."

By the time they descended into the entrance hall, Minerva had spoken with Figgs and now stood ready for the butler to open the tall double doors. Creighton gave Sebastian a shove and he had no choice but to join her.

"I told you not to do this," he muttered under his breath.

"I am not a soldier under your command, Colonel. Do try and smile," Minerva said and slipped her arm through his.

He gritted his teeth and curled his lips back.

"On second thoughts, don't smile. You'll frighten the poor man to death."

"A smile is far less messy than pistols at dawn." Sebastian grunted as his loving wife elbowed him in the ribs.

"You will not do your brother bodily harm two days before Christmas."

"What about Boxing Day?"

Minerva sighed. "I am afraid I must forbid you spending so much time with Edward. You become more like him every day."

Figgs cleared his throat and opened the doors to Chesnick Wharton wide. "His lordship, the Earl of Haddonfield," the butler announced with a dignity far more appropriate to a London town-house. Minerva fully intended Sebastian's brother to feel at home.

The earl removed his hat and stepped into the entrance hall. Minerva gave Sebastian's arm a squeeze and stepped forward, her hands outstretched in welcome. He looked like their father, more so than Sebastian ever did. The hair at his temples was greying. His eyes were a sort of hazel green. And it was those eyes that did it.

Twenty years disappeared as nothing. Sebastian was eight years old and standing in this exact spot as his then ten-year-old brother stood at the top of the stairs and banished him and his mother from the only home Sebastian had ever known. Their father had been dead less than a day.

"You cannot do this, Anthony," his mother whispered, tears standing in her eyes. "I am your mother. Sebastian is your brother."

"I am the Earl of Haddonfield now, madam, and my mother is long dead."

"Where will we go? What will we do? You cannot send us away with no money, with no means to make our way."

"Goodbye, madam. I wish you and your son well."

Sebastian still remembered the boy's stoic face and their grand-mother's triumphant visage as she stood with her hand on Anthony's shoulder. The servants' faces, stricken and pitying. The dust of the road as he and his mother walked five miles to the village.

They'd spent the first night in the local church. Four years later his mother was dead and Sebastian was alone.

"Sebastian, will you not greet your brother?" Minerva's voice sounded so far away. She stood with her arm through his brother's and the man smiled. He actually smiled and extended his hand.

"It is good to see you again, Sebastian." He even sounded like their father, damn him. Damn him to hell.

Sebastian, his head swimming, turned and walked away. He commanded his feet to move, one foot in front of the other. He wanted to run. He wanted to scream. He wanted the images in his head—his mother growing thinner and more ill, Anthony standing at the top of those stairs, and Minerva, her face stricken as he walked away—to fade away and leave him. Someone was calling his name and he kept walking towards the back of the house. He reached the French windows into the conservatory and stopped, his hand on the latch.

"Papa!" The thick Turkish carpets muffled his stepson's footsteps as he ran towards him. Sebastian turned to be pummeled by a series of small punches to his stomach. "You made Mama cry. You promised. You promised never to make Mama cry."

He stared into Edward's face, tearstained and determined. He had promised the boy. And he'd broken that promise. No words came to him. Sebastian was lost, lost in memory and guilt and shame.

"Edward." Minerva, her eyes bright with furious tears, stood in the middle of the corridor and beckoned to her son. "Go with Uncle Fitzhugh. He wishes to see your pony."

Edward dragged his sleeve across his face. "You will make it right?"

"I will try, Edward," Sebastian replied, his chest aching so badly he could hardly speak.

Fitzhugh, standing just behind Minerva extended his hand. "Come along, Master Faircloth. I dare not visit the stables without you to protect me from that vicious horse of his."

"Lovey isn't vicious," Edward declared as they walked away, hand in hand. "She is merely misunderstood."

"She is a menace." Fitzhugh looked back at Sebastian and mouthed *"Don't muck this up!"*

Minerva, as glorious as redemption and as fierce as an avenging angel, stared at Sebastian even as she spoke to Creighton who had followed them all from the entrance hall. "I have left Lord Haddonfield in Aphrodite's care, Harry. Could you make certain she hasn't driven him to distraction so early in his visit? I wish to speak to my husband."

"If you are certain, Minerva." Creighton glanced at Sebastian. "You do not want me to stay?"

She touched her hand to Creighton's sleeve. "I will be fine, Harry."

"It isn't you I am worried about, my dear."

Once they were truly alone in the corridor, Minerva marched to the conservatory entrance, grabbed Sebastian's arm and pulled him inside. She dragged him through the thick avenue of banana trees and towering ferns until they reached an arrangement of chairs in an alcove surrounded by towering potted laburnum.

"Minerva, I—"

"Sit."

Sebastian did as he was told. Sometimes discretion was the better part of valor. When it came to women, it was always the better part.

She took a moment to settle herself into the comfortable damask-covered chair opposite him. "You are not leaving this room until you make me understand why you would humiliate me, insult your brother who has made a long journey to be here, made my son cry, and distressed our friends to the point even Fitzhugh is serious and all the day before Christmas Eve." She folded her arms across her chest. No woman had a right to such beauty when consumed by righteous indignation.

"Stop it," she snapped.

"Stop what? I didn't say anything."

"Stop looking at me like that, as if I am the most beautiful woman in the world. I have been crying. I am fat. My ankles are swollen. And I am so angry with you I want to punch you in the nose."

"You are the most beautiful woman in the world, Minerva." He reached across and took her hands. "I know that, even if I don't know anything else."

"What happened, Sebastian? We cannot go on like this. I won't go on like this. I have given myself to you—mind, body, heart, and soul. Until you free yourself of these demons, you will never be wholly mine." Her face in all of its anger, pain, patience, and love was his refuge. She was his refuge. She always had been. And suddenly he was so very tired of bearing this last burden alone.

"He sent us away, Minerva. The fever that took your father and half the village took my father, and the next day Anthony stood in that hall and sent my mother and me away with nothing. She raised him until he went to live with our grandmother. Mama was his mother for eight years and he looked her in the eye and sent her away to starve to death. I cannot forgive him. I can't."

"Oh, Sebastian." She raised his hand to her lips and kissed it. "I knew you were sent away. I had no idea how awful it was. I had no idea it happened here. Why would you ever come back?"

He stood and let her hands slip from his. Outside the glass panes of the conservatory it had started to snow. The sky was grey and still. "It is the only place I remember my father. It was the perfect place to be a boy. I met you in the village, remember? And there is the library. I don't know. It was the first property my brother offered and I took it."

She laughed at his mention of the library and then grew serious. "Why do you think he offered you Chesnick Wharton first?"

"What?" Her question had startled him. Minerva was thinking. Never a good thing for him.

"He has half a dozen unentailed properties, several smaller than this one. Why did he offer you this one?"

"How the devil do you know… I take it your letters have not only been discussions of the weather."

"I am not only a pretty face, Colonel."

Sebastian let loose a bark of laughter. "No one knows that better than I do, Mrs. Brightworth."

"How old was Lord Haddonfield when your father died?" This was typical Minerva. She distracted him with humor and gentle cajoling and then returned to her point. A point that pricked at his memory, and worse, his conscience.

"He was ten. He went to live with Grandmama after our grandfather died and Papa became the earl. He lived with her two years and then Papa died and Anthony became the earl. What difference does it make?" Irritation walked across the back of his neck like the brush of nettles.

"Why? Why did he go to live with that horrible woman?"

"I don't remember. He wanted to, I suppose. God knows, he has always done as she commands."

"And he was ten when he sent you and your mother away." She folded her hands in her lap, her face a composed mask of simple inquiry. Minerva was many things. Simple was never one of them.

"Yes, old enough to know what he was doing." Sebastian turned to gaze out over the wintery back lawn.

"How do you know, Sebastian? Were you old enough to know what you were doing when you were ten?"

"I don't know, Minerva. I was too busy gathering firewood at the side of the road and trying to find food enough for Mother and me to eat. He knew what he was doing. He knew he was sending us away to die."

"At what rank in Wellington's cavalry does an officer obtain omniscience? You will never know what your brother was thinking until you ask him. Your grandmother is one of the most formidable and evil women in England. What chance did a ten-year-old boy have against her?"

"You don't understand." Even as he said it, Sebastian marveled at

Minerva's willingness to see the best in people. It frightened him to think where he would be now if she didn't.

She struggled to push out of the chair. He stepped to her side and took her arm to help her. "I do understand, Sebastian." She touched her fingertips to the side of his face and kissed him gently. "Talk to him. This is hurting you both. And you need to remember, what hurts you, hurts me as well. This is the perfect time of year to make things right. Please try."

"Why is it women think Christmas can change everything?"

"Because it is the season of miracles. Anything can happen. Even if that thing is for a stubborn beyond reason man to attempt to talk to his brother after all these years.

"What if I can't? He had to know, Minerva. He had to know."

"Well then, apparently your omniscience is selective, Colonel Brightworth. For if you knew what I was thinking at this moment you would not be standing here." She delivered a loud smack of a kiss to his cheek. "I expect you to be charming and polite at dinner tonight. And I expect you to think about what I have said." Far too quickly for a woman in her condition she disappeared through the foliage.

"Do I have a choice?" Sebastian asked the nearest banana tree.

"Probably not," Creighton said as he strolled into view from the other side of the conservatory. "I am pleased to see you are unscathed for the most part."

"Is everyone else settled?" Sebastian flushed slightly. He'd made a hash of the morning's festivities to be sure. And Creighton had ever been the one to clean up their messes.

"Of course. Your brother seems quite smitten with Aphrodite. Should I warn him about Mama now or wait to see if my dear sister frightens him away?"

"Haddonfield can take care of himself. He always has." Sebastian indicated the path back to the French windows and Creighton joined him as they walked the colorfully paved path.

"So, you have no intention of taking your wife's suggestion."

"How long were you lurking in the ferns listening to my conversation with Minerva?"

"Long enough." Creighton stopped just short of the entrance back into the house. "I am the last person in the world to lecture anyone on forgiveness. Over the last ten years my hatred of my parents for what they have done is often the only thing that keeps me alive."

"You will find her, Creighton. One day, you *will* find her." Sebastian did not want to think what his life would be if someone had hidden Minerva away from him for ten years with no hope of ever seeing her again. Creighton had been searching for the love of his life for all these years, knowing all the while his late father had sent her away, and his all-too-alive mother knew where she was.

"I don't know anymore, Brightworth. But this I do know. As the years go by… with no hint of a sign she is even alive, I find I need my friends—you, Fitzhugh, your loved ones, and even my hoyden of a sister more and more. Can any of us afford to throw away even one person who wants to love us?"

Sebastian snorted. "After all this time what makes you think Anthony gives a damn about me?"

"He's here. Why don't you ask him?"

They left the conservatory and made their way into the library.

"Oh, and Brightworth?" Creighton said as Sebastian turned to ask him if he cared for a brandy.

"Yes?" The next thing he knew, he was on the floor with a bloody nose.

"I told you if you embarrassed her I would draw your cork. Do you want some ice for that?"

Christmas Eve

Somehow, they'd made it through the last two days with no violence and an inordinate amount of painfully polite conversation. Lord Haddonfield was an amusing and considerate guest. Minerva had not failed to notice his interest in Aphrodite. Unfortunately, no one knew what Aphrodite was thinking from one moment to the next. Poor Lord Haddonfield was in for it.

And Sebastian? Sebastian had kept his peace and spent a great deal of time in the library or the billiards room. Alone. She'd allowed him back into her bed for her sake as much as for his. She did not sleep well away from him, and the man's body and kisses were warmer than any coal-fueled stove.

But he did not sleep well, in spite of his protestations to the contrary. He rose in the middle of the night when he believed her to be asleep. Sometimes he stood at the window and looked out over the snow-covered lawns in the moonlight. Sometimes he left their chambers and wandered the corridors. She feared his brother's arrival had not put any ghosts to rest, but had rather drawn them out of the very walls. Any other woman would have begged him to share his troubles with her. Minerva knew this man intimately. Some things he had to work out for himself. Her interference would only make matters worse.

The entire party had gone out to gather greenery this morning and with a great deal of laughter and teasing had returned to the house with half the forest. Minerva had been bundled into a landau under a mound of lap rugs and blankets with half a dozen hot bricks at her feet. From there she had supervised the gathering of holly, mistletoe, and other assorted greenery. Each time his brother came to ask her approval, Minerva noticed Sebastian watching him, wary and confused all at once.

Now from her spot on the most comfortable sofa in the upstairs parlor, Minerva surveyed the room as everyone save Sebastian set about creating kissing boughs, holly sprigs and swags of greenery to bedeck the parlor. The servants had taken care of the rest of the house and done a beautiful job. And Cook had undone herself both with dinner and with the buffet of Christmas delicacies set up on the sideboard across the room. Fitzhugh divided his time between there and helping Edward to tie kissing boughs over the doorways.

It was not perfect, but it was not the disaster she'd feared.

Perhaps this year she would settle for that. There was always next Christmas.

A quiet knock announced the arrival of Figgs who ushered in two footmen bearing what appeared to be a large painting in an ornate frame. A holland cover was draped over it, obscuring the painting from view.

"It arrived only moments ago, my lord." Figgs addressed Lord Haddonfield, whose expression might only be described as one of utter trepidation. "Was this where you wanted it?"

"Yes, Figgs. Here will do."

"What on earth is it, Lord Haddonfield?" Aphrodite settled herself on the arm of the sofa next to Minerva.

"It is a gift, my lady. For my brother and his lovely wife. Would you like to do the honors... Sebastian?"

With deliberate care, her husband placed his glass of brandy on the mantelpiece. He and Creighton exchanged a look. Sebastian crossed the room and stopped before the covered painting.

"Happy Christmas, brother," Lord Haddonfield said softly.

Sebastian tugged at the cover, which slid to the floor with an audible *shush*. It was a portrait. A Gainsborough by the look of it. The subject was an exquisite dark-haired lady, dressed in a vibrant blue riding habit. One arm propped on the withers of a magnificent grey her smile was breathtaking. The front façade of Chesnick Wharton stood in the distance.

"Who is she?" Fitzhugh asked. "She is a diamond and no mistake."

"My mother," Sebastian murmured. "It is a portrait of my mother." He turned on Lord Haddonfield. "Where did you find this? Where has it been all these years?"

"I found it here. I had it removed to the estate in Wales for safekeeping."

"Safekeeping? This was mine. My father left it to me, but no one could find it. You stole it. After what you did to her you had no business keeping her portrait from me."

"Sebastian, stop this," Minerva took three tries to rise from the sofa. "It doesn't matter where it was, it is here now."

"It matters to me dammit. It wasn't enough you sent her to her death, you had to take the only thing I had to remember her by too?" Sebastian stood, chest heaving and fists clenched. It broke Minerva's heart. Would he ever forgive himself for his mother's death? For that is what his rage was all about. How could he forgive his brother when he could not forgive himself?

"I cannot do this," he muttered and strode towards the parlor door.

"Stop. Sebastian wait," Lord Haddonfield said. "This is your home, your family, your friends. You stay. I'll go." He reached the door before Sebastian and raised the latch.

"Anthony, no. There is no need for anyone to leave," Minerva blinked against the hot tears pushing at the backs of her eyes.

He turned to face Sebastian. "I took the portrait because I knew Grandmama would destroy it. I ordered Old Foster and two footmen to load it on a cart and take it to Wales because I knew she'd never visit the estate there. She hates Wales."

"When did you take it?" Sebastian asked softly.

"The day after she made me send you away. I wrote out orders for the servants who took it to serve the estate in Wales for the rest of their lives. I knew she'd punish them if they returned. She was my mother for eight years, Sebastian. She is the only mother I have any memory of and I loved her."

"You chose to live with grandmother. After grandfather died and you became Papa's heir you chose..."

Lord Haddonfield shook his head.

"She had control of the money," Creighton half-asked.

"She did, Lord Creighton. To a certain degree she still does."

"I don't understand," Sebastian turned towards Minerva, his face a mask of confusion. Always in command—of himself, of his life, of what he knew to be true. Her strong and stubborn husband had no idea what to say or do.

"I know now she blackmailed them, but then I didn't understand. They sent me away with a cold-hearted fiend of a woman and

I blamed them. I blamed her, Sebastian, our mother. In my mind she chose to keep you, her real son, and she sent me away. When Father died I was still angry. I was angry at her for leaving me and angry at you because she chose you. I had no idea it would end the way it did and there was nothing I could do until it was far too late. I should have been stronger. You survived. You made your life on your own. You beat Grandmama, when I never could. And I am so very sorry." He bowed in Minerva's direction. "Thank you for inviting me, Minerva. My brother is lucky to have you." With a quick glance at Aphrodite he quit the room.

Sebastian returned to the portrait, staring at it as if some answer lay there. Minerva came to stand beside him. She rubbed her hand along his back. Sometimes the only thing worse than believing a horrible lie was to finally hear the truth.

Edward was asking one question after another. Minerva wanted to be the one to answer them for him, but in this moment, Sebastian needed her more. She smiled as she heard Fitzhugh's attempt at answers and Aphrodite's derisive assessments of those answers.

"Sebastian," she finally said, stilling her hand against his back.

"I really hate it when you are right, Mrs. Brightworth. It happens so often, however, I should be used to it." He took her in his arms and kissed her. His lips seared hers in a kiss so fiery and passionate she wanted to melt into the floor.

"There is no mistletoe there, Papa. That isn't fair."

Sebastian laughed against her mouth and rested his forehead against hers. "I shall have to remedy the mistletoe situation, but right now I am going after my brother."

This time she kissed him, but only for a moment. "Go. Go and find him."

"Someone keep Fitzhugh away from the food," Sebastian said as he left the parlor. "My brother and I might like to eat when we return."

Minerva pressed her fingertips to her mouth and ceased fighting her tears. Creighton strolled over and handed her his handkerchief.

"Well done, Mrs. Brightworth. Very well done indeed."

"*Ouch!* What the hell!"

Sebastian dashed into the stables to find his brother shrugging out of his coat to inspect a nasty bite on his arm.

"I see you've met, Lovey," he said with a grin.

"Lovey?" Anthony shook his arm and checked it again. "She nearly broke my arm. Yours, I take it?"

"I had her at a very good price."

"Someone should have paid *you*."

Sebastian laughed.

"I didn't mean to—"

"I owe you an—"

Sebastian dropped his head and shoved his hands in the pockets of his greatcoat. When he looked up Anthony had done the exact same thing.

"I remember you, Anthony. You looked out for me. You never ran out of patience. I remember that now. I don't know how I could have forgotten."

"Our grandmother knew exactly what she was doing. She knew you'd hate me and that is what she wanted. She didn't give us any choice. She knew I loved your mother."

"Our mother."

"Yes. Our mother. And it drove her mad. And even after Mama died Grandmama was afraid of you. She knew I'd be stronger if I had you in my corner."

"Well," Sebastian said as he slung an arm across his brother's shoulder. "She has every reason to be afraid now. I rather like the idea. Come inside before Fitzhugh finishes off the buffet."

"Does he always eat like that?"

"God, yes."

"Wait," Anthony said as they passed Lovey's stall. "Is this the horse you rode into the church to steal Creighton's bride in the presence of his mother?"

"She is."

"Good God, man. You may well be the bravest man I know."

"Lady Creighton is nothing. Wait until you have to face down my wife."

They crossed the stable yard and crossed the front terrace to the portico. The night was bitter cold and the snow had begun to fall once more. Sebastian stopped and they gazed out over the white-covered front gardens.

"I can go, Sebastian. If you'd rather spend Christmas with your family."

"Absolutely not. You have to come back with me. The bed in the master's bedchamber is damned uncomfortable and I don't want to be banished there again."

"Actually, I heard grandfather made that bed uncomfortable on purpose, so Grandmama would not join him there."

"Wise man."

MINERVA PROPPED HERSELF ON HER ELBOWS AND WATCHED AS Sebastian added a few logs to the fire and then placed the guard before it. He'd shed his dressing gown and she did so love the long line of his back as it tapered to his waist and curved into the muscles of his—

"Woman, if you do not stop staring at my *arse* as if it is a Christmas pudding I will not be responsible for my actions," he warned.

"I cannot help myself. Get into bed and I won't be able to look."

He leapt under the covers and dragged her across the bed to him. "You may look all you like once this little one arrives." He patted her belly and pressed a kiss to her temple. "Thank you, by the way."

"For what?" She snuggled into his embrace.

"My Christmas gift. The one I said I never wanted."

"Your brother."

"Yes. And my family and the best part of my childhood. And my home. What gift can I give you to compare to that?"

"You already have, my love. You are happy. That is all I ever wanted for Christmas."

"He-e-elp! Someone, help me! Get this fiend off me!"

Minerva tried to sit up, but Sebastian would not let her go.

"Precious is after Fitzhugh again," she said. "We have to save him."

"That isn't Fitzhugh," Sebastian replied. "That's Anthony."

"Sebastian, come out here and tell this devil dog to release me."

"Ask Creighton to help you. He excels at dealing with Precious."

Minerva struggled not to laugh. "You should not have told him that, Sebastian. You are awful."

"What should I tell him? I am warm and comfortable in bed with my wife."

"It is Christmas, Colonel Brightworth."

"So it is. Happy Christmas, Anthony. Welcome to the family."

The sounds of running feet, shouts, and a dog barking echoed in the corridor.

"It will be a miracle if we get to sleep tonight," Minerva said with a sigh.

"It's the season of miracles, Mrs. Brightworth. Anything can happen."

Colonel and Mrs. Sebastian Brightworth
are pleased to announce
the christening of their son
Anthony Harold Xavier Brightworth
14th February, 1818

The End

If you enjoyed *Stealing Christmas* by Louisa Cornell
be sure to look for *Stealing Minerva*
for the story of Sebastian and Minerva's scandalous courtship.

OTHER BOOKS BY LOUISA CORNELL

Lost in Love

Christmas Revels

Christmas Revels II

Christmas Revels IV

Christmas Revels V

A Lady's Book of Love

Between Duty and the Devil's Desires

Louisa loves to connect with readers! For more about Louisa and updates on future books by Louisa Cornell stop by any of her online homes!

facebook.com/RegencyWriterLouisaCornell

numberonelondon.net

twitter.com/LouisaCornell

pinterest.com/louisacornell

JOY TO THE DUKE

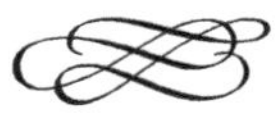

A DUKE'S SECRET STORY

EVA DEVON

For you, dear reader.
May your season be full of peace and may joy find you.

CHAPTER 1

Robert Deverall, the Duke of Blackstone, pulled down the delicate carriage window and leaned out into the soft falling snow. In the frigid winter air, his breath puffed out white before him. He stared straight ahead, the beautiful landscape dusted with snow unfolding before him. He paid no mind to the cold wind whipping against his cheeks. No, he was waiting for her to approve it, waiting to go over the rise and slip over the hill. Because then, as soon as the perfectly-appointed coach followed the curved path that wove through ancient oaks. . . Blackdown would appear, like a floating jewel.

He stilled his breathing and gripped the door with black-gloved hands. Just as he recalled, almost magically, a vast field of snow appeared before them. . . except, as most things at Blackdown House, it was a deception.

For under the fluffed clouds of snow, a large, manmade lake was hiding. Of course, now it was frozen solid.

Once, he, his sister, and their friends had skated upon it, reveling in the feel of flying across the ice and the cold winter wind whipping against their faces and woolen clothes.

There had been almost nothing like it, that pure freedom and speed as he had sped over the ice. It was one of his happiest memories.

It had been some years now since joy had touched this winter landscape. His father had seen to that.

But that was about to change. And all because of one woman. One daring, marvelous woman. His wife.

"I'm turning into an icicle."

The sound of his darling wife's voice warmed Rob's heart and he turned to her.

She gave an elaborate shiver.

"Well, let me warm you then," he replied happily, savoring the sight of her.

Harriet, or Harry to her intimates and he was the most intimate of all, sat cuddled in scarlet wool blankets up to her chin, her booted toes pressed to a small coal brazier. Even so, her cheeks were a bright red from the cold and did a remarkable job of matching the blankets tucked about her.

She flashed him a saucy look and held out a gloved hand to him. "You shall do a far better job of it than any blanket."

He slipped her hand into his palm and settled down beside her curved form. Nestling her close, he readjusted the blankets about him and tucked her head under his chin. Then he pulled her tightly to him, savoring the feel of their bodies pressed together. For Harriet's nearness not only warmed him, it soothed his soul.

She let out a contented sigh. "Are we mad to take to the roads?"

He laughed. "I thought our madness was already agreed upon." He sobered. "But I do not envy those upon the highways who do not have the comforts that we do."

Traveling in winter was no easy thing. Even for the very wealthy.

The appalling state of English country roads was a rather shocking thing. There was no middle ground to them in the months between October and March. From day to day throughout the long winter months, they either proved bogs of mud or frozen ruts as deep as the bloody Thames.

Only the determination of horses bred for it, along with coaches that cost a fortune and were designed to endure such hardship, made such a thing even possible. There was also the strength and tenacity of the driver and footmen.

Still, Christmas was the time to face the dismaying roads framed with hedgerows and stone walls. He had to do as had traditionally been done for hundreds of years.

He had not been home to Blackdown in some time. Not since he had seen how terribly it had begun to fall to rack and ruin. A thing done primarily by his father through a terrifying misuse of funds. He'd never forget standing in the great hall, the rain leaking in due to the lack of repair.

His father had very nearly destroyed everything.

Rob had not been able to face it. It had amazed him how quickly such a beautiful place could be brought to its knees by the misdeeds of one man.

Harry had managed to change all that.

She had taken on the restoration of the house with vigor and she was all but humming with excitement at the prospect of revealing it to him.

Harriet was a marvel. She'd restored him, too.

He pulled her closer and tilted her head back.

Though he was loath to admit it, part of him wished they had stayed in London for Christmas.

The ghost of his father had been mostly exorcised. But at Blackdown?

Surely, his father's ghost might be in every corner. No. He refused to let such a thing happen. For truly, it was he and he alone that could banish all such sadness and he had given his father enough time. Now was the time for joy, for he had so very much to be grateful for. He would not insult his good fortune with self-indulgence in gloom.

Robert swallowed then kissed his wife, determined to drive the hint of darkness away. For he had always loved Christmas. As had Harry.

They'd celebrated it together as children given that their family estates were side by side.

Now, they would once again make Blackdown a jewel of revelry and happiness for all those who lived on his lands at Christmastime.

He deepened their kiss, focusing all his will into pleasing her.

Harry's soft mouth parted beneath his and she tenderly stroked his hair.

As she leaned back against the velvet squabs, she cupped her small hand against his cheek.

"I love you dearly, Your Grace," she said with a wicked grin. But her eyes spoke of the depth of her feeling and the clear understanding that she recognized that this was no ordinary homecoming.

He wrapped his arms about her slight form and pressed her to his heart as if that could somehow anchor him to this moment and keep the past far, far away. It could. It already did. "I love you, too, Wife."

"Just you remember that," she teased, poking him lightly in the chest. "And you remember that if the past decides to pull at you this Christmas, I am holding your hand and will happily pull you back."

"Don't let go," he whispered.

"Never," she replied.

And he knew, deep in his bones, her help would be more than enough. For despite the darkness of the corridors of Blackdown and the tarnished pain of his family's descent into deepest misery, they had all emerged phoenix-like from the ashes to a new and glorious day.

This Christmas, together, they would light the Yule log and bring in the mistletoe. . . and cast out all ghosts for good.

CHAPTER 2

Harry all but danced up the stone steps of the towering, great house, not giving a whit for what anyone might think of her. Luckily, there wasn't a trace of ice on the stone, having been well sanded. The servants of the ancient seat were once again a force to be reckoned with, keeping the house in perfect working order.

Good wages, board, particularly good fare and a cheerful environment had done a wonder of good.

It had not been easy to assure the servants that Blackdown was to see a new day. She had worked long and hard to ensure that the estate shed the layers of tragedy it had absorbed just as thoroughly as she had seen the wrecked plaster and stained silk wall hangings be swept away.

While Rob had spent some extremely important hours working in Parliament changing the fate of nations, she had come down to the country and assessed how terrible it truly was. To her surprise and happiness, she'd discovered in herself what she'd realized was quite a remarkable talent for restoration.

Poring over plans, silk swatches, plasterwork designs, marble, and wood samples had not bored her. Not one bit. It had excited her. It had been clear to her that she was making choices which might, one day, please people hundreds of years in the future. Such a thing had been thrilling.

Each day had not been a trial of work and setbacks. No, it had been a revelation in her own ability and in the way art was created to last. She'd thrived in the discovery of each new beautiful element of the house. 'Twas as if she were befriending the old place, seeing its scars, loving it in any case, and helping it to heal. No, it had not just healed. Now, it positively shone.

She could not wait to show Rob. Not only was the house a stunning tribute to history now, and a quite comfortable place to live, she had also sent orders for festive decorating to be implemented.

Mary, her sister-in-law, and her mother-in-law, the dowager duchess, had been in the country now for two weeks, preparing for the Christmas season, too.

It had been, in the very end, a joint effort of the Deverall women to rejuvenate the ancient estate. An effort they were all very proud of. The spirit of the servants and tenants was now one of hope for the future.

Rob had been far more wary, as if the possibility of being within the vicinity of his childhood home might open a tide of memory and emotion he'd hoped to keep dammed up quite safely.

Still, he was here now, right behind her and he did not seem like a man being led to the gallows. In fact, his strong step was sprightly. He seemed cheerful even. Which was a good thing, for her own emotions had been rather full these last weeks. His steadiness had been most helpful as she had begun to feel waves of great happiness and waves of great irritation. Still, she knew she was going to have to become used to the unreliability of her emotions for several months.

She smiled to herself at the thought.

The double doors at the head of the wide stairs opened, revealing the marvelous butler, Stevenson. Much to her good fortune, they had formed an immediate accord and the long-suffering family servant had been eager to help her to return Blackdown to its former glory. At first, she had been frightened that she would tire him with her efforts given his years. Instead, he had only increased in vigor at the task.

She smiled then felt Rob's hand touch her back as they stepped into the spacious foyer which was as large as some people's entire houses. The ceiling soared above them and their footsteps echoed on the ornate, green, marble floor.

Unlike so many of the newer, prestigious houses of the *ton*, this beautiful place had been built before Henry VIII. Somehow, it had survived almost entirely intact and the ceiling fairly glittered what with its elaborate gold cornices and carved wood.

Painted a brilliant blue, flowers of all of England's counties twined about the arched ceiling, but there was no mistaking the Tudor Rose in several prominent places which showed the loyalty of the Blackstone family.

That loyalty had seen the family through several revolts and uprisings of many of the most powerful families of England.

Others had fallen to the dust. The Blackstones had remained.

There was no doubt in her mind that there would be a Blackstone at the helm of the English government for all time.

Still, she hesitated, unsure how Rob might take to the changes. The tall windows had been replaced with perfect panes, and many of the blackened tapestries had been taken down and sent away for restoration which might take years. In the meantime, a series of paintings featuring the great deeds of the first Blackstones hung upon the walls.

She glanced back over her shoulder, hoping to see some sign of acceptance.

She did not see it. No, it was not acceptance. His face had all but transformed with pleasure. A wide smile parted his wicked lips and his eyes, so often given to mischief, lit with delight.

"What a marvel," he declared. "How proud you both must be."

The butler all but bounced on his ancient toes, unable to hide his glee. "We are, Your Grace. We are. But it is Her Grace who is most responsible. She has brought the place to life again."

"She has brought us all to life again," Rob corrected kindly.

"No ghosts could dwell here," he whispered very quietly before giving himself a little shake.

Harriet barely heard his declaration but hear it she did, and her heart warmed. It was no easy thing for him to choose happiness. Her heart swelled with pride at his strength.

"Now," Rob proclaimed, clasping her to him, "show me our home, Your Grace."

Harry all but hummed with relief and joy at his reaction. Rob had always danced on the edge of the sadness of his childhood. But when one had known such tragedy as he had, it was to be expected. The horrific depths of dissipation to which Rob's father had descended and which Rob had witnessed would be the heart break of any son.

As of late, the shadows of the past had released him more and more.

So, delighted, she took his hand and began pulling him towards the curved stairs.

"Where to first?" he asked, following happily.

She stopped and popped onto the tips of her boots. Pressing a kiss to his cheek, she then whispered, "The bedrooms, I'd think. Don't you agree?"

CHAPTER 3

Mary scribbled fiercely at her writing desk before the frost-tinged windows. A soft blue, winter light bathed her room and the single taper she'd lit to illuminate her pages danced cheerfully.

The guests had been arriving all afternoon and she knew she should be glad. She was! For they were all free now of the prison her father had made for her, Rob, and their mother.

That darkness was gone now forever with her father's passing. Bitterness had given way to joy. Dawn had come to Blackdown. Even now, cloudless blue sky caused the snow-blanketed ground to wink as if covered by millions of priceless diamonds. Everything fairly glittered.

She bit the end of her wooden quill as she contemplated the vast estate unrolling before her.

No. She would not think about *him*. The man who had changed everything from the moment she had set eyes upon him.

His rough voice and rough hands were not her concern.

Mary looked back to the parchment, half-filled with quickly scrawled words.

Richard Heath...

Her heart all but skipped in anticipation.

He was coming for Christmas.

What ever would she do?

She had not seen him since he had so bluntly proclaimed that a lady such as she was no longer to keep company with a man such as he.

But it was his company she preferred to all. It drove her mad that she could not make him see that.

Truly, it amazed her he had agreed to leave London for the polished halls of aristocrats at all given his general dislike of the upper classes. But he had formed the most unlikely of friendships with her brother and his closest friends.

And that made everything all the more complicated. What would Rob truly think of her friendship with Heath? Was friendship truly the proper word? Of that, she was not certain.

Sighing, Mary flung her quill down. Ink spattered the ivory page and she folded her arms beneath her breasts.

It did seem that she was destined to play a role she had no interest in. Even Heath had made it seem like that was what she should do.

Duke's daughter, indeed. She snorted.

The very idea. For far too long, she had been forced into a submissive guise, unable to be herself. Now was her chance to shed all that and choose her own path.

No, it was not her fate to marry some silly arse of a man who cared naught but for dogs, lace, and snuff boxes.

Oh, how she longed for a man who had looked into this hellish life and laughed, unbowed.

As if the bidden devil had heard his name, Heath's voice boomed up from the drive and she realized that the most recent coach to arrive was his!

Mary bounded up from her chair, all but knocking it over. She pressed her face to the cold glass, desperate to catch sight of him.

To no avail.

His voice filled the frigid air, but he was already mounting the steps, vanishing beneath the elaborate portico.

What to do? She bit the inside of her cheek.

Stay here?

No. She would not hide. He might have told her to avoid him, but surely even he would agree such a thing would be impossible at a Christmas party?

And so, anticipation lacing through her veins, Mary dashed out of the room, certain that this Christmas, Richard Heath's presence was almost certainly the greatest present of all.

CHAPTER 4

Richard Heath hated Christmas presents. Rightly, he should have hated Christmas, too, having spent more than a few of his sleeping in gutters, guarding whore houses, or cleaning up dubious liquids in taverns.

For whatever reason, he'd never quite been able to hate it the way some people he knew did. For, whilst it had been a sort of hell, he'd always been swept away by the way his sort could still lift a cup of gin, salute the season, and revel in a few hours of undiluted joy.

Christmas, he knew, was not about the goose, pudding, marble halls, or oranges.

No, it was about the company one kept.

That was the only reason he'd stepped into this gilded box which usually would have made him wish to snarl with disgust.

No, the people in this house were most acceptable to him, unlike most of the upper classes.

It was still a marvel to him the way he had taken in Rob, who had come to him lost, and looking as if a cannon had exploded right before him. There was no good reason that he could recall to deciding to guide the young duke through the rings of debt and trouble his father had immersed himself in. Rob hadn't been arrogant or superior. He'd been curious, determined to learn, and terrifyingly clear that he would not be repeating the disastrous mistakes of his sire.

And he clearly cared about Mary. Unlike the man who'd tried to all but sell her away to clear his debts.

Richard admired Rob for his sheer determination to do the right thing, though Richard had been loath to admit it at first.

And then, he'd been pulled inexplicably into the small, secret circle of the Number 79 club. He still wasn't sure how he'd become a member. It boggled even his jaded mind.

After all, only dukes were members. . . all but him.

Footsteps clattered down the ornate stairs at the center of the sprawling foyer and his heart suddenly did a damned inconvenient stutter.

Lady Mary stopped at the center of the landing, her green silk skirts, edged with gold, swinging about her legs. The swish of the fabric bared white, silk-stockinged ankles and green slippers.

Her dark hair was wild about her face, as if she had not bothered with an elaborate coiffure.

She looked completely different than the timid girl he'd first met. God, how she had infiltrated his sympathies. He'd been appalled by his sentimentality. But now, he knew it was because he had seen the survivor in her.

Mary was not a mouse, following the bidding of her monstrous sire. Instead, she was a lioness ready to tear all apart to protect her mother.

That realization had solidified his deep admiration and devotion to her.

She'd never known that. She never would.

It was imperative he keep the damned high kick away from him. A brutish fellow, no matter how smoothed out with highly applied gloss, was not for her.

In the end, for all his schooling, for all his practiced airs, he was a man of the gutter.

He would not drag her deeper into his sordid world. No, her

beauty would not be marred by it. Her heart had known enough suffering without him causing her more.

"Hello, Richard," she said, the corner of her mouth quirking up in the way it did when she was secretly thinking thoughts that titled young ladies were not supposed to think.

He knew that smile. It had nearly led him down a path he could not return from.

He inclined his dark head. "Lady Mary," he replied.

Sighing, she started down the steps, head held high. A slight red colored her pearl white cheeks. Not rouge, not the color of the women of his birth, which was meant to feign desire.

This color. . . this color was pleasure at the sight of him.

His breath all but stopped. How had he ever thought he could be in her proximity again and not be tempted?

He clenched his jaw. Damnation. He was stronger than that. He was Richard Heath, ruler of the bloody underworld of London. A chit of a girl, an aristocrat, was not going to move him.

Except. . . except, he knew in his soul, in his bones, in what little was left of his heart, she was so much more than that.

Mary was glorious.

She was the sort of creature that made men kneel, breathless, ready to worship, and give their hearts over even when they knew only hell would result.

Luckily, he had more self-discipline than most.

"Now," she began, her voice surprisingly deep for one of her years. Richard—"

"Heath," he cut in quickly.

She cocked her head to the side. "Surely not."

"Surely yes," he countered, every inch of him aching at her sudden nearness. He fairly towered over her. She had to crane her head back to meet his eyes, causing her dark hair to spill over her ivory shoulders. It didn't seem to bother her in the slightest, his height.

Her brow furrowed. "But—"

"We are not friends, Lady Mary," he said with forced gentleness. "And only friends use each other's given names."

"*Only* friends?" she asked, her brows rising as she teased him.

The two words which should have been so completely ineffective with a man who had known every type of seduction or intimation of desire, sent a wave of longing through him.

Bloody hell, how had he ever let it get this far? How had he ever let her think she could be so intimate with him?

He leaned down and whispered, "We are not lovers, either, Lady Mary."

She smiled up at him, unrepentant. "Alas."

"Get yourself a husband," he growled, suddenly impatient and desperate to be away from her lest she see the power of her effect upon him. "And then, if you're still after your bit of rough, you'll know where to find me."

She winced. "I—"

For one moment, he hated himself. For one moment, he started to reach out to her and tell her how much he hungered for her, how he admired her above all others. But he never could and never would.

And he sure as hell would not be the one to ruin her.

With that, he forced himself to turn and leave her. One foot stepped after the next, having no bloody clue where he was going, as long as it was away from the only woman he'd truly ever wanted.

CHAPTER 5

The close friendship of Harry's husband, the Duke of Blackstone, to the Duke of Drake had begun in a hospital tent, on the edge of a battlefield, just before Christmas. It had not been on England's green shores that their powerful alliance had begun but at war on a far-flung field.

She could only imagine that the air had not smelled of evergreen, cinnamon, oranges, and a good fire. Surely, the air had smelled of gunpowder and dying men.

But as Harriet understood, it had been in that tent that the Duke of Blackstone and the Duke of Drake assessed each other warily then committed to what would soon be an undeniable tradition.

She'd always been rather fond of the distant, wickedly sharp Duke of Drake. He'd held himself with such power, such cleverness, and stayed above the antics of everyone else about him. And yet, he'd often spared kind smiles for her. Most recently, she'd begun to believe that he was not nearly as jaded as he liked others to believe. In fact, she was almost certain that his cutting stare and blade of a tongue stemmed from a kind heart that had been sorely misused.

It had been known to all and sundry when he and her husband had first begun their friendship that Damian, then future Duke of

Drake, was not welcome at his own estate. He had been hated by his own parents who had decried him to all of society.

So it had been decided that Damian would go home with Rob from war since he had nowhere else to go. And every Christmas since, the dangerous young man, cast out from his family but still destined to inherit, had spent every Yuletide with the Blackstone family.

Much to Harry's delight, the Duke of Drake now sat at the pianoforte in the long hall, pounding out *God Rest Ye Merry Gentlemen* in dramatic and passionate tones.

He played it with a vigor that seemed to encourage cheer and all about chattered with happiness as they played cards.

A smile tilted her lips as she gazed upon him and his strong fingers dancing over the keys. No one could play like Drake.

He paused mid-chord and took a long drink from the snifter of brandy perched on the table beside him before he transitioned into a rousing reel.

Harry almost laughed, for he did so with such ease. Not a note was missed.

The Duke of Drake was a man she knew she'd never understand. He hid his truths under a mask of wicked quips and sardonic smiles. His gaze spoke untold knowledge of wonders most would never know. But he seldom said a serious word, preferring to drawl his way through most conversations.

How she hoped he would find the sort of happiness that she and Rob had found. According to her dear husband, Drake had known very little joy in his life.

She looked about the room which fairly glowed with good humor and surveyed her guests. A feeling of great contentment settled over her. A year ago, she'd known she would wed, but it had never occurred to her that she would wed her childhood friend, or that she would find both passion and happiness.

Were there any two as lucky as she and Rob? She casually walked along the length of the red, silk brocaded room, taking in the happiness of those who had been invited to Blackdown.

A hearty fire crackled in the massive Carrara marble fireplace which was decked with holly and ivy. Massive mirrors in gilded frames hung from every bit of the wall, increasing the light within the room. They, too, had been decked with Yuletide finery.

In fact, bows of greenery swung from every place she could see and the scent of mulled wine filled the room with citrus, cloves, and cinnamon as it simmered in a pot by the fire.

It was almost shocking to see an item cooking in such a room.

But she loathed cold wine that was supposed to be hot. And there was simply no way to keep mulled wine as warm as it should be on the journey from the kitchens to the salons.

So, she had decreed it would be good fun to mull it themselves.

Richard Heath had all but rolled his eyes as he'd witnessed the attempts of the ladies to *cook*.

And since the dukes had always had servants, even at war, they were no better. None of them had ever had to boil water let alone mull wine.

So, much to everyone's deep gratitude, they had stood aside as Heath had poured in the wine, cut the oranges, grated the cinnamon, and stirred the whole lot into a punch. And then he'd poured in a good deal of brandy from a decanter on the grog tray and set it to simmer over the blazing fire.

Harry had all but gulped at the vast amounts of brandy that had been used.

"If you want someone from the East End to make your punch, you'd best be prepared for it to have a bite," Richard had proclaimed.

And as if the good man who ruled the dark night of London could hardly bear to be at ease, he stood beside the fire, his dark eyes flicking over the company.

His gaze landed upon Mary and, much to Harriet's astonishment, his gaze. . . softened.

Harry nearly gasped as she swung her own attention from Mary to Heath.

Surely, she was mistaken.

They hardly knew each other.

But she observed the way in which Heath looked with utter admiration upon Rob's sister. His dark gaze became pools of emotion as he took in her coiled, black hair and ivory face.

It was discernible, the depth of his feeling, in the subtle flexing of his hands into fists and the tightening of his jaw. It was not anger that caused such actions, but. . . longing.

Clearly, his admiration did not give him pleasure.

Harriet stared at the man who had come to her husband's aid when she had been kidnapped and suddenly wished that he, too, could be as happy as she. For surely, those who had suffered so terribly and known so little happiness, deserved joy most of all.

But would he be a good match for Mary?

Did she reciprocate his feelings?

Suddenly, Harry felt rather flummoxed. She gazed upon her enigmatic sister-in-law.

As if in answer to her question, Mary's face tilted upward, and her sapphire gaze met Heath's. Her cheeks blossomed apple red, her pink lips parted, and the connection between the two fairly sang.

"My love, will you not dance with me?"

She whipped around, laughing. "You startled me."

Rob gave her a warm smile. "Woolgathering were you?"

"Something like that."

Rob arched a dark brow. "I know that look, Wife. You're scheming."

"I do not scheme," she corrected playfully. Harriet gave his accusation further consideration and added. "I plan. In detail."

He threw back his head and roared with laughter. "Indeed, you do. Now, come and dance. We must set the tone, after all. And it is imperative that Blackdown be merry and bright."

"I heartily agree," she replied, tucking her ivory-gloved hand into his.

He leaned towards her and whispered, "Do you think we should change the name?"

"The name?" she queried.

"Of the house," he explained lightly. "Blackdown is so very dreary."

She considered his question. "It is tradition, I suppose."

He harrumphed. "Tradition is dreadful."

Harry heard the wish in his voice, the wish for something better than the past and so she smiled up at him. "Rob, now listen and listen well. You are a duke. You make tradition. If you so like we can call this house *Sun Hall* or *Jolly Manor* or—"

"Have done! Have done, my love." He laughed again and whisked her towards the open space before the pianoforte. "I take your point. *What's in a name* and all that."

"Good," she replied, happy he had so easily agreed. "Now, we can't possibly dance alone. Not if we are to set the precedence for merriment."

Rob nodded then cast his gaze about. "Heath," he called. "Come and dance. I'm certain Mary longs to do more than sit."

Harriet nibbled her lower lip and waited for Heath's reply. Perhaps, such a man as he shunned dancing. After all, there likely was not a great deal of cause for such a thing where he spent the vast majority of his time. At least not formal reels.

But to her delight, Heath took up the challenge and crossed silently to Mary.

Rob's sister's lips curved in a strange smile before she slipped her fingers into Heath's.

Damian looked at the four of them now awaiting him to continue in his dancing tunes. He lifted his hands and brought them down dramatically. The notes of a dirge began.

"Drake," roared Rob.

Drake's brows rose ever so innocently. But then he laughed and launched into a sprightly air.

Harry and Rob lined up opposite Mary and Heath. A strange sense of anticipation danced through Harriet as they began the intricate and cheerful turns of the dance. Weaving from partner to partner, touching hand to hand, she was certain that she noticed sheer delight color Mary's cheeks.

Yes, Mary liked Richard Heath.

Harriet nearly laughed. She was far too young to be a matchmaker, was she not?

But as she considered her own happiness, she thought, perhaps not. What better role than to make others merry?

CHAPTER 6

A sense of unease slipped through Rob as he propped himself up on one arm in the great bed which dominated the ducal bedroom. Rare winter sunlight had just begun to spill through the window and onto the Aubusson rug. The night before had been perfection. Now. . . he could not fight back the worry that had been slipping through him the last days.

"Are you unwell, my love?" he ventured, attempting to keep his deep concern from his voice.

She sighed, then strode back to the bed, her night rail slipping over one shoulder. She looked quite pale and she took up the glass decanter of water beside the bed and poured herself a glass. Slowly, she took a delicate sip.

"Harry?" he prompted.

"It is just my stomach," she confessed.

Rob's brow furrowed with inescapable worry. His happiness had never been sound and now that he had it, he had to make every effort not to fear its loss.

For days, Harriet had leapt from the bed and scurried away, seemingly unwell. In fact, it happened several times a day recently and then she would quite recover. Plus, she had taken to quick naps on a chair in their rooms, something that she had never done before.

He tossed the blankets back and padded barefoot over the Aubusson rug to her side. Carefully, he smoothed her blonde curls back from her face.

"You look a bit done in, my darling." He gazed down at her lovingly, not wanting her to sense his true concern. "Should we send for the physician?"

"It is nothing," she protested easily, placing her glass down.

"But you've been unwell—"

Gently, she took his hands and carefully studied his face.

His heart slammed with terror for, surely, she was contemplating how best to tell him some piece of bad news.

Rob swallowed. "Harry... please tell me you are not... *ill.*"

"I am not ill," she said quickly and, suddenly, her face bloomed with a bright smile. "Quite the contrary. I am in robust health."

He shook his head, struggling to understand. "Then why?"

Her eyes all but sparkled. "I am with child."

He stared at her, his mouth dropping open. All his wits abandoned him then. "W-w-with—"

"Child," she finished for him. She bit her lower lip. "Are you pleased?"

It had been a mark of darkness between them in their early marriage. He had been utterly determined not to have a child, to end the Blackstone line. With her help, he'd managed to come to terms with his fears, and he'd agreed to the possibility.

Now that it was here?

His hearted hammered against his chest. Then without further thought, he was grinning. Harriet's child. His child. *Theirs.*

"She will look exactly like you," he proclaimed. "And no other child shall be as loved."

She sighed with relief. The breath that exhaled was a long one and the tension that had held her evaporated under his words.

"Harry, this is the best Christmas gift I could ever receive," he said softly, holding her close.

She laughed. "It is not my doing, the timing of it, but it is a marvelous present for us both."

He folded his arms about her waist. "I cannot countenance how lucky we are."

"Nor I," she agreed, slipping her hands up his shoulders.

"The whole world should be as happy as we are," he declared, so full of love he wished such a state for everyone.

"Indeed, it should," she agreed. "What say you? Should we partner up all of mankind?"

Rob laughed again. How he loved her turn of mind. "Whenever would we find the time?"

She pursed her lips in thought. For it was true. Both of them were immersed in never-ending meetings, councils, charities, political dinners, and attempts to make England and, thus, the world a better place.

"True," she sighed. "Perhaps then, we should just find a husband for Mary."

Rob shook his head. "Dear wife, let me take in our news before we go on to greater ventures."

Harry leaned forward and linked her hands behind his neck. Heart swelling, he held her carefully, amazed that such a thing could be happening to him, and gazed down into his wife's perfect visage.

"I thought," she whispered. "I thought—"

"Yes, Harry?" he encouraged, sensing her need to be soothed.

She nibbled her bottom lip then she began, "I thought coming here... that fatherhood... that it might..."

He caught her chin. "Darling Harry, there is no going back. I have seen those dark ways and have no wish to traverse them again. You took me by the hand and led me out of the shadows. With you, my love, there is only one place in which we shall go and that is forward. Forward with our love and forward with our family."

A sheen of tears filled her eyes, but they were tears of joy as she replied, "I love you, Rob."

"And I you, with every beat of my heart."

CHAPTER 7

Damian Avonby, Duke of Drake, strode through the snow, determined not to devolve into trudging or self-woe.

Perhaps Christmas with his friend and compatriot, the Duke of Blackstone, had been a mistake this year. But he had come every year for some time. Each visit in the past had been the highlight of his year, offering a family. Something he had never truly had.

He adored his friend's happiness. For Damian was not a believer in continued or prolonged suffering and he was delighted beyond measure that his friend had shed the pain of the past. In fact, Rob seemed happier than he'd ever been.

Damian certainly didn't begrudge him that. If anything, Damian had shoved his friend towards it. . . as he was attempting to do to all the men who had pulled him out of a lonely hell and included him in their brethren. Whether they knew it or not, he was bloody determined that nothing should stand in their way to happiness.

Even so, it did now seem to provide a stark and unavoidable contrast to his own state.

Damian knew one thing and knew it well. He would never be happy. The most he could hope for was a lack of pain and, perhaps, one day a sort of contentment. The condition had been with him for so long that he no longer gave it much thought. He'd simply accepted it.

Now, it was. . . both wonderful and wearing to see the happiness about him that he'd had such a distinct part in.

He gazed up at the soft grey-white sky, crystal flakes floating softly to the blanket of snow unrolling before them.

He, Rob, and Heath cut through the white-hued meadow hunting for oak trees.

Well, not hunting. Oak trees could not leap about, hide, or suddenly take up root and choose a new location as humans did. No, the oak trees on this estate had been here since Henry Tudor had unfurled his banners in Wales and England and had bid a final adieu to the great Lancasters.

The roots of the trees ran as deep into the ground as did Rob's ancestors into the tapestry of England.

Damian clenched his jaw, then immediately forced himself to relax. He dared not tense. He dared not think of how he did not belong here and never truly would. For if he did, the stutter he had worked so very hard to conquer would claim him and then he'd never hear the end of it from Rob until he confessed what ailed him.

There were curses to having friends.

A friend's concern could be one of them.

"There!" Rob shouted happily pointing to the west.

Rob's good humor was so bright, so full, that a different man would have found it rather annoying. Damian certainly would have before he'd had the good fortune to make Rob's acquaintance.

Now, he took it without cynicism. Some people were happy without being foolish. One was not synonymous with the other.

He followed Rob and Heath as they came upon the great oak, its branches wild and bare. Like gnarled arms, they twisted into the air, home to birds and. . . mistletoe.

The three men leaned back, their great coats flying slightly in the winter wind, and stared up at the twisting branches. The green leaves that grew in the otherwise naked tree were quite visible and high.

"Right then," Heath said. "Who's climbing?"

"Surely you, Heath," Damian drawled.

Heath eyed the tree as though it might attack him.

Damian studied Heath then observed, "You've never climbed a tree."

"There aren't trees in East London," Heath countered. "So, the opportunity never presented itself. Some of us weren't born to romp through bucolic, green fields."

"Point taken," Damian replied, though he could have added that he could not recall a single moment of frolic in his childhood though there had been many, many green hills. Most of them rugged and unforgiving in the northernmost corner of England.

Still, self-pity was for idiots, and Damian didn't suffer idiocy. So, he turned to Rob and quipped, "And you are a newly-married man. I won't face Harry if you break your leg."

Rob scoffed. "Break my—"

"I won't risk vexing Harry. Or your mother." Damian gave a dramatic shiver. "I like my person the way it is."

Quickly, Damian assessed the tree then with little ado, he grabbed the best handholds and footholds and vaulted up the tree. He balanced easily over the damp branches and made his way to the clusters of green leaves.

Allowing nothing to distract him from his precarious position, he whipped out a knife and began cutting.

The two men below shouted cheers of encouragement with each set of falling greenery until there was quite a pile on the snow-covered ground.

"Is that enough?" he called down.

"I'll kiss my wife in every corner," returned Rob.

"You already do that," Damian drawled.

Rob merely grinned. "Wait until you've a wife, old boy. You'll see. Any excuse to kiss her will do."

Damian clasped a final bunch of the plant which had been part of the Yuletide season for as long as could be remembered on this isle and fought a wince. Marriage? Would he ever dare? What chance had he of such happiness?

For one moment, he felt a flame of hope light in his chest. Perhaps, one day, he could be loved, could he not?

But then, he shook the thought away and allowed the mistletoe to fall to the ground.

CHAPTER 8

Full to the brim with joy, Harry fairly danced down the hall. Any worry she'd had about Rob and their visit had vanished entirely with this morning's confession. She had waited to tell him of her condition, both because she had wanted to be absolutely certain the life had taken root and because she had no idea how to tell him. It had been far easier and sweeter than she could have imagined.

Now, all was well and the sun was setting.

Christmas Eve had arrived, as had almost all their guests. The preparations were well underway for the evening's festivities and tomorrow's elaborate dinner. Cook had seemed in very good spirits, too. After years of cooking for only the family, or just the servants on staff, she was reveling in the large party and decadent meals she was preparing.

While all this to-do did cause Harry great happiness, in the end, it was Rob's reaction to her news and his general good cheer at his country seat that caused her to fly down the corridor. If ever she had cause to worry about this visit, that seemed to be gone now.

It seemed almost foolish now to have doubted.

She had always loved Christmas. It was a time of year that had filled her with so much joy throughout her life. But it was also the first Christmas she had not spent with her own family and, suddenly, she hesitated in her near skipping down the hall. She paused before a tall window which looked out to the frozen lake.

She contemplated the still view before her, wondering what was transpiring at the Harley estate across the hills. Likely, they were all scurrying about preparing for minced pies and game fowl for their dinner. Certainly, there would be all sorts of games to amuse the children.

Her mother and father had made every Christmas one of happiness for their children and their tenants.

It had been quite a blow when her father had died. For he had always been the kindest of men. Every year, he and her mother had gone to the tenants, giving out presents which were dearly necessary. The baskets had been laden with provisions and oranges. She had taken up that very tradition herself at Blackdown, having gone out with Rob after breakfast. He had tried to protest, insisting she rest. She had scoffed and proclaimed a bit of bracing air would be just the thing. It had. For her spirits had felt light in continuing a tradition her parents had instilled in her.

Now, she could still recall the feel of her family, all standing about the harpsichord, singing in Latin, as the candles flickered and Christmas Day drew close.

Her dear brother was the duke now and married to her closest friend. And it felt so very strange to be so near to them, for the estate she had grown up on abutted her husband's, and yet, not be with them.

It was. . . the only ill thing in such a wonderful Christmastide.

She lifted her hand and touched the cold glass. It was the oddest sensation coming over her. Part of her felt such joy at her new situation, and another felt the slight melancholy of memory.

A wry smile tilted her lips.

How lucky she was to have so much family and so many who loved her and that she could love. Yes, that was how she would manage those strange, slightly unwanted feelings at the loss of the past. She would count her blessing, and ensure the Yuletide spirit of those around her.

"Harry?" Mary called from down the long corridor. "Are you well?"

Harry turned to her sister-in-law and nodded. "I could not be better."

Mary tilted her head to the side, firelight from one of the wall sconces catching her dark hair. "You looked. . . sad."

Harry nodded, not bothering to deny it. "I was thinking of my father."

"He was a good man," Mary said kindly before she added, "unlike mine."

"My father was exceptional, it is true," Harry agreed and she extended her hand to her sister-in-law. "I wish yours could have been, too."

Mary sighed as she strode forward, the red silk skirts shot with gold braid swishing about her legs. "Indeed, I should wish it but cannot. For if he had been different, I would not be me. Who knows if Rob would have married you and then we should not be sisters."

"How true," Harriet declared. "You bear your pain very well."

Mary merely smiled before she linked arms with Harriet. "When will the last guests be arriving?"

"Any moment, I should think," Harry replied as they began to head down the hall that led to the central stairs. "Can you imagine?"

"What?" Mary asked.

Harriet guffawed. "A house full of dukes at Christmas."

"It is rather surprising." Mary squeezed Harry's arm and said with exaggerated seriousness, "Thank goodness they're all handsome, witty fellows. Not a crusty sot among them!"

"Mary, for all your seeming quietness in the past, you really have the most marvelously wicked tongue."

"Why, thank you. I always wanted to unleash it upon the world."

"And now you can," observed Harry as they turned and stepped out to the landing, the red and gold carpet stretching before them.

Mary nodded. The unspoken words that it was the death of her father, a destructive and cruel man, which had prevented such a thing played in her mind.

"Let us go down then and await them." Mary waggled her brows. "For, in but a few hours' time, the revelry shall begin!"

CHAPTER 9

While the house was not bursting at the seams, as some might say, Rob adored the sense of goodwill radiating from every hall, every corridor, every nook, and every cranny. It was so very far from the darkness of his life but a year ago that he could not cease smiling.

Everyone was smiling. Even Heath and Drake were making pleasantries. The two were more alike than they'd ever likely admit but they both had a gift for cynicism, quips, and well. . . though they'd bash Rob's brain in for saying such a thing aloud. . . they both had wounded souls.

Their efforts to be, if not joyous, but good company was duly noted.

It was hard to believe that Blackdown had been so. . . well, black such a short time ago.

A year ago, one could not have paid him any sum which would have induced or compelled his presence here. After the death of his father, he had stopped coming and thought he might never come home again.

Now? Now, he could imagine spending every Christmas here with his family.

His family. What a remarkable thing. Soon, that would be more than his wife, his sister, and his mother. Soon, his family would include a child.

His insides humming with amazement, Rob climbed the side stairs to a small but beautifully decorated study. Notes had been sent out about the house.

Perhaps there would be no visit to Number 79 but the friends who had come together over impending dukedoms would still gather here in this house. They were almost all present, after all.

As he entered through the soaring, arched doorway, and stepped into the golden-red glow of lamps and firelight, he could not help but inhale and bathe in a feeling of contentment.

The deep, leather chairs studded with brass tacks were arranged before the cheerful fire. It was a room that was the height of comfort. It was quite simple without any fuss to it.

Dark wood, green curtains, and paintings of the horses that had graced Blackdown's stables made the room a refuge. As did the books. Hundreds of books lined the walls, their gold-titled spines facing the room.

As he stepped inside, contemplating how the world could change so drastically in but a brief amount of time, the sound of male voices, laughing, filled the air.

Royland, Raventon, and Drake charged in just behind him.

Royland strode forward and clapped Rob on the back. "Brandy, old man. It's deuced cold out this night."

Feeling all was ridiculously right with the world, Rob did as he was bid. He crossed to the grog tray by the fire, laden with crystal decanters of various spirits and glasses of myriad shapes.

"Encounter any highwaymen, Royland?" Drake drawled, eyeing his fingernails before he gave Rob a mocking wink.

Rob arched a brow.

"Not a one," intoned Royland.

"Except the one who stands before me," pointed out Raventon.

"Those days are done," Rob protested.

"I did hear you kept your hat," Drake said as he crossed towards the grog tray and collected a glass.

Rob cleared his throat. The truth was, Harry liked his hat, and well. . . he rather liked sweeping her away.

"You're blushing," crowed Royland.

"Don't be absurd," returned Rob.

"No doubt, it is the fire," Drake drawled.

"Exactly," Rob cut in. "The fire."

Despite their usual stoicism, his friends grinned, all knowing when to stop. Their jests were always in good humor and never meant to cause pain.

Brandy was quickly passed about, the crystal snifters winking like diamonds in the firelight. Night had now truly fallen. The dark night sky would have left the park as dark as black velvet save for the countless shining stars and bright moon.

But as the night progressed, the room had closed in to a warm, familiar glow.

"Where the devil is Harley?" Royland asked.

Rob frowned momentarily. "I thought he would—"

And as if summoned by the words, the Duke of Harley strode through the door. His eyes were bright, his hair was wild, and his face was merry. It was the face of a man deeply happy with his wife. Rob knew it well.

A chorus of "Harley!" went around and before they could think twice, there was a good deal of back clapping again and toasting. It had been too many weeks for Rob's liking since they'd all been together.

"Is that Scot, Ardore, ever coming back?" Harley challenged before he took a long drink of the rich French spirit.

Drake shrugged. "Perhaps he has given up the aristocracy in favor of a republic."

Harley shuddered. "Americans."

Royland laughed. "They're not so very terrible."

"And one must admit, they have a certain daring," Rob agreed.

"A sense of panache," put in Raventon.

Royland lifted his glass as if in salute of the rebels. "And they know how to write a damned good declaration."

A moment of silence fell as they realized that if any of them had been born just a decade or so earlier, that they would never be jesting like this about the former colony and Ardore wouldn't be there to visit at all. It didn't matter that their political party had supported the separation of the colony. As soldiers, they would have had to go.

Raventon broke the reverie. "In all events, you'll never catch me across the pond. Panache or no. Too many Puritans."

Royland rolled his eyes. "We all know you're afraid of sailing."

"Oh, indeed. I'd clutch the main mast the whole of the way," jested Raventon who was, in fact, an excellent sailor. One might have thought he'd been a naval officer rather than a rifleman but he'd fought on land, not on sea.

"In all events, you and Harley looked damned pleased with yourselves," Heath observed from the doorway, leaning against the frame.

"Get in here, Heath!" Harley called, bidding him with a wave of his hand.

Heath and Harley clasped hands in a firm shake and Rob handed the London man a glass.

"Heath's right. You both *do* look rather pleased," Drake observed through exaggeratedly narrowed eyes.

"It is Christmas," Harley said over the rim of his glass.

"It's not that," put in Royland. His eyes narrowed as he, no doubt, tried to assess what they were missing.

Heath cocked his head to the side. "You both look like cats that have gotten the cream."

"Don't tell me," Drake began, his stoic face parting with a genuine smile. "We have a pair of fathers in our midst."

"I swear you pay my servants," Harley breathed. "You know far too much."

"No need. Your face has always been an open book, Harley," Drake informed.

"Is it true?" Royland asked, stunned.

Rob stared at Harley, amazed. Could he? Could *they*? Was it possible? Would they both be expecting at the same time? It would certainly make the whole of it easier with a friend to share his worries and anticipations with.

"It is," declared Harley. "Or at least, Eglantine is enceinte."

"As is Harry," said Rob, fairly reeling. "Though I never should have confessed it without your guess."

"Why not?" asked Royland. "For we are all friends. And we wish to share your joy."

And as if on cue, Rob and Harley were surrounded by their friends, glasses raised.

"To Harriet and Eglantine," said Drake quite seriously. "Bringers of happiness. And to you two devils, who've found joy."

"To joy!" Rob's friends toasted.

He turned to Harley and they gave a quick clap to each other's backs before they shrugged and then abruptly hugged each other, laughing. Then they were all loudly clapping each other's backs and declaring how happy they all were.

It seemed a perpetual grin had affixed itself to Rob's visage.

"Two down," Harley said, waggling his brows and surveying the bachelors in the room. "Which one of you is next?"

Rob nearly choked on his laughter at the look of horror on the other men's faces.

It was going to be a Merry Christmas, indeed.

CHAPTER 10

The festivities of the Christmas Eve party were everything that Harriet could have hoped for and more. To her absolute delight, her sisters, mother, and dearest friend, Eglantine, had come through the door in a burst of bright skirts, bouncing curls, and infectious smiles.

The cries of "Happy Christmas" that had surrounded her had nearly done her in. Could there be too much happiness? She knew not, but tears of joy had stung her eyes as she had been enveloped in their embraces.

"Why, you are here!" she declared as her young sisters bounced around her, their eyes dancing.

"We could not stay away," Marianne said brightly, her blonde curls bobbing.

"You should see the state of the roads," Calliope added oh so seriously.

Her youngest sister, Edith, looked at her, wide-eyed. "You are glowing like the stars outside tonight."

Harriet knelt down and pulled her smallest sister close. Edith fit snuggly against her. Had she thought she couldn't feel anymore pleasure at the Yuletide season? If she had, with her sister tucked against her, she realized she would have been most mistaken.

Harry gazed into Edith's eyes and said lovingly, "Because I am so very, very happy and happier still that you are here."

"Rob insisted we come," her mother declared, clearly proud of her son-in-law. "And you will come to us in the morning before your Christmas dinner."

More tears stung Harriet's eyes. Goodness, she was tearful quite often now. She imagined it was the emotions that came with the gift growing inside her. As she lifted her arm and circled it about her mother's waist, she rested her head for a moment against her hip and savored the contentment flowing through her at being with her entire family.

How had she been so full of good fortune in her choice of husband?

How had Rob known that she would so miss her family? But, of course, he knew. He knew her. Knew her so very well.

At that moment, as if her thoughts had summoned him to their company, her husband and his group of friends came into the room, their spirits high.

She caught his eye and knew her eyes shone with her gratitude at his thoughtfulness.

He smiled at her, a knowing smile. They needed to exchange no words for Rob to understand that *this* was truly his gift to her. No bauble could ever surpass it.

She caught Heath and Mary exchange a quick glance before they both looked away and busied themselves with other activities.

Harriet knew then that there was a deep connection between the two. And whilst all the world might not understand a man like Richard Heath with a woman like her sister-in-law, Harry did. Richard Heath was a hero of a man, even if he preferred the rest of society not to know it.

As the gentlemen neared, wine was served and they all made merry about the room. They were playing cards, singing carols, and dancing when it pleased them for, as always, Drake chose his place at the pianoforte.

It was not until the clock began to near the stroke of midnight that they all gathered around the pianoforte and began to sing together the ancient carol *Good King Wenceslas.*

The rich tones of baritone and tenor blended with the ladies' and children's voices. And like bells, they rang through the room.

Harry's breath caught in her throat as she looked towards the windows.

Some force she did not quite understand pulled her towards it. And as the tones of the carol reverberated behind her, she gazed up and caught sight of a single star, larger than the rest, a diamond in the darkness.

Her heart swelled and, with all her might, she wished a Christmas wish. "Dear star," she breathed, "bring love and joy to our friends. Every single one but, especially, shine your blessings on our good friend Drake. . . and Mary and Heath. Let them know joy."

"Whatever are you doing, my love?"

She smiled softly as Rob's arms encircled her waist. His hands came to rest on her belly, resting gently. "Oh," she replied, her lips quirking in a smile. "Scheming, my darling. Scheming."

A low laugh rumbled from him.

At her words, the golden clock above the mantel began to chime midnight and as if in answer to her wish, the star so high above winked.

She gasped as she witnessed the sight, hardly daring to believe her eyes. Then she turned and slid her hands about Rob's shoulders.

"Happy Christmas, Rob."

"The happiest," he whispered.

And then he lowered his lips to hers in the sweetest, most passionate kiss they'd yet to share.

As she leaned back, she added, "With many more to come, Rob. With many more to come."

OTHER BOOKS BY EVA DEVON

The Must Love Rogues Series

The Rogue and I

If the Rogue Fits

Duke Goes Rogue

Live and Let Rogue

Rogues Like it Scot

A Rogue's Christmas Kiss

Rogue Be A Lady

The Dukes' Club Series

Once Upon A Duke

Dreaming of The Duke

Wish Upon A Duke

All About the Duke

Duke Ever After

Not Quite A Duke

A Duke By Any Other Name

My Wild Duke

If I Were a Duke

The Duke's Secret Series

A Duke for the Road

How to Marry a Duke Without Really Trying

THE EARL'S CHRISTMAS BRIDE

THE CAVENSHAM HEIRESSES

JANNA MACGREGOR

CHAPTER 1

The nobs, fobs, and fops careened around Cameron Dunmore, the Earl of Queensgrace, like spinning tops set loose on the streets of London. Hither and thither, grown men raced from shop to shop on Bond Street, packages overflowing from their arms. Since Scotland really didn't celebrate Christmas, such a sight should have been highly entertaining.

However, Cam ignored the bustle as he'd found what he was looking for, and she was definitely more intriguing than spinning tops. He leaned close to the boy selling roasted chestnuts from the small cart beside him. "See that lass yonder?"

The boy scrunched his nose then followed Cam's pointed finger. "Yes, m' lord." The boy's gaze jerked back to Cam. "You are a lord, ain' you?"

Cam nodded gently. "Scottish."

The boy nodded once in answer as if that one word explained everything, then rubbed his hands over the fire where he roasted his chestnuts. He blew out a breath, and a wave of white steam escaped.

"Now, I have a job for you." Cam pulled out a brand-new guinea and held it between his thumb and forefinger. "This is yours if you approach that bonnie lass and give her a bag of chestnuts." Magically, he pulled another from his cuff. "They're both yours if you give her the nuts and this." Gently, he reached into his waistcoat pocket and retrieved a rose posy, somewhat smashed but still vibrant in color.

The boy tilted his head and regarded him. With fingerless gloves on his hands, he nimbly took the posy, then straightened the flowers and tidied the lace ribbon holding the small bouquet together. Satisfied with his work, he tipped his hat to Cam. "I'll have 'er eatin' out of m' hand. Watch m' cart." Without waiting for a reply, he set off to give the tokens to the lovely lady not ten paces away.

Cam's gut tightened. He'd have approached her himself, but after the way he'd made a mash of proposing to her, he didn't want to cause her further embarrassment. He'd told her sister, Miss March Lawson, that he'd planned to come the next day and propose, but his only sister, Lara, had summoned him immediately.

Her husband of twelve years, Ewan MacFarland, had died of a lung infection. Beside herself with no one except Cam to turn to, Lara had begged for him to return to Edinburgh. Stupidly, Cam had sent a note to his one true love's sister, but not to her. He blinked and said a little prayer.

Father, give me another chance. It's all I'll ever ask for this Christmastide.

His hands tightened into fists by his sides as the boy spoke to Miss Julia Lawson, the fairest lass in all the kingdom. Even London, the most jaded town in all the British Isles, proclaimed her the bonniest lass of all. Even *The Midnight Cryer,* the vilest gossip rag ever to have been printed, had crowned her a diamond of the first water.

Cam had never understood the expression, but he knew it was something rare and beautiful—just like her. With eyes bluer than sapphires and hair that would rival the most brilliant sun, she stood at an angle that allowed him to gaze his fill.

He tried to shake the trepidation that felt like a dead weight on his shoulders. That Julia would welcome him with open arms was highly doubtful. After he'd raced back from Scotland, he'd called upon her twice at McCalpin House. Always she'd been "out" and unavailable. Both times when Cam had left, he'd felt as if someone was watching him. He'd always wondered if it was her, or just his wishful imagination. But today he'd found her and wouldn't let her go without first explaining himself. He could only hope that she'd not cut him directly and walk out of his life forever.

"Miss, I have somethin' for ye." The small boy who sold chestnuts on the street corner had left his post and stood before Julia. His big brown eyes and soft brown curls could melt an iceberg in the Arctic Sea. He handed her a bag of still-warm chestnuts, and a rather smashed but brilliant posy made up of red roses, her favorite. The roses reminded her of the bouquet that arrived on her doorstep every week.

"Oh, how thoughtful." She opened her reticule to retrieve a coin for payment. "Thank you. How did you know that I was hungry?"

Though he was only ten years old, her brother, Lord Bennett Lawson had accompanied her on the shopping trip for a few presents for their sisters and brothers-in-law. She had the perfect present, a new chess set, picked out for him, but she couldn't buy it with him here.

Bennett bent over the bag and examined the treasures inside. With an exaggerated inhale he declared, "Amazing that the vendors now offer curb service."

The boy selling chestnuts shook his head slightly as if unamused with her brother's quip. "It's from his lordship over thar." The boy jabbed a thumb behind his shoulder.

When Julia smiled then glanced to see who'd sent such delightful gifts, she'd half expected one of her sisters and their husbands to be the responsible party.

She definitely didn't expect to find *him* staring at her. From across the street, his gray eyes sparkled with a heat designed to melt away any remaining anger she possessed. His black greatcoat and beaver hat emphasized his towering height. The wind teased the long length of his chestnut-colored hair that brushed his shoulders. Why had he let it grow so long? He'd always been meticulous with his appearance, but truthfully, it only enhanced his masculine looks. Her heart always skipped a beat when she gazed at his sharply angled cheeks and handsome visage. Even with a slight bend on the bridge of his nose, he was striking. Ever since he'd told her that he'd broken it as a boy when his horse shied from making a jump, she'd been enthralled with him.

She pursed her lips. She didn't have time to waste another second with thoughts of Cameron Dunmore, the Earl of Queensgrace—the man who'd jilted her even before he'd asked her to marry him.

"Will he ever leave you alone, Jules?" Bennett asked with his green eyes trained on Queensgrace. "Don't worry. I'll handle this man-to-man."

Julia shot her hand out and grabbed Bennett by the arm stopping him from crossing the street. Unfortunately, it did little to tame the anger that had his nostrils flaring. "I appreciate what you're doing, but allow me to discourage Lord—"

"Lord Lawson." The earl stood before them, then elegantly nodded his greeting.

In retaliation, the young viscount lifted his chin another inch in the air.

Ignoring her brother's rebuff, Lord Queensgrace settled his brilliant gaze on hers. "Miss Lawson, may I say that you are a ray of warm sunshine from the heavens on this cold, dreary London morning." The earl took her hand and gently squeezed it in greeting, then executed a perfect bow.

Bennett rolled his eyes.

The earl witnessed her brother's dramatic gesture and laughed in response. The rich baritone wrapped around her like a heated blanket.

Which was appropriate as fire bludgeoned her cheeks. *Bother it all.* She didn't want any part of his six-foot three-inch lean muscular body to have an effect on her. Yet here she stood on a London street corner blushing like a school girl with her first crush—*never mind that he was her one and only crush.* At first sight, she'd fallen in love with him. She'd have followed him to the ends of the earth until he'd crushed her with a broken promise of marriage.

Discreetly, the earl slipped something into the boy's hand, and the little vendor skipped back to his cart. The earl's gaze strayed to his boots as if struggling to find something to say. He rocked back on his heels.

"Julia—"

"Cam—"

They both chuckled awkwardly at speaking over the other. But when their gazes caught, the familiar magical electricity that always coursed through her body when he was near, laid claim over her. Then their silence turned from tongue-tied to familiar. It was more like an unspoken conversation between them.

His gray eyes softened. *I missed you.*

And I you. Hot tears gathered in her eyes. *Every day since you left me.*

Don't cry, sweetheart. Give me another chance.

"Julia, we should leave." Bennett tugged his gloves tightly as he waited for her to lead the way.

"One moment, Bennett." To encourage her tears to evaporate, she turned her head into the biting December wind. It was pure madness to even consider allowing him back into her heart and into her life after he'd hurt her so.

The earl reached into his waistcoat pocket and withdrew a pristine embroidered handkerchief. Instead of blotting her eyes, she held it to her nose and inhaled. His fragrance of fresh cedar and sandalwood filled her lungs. It reminded her of the season and all those nights when he'd danced with her at the various *ton* events, practically declaring in front of London society that she was his.

She held his scent as long as she could. Another simple pleasure she'd missed in her life.

If she continued in such a manner, she'd make herself sick with grief. She was long past shedding tears and losing sleep over this man. "It's good to see you, Queensgrace. I wish you a happy Christmastide."

She clutched the handkerchief tight while she slipped her other hand through Bennett's fingers. In response, he opened his mouth to protest such an act. She could recite his protest from memory since she'd heard it so many times. He was a man and didn't need his sisters to look after him. She squeezed his hand with hers.

"Please, Bennett." She lowered her voice to a whisper. "It's not for you, but for me. I *need* to hold your hand." She'd steal whatever strength she could from his warmth.

"Wait. Please." Queensgrace took a step nearer decreasing the distance between them. His tall and broad physique blocked the north wind's assault. "Please, Julia...Jules. I beg of you."

Her gaze snapped to his. Her family's chosen nickname for Julia resonated like an invitation to sin when his deep heavy voice whispered her name. But the pleading in his words caught her by surprise.

"I'll get down on my hands and knees, if that's what it'll take. Let me at least have a chance to explain what happened."

She nodded once while still squeezing Bennett's hand. "Come tomorrow at nine."

It was Christmastide, and even Scottish louts, who were too handsome for their own good, deserved a little goodwill and glad tidings.

CHAPTER 2

The next morning, Julia and Bennett sat in the small breakfast room. Though the bold navy and red furnishings normally captured her attention, all Julia could do was stare out the window. Each tick from the longcase clock brought her closer to her meeting with Cameron.

Just seeing him after these six long months brought a plethora of emotions to the surface. Pleasure, pain, joy, and doubt mixed together in a perfect recipe for misery. For icing on the cake, her stomach had twisted into knots that even the most experienced sailor could never untangle.

Bennett leaned back in his chair and stroked the silky black fur of his cat, Maximus. Since the rest of family were out all day, Julia allowed Maximus the run of the dining room. When they lived at their ancestral seat of Lawson Abbey in Leyton, Maximus always found a way to join the family for meals. But when her oldest sister, March Lawson, had married the Marquess of McCalpin, the entire family, including her, their other sister Faith, and Bennett, had joined them. Julia closed her eyes and sighed.

Growing up at the Abbey was a fond memory. In their hometown of Leyton, she never had to worry with gossip or innuendos.

But London had taught her how plain meanness and vile rumors could ooze from society—particularly whenever they saw her. Six long months ago, everyone within the *ton* along with her two sisters, March and Faith, thought Julia would marry Cameron.

But then Cameron had disappeared like a ghost into a wall leaving Julia the one left with the carnage. The gossip rag, *The Midnight Cryer*, repeatedly said she'd been jilted. Within a week, she'd received a houseful of flowers from Cameron begging her forgiveness, but he'd never called upon her. A month later he sent another note explaining his sister had been ill. Because her complete recovery was questionable, he thought it unfair to keep Julia waiting for his return. Though they weren't officially betrothed, Cam released her from any promises that existed between them. He'd ended the note with a heartfelt wish that she find happiness in her life.

Julia had been devastated when she received his message. She'd always wondered if it was some excuse to hide the fact that he didn't want her anymore. But starting two months ago, beautiful red rose bouquets were delivered every week with a card simply signed, "Queensgrace."

Days then weeks passed by and eventually, her sister Faith had married the love of her life, Dr. Mark Kennett, a successful London physician. Both March and Faith had found the true loves of their lives while Julia had just mildewed like a piece of stale bread. But truth be told, Julia was ecstatic that her sisters had married such fine men. Secretly, she'd always held out hope there was a marvelous man for her to take as a husband.

Yet because of Cameron, damage had been done. Her reputation for one. After Cameron had left, no other suitor feigned any interest in her, the last unmarried Lawson sister. Which made it all the more understandable that she was angry with him. But if she was honest with herself, yesterday after she saw him, the anger that had festered for months slowly started to whither.

Her fickle heart.

"Since I'm the man of the house, I'll not allow that vagabond to upset you any further." Bennett straightened the simple knot of his cravat, then pulled down his waistcoat as if he'd not tolerate any nonsense from the earl.

"You're the man of the house because the marquess is out with March." She reached out and petted Maximus. The black cat slowly blinked his gold eyes, then rewarded her with a purr.

"You should have told March and McCalpin that Queensgrace would call this morning."

"I did." Julia slowly shook her head. "However, I need to talk to him by myself."

"Let me deal with him." Her ten-year-old brother announced. "I'll have him thrown out quicker than Maximus can catch a mouse."

She shouldn't be surprised at Bennett's reaction. He'd inherited their father's viscountcy when he was less than a year old. Every day, he became more and more comfortable in that role. Still, it amazed her that her little brother had turned into a very proper and very protective young man who would shield her at any cost.

"Bennett, what would I do without you?" Truly, Julia loved her little brother with all her heart. Though he irritated her at times, he was her *only* brother. She glanced around at the opulence of the room, but her gaze froze at the window. It looked like a blizzard had hit Mayfair. "Look it's snowing."

At the word "snow," Bennett put Maximus down then rushed to the window, proving he was still a boy interested in the season's delights.

"*Snow.*" Bennett motioned her forward. "Just look at it, Jules!"

She joined Bennett at the window and gazed at the sparkling blanket of white before them. Such a snowfall was rare in London, but this would guarantee a white Christmas since it was only three days away.

The clock struck half past the hour indicating that Cameron was late. A round of goosebumps prickled her skin like thousands of tiny icicle shards pelting her. She rubbed her hands on the upper part of her arms to keep the cold away. But it still didn't lessen the fear that he wouldn't come.

No matter what, this was the last chance she'd give him. She exhaled. Was she really considering giving him another chance? She shook her head to clear such thoughts.

She glanced down at Bennett fully expecting him to still be inspecting the snow. Instead her brother silently studied his shoe. "Julia?"

"Hmm?" A thick black curl had fallen across his forehead. With her fingers, she gently combed it back in place.

"Don't marry him," Bennett said softly. "I don't want to lose you, too."

She leaned closer until they were almost eye level. "What do mean 'lose me'?"

"Now that March and Faith are married, it's just you and me. You're the one who always quizzes me on my lessons. You correct my grammar and spelling." His cheeks blossomed into a fiery red. "You read to me."

"We read together," she added.

Discreetly, he nodded in answer. "You make time for me."

Really, this was so unlike Bennett to feel this insecure. Normally, he was the one who gave the orders to his three sisters when the siblings all gathered together.

"You and I are all that's left of the Lawson family." His voice cracked on the last two words which caused another bout of red cheeks. "He'll take you to Scotland, and I'll never see you. You're the only one I have left."

Those softly spoken words hit her square in the stomach and gutted her. She slowly blinked as she struggled for equilibrium.

When she'd been a little girl, Julia had felt the same fear when their parents had died. After suffering such a devastating loss, her place in the world had become untethered like an unmoored boat drifting aimlessly without the security of an anchor. Julia hadn't let her oldest sister, March, or her other sister, Faith, out of her sight for months. How could she even allow her darling brother to suffer the same?

She pulled him into her embrace and pressed a kiss on top of his head. His arms clenched her waist with a grip that defied his age.

"Bennett, look at me." She pulled away and tilted his chin until their gazes met. His eyes glistened with emotion, and her heart lurched at the sight. "The earl hasn't asked me to marry him. Don't worry about things that haven't happened. As long as you need me, I'll be by your side. Understand?"

He nodded once.

A footman cleared his throat. "Miss Lawson, the Earl of Queensland is calling. I put him in the front sitting room. Are you receiving?"

"Yes, I'll see him." She squeezed Bennett once more, then slowly released her hold. Instead of looking at her, he studied the falling snow outside. But she saw the lone tear that cascaded down his cheek.

He quickly dashed it away. "I'm going outside."

"After I finish with Queensgrace, I'll join you."

"I'd like that," he said softly, then quickly ran from the room.

Taking her heart with him.

CHAPTER 3

Cam stared at the falling snow outside the window that looked over the private courtyard at McCalpin House. Such a serene sight did little to calm his racing heartbeat that pounded in time with each movement of the second hand on his pocket watch. Each tick reminded him that he had to make the most of this chance to win Julia's hand.

"Hello, Cam."

Such a mellifluous sound instantly slowed the battering inside his chest. He turned and found a vision before him that would have made angels sing praise to the heavens.

His Julia.

All five feet five inches of her regally stood before him. Dressed in an azure brocade gown with a silver lace overlay, she was a vision of beauty.

God, how he'd missed her. When he'd left to attend his sister at the sudden death of her husband, he'd left his heart in her possession. Did she have any idea the power she held over him? Her incomparable beauty could make a man mute. But he couldn't let it overshadow what he'd come to accomplish today. He'd not leave without her agreeing to allow him another chance. Nor would he leave without giving her the proper kiss he'd meant to give her before he left.

"Julia—" His traitorous throat thickened. In an attempt to tame the riot of emotions, he cleared his voice.

Before he could say another word, she closed the distance between them.

With an elegant ease that betrayed the turmoil running amok through him, he took her hand and brought it to his lips. The warmth of her skin could soothe the most jaded of beasts, and he allowed his lips to linger and savor the softness that resided there.

"Would you care to sit, or will your visit be short?" she asked serenely. The blue of her eyes sparkled, and a smile tugged at her lips.

Her inner imp was in rare form today. She knew *bloody* well that he wanted to spend every moment of his life with her starting now, and if she didn't, she soon would. "My visit will be as long as necessary to convince you to give me a second chance at wooing you, lass."

The smile on her face could light the entire end of East London with its brilliance. "Ah well, then I don't think I have enough refreshments to serve you forever."

"Refreshments might only be a nuisance for what I have planned." Unable to hold his mirth at her antics inside, he laughed. Her eyes widened. But the feigned shock didn't fool him as her gaze grew even brighter.

"Why is that?" She walked to a Louis XV settee, then sat.

He settled beside her, then angled his body so he could see every glorious inch of her. "Because I plan to kiss you until you forgive me." He leaned closer until an inch separated their lips.

Her mouth formed a perfect and endearing "o." Her gentle breath brushed his cheek. He took a deep breath, then slowly released it to keep from possessing her on the sofa that very instant. Every blond hair, eyelash, and inch of her perfect skin was his, and he'd do his damnedest to convince her of it. "Julia, I've thought of this moment every single day since I left London." Gently, he took her hands in his. "I've thought of *you* every hour and minute of the day. I've dreamt of *you* every night."

One perfect eyebrow arched in disbelief, but she didn't release his hand which gave him hope.

"It wasn't fear of marriage or unwanted gossip that kept me from coming to ask for your hand last May." He bit the side of his cheek and hoped he'd find the words to convince her. "You must know that I'd have never left you to fend on your own had I known what those heathens at *The Midnight Cryer* were capable of printing about you and me."

Her face remained frozen, and she didn't offer a word.

"My heart was ripped in two by what they said I'd done to you. I never left you, lass."

"Yes, you did," she answered curtly. "For over six *long* months. Besides, your last letter released me from a betrothal that never existed."

"No." He shook his head. "Never. Do you know why?"

She bit one adorable lip in answer.

Unable to resist, he brushed his thumb across her plush lower lip. "Because I left my heart with you."

She slowly blinked her eyes and took a ragged breath. His Julia was strong, but she was hurting now. He hated to cause her pain, but as his dear mother had always said, *you must lance the wound before it can heal.*

"Then why didn't you come back for me?" she asked softly. "Why didn't you at least write more than the note that your sister was ill and might never recover? If I meant that much to you...was it just an excuse?"

"No, sweetheart." He ran a hand through his hair as he struggled to explain his actions. How to share the fact his sister had gone practically stark-raving mad after her husband had died? He'd never felt so alone or so helpless when he'd returned home to Edinburgh.

"It's true my notes were vague, but it wasn't something I could write about. In my missives, I told you part of the story but not all." Cam rested his elbows on his legs and studied his hands. He'd always been strong with brawny muscles and stamina, but Lara had taught him that physical strength meant nothing if you didn't have emotional fortitude. "After my sister's husband died, she called me home. What I found there would have made even a witch's toes curl."

Julia put one delicate hand over his. "If you're not comfortable sharing, I understand."

"No, I'll hide nothing from you." He placed his other hand atop hers. His were so much larger than hers, but the warmth of her skin beckoned him to tell her everything. "Lara had always put her family first. Her husband and her sons were everything in the world to her. I had always thought of her as the glue that held the family together. She'd always been able to handle anything that life could throw her way. When Ewan died that hadn't been the case—not when she left her two small boys alone to care for themselves when she disappeared."

"What happened?" Julia's voice had softened, but her eyes warmed with an unmistakable empathy at his words. "Where did she go?"

"I don't know. When I went to their home, I found my nephews alone, hungry, and dirty. She'd been gone for at least a week. I took Kinnon and Tavis to my estate. Once they were safe and sound, I assigned my housekeeper to look after them while I rode over practically every stream and crag in the highlands to find their mother. This went on for weeks. I couldn't trust that what I wrote to you wouldn't fall into the wrong hands." He shook his head gently as the feelings of helplessness and agony threatened to take his words. "I found her alone in a rundown shack not far from Edinburgh. I thought she'd be ruined if anyone found out about her disappearance." He swallowed the grip of emotion that held tight. "I didn't want any of it to taint you." He huffed a feigned laugh. "But I only put you in a worse situation."

"Oh, Cam. I'm so sorry," she said gently. "That must have been horrible for her sons...and for you. Where are Lara and the boys now?"

"I brought them with me to London. I couldn't leave them alone, but I couldn't stay in Scotland with you here."

She contemplated him with a depth that cut straight through him. In that instant, she saw all his faults and fears, and the truth hit him square in the chest. She'd never judge him or his sister. "I'm not certain I can find the words, but I hope you'll forgive me."

"Of course." A sad smile tugged at her lips. "I'd like to meet Lara. I'd welcome her as a friend and so would my family. And of course, your nephews."

"They'd be delighted, I'm sure. She's better now, but I can't leave her alone." Cam nodded. "Perhaps we can share a special Christmas celebration for all of us?"

An adorable expression of befuddlement crossed her face. "I didn't think Scots celebrated Christmas the way the English do."

"My mother was English and brought all the lovely traditions with her. Mince pies, mulled wine." His voice deepened as the urge to take her in his arms became overpowering. "Of course, the Scots brought the Yule log and mistletoe for sweet passionate kisses."

A soothing silence descended around them wrapping them in the safety of its comfort. A log fell on the fire, and her eyes brightened. It was the perfect timing to bring out the small gift he'd brought her. Truthfully, it was as much for him as for her, but it would bring her pleasure, or his name wasn't Cameron Dunmore. He reached into his morning coat pocket and pulled out the mistletoe posy tied with the ribbon she'd given him last spring as a token of her affection.

"Cam…you kept my ribbon?" she asked incredulously. Her eyes flashed as if truly happy making her even more beautiful.

"Next to my heart this entire time." He held the posy above her head and leaned close until no more than an inch separated them.

Her lips parted slightly, and he took that as a blessed sign from heaven that this Christmas celebration would be one forever engraved upon his heart.

He leaned until his mouth touched hers. The supple warmth from her lips was ambrosia, and he gently rubbed his against hers until the sweetest moan escaped her. Still holding the mistletoe, he wrapped her in his embrace and brought her close until her softness melded with his hardness. A perfect fit that he'd never tire of. Nor would he ever tire of her kisses. They had so much lost time to make up for. With his tongue, he traced the crease of her lips, begging for entry into her sweet mouth. With a soft breath she sighed, and he deepened the kiss.

"*Julia.*" A curt voice called from behind them.

Cam softly groaned before slowly pulling away. The desire in her eyes and the slight swelling of her lips from their kiss made him want to throw the intruder out so they could continue losing themselves in each other's arms.

"Queensland, I'll have you take your hands off my sister."

"Bennett, stop," she protested. "The earl is—"

"Mauling you," her little brother declared as he approached.

A perfect crimson blush colored her cheeks reminding Cam of the hot house roses he'd ordered for her to be delivered today. Reluctantly, he let her go and turned to face her irate brother. Though the boy only came to his chest, his demeanor indicated the young viscount had the anger of a man. Frankly, Cam couldn't fault him. If it was his sister who was being kissed like there was no tomorrow, he'd object too.

"Lawson, I apologize for getting carried away. But I can assure you that I have the best intentions here." Cam extended his hand for a shake man-to-man. "I want to marry your sister."

"You pig." The grimace on the boy's face was pure disgust. "Never in a million years will I allow that."

Julia seemed to come out of the sensual fog they'd created together. "Bennett, apologize to his lordship this instant," she demanded.

"That was ill-mannered of me. I apologize," he murmured. The young viscount's cheeks turned a color reminiscent of holly berries.

"Lovely." Julia's exuberant smile was a little too bright. "Then let's all go for a walk in the snow."

"No," Bennett declared.

Cam bit his lip so he wouldn't respond to the young lord's outburst. "Miss Lawson, perhaps another time."

Julia's brow creased. "Perhaps another time?"

Cam nodded. "May I stop by tomorrow?"

"Could you come this afternoon? I think the sooner we finish our discussion, the better."

An excellent sign that she wanted him back so quickly. "I agree."

"Come for tea?" she asked.

"It would be my pleasure," Cam said softly while ignoring the young viscount's look of outrage.

CHAPTER 4

That afternoon, Julia inspected the front salon and found it perfectly situated for the tea she would host. She plumped the red silk pillows that adorned the deep green sofas, then counted the plates, cups and saucers in the McCalpin china. Pleased with the festive look of the room, she walked to the side table where another massive arrangement of red roses accompanied by boughs of holly stood guard in a silver vase. She inhaled the sweet fragrance and instantly, all thoughts turned to Cam.

Her heart skipped a beat or two. Cam had made his intentions clear—he was once again her suitor. Secretly, she was thrilled that he was pursuing her so vigorously. If she'd only had to be concerned with herself, then her decision would be easy. But she'd not allow Bennett to feel discarded or ignored. Her brother was too precious to her.

But so was Cam. Though she'd been angry at him when she first saw him, once he'd explained his reasons for being vague in his letters because of his sister's disappearance, she'd been able to forgive him. Life was too short to hold such anger.

When he'd held her arms and kissed her, it'd been heaven. She realized her decision to let go of her anger was the right one. Their morning kiss had set a fire inside of her, and all she wanted for Christmas was more. Once their lips had touched, it had kindled the familiar yearning she had always carried for him. Any doubts she had about loving him evaporated like snow on a May day. She loved him with everything she possessed. Her heart, her happiness, her sorrow, and all her desires for life were his.

"Hello lass, I'm back." The deep reverberation of Cameron's voice pulled her from her musings, and she turned to greet him.

Resplendent in an iron gray dress coat and a green velvet waistcoat that magnified the color of his eyes and his chestnut hair, Cam was her very own Christmas present come calling.

She rushed to his side with her arms held out in greeting. "Cam, welcome." The breathlessness in her own voice couldn't be helped as she was delighted that he was here once again. Heat bludgeoned her cheeks from the intensity of his devouring gaze.

"Julia, you're more beautiful than the last time I saw you." He took her in his embrace, then gently kissed her cheek in welcome. When his cool cheek pressed against hers, it did little to bank the fire that had roared to life when she saw him.

"It's only been hours since we last saw each other." She took his hand and led him to the sitting area. "Come. Are you hungry?"

"Only for you," he whispered as he followed her.

Another blistering heat rolled through her. "Stop that or I'll not be able to serve you a proper tea."

A charming self-satisfied smile tugged at one corner of his mouth. "Hmm, I like the sound of 'not proper.'"

After they sat, Julia poured the tea and served Cam several pastries including a delicate mille-feuille filled with raspberry jam and several almond cakes sprinkled with crushed nuts. He accepted the plate without a word, then gently tugged her hand where a spot of jam stained her forefinger. Holding her gaze to his, he took her finger into his mouth and gently sucked.

She inhaled sharply as a bolt of electricity shot through her. The warmth of his mouth surrounding her skin melted her insides. But when his tongue moved against the sensitive skin, her gaze latched on his perfect lips and the slight indentation of his cheeks.

If she thought she'd experienced heat from his teasing, the sensations he summoned forth now could only be described as an inferno. Her heart pounded while her breath grew shallow. The force of their desire for one another caused a deep throbbing low in her middle. She closed her eyes so that all her concentration was focused on his mouth sucking her finger. Instantly, wicked thoughts of his mouth all over body threatened to consume her.

"Cam...I...we..."

He slowly withdrew her finger from his mouth but pressed it against his lips. "Hmm, I like that last bit, 'we.' Such a clever lass. I don't think I'll let you go."

The vibrations of his words against her wet skin caused her to shiver, but then his words registered. "What do you mean you won't let me go?"

"I want you all the days of my life and beyond, Miss Julia Lawson." He clasped her hand in his, then covered it with his other. "There is a solution to my dilemma, sweetheart."

The rumble of the endearment from his lips beguiled her, and she leaned forward. The smell of peppermint and male rose to greet her, and she breathed deeply.

"Marry me." He brought her hand to his lips. "Tell me you will, and I'll wait all day and all night outside McCalpin House so I won't miss your sister and brother-in-law's arrival. I'll fall to my knees in the snow and beg their permission." He pressed another kiss to the top of her hand. "I should have asked them before I spoke with you." He raked his free hand through his chestnut locks, the act causing a riot of curls to revolt by falling askew about his face. "But I love you, Julia. I don't want to lose you again."

The sincerity in his eyes caused her heart to pound against her ribs in a desperate act to reach him. "I love you," she said gently as tears flooded her eyes. "I always have and always will."

With the utmost care, he wiped one renegade tear that slid down her cheek, then pressed his lips against hers. With a sigh, she opened to him and he deepened the kiss. His sweet taste and gentle lips told her how much he cared. In return, she kissed him with the same tender affection.

When he pulled away, he released an anguished breath, then pressed his forehead to hers. "I take that as a 'yes?'"

She could only nod.

He pulled her to him, and she pressed her ear against the middle of his chest. His heartbeat pounded like a coach and four barreling through the English countryside.

"Julia, let's not wait. I'll secure a special license. We can marry tomorrow morning, then head to Scotland directly after. If the fates and weather are kind, we can be nestled in bed together at Dunmore Castle within five days." He pulled away and cupped his cheeks in her hands. "We can be home. We'll spend our first Christmas and then every single one thereafter that the good Lord gives us in Edinburgh."

"Wait! No." She shook her head gently. "I can't leave Bennett."

His brow creased into neat lines.

She swallowed taking the moment to find the right words. "Bennett will feel abandoned, and I can't do that to him. You see, after we lost our parents and March and Faith married, he and I have become very close. He'd feel as if I've broken my vow to him. I just promised him this morning that I'd never leave him."

A beautiful smile lit his face. "There is no cause for concern. He'll come with us. Does he have a tutor or a governess? They'll come with us. If not, then we'll find the best tutor that Edinburgh has to offer. My nephews will need one, too. They can all study together."

The beguiling gleam in his startling gray eyes took her breath. Her beating heart pounded against her chest to reach his. She wanted to agree, but for all her worth, she simply couldn't. "Cameron, no. I can't take him from my sisters. The three of us are his security. He's learning how to be a man. Our brother-in-law, McCalpin, has personally taken him under his wing. He's teaching him what it means to be a peer and what those responsibilities entail."

Cam's eyebrow shot up, and his voice deepened. "I could teach him those skills, my love."

"Of course, you can. But it's more than that." If she navigated successfully through their conversation, perhaps they'd find a solution that would be satisfactory for them all. "Cam, you're an honorable and caring man. I wouldn't have fallen in love with you otherwise. It's just"—she twisted her fingers together—"that he's lost so much in his short life. I can't take him from his family."

He let out a soulful sigh. "Jules, if I was only responsible for myself, I'd say yes to staying in London. But I have my sister and my nephews to consider. I'm the only man in their lives now. I finally have Lara settled where she's able to grieve without the need to flee. I brought her and the boys with me so I could keep an eye on them. I can't ask her to stay in London. She might become distraught or fall ill again. If that happens, I'm not certain I can put the pieces together." He took her hands in his and gazed deeply into her eyes. "I can't jeopardize my family's safety and happiness. Perhaps in a year or so, we could spend more time in London. Until then, Bennett is always welcome in our home."

She blinked twice to defeat the sting of hot tears that threatened to escape. She had no conception that love could be so painful. Though she desperately wanted a life with him, her promise and duty were to her little brother. Just as Cam's duty required he care for his sister and nephews. Burrowed within her chest, her heart revolted by skipping a beat, but there remained only one right decision.

"I'm sorry, Cameron, but I can't marry you unless we stay in London and Bennett lives with us." She released his hands. The movement made her feel adrift in a sea of doubt as her heart and her mind battled against one another until there was only one clear victor who would take all the spoils of war, or perhaps more appropriately, the spoils of her heart. "Perhaps too much has transpired between the two of us in the six months that we've been separated."

He picked up the sprig of mistletoe that had fallen to the floor, then stood slowly. He studied the small posy as if it held answers to all their dilemmas. Finally, his sigh broke the silence between them. "I'm sorry too, Julia. I thought we'd be able to see our way through my mistakes…but perhaps I was foolish to hope for a Christmas miracle."

With a quick bow, he took his leave. The logs in the fireplace crackled before a flurry of sparks exploded.

Exactly what had happened to her heart when he exited the room. It shattered into a million pieces, and she had no idea how to put it together again.

CHAPTER 5

Julia sat in the salon not seeing or hearing anything until she found herself surrounded by her sisters, March and Faith. Her oldest sister March had brown hair that only enhanced her exquisite attractiveness. Julia favored her other sister in looks, but Faith's real beauty derived from her endless patience and kindness to all.

The concern on their faces opened the floodgates of grief and tears over losing Cameron. March rocked her in her arms as she'd done countless times when Julia was little and needed comfort. But there was no comfort and joy to be found this holiday.

After she had no more tears to expend, she released a deep breath. "It's over."

"What is?" Faith asked. She pushed a perfectly pressed linen square into Julia's hand.

"Queensgrace's and my betrothal. He asked me to marry him today, and I said yes. Then within a minute, it was over." The words sounded caustic to her ears, but she wanted to share her brief elation that had turned into such painful sorrow. If love could be so cruel, then she'd vowed she'd never subject herself to such agony again. But both March and Faith were the most level-headed women she knew. If anyone could help her heal, it would be them. Lucky for her they were her best friends as well as sisters. "He wanted to marry quickly, then move to Edinburgh as soon as possible." She forced herself not to succumbed to another sob that threatened.

"Why?" March asked as she brushed the wisps of Julia's hair that had escaped from the simple chignon she'd crafted this morning. "When you told us that he was coming today, we were thrilled that things seemed to be working out for the two of you. Don't you want to marry him?"

Julia shuddered in her arms, then pulled away. "More than anything. He explained why he hadn't written to me with more information. His sister was ill." That's all she felt comfortable sharing of the Queengrace family's misfortunes. "It's all I've ever wanted, but I made a promise to Bennett that I'd not leave him. Nor would I take him away from you both."

"Our brother is keeping you from marrying Queensgrace?" Faith tilted her head and studied her. "Julia, the earl loves you."

"I doubted him after he left me, but I have no doubt he loves me now," she murmured. "Sometimes love isn't enough. There are too many obstacles." Julia rose from her seat and began to pace. "Once Bennett discovered Cameron was in town, he's become very protective of me."

"That sounds like our brother," Faith agreed.

March's eyebrows lifted. "He's always done that. Is there more?"

She nodded. "He shared that he was frightened that I'd leave him. He believes we're the last of the Lawson family, and if I married and left to live with Queensgrace, then he'd be alone."

March sighed woefully, and little lines of worry creased Faith eyes.

"I've neglected him," March declared. Elegantly tall, she rose from her seat and joined Julia beside the fireplace.

"No, March. After all you've done to hold our family together, it was time for you to find happiness with McCalpin. I've never seen you so happy," Julia wouldn't let their oldest sister bear this burden —not after everything she'd done for the family. For years, she'd been the father, mother, estate manager, and governess to her brother and sisters.

Faith released a deep breath, then joined her sisters before the warmth of the fire. "Since I married Mark, I've been helping him as the demand for his services as a physician is increasing weekly. Perhaps, we could find someone else to help."

"No." Julia grasped her middle sister's hand in hers. "When you're with your husband, you absolutely glow with brilliance. You deserve such joy and more."

Julia bit her lip as the memory of Cam's mouth against hers cascaded through her thoughts. All afternoon she'd replayed their kiss. She promised herself she would never forget the soft sweep of his lips against hers or the way he deepened their kiss with his tongue as it tangled with hers. Now she knew how perfect such a heartfelt caress could be. No wonder poets were so effusive in their praise of the act. To forego Cam's kisses forever was her definition of purgatory, but her first responsibility was to Bennett.

"Perhaps we should call a family meeting," March offered. "Bennett's never been shy about telling any of us what he wants or needs. With the four of us, perhaps we can come up with a solution that will benefit us all?"

Faith nodded. "Just like in the old days."

Julia smiled at the fond memories. Though they were once a ragtag family, they always had loved each other deeply, and even when their circumstances had changed from dire to everything spectacular, they were loyal to one another. That's why she couldn't forsake her little brother.

She smoothed her hands over her shirt. "A family meeting won't change my mind. I'll not leave Bennett. All my life you two have provided the security for our family. It's my turn. It's a promise I intend to keep."

March stared at her. "Julia, even if it means you'll lose the love of your life?"

Gathering certainty in her decision, Julia attended to the fire, then turned to face her sisters. "How could I leave our brother after I promised him I wouldn't? I above all understand that feeling of abandonment."

The pain on March's face didn't escape Julia.

"March, you were everything to me when I was Bennett's age. I hate to think how I would have survived the loss of our parents without knowing that you were there for me. Always." She straightened her shoulders in a sign of strength. "You both have your husbands and other responsibilities that you're responsible for now just as I have mine. I want to be there for Bennett. Even though he acts like a man, he's still a little boy that deserves comfort, love, and a sense of belonging. I can provide that stability if I'm here in London. I can't do that in Edinburgh. Cam even offered to have Bennett live with us, but I'll not take him away from both of you."

Their eyes widened in shock. Even the suggestion of taking their little brother from them was inconceivable.

"Even if it means you're the one that sacrifices your happiness?" Faith asked softly.

"Yes. Christmas is the season where we should think of others first," Julia answered. Her chest tightened.

Even if marrying Cam was the only thing she'd ever wanted for Christmas.

CAM'S LONDON TOWNHOUSE HAD ALWAYS BEEN A COMFORTABLE haven since he'd had it redecorated the first year he took his seat in the House of Lords. But the contentment he normally found within its walls had vanished. Even the Scottish tea he enjoyed first thing in the morning tasted like yesterday's bathwater.

He let out a deep breath as he studied the blanket of snow that covered the London streets outside his window. Would he ever find joy in the simple things in life again?

The inevitable answer of 'no' echoed throughout his musings. It'd been less than twenty-four hours since Julia had rejected his proposal. In that time, he hadn't come up with any additional arguments, let alone a sound solution to their problem. She needed London for her family, and he needed Scotland for his. Her sense of family and loyalty were some of her most endearing qualities. She'd shown that trait in abundance when they'd first met, and he'd been immediately smitten. That's why he could share so much and wanted to build a life with her.

He rested his head against the back of his chair and closed his eyes. He could propose that they marry, and she could stay in London when he had to travel to Scotland, but that left a bitter taste in his mouth.

He'd not leave his wife—his Julia again—ever.

But the truth was, she wasn't his.

"Cameron Alan Dunmore." Lara glided into the study. With her red hair and flashing blue eyes, she was a force to be reckoned with. "What have you done?"

Cam stood and studied her face. "Is something wrong?"

"Yes, something's wrong. I'm aghast. Are you really thinking of leaving London without your bride?" Lara softened her voice. "You love her, Cam."

He came around the desk and led her to the two matching chairs in front of the fire. After she was seated, he took the other. "Too much has passed between Julia and me."

Her brow creased. "Is it because of me and my illness that you can't see your way clear to marry Julia?"

He took his younger sister's hand and squeezed. "No. She won't move to Scotland, lass, and I won't leave you and the boys."

She took a deep breath and sighed. "You were always the protector, Cam." She leaned close to him and held his gaze. "But let me take that role now. I thank you for everything you've done for me and mine, but it's time to live your own life. I'm better now. I'd even say I'm stronger now than ever before."

He had to make the right decision. Lara had only recently sewed the pieces of her life together with a proverbial thread that was still new and probably fragile. He couldn't live with himself if she fell ill again because of him. "There's no denying you're stronger," Cam said softly. "But I'd never leave you and the boys. You're my family."

"And so is Julia," Lara answered with a smile, but she held his gaze. "Listen to me, Cameron." She squeezed his hand in a show of strength. "I know what it's like to lose the love of your life. I'll not let you forgo such a gift as true love."

"My lord, a boy who calls himself Lord Lawson is here to see you." His butler and man-of-affairs, Dougan Campbell announced. "What shall I tell him?"

Lara stood and kissed his cheek. A breathtaking smile lit her face. Such a rare sight was a brilliant present in itself. "Find a way, Cam. It's what I want for Christmas," she said softly. "Now, see to your visitor."

"Send him in." Cam answered. As Lara left, he dropped his shoulders. The young viscount probably still wanted to wring his neck for kissing his sister. Perhaps he should allow Bennett to do it. The pain wouldn't be any worse than the way his heart had been ripped in two after his last visit with his Julia. He closed his eyes. He was making himself sick with such thoughts. She wasn't his, and it appeared she never would be.

What a *bloody* happy Christmas this would be.

"Queensgrace?" Lawson entered the room.

Cam motioned him forward. The boy's normal bravado and keen sense of wicked humor were notably absent. Before Cam stood a tentative young boy, who seemed defeated.

"Lawson, I'm surprised you're here. What may I do for you this morning?"

"We need to talk man-to-man." Bennett's cheeks flushed, and he cleared his throat after his voice broke uncontrollably. A sign that the young boy in front of him would soon be on his way to manhood.

Cam blinked, then narrowed his eyes. The boy's face looked worried and a bit apprehensive. But Julia loved this boy with all her heart, and because she did, he'd welcome her brother into his home even though they both were aware that Bennett didn't trust him. "Come sit in front of my desk. Would you care for a tea or chocolate? The wind is particularly biting today."

The boy shook his head. "Thank you, but no. I'll be brief. Julia doesn't know that I'm here, and I'd like to keep it that way."

The boy's serious face gave Cam pause. "Would she disapprove?"

Lawson nodded gently. "After you left yesterday, Julia cried. I heard her tell my sisters that she couldn't marry you because of me."

The words were a direct punch in Cam's stomach, and he sucked a gulp of air. In all his years, he never recalled making a woman cry, and the fact that he'd made Julia, his love, cry left him reeling. "Lawson, I swear I never meant to hurt her."

With a slight nod that sent his black curls waving, the boy continued, "I'm aware that you love her, and this makes my confession doubly hard. I'm the one that made her cry. You see, I made her promise that she'd stay with me. But it was selfishness on my part. Julia, just like my other sisters, deserves happiness, and I know she'll have a happy life with you as your wife."

Cam leaned back in the massive study chair he'd had custom made to accommodate his long legs. The boy's solemn words were laced with contriteness. "That's very noble on your part, but I've never seen your sister as one who could be swayed if her mind and heart had decided another course." He leaned forward and rested his elbows on the desk as he regarded Bennett. "And if I could find a way around this predicament, trust me, I'd be on my knees in front of your sister right this minute begging her to marry me."

Bennett straightened in his seat and regarded Cam. "I've found a way. I've asked my tutor to recommend that I be admitted to Eton early for next term. March thought it best if I wait a year so I had the necessary academic foundation, but I don't want Julia to suffer because I'm still at home. I'll see if there are private tutors that can help me acclimate to the academics required by the school."

Cam sat there dumbfounded. The boy sitting before him would

make such a sacrifice for his own sister's happiness? "Bennett, you can come live with us in Scotland."

He shook his head. "I appreciate the offer, Queensgrace, but I need to think about what's right for my sisters. If I'm in school, then they can concentrate on their new families." The tiniest hint of an Adam's apple bobbed up and down on his thin neck. "They're all I have, and I'll see every one of them happy," he declared.

The unwavering strength in his voice that his decision was steadfast showed a maturity that grown men didn't possess. The Lawson sisters had raised a fine boy who would turn into a great man—sooner rather than later.

"It's my Christmas gift to all of them," he said. "Now, let me give you a piece of advice." He leaned close to Cam's desk, then lowered his voice. "Julia is shopping on Bond street for my present. Find her and walk with her a bit. She'll see how much she misses you. Tomorrow, McCalpin and March are having a Christmas Eve gathering for family and friends. I'm inviting you. You should ask her to marry you then." He winked, then delivered a sly smile. "No one can resist saying yes to a proposal on Christmas Eve."

Cam laughed at such an audacious comment coming from a ten-year-old boy. The charm he exuded would only increase the older and more confident he became. Ladies would soon be swooning at his feet. "And you know she'll say yes just because it's Christmas Eve, or is it because you have experience with the ladies?" He arched an eyebrow in obvious teasing.

"Well, McCalpin's cook is making me my very own Christmas pudding because she thinks I'm *enchanting*." Bennett waggled his eyebrows playfully. "But the answer to your question, Queensgrace, is no." He laughed in return. "Julia will say yes because she's madly in love with you."

Cam's heart swooped like a swallow returning home. Bennett truly knew the meaning of Christmas and the fact he was willing to sacrifice his own happiness for his sisters, particularly Julia, was awe-inspiring.

Having his heart desire's hand in marriage was everything Cam wanted this Christmas. Suddenly, a thought hatched that might make everyone's Christmas the best holiday ever.

"You're a man to be admired, Lord Lawson," Cam said. "You've given me some ideas. Where exactly did you say your sister is shopping?"

CHAPTER 6

Julia sensed Cam everywhere around her. From the scent of peppermint that reminded her of his kisses to the soft wool scarves that reminded her of his morning coat when his strong arms had held her. She could find a connection to Cam in every single item that surrounded her at Grigby's Haberdashery. With a deep sigh, she forced herself to admit it. After telling the earl she couldn't marry him, he haunted her day and night, particularly in her dreams when he'd take her in his arms and whisper sweet nothings while kissing her under boughs of mistletoe.

She shook her head slightly. She was a sorry example of a lovelorn goose. The quicker she finished her shopping, then the quicker she could prepare for tomorrow's small soiree at March and McCalpin's house. Most of McCalpin's family had traveled to Falmont, the Duke of Langham's ancestral home, for the holidays. But McCalpin and March, along with Faith and Mark, had friends who would visit tomorrow evening in celebration of Christmas.

Normally, she'd be overcome with excitement, but these past several days had taken the joy out of the simplest things, including the holiday.

"Hello, Miss Lawson," a whisky dark voice murmured.

Without looking up, she'd recognize that deep cadence anywhere. It was *him*. Her heartbeat accelerated that Cam stood beside her. She forced herself to look up, and the sight stole her breath. He was magnificent in a subtle plaid morning coat with a deep red waistcoat and dark grey pantaloons. His Hoby boots glistened even though the London streets were somewhat mushy from the snow that had fallen two days ago.

"My lord," she answered. She straightened her shoulders and forced herself to smile. Though she couldn't marry him, at the very least, they should be friends, even if her contrary heart protested such an outcome. "It's good to see you."

"Is it?" he asked. A wry smile tugged at the corner of his lips.

She blushed at his obvious teasing. "You know that it is true. Every time..."

He leaned down and his grey eyes studied her. Her heart fluttered in her chest as if desperate to break free and reach him.

"Every time what, sweetheart?" His words floated over her, then he did the unthinkable. He caressed her cheek with the back of his finger, the touch soothing but at the same time making her want more, causing a heat that could never be satisfied.

"Whenever you're near, I'm happy. But you know that." Unable to control her joy at seeing him, a tremulous smile crossed her lips. "When are you going back to Scotland?"

"I'm not certain." A scowl marred his handsome face. "My plans have been upended."

"Because of me. I apologize that caused you such an inconvenience." She bit one lip, and his gaze narrowed to her mouth causing a heated blush to bludgeon her cheeks. "I wanted to say 'yes.' You believe me, don't you?"

She loved him so much that her heart ached. How could fate be so capricious and cruel at the same time, particularly at Christmas, when it brought him back into her life, but then not allow them to be together.

"Julia, I do. At first, I wasn't certain after we last parted. But just seeing your beautiful face light up"—his gaze caressed every inch of her face as if committing it to memory—"makes me believe you love me."

They would soon part for good, and she never wanted him to doubt her true feelings for him. In the past, when she'd thought these last six months were hard, she had no idea what would face her. The next six months without him promised to be unbearable. She could only survive it, and the years that would follow, if he realized that she would always love him. She didn't expect him to wait for her while Bennett grew to adulthood. But she also didn't want him to think that she'd rejected him because she didn't love him.

He caressed her cheek again. "You're so precious to me."

A hateful tear crept into her eye as his words surrounded her. How could she give him up? Then reason took over from her wayward emotions, and she remembered her commitment to Bennett. She put her gloved hand over his and squeezed. "I want you to promise me something." Before he could answer, she leaned close. "Never forget that I love you and always will. You'll never be alone. Miles may separate us, but you have my heart forever."

Without giving him a chance to respond, she quickly leaned up on tiptoes and gently pressed a kiss against his mouth. No well-respected young woman did such an outlandish thing out in public, but she didn't care. Deep in her heart, the truth couldn't be denied. If she couldn't marry Cam, then she'd never marry. There was only man who could ever possess her heart, and she couldn't have him.

Before she said anything foolish or changed her mind, she darted out of the shop clutching the presents she'd carefully selected for Bennett.

At this moment, if she never celebrated Christmas again, it would be too soon. For the holiday only meant one thing to her now.

The day she lost the love of her life forever.

THE LASS'S BEHAVIOR LEFT CAM BEMUSED AND SOMEWHAT flummoxed. All he'd wanted to do was to inform her of his plans for how they could be together. He rubbed a hand down his weary face before he suddenly realized what had occurred. It was his very own Christmas miracle. Julia Lawson would love him, Cameron Dunmore, forever with every fiber of her being.

Just like he would for her.

Unable to control his glee, he laughed aloud. The shopkeepers, Mr. and Mrs. Grigby, looked up from their work and smiled at the sound.

He nodded his greeting to the middle-aged couple, then turned his attention to the shop window. His darling, the lovely woman who had captured his heart, beat a fast retreat down the London street as if the devil himself were ready to claim her. But Cam had no cause to worry as he'd already claimed that enviable spot.

Julia Lawson was his now and forever, and he knew exactly how to woo his Christmas bride.

She'd see exactly what a Scotsman does when he wants a woman to take notice.

CHAPTER 7

A new snow fell outside bestowing a holiday sparkle to the grounds of McCalpin House, but Julia couldn't muster any excitement. Crisp smells of the evergreen garlands and greenery that decorated the house filled the air. Guests surrounded her, and the sounds of holiday cheer melted together into a soft cacophony of merriment.

Never had she felt so alone.

March and McCalpin ushered a beautiful woman and two young boys into the sitting room. The woman was tall with dark red hair, and the boys resembled her. They were probably the wife and sons of some distinguished member of the House of Commons who her sister and husband had invited. The look of joy and contentment on her face pierced Julia's heart. Would she ever experience such feelings again? Not likely as her heart felt as if it had broken into a million pieces.

McCalpin stole a quick kiss from March under one of the bountiful boughs of mistletoe that seemed to reside over every doorway of the house. Those two were so in love, and their every action and deed seemed to magnify that fact.

Julia turned back to her study of the snow wanting the night to be over with. She was surrounded by Christmas cheer, holiday love, and she wanted no part of it. Tomorrow she'd go to church and pray that her heartache would lessen, but it was unlikely. Every breath and thought reminded her of Cam.

"Julia, may I introduce Mrs. Lara MacFarland?" Somehow March had sidled up beside her with the woman and her two boys. Bennett stood next to the boys with a beaming smile.

"How do—" Julia gasped in a very unladylike manner. "You're Cam's sister?"

The woman smiled. "Indeed, Miss Lawson. It's lovely to meet you." She leaned close as if divulging a secret. "I've wanted to see for myself the woman who had enchanted my brother all this time." Her warm blue eyes twinkled in high spirits. "I can see why." She turned her gaze to the two boys beside her. "May I introduce my sons, Ewan, age eight, and Cameron, age six."

Julia smiled. They'd been named after Lara's husband and brother. "Hello. I'm—"

"She's my sister," Bennett announced, then turned to the guests. "Follow me. I know where the mince pies are. They're the best in London."

The boys' eyes widened in awe at Bennett.

"Do you know how to play chess?" Bennett asked.

"Uncle Cam is teaching us," Ewan answered.

Cam MacFarland nodded. "But I don't understand it yet."

Bennett waved his hand beckoning the boys to follow. "Come on then. Let's pile a plate full of sweets, then adjourn to the library. My old chess set is there. It's missing several pieces, but we can still play." Bennett put his arm around the littlest MacFarland lad. "Don't worry, I'll help you." He led the boys away all the while chatting about his prowess as a chess master.

Lara's smile made her radiant as she watched her sons retreat with Julia's little brother. "Lord Lawson has captivated my sons. I think they both have a serious case of hero-worship."

Julia smiled in answer. It was the first hint of lightness she'd felt all evening. "Thank you. My sisters and I adore him. I'm afraid we've probably spoiled him."

Lara leaned close. "That's what we're supposed to do with the irresistible men in our lives. Of course, that's my opinion, but wouldn't you agree?"

Julia grinned. "As long as they spoil us on occasion."

Lara laughed in answer. "I concur." Then her eyes grew misty. "I always spoiled my Ewan, and he did the same for me."

Julia grabbed her hand and squeezed. "Queensgrace told me about your loss. I'm so sorry."

Lara blinked rapidly, then squeezed in return. "I was fortunate that I had so many lovely years with him. After my husband died, I was so lost and ready to give up everything, but my brother made me realize that those two little men needed me to spoil them, too." She glanced around the room and took a deep breath. "May I call you Julia?"

"Of course," she replied.

"Julia, the one thing I've learned in this life is that when love is yours, you must hold on to it for as long as you have and cherish it." Her eyes glistened with emotion. "I lost my true love, but I never had any regrets. My husband and his love were the most precious gifts I'd ever received."

Before Julia could respond, a murmur went through the room, then complete silence. She looked up and immediately brought a hand to her mouth. Somehow, while she was talking with Lara, the entire room behind her had become flooded with vases of various shapes and sizes. Big bouquets of red roses crowded with boughs of mistletoe decorated the floor, the tables, even the fireplace. In the midst of all the green and red, Cameron stood in the doorway in full Scottish dress. With snow covering his long hair, he looked like an ancient warrior prepared to win at any cost.

Instantly, her heart skipped a beat at the magnificent sight. But he stole her breath when his gaze captured hers. With heat and fire in his eyes, he came toward her without glancing at anyone else. Everyone stood off to the side to allow him a clear path.

In an instant, he stood before her. With his navy velvet evening coat, red and blue kilt, and matching waistcoat, he towered over everyone. The adornments on his sporran and the silver hilt of sgian-dubh glittered in the candlelight. Her breath caught at such a magnificent sight, and all she could do was stare.

"Julia, my love," he said tenderly. "Your brother and my sister helped me come up with a solution to our dilemma."

"What? When did they do that?" she asked incredulously as her breath grew shallow.

"Bennett came to see me yesterday right after Lara did." Cam took her hand in his and raised it to his lips. "Your brother loves you dearly. He offered to go to Eton early so we could marry."

Tears came to her eyes at her darling brother's action. Just then, she caught Bennett's gaze when he entered the room with Cam's nephews. He slightly bowed his head in acknowledgment.

"But I couldn't let the lad make such a sacrifice. Not when it came to his lovely sister. But with his and Lara's help, I thought of another solution."

Her heart was thudding against her ribs. Was it possible that she'd have her Christmas wish and be able to marry the man she'd fallen in love with? Tear streamed down her face, and Cam gently wiped them away.

"Don't cry, love. I promise you'll be happy if you still want me." The tenderness in his words flooded her with emotion.

"I'll always want you." She took the lapels of his jacket in her hands and gently pulled him closer. "Don't you know that? I love you with all my heart."

"And I love you with everything I am and everything I have to offer." He brushed his lips against hers, then pulled away.

The sound of happy sighs and gentle laughter filled the room, but she concentrated on the man she loved with every ounce of her being who stood before her offering the world.

Suddenly, he dropped to one knee while holding her hands. His strength and vibrance apparent in the heat of his large hands. "I've spoken with Lara and her sons. I told them I couldn't lose you, and like Bennett, they helped me find a way."

She couldn't answer as her throat tightened. Tears streamed down her face.

"They want to move to London. Lara wants a fresh start for herself and the boys here. Edinburgh holds too many painful memories for her. I don't have to return."

One of her hands flew to her mouth at his words.

"Now, I can do this properly and with the blessings of your family."

Julia's gaze darted to where Bennett, March and McCalpin, Faith and Mark stood. March and Faith's eyes glistened with emotion. McCalpin and Mark wore endearing smiles, but Bennett's smile took her breath away. He was beaming.

"Cam," she whispered.

He brushed another wayward tear from her cheek.

"Miss Julia Lawson, will you do me the greatest honor I could ever receive and be my wife?" The richness of his deep voice held a tenderness she'd never heard before. It filled the room with love and affection. "I bequeath my heart, my love, and everything I am to you. I promise to love you more each day and ensure your happiness to my utmost best. Please, give me your heart and hand in return."

"Forever," she whispered while she nodded for the crowd.

As applause and cries of good spirits rang out, Cam gracefully came to his feet and took her into his embrace. It felt like home, and Julia lifted her lips to his.

When his lips met hers, he tenderly kissed her. But as they stood in each other's arms, their passion swirled around them, binding them together in love while encompassing them in a cherished desire that would last forever.

Gently, Cam pulled away and cupped her cheeks in his warm hands. "I've got a special license in my pocket. We can marry tomorrow and make Christmas our special day always."

"I'd like that," she said shyly. "I don't want to spend another night alone without you."

"Clever lass." A grin spread across his face that could only be described as pure sin. "I was thinking the same. Come. Let's go somewhere we can have a little privacy."

Cam led her through the French doors to a balcony overlooking the main courtyard of McCalpin House. As he wrapped her in his arms, she forgot the cold and everything else except the man holding her tenderly.

"I love you, Cameron Dunmore. You've made me the happiest woman in London."

"I love you, Julia Lawson." He dipped his head to hers and gently rubbed his nose against hers. "You've made me the happiest man in Edinburgh. I've rented two townhouses next to each other. Lara and the boys will move into one, and we'll move into the other with Bennett." He pulled her tighter and pressed his lips to her temple. "We can move in immediately. Tomorrow if you like."

Julia tilted her head. "I hope I can wait that long."

Just then snowflakes danced through the air proving how magical the night had turned.

Cam chuckled as he looked up at the snow dancing in the sky. "Julia, look." He pointed above where a bouquet of mistletoe hung from the overhang above them.

"Did you put that there," she teased.

"And ordered the snow." Gently, he kissed the tender spot below her ear. "Anything for my Christmas bride."

He took her lips with his and kissed her with a tender passion that made her believe all her dreams had come true. She returned his kiss with an equal passion that told him she'd never let him go. In that perfect moment, their lips met in a searing kiss that bespoke of Christmas, magic, and the promise that such miracles would always be a part of their lives—forever.

ALSO BY JANNA MACGREGOR

If you enjoyed *The Earl's Christmas Bride* (The Cavensham Heiresses) by Janna MacGregor be sure to look for other titles in this series.

THE BAD LUCK BRIDE

THE BRIDE WHO GOT LUCKY

THE LUCK OF THE BRIDE

THE GOOD, THE BAD, AND THE DUKE

where you'll find the next thrilling installment in this series—

available November 28, 2018.

To find out more about Janna or to sign up for her newsletter visit www.jannamacgregor.com. For reminders when new books come out and when backlist titles go on sale, follow her on BookBub @JannaMacGregor.

EXCERPT: THE GOOD, THE BAD, AND THE DUKE

Book 4 in The Cavensham Heiresses Series
by Janna MacGregor

"Now just a minute, sir," Daphne interrupted. "I happen to be—"

"Lady Moonbeam," a voice behind her announced. "My escort for the evening."

The deep sound wrapped around her in a polished smoothness that reminded Daphne of a calm bay at night off the Adriatic Sea. It was smooth as glass, but she knew that beneath the surface there lurked unfathomable danger. The Duke of Southart could blow everything out of the water for her with one word or command.

Why had she even wanted him to be here?

She turned and faced him. He moved in front of her and blocked the view of the gaming room. His cool gaze locked on hers, and the slight smile made him even more handsome than she remembered. Lit from within, his eyes blazed with a hint of temptation or mayhap seduction.

Most likely, it was just surprise.

Daphne exhaled and pushed her consternation aside for another day. She had to find the kitchen. The cook would know the whereabouts of the boy.

"Come, Moonbeam," Paul whispered. He'd leaned close enough that she could smell his fresh, clean sandalwood scent. He extended his arm in a command for her to take it, then directed his attention to the major baboon. "Why don't you alert my footman that Lady Moonbeam and I are ready to retire for the evening."

"Yes, Your Grace." The majordomo nodded and snapped his fingers at one of the attendants who worked the floor of the gambling hell.

Before she could say a word, the summoned attendant was halfway out the door.

She and Paul faced each other like two ships ready to commence fire on the open seas. "You had no right to interfere." She ignored Paul's offered arm, and there was enough hiss in her voice to alert him that she wasn't happy. "And quit calling me that ridiculous name."

Paul grinned, and it transformed him from an arrogant aristocrat accustomed to getting his way into a man who took her breath away. Without taking his eyes from hers, he addressed the majordomo. "My good man, you've seen what type of mood she's in. Might there be a place where Lady Moonbeam and I might have an intimate conversation for a few minutes before the carriage is brought to the door?"

"Of course, Your Grace. If you and *Lady Moonbeam* will follow me."

PAUL WAITED UNTIL THE MAJORDOMO SHUT THE DOOR TO THE PRIVATE room before he addressed Daphne. "Imagine my surprise and pleasure to find you standing in the middle of the Reynolds. Unfortunately, for both of us, women aren't allowed, and there's no exception for the sister of the Marquess of Pembrooke." With a purposeful insouciance, he strolled to the side table against the wall where an open bottle of chilled champagne waited for him. He'd say one thing for the Reynolds brothers—they took care of their guests whether expected or not. "May I pour you a glass?"

"No, thank you." Daphne straightened her shoulders.

Her prickly mood and appearance reminded him of an inquisition, and he was the examiner.

Interesting, since he hadn't asked her a single question—yet. He poured a glass and, without taking his eyes from hers, took a sip. An excellent vintage, but too sweet for his tastes. He much preferred the brut variety, so he replaced the glass.

"Moonbeam, I thought with our history, you'd share without me having to ask." He feigned a sigh and placed his hand over the middle of his chest.

"Please stop calling me Moonbeam." She tipped her head and regarded him like an unwanted interruption. "To answer your question, I'm looking for someone."

"Aha." Though he said it in a lighthearted manner, his stomach twisted at her confession.

The thought that Daphne Hallworth would risk her reputation for some reprobate who frequented a place such as the Reynolds made him want to curse the vilest oaths he could conjure. There wasn't a single man in the place he'd allow to attend her.

Shocked at the intensity of his feelings, he drew a deep breath. The only reason for such a strong reaction had to be his protective instincts. He was simply concerned for her welfare much like a brother. Granted, he'd seen her at Langham's house and at a handful of social events, but they barely spoke. Yet she'd always left an indelible impression on him. The reason didn't escape him. She was striking.

He shook his head to clear such inane thoughts. He would never *ever* in his entire life as a reprobate consider Daphne Hallworth a sister. "Who is it?" He asked the words with a nuance designed to learn her secrets.

"No one you would know." She turned toward the door. "I'll leave you to your evening, *Your Grace.*"

"Stop, please. Someone might recognize you." In a stealth move, he followed her. By the time she'd twisted the knob, he rested his palm against the door, thwarting her escape.

"Moonbeam, you can't go out there without a proper escort. Where you go I go."

She turned around and flattened her back against the door in a show of defiance. "Please, I would hate to ruin your plans or festivities."

The urge to whip out a witty quip fell silent when he caught Daphne's gaze. She looked like a devil's angel with her dark hair, ethereal silver eyes, and those strawberry-colored lips.

Any sin she offered, he'd have no hesitation rising to the challenge.

He leaned in close. Her chest rose and fell with a rhythm that drummed like a well-crafted metronome, and his heartbeat joined into the melee with abandon. Daphne's warmth and her delightful scent of lavender and woman transformed into a witchery he couldn't resist. He drew nearer until his breath mingled with hers.

"You're not ruining anything." He lowered his voice. "In fact, my night became much more interesting since a beautiful moonbeam appeared."

Her black lashes drifted down when she leaned just a fraction closer. His chest swelled in response. She was affected as much as he was.

"Shall we sit until your carriage is ready?" Her breathless sigh was a welcome distraction and indicated her wariness was fading.

"After you." Taking several steps back, he swept his arm toward a matching pair of club chairs that faced the fire. Her quick acquiescence meant it would take little effort on his part to find out whom she intended to meet.

A gentle smile adorned her face and locked him in place. She charmed him in returning one to her. When she held her smile a little too long, he instantly recognized his mistake. With her hand behind her, she opened the door and flew down the hall without a look back.

"Bloody hell," he muttered. If she returned to the game floor, her reputation would be in tatters if some lowlife libertine recognized her. There was only one thing he could do—he gave chase.

He, the Duke of Southart, had to catch a moonbeam.

SILENT NIGHT

A 1797 CLUB STORY

JESS MICHAELS

CHAPTER 1

December 1815

Charlotte Hoffstead, Duchess of Donburrow, moved through the quiet halls of her country home with a soft smile. She loved this place. It was a beautiful estate, situated on a cliff above the sea. The views were magnificent and the grounds well-tended and stunning.

Right now it was a quiet place, with just her little family in residence, but that was all about to change. In two days, these rooms would be filled with laughing family and friends, and their giggling children. They would boisterously sing carols by the fire, she had heard a rumor that the Crestwood family intended to put on a play for an entertainment, and there were a dozen other Christmas Day excitements to look forward to.

Yet today a cold rain fell outside, rapping on the windows and it put her to mind of a Christmas five years past now. A long time ago, before she had married the duke. Before she had called this house her home.

A Christmas when she'd thrown caution to the wind and made seduction a weapon against her now-husband, Ewan. It had been a scandalous plan, one that could have just as easily destroyed her hopes rather than given her the future she'd dreamed of.

And yet, somehow, it had worked. Ewan had surrendered to her, despite the years of heartbreak and rejection that had once separated them. They had fallen deeply in love and married swiftly enough to cause gossip in every corner, and the past five years of their marriage had been filled with love and laughter and joy beyond compare.

So she loved this time of year. Loved it for the traditions and the gaiety, yes, but loved it more because the holiday had given her the opportunity all those years ago to receive the greatest gift of her life: the man she loved to distraction.

Now she could only hope he would equally love the present she had in mind for him this year.

She smiled as she began to pass by the music room. Before she could fully do so, a hand snaked out from the chamber and caught her elbow. She laughed as she was tugged inside by her husband. He wrapped his arms around her as he used their combined weight to shut the heavy door. As he kissed her—gently at first, sweetly, then with more force, more promise—he reached around her backside to lock the door.

"Your Grace," she giggled breathlessly as his warm mouth slid to her throat. His hands cupped her bottom as he lifted her to grind against her gently. "Is *this* my gift?"

He lifted his head from her throat and speared her with a pointed and playful glare. He didn't respond in words, though. Ewan had been born without the ability to speak. That fact had caused him a great deal of pain over the years. His mother and father had abandoned him and his family had fought to keep him from inheriting.

Charlotte had never thought anything less of him, though. As children, he had been close friends with her brother Baldwin, the Duke of Sheffield. Charlotte had even helped Ewan develop a complicated hand language she and Ewan still used to this day.

But in this moment, he needed no words, nor did she as he

pushed her toward the settee in the back corner of the room. So often that was true. They were so connected now, so in sync that they only needed a look or a smile or a touch to convey a hundred magical experiences.

This was one of those times. She shuddered with pleasure as he laid her back against the settee, covering her with his weight. Her arms came around his back and she smoothed the lines of muscle there, whispering crooning sounds of pleasure and encouragement. He responded by catching the fine silk of the edge of her dress and hitching her skirt up while his mouth continued to plunder hers.

She sank into the passion, something that had never faded since the first time she'd dared test him with it. Not even all the years they'd shared, nor the children who demanded their time, nor anything else that had passed between them could cool it. Their desire was as constant as their love.

He found the slit in her drawers and drew back to meet her eyes as he pushed his fingers past it. She opened her legs a fraction to allow him greater access. He traced the shape of her sex gently. She shivered. He knew exactly how to touch her. Exactly how to move those rough fingertips across her lower lips, then spread them open, then stroke her once, twice, swirling his thick thumb around the sensitive bud of her clitoris.

"Ewan," she gasped, turning her face into his neck as pleasure began to mount. "Please, please."

He grunted from deep within his chest, then stood up. She held his gaze as he slowly unfastened his trousers and let his cock bounce free. She sat up slightly, reaching for him, stroking him with her hand, then smiling at him with wicked intent before she let the tip of her tongue trace the head of him.

His eyes widened, pupils dilating with pleasure, but then he shook his head at her. He pushed her hands away as he caged himself over her. His mouth found hers, driving hard and insistent. She felt him position himself at her entrance, and then he was sliding home.

She arched beneath him as he seated himself fully, moaning

against his kiss as he ground his hips just right. The man was magical, made for her. She for him.

He stroked, over and over, heavy and hard, grinding against her to stimulate her perfectly.

She came in a rush, jolting against him as he continued to thrust, thrust, thrust until she feared she would go mad with the pleasure that never ended. Only when he stiffened above her, his seed spilling hot inside her clenching body, did she find full relief from the mobbing crest of sensation.

He collapsed down over her with a guttural sound of relief. He kissed her neck, stroking his hands over her sides, feeling her body almost like it was the first time they'd done this. Like it was all new and wonderous. For a little while, they just lay that way, the silence comfortable, as it always was.

At last he sat up, giving her a little more room. His face lit up as he smiled at her, then he signed, "You cannot truly think that orgasms are your Christmas gift, Charlotte."

She giggled at his return to the conversation from before her surrender.

"I would not mind if they were," she said. "Although, to be fair, you are so good at giving them, they're really a regular gift. I will have to keep needling the truth out of you and guessing what it is you have in mind for me." She glanced over at the clock on the mantel. "Oh damn, you do make me forget the time. The children will be awake from their nap soon."

She knew their family was an oddity in some ways. Outside of their group of closest friends and family, most lords and ladies were not close to their children. Detached affection was the popular method of childrearing. But her own closeness to her family and his terrible distance from his had made them both thwart the common wisdom. And their home life was better for the deep and powerful attachment they both felt for their children.

Ewan's eyes danced even as he signed, "Are you certain we cannot send them off to the village or something for a few hours and continue to explore this orgasm as gift idea of yours?"

She swatted him playfully. "Jonathon is three and Abigail is not even two. Great God, what would you have them do alone in the village?"

"Entertain everyone with how adorable they are?"

She shook her head and sat up, adjusting her skirts before she got up and moved to the mirror along one wall. She fixed her hair and watched in the reflection as Ewan got up and trudged his way through fixing himself, as well.

She turned to stick her tongue out at him playfully. "Come now, don't act as though I *never* indulge you. You know I would spend a whole week in bed with you if we could."

"Soon," he signed with a wicked wink.

She laughed. "Yes, I cannot wait. Isabel and Matthew are taking the children in February so you and I can have an extra special escape to London." She could already picture all the romantic fun they could have together. "But this is *Christmas,* Ewan! There are a hundred wonderful things to do with our family and you will not convince me to run away with you now."

He waved his hand, as if he were surrendering even though he knew she was wrong. She giggled as she stepped up, settling against his side as he slung an arm around her. They walked to the door together. He unlocked it, and they stepped into the hall.

CHAPTER 2

Ewan loved the feel of Charlotte tucked into his side. She just fit so perfectly there. It was strange to think that anything had ever made him believe she didn't belong with him, or more aptly, that *he* did not belong with her. But a lifetime of abuse from his father and brothers over the mutism he could not change had damaged his view of himself.

And yet Charlotte had seen through it all. Seen the man he really was. Seen the man he could be. She had taught him, day by day, year by year, to love himself as much as she loved him. That he was worthy of it.

He squeezed her a bit tighter as they stepped forward, but they had not made it three steps when there was a great sound of screeching from down the hallway that could predict only one thing. Charlotte laughed as their two children, Jonathon and Abigail, came rushing up the hallway at full speed. Little Abby's hair bobbed around her face, the fine locks free from their ribbons as usual.

Ewan released his wife and dropped down to his haunches, opening his arms as the two hit him at full force. He toppled backward, clutching his chest playfully as if he had been shot down by their attack.

"Papa, Papa!" Jonathon squealed, his fingers moving wildly in the same finger language Charlotte and Ewan had designed decades ago.

It warmed Ewan's heart to see it. No one else in his life understood more than a word or two, not even their friends or family, but Ewan's children had picked it up at the same time they were learning words. Both had fallen into its use as if it were second nature. Sometimes he wasn't even sure they knew they were signing while they spoke.

Ewan grinned as he signed out, "You are screaming the house down. What is it? Are the dogs loose? Is the house on fire?"

As he signed, their youngest child, Abigail stared and moved her fingers in time with his, mimicking his movements, expanding her understanding of the family vocabulary. His heart swelled at the sight.

"We don't have dogs, Papa!" Jonathon said, his tone filled with incredulity.

"Of course, yes," Ewan signed as he glanced up with a grin at Charlotte. She was beaming back at him. "How silly of Papa not to remember. Perhaps we should get a dog, though, yes?"

Both the children's eyes lit up, and Ewan could hardly contain his glee at their reaction. He and Charlotte were planning just that as their gift for the holiday. His cousin Matthew would bring the pup today when their family arrived from London. He could hardly wait to see the reaction when they arrived.

Charlotte leaned down and touched his shoulder. "I have a few things to attend to," she said softly. "I'll come find you later."

He nodded. She blew him a kiss as she headed up the hall to continue whatever duty he had interrupted with his insistence that they explore pleasure earlier. He stood, reached out to catch each child's hand, and together they walked up the hall together to the parlor.

Perhaps other members of the *ton* would have found this bond he shared with his children to be odd. But he had felt the sting of hate from his family, he was determined that his children only experience the deepest love. Aside from that, he adored the time they spent together, playing and growing closer.

Even now, they sat on the floor in the parlor together, happy as three peas in a fire-warmed pod. The children had been playing here earlier in the day, and the toys that had been left behind were still there to enjoy together. He helped them build a block tower, changed the nappy of one of Abby's dolls and engaged in a battle with militia on horseback where he was trounced by the other side.

But after a while, Ewan touched each child's hand to get their attention and signed, "We have serious business to attend to."

Abigail's wide eyes, blue as her mother's were solemn. "What Papa?" she asked, her tone still soft and babylike.

"Two days until Christmas," he signed. "And we need to figure out what you two are giving to Mama as a gift."

Jonathon puffed out his chest with pride. "I drew her a picture," he said, "of you fighting a dragon, Papa."

Ewan nodded his head slowly. So that was what the scribbles he'd seen a few days before were meant to be. He would be sure to mention it to Charlotte so she could properly identify the gift upon opening it.

"What about you, sweet?" he signed to Abigail. "Miss Foster said you were working on a song."

"Song!" Abigail repeated, and then proceeded to launch into an off-key and boisterous singsong about a mama who was so pretty. It seemed to go nowhere in particular and there were no verses to speak of, but he was certain Charlotte would know all the words before Christmas day had ended.

He grinned as she finished the rambling performance and clapped his hands before he signed, "Wonderful. Good, that is taken care of. I know she'll love it all."

"What are *you* getting Mama?" Jonathon asked as he turned his attention back briefly to the blocks on the floor.

When he looked up again, Ewan signed, "I have a beautiful ring for Mama, with a stone that is as pretty as her eyes. Do you think she'll like that?"

"Pretty wing?" Abigail clapped her hands, for she was just becoming interested in dresses and hair ribbons and her mother's jewelry. "Oh yes, Papa."

"That's a secret, though," Ewan signed. "No telling."

"Yes, Papa," the children repeated.

"Mama has a secret," Jonathon said absently, as he picked at the paint on the block in his hand.

Ewan wrinkled his brow at that idea. Charlotte did not keep secrets, he knew that. Of course, the boy likely meant a secret about her gift for him. She had been looking very sly every time she teased him about it.

"Oh yes, what secret is that?" he signed.

"A baby," Jonathon said.

Ewan blinked. Jonathon had to be wrong, of course. Not because it wasn't possible. They made love often and were never careful, but Charlotte had said nothing about being with child again. "What?" he signed.

Jonathon stacked his blocks so slowly that Ewan was tempted to draw his attention. But at last he said, "She was talking to Miss Foster about needing to ready a room for the baby. They were talking about colors and finding the cradle in the attic. Then she said to be sure to be quiet because it was a secret."

Ewan's lips parted at his son's innocent words sank in to his mind and spirit. This seemed like far more than just some misunderstood comment. There was so much detail in Jonathon's tale.

Could it be true? He racked his mind for the signs he might have missed. And found them. Charlotte *had* been a little more tired as of late. She slept a bit longer in the morning and started yawning earlier in the night. He'd dismissed it as a reaction to the cold winter up here by the sea. Now it made more sense.

She'd also occasionally felt ill during the last few weeks, especially before she ate in the morning. During her prior pregnancies, both those things had been the signs that she was breeding.

He paced away to the window, staring out at the foggy rain and the swirling sea beyond it. He hardly registered any of it. All he could think about was the fact that Jonathon might be right in what he had overheard. Ewan would be a father again.

Delight was his first reaction, rushing through him from head to toe like the flush of new love.

But it was swiftly followed by another emotion. One that pushed aside the first and made itself more known. Concern. Why would Charlotte tell their nurse about the baby before him? Why would she want this news to be a secret from him?

He glanced over. The children were oblivious to his changed mood as they continued to play on the rug. He moved to the fire. Above it a portrait of him and Charlotte hung. It had been painted just after their marriage five years ago. He could see the lines of worry about his eyes, captured unknowingly by the painter.

And there *had* been worry for him then. His early childhood before he was taken in by his cousin Matthew's family had been so miserable. He had still been anxious about his lack of ability to speak that the idea of bringing a child into the world who might share his affliction was almost unbearable. He'd pushed Charlotte away because of it, nearly lost her.

Even now the idea of that took his breath away.

When she'd told him she was pregnant with Jonathon, he knew his reaction had disappointed her. They had been happily married for months, and yet his old fears had rushed forward and spoiled that happy day. He'd spent the remaining time before his son's birth apprehensive and afraid. Only Jonathon's first cries, the ones that proved he would have the voice Ewan never had, freed him from his terror.

When she'd told him about Abigail a little more than a year later, he had tried so hard to be happy, and it had been a little better. But he still hadn't exactly celebrated as he waited for their child to be born and for the moment to come when he would know if she would one day be able to speak.

And perhaps *that* was why Charlotte had kept this from him. His heart sank. At Christmas, her favorite holiday thanks to the history this time of year held for them, she didn't want to face his worry, his fear. She didn't want to be disappointed by his lack of joy over her pregnancy.

They were happy. And he knew that there were few areas where he failed her. This was obviously one of them.

He turned to look at the children. They were now half-heartedly fighting over who would put the last block on their tower. Their nurse entered the room and smiled at him before she scolded, "There now! You two best not fight, for what will the Christmas spirits think of it?"

That seemed to snap the children back into line and Jonathon handed over the block to allow Abby to finish their tower.

"May I take them, Your Grace?" Miss Foster asked with a smile.

He nodded. Though the nurse didn't know their family hand language, if she needed more of a response he could bring out the silver notebook Charlotte had given to him years ago and write his responses to her queries. But she seemed to have none. She simply helped the children gather up their toys to be put away.

They waved to him as they were ushered from the room, leaving him alone to ponder the thoughts that now clouded his mind.

If he had let Charlotte down on this subject in the past, he needed to make it up to her. He needed to do it as soon as possible.

CHAPTER 3

Charlotte sat on the settee in utter comfort. She had long ago discarded her slippers, and her stockinged feet were tucked beneath her. At present she was being entertained by her husband and two children. The threesome sat on the floor before the fire, making shadow animals on the opposite wall together. From time to time, Ewan would lean over and subtly adjust Abigail's hands. The effect was to transform her shadows from mere blobs to something more akin to birds. Abby giggled when he did so, and he dropped a playful kiss to her nose every time.

Love swelled up in Charlotte, utterly powerful and infinitely true.

She had always felt that emotion when it came to Ewan. Even when they were children it had been there, innocent and hopeful. Her love for him had moved her to help him create a language all their own, in the hopes that she could find a place in his world. Or at least ease that troubled world a fraction.

As a young woman, she had confessed what she felt to him once, only to be rebuffed and brokenhearted by his response. He hadn't been ready. She had been almost destroyed.

And yet the love in her heart had survived. She had married

another man, but her feelings for Ewan had always been there. They'd grown every time they wrote letters where they pretended to be friends. It had pulsated within her when she saw him or heard his name from the lips of her friends or family. When her husband was gone…

Well, that love inside her had driven her to take a chance. And here they were. The day she married Ewan, Charlotte had thought she couldn't love him more. Five years proved that belief very wrong. Each day she found something new to love about him. Something bigger and stronger blossomed between them. And these moments with their children also made that love increase, transform and mature.

Soon there would be another child to add to their family. A fact she was very pleased about, though she did worry a little over Ewan's reaction. He was always concerned that his mutism would be passed to one of his children. Her pregnancies had been only marred by his haunted looks.

The nurse, Miss Foster, stepped into the room quietly. Charlotte knew their family was a little odd. Most in Society didn't spend each evening in some kind of family activity. She didn't care. She wanted these beautiful moments with the children, with Ewan. And Miss Foster had long ago stopped looking like it wasn't normal.

Charlotte smiled at the young woman, nodding slightly before she got to her feet.

"The night is getting long, my lovelies!" she teased, as she often did on these winter nights. "And Miss Foster is here to spirit you both away to dreamland."

"Awww," Abigail and Jonathon groaned at once.

"Yes, awwww," Ewan spelled out with a wink in her direction.

She laughed at his teasing, even as she shook her head. "You must go to bed."

"Why, Mama? Can't we stay up just a little longer?" Jonathon asked, giving his best pleading look that she was certain would melt hearts before she knew it.

"Because, my love, tomorrow is an exciting day and you need

your rest. Uncle Matthew and Aunt Isabel will be here with Daniel and Grandmother first thing in the morning." She referred to Ewan's aunt as grandmother and his cousin as his brother because that was what they were. They had raised him and loved him as that for most of his life.

Abigail's face lit up like she had forgotten her family was coming and now it was a marvelous surprise. "And da baby, Mama?"

Charlotte smiled at Ewan, but he had turned his face and was now focused on a loose string on the carpet. Abigail was currently very interested in Charlotte's brother's family. She saw their new daughter as a dolly, in a way. "Uncle Baldwin and Aunt Helena are coming before luncheon with the new baby and your other grandmother. And then all our other friends before nightfall. You'll see all the children and this house will be filled to the brim with excitement. So the sooner you sleep, the sooner we wake up and everyone will be here."

The children exchanged a look, like they were contemplating if this was a good enough reason not to argue for more time.

Ewan arched a brow toward them. "Listen to Mama," he signed with just enough sternness in his expression. "Say goodnight."

They knew the look. Both knew it brooked no refusal. That seemed to put an end to any attempt at arguing. The children sighed before they got up to tackle Ewan just as they had earlier in the hallway, all but smothering their father with goodnight kisses.

When they were finished with him, Charlotte dropped to her knees as they flew at her, gathering them into her arms. She loved the warmth of their little bodies, the sweet smell of their skin that still retained some of that baby perfection. She whispered words of love and good night to them before she let them go, turned them and gave them a gentle push toward Miss Foster.

"Race you!" Jonathon shouted as he took off past their nurse.

"No fair, Jonny!" Abigail wailed as she followed him.

Miss Foster inclined her head with a laugh. "Good night, Your Graces."

"Good luck, Miss Foster," Ewan signed, and Charlotte translated with a chuckle that their servant echoed as she followed her rambunctious charges.

When she was gone, Charlotte got up and moved to close the door. She faced Ewan, who was still reclining on the floor. He was watching her closely, though not with a look that said seduction. Like he was reading her.

He could do that so easily. She wasn't even shocked by it anymore when he read her mind by examining some turn of her lips or cock of her head.

"They're excited for the holiday," she said with a heavy sigh. "But I think we must talk to Jonathon about beginning to practice some calm. When he goes wild like that, he is a bad influence on Abby."

Ewan shrugged, though he was clearly not dismissing her concern. "When the new year starts, I will begin to work on it," he signed. "Although he's three. It is an age."

She laughed. "It is that. Great God."

He stretched his back. "I'm sure most of this behavior he'll grow out of naturally."

"I know," she said, watching as he slowly pushed to his feet.

It was funny, but even after all this time, she still wondered at the muscular unfolding of his long limbs, the way his chest flexed against his shirt. When he caught her looking at him, he arched a brow, his expression telling her she'd been caught ogling him.

"What?" she teased. "I like ogling you. I will never stop."

He smiled as he shook his head and reached out a hand to her. She took it, letting him lead her to the settee where he sat, drawing her down into his lap. She rested her head against his with a contented sigh. For a little while they let the silence hang between them.

"I'm almost ready for our guests," she said at last. "I finished the menus this afternoon."

He caught her hands between his and held them there before he began to sign around them. "Is there anything I can do to help?"

She pondered the question, knowing she was lucky have a husband who took such a great deal of the load from her shoulders.

"Well, all the dukes will want to hole up and play billiards together. I don't mind, of course. I don't think any of the duchesses do, for you don't all end up in the same room nearly enough."

He nodded. "Now that everyone is married and having children, we do see each other less. Perhaps we should arrange for some kind of 1797 Club gathering, just the gentlemen. Next year at the hunting lodge in Scotland?"

"I love that idea," she said. "We'll talk to them about it this week. However, if you want to help during the visit, be certain to encourage them to be social with the rest of us."

He shook his head. "You know none of them can be apart from their brides very long. I'm certain it will take no convincing whatsoever. But I will be mindful of the time."

She leaned in and kissed his temple, felt him shift beneath her as he turned his mouth up for her. She claimed it, kissing him gently before she cuddled a bit closer.

He cupped her hands between his again, staring as her fingers disappeared within the cocoon of his. Then he let out a long breath.

"I'm sorry," he signed.

She jolted at the way he signed those two words. Slowly, regretfully. His expression as he glanced at her was a little dark, a little sad.

"Why?" she asked, her voice barely above a whisper.

He stared into her face for a moment, his mouth still a deep frown. "I love our life, you know," he signed, his fingers slashing the words as they always did when he was frustrated or upset. She rarely saw that kind of movement from him anymore. She had no idea why he would exhibit it now.

"Of course you do," she reassured him. "I know that."

"Do you?" he asked. "Do you truly know? Do you truly understand how much waking up beside you means to me? That I sometimes just stare at you while you sleep and wonder if this is all some long, wonderful dream. That when I hold our children, it's like a part of me I never knew existed is brought to life?"

Tears swelled in her eyes at those lovely words. At his expression when he said them. They meant the world to her. "What's brought this on?" she asked, wiping at the tears that had begun to fall. "Not that I am complaining. If you want to wax poetic about our life together, you may do so at any time—it's very romantic."

He shifted, turning his face away a little. "I've just been thinking of how things were back when you came here five years ago, filled with spitfire determination to seduce me and force me to see what our future could be like."

"This time of year always makes me think of those days, too," she admitted. "I was so terrified you'd turn me away when I made the first attempt to seduce you."

He frowned. "You shouldn't have had to be. I loved you, I'd always loved you. I should have been strong enough to let that happen without forcing you to fight so hard for what we both wanted."

"Ewan," she said, sliding from this lap and taking a spot beside him on the settee. She turned to face him, catching both his hands and lifting them to her heart. "I don't know what brought this reflection on and the self-recrimination along with it, but you cannot beat yourself up like this. There were a great many good reasons for you to be uncertain of what I was offering. Was it a battle at times? Yes. But not one I ever regretted. Ultimately you accepted it."

His frown didn't lighten. There was a long hesitation, a silence that was not comfortable. She could see him struggling, and it broke her heart.

"I didn't accept it entirely, though, did I?" he signed at last.

She stared at him, confused. "What do you mean?"

"The children," he signed. "When you told me you were pregnant with Jonny and later Abby, my reaction was...well, I know it hurt you."

She moved her hands to cup his cheeks, feeling the roughness of his beard against her palms, smoothing her thumbs along his cheekbones. "The only thing that has ever truly hurt me is that you couldn't see your own worth."

He smiled then, briefly, a shadow. "You taught me that. Back then you put me on a path, and it's different now, I hope you know that. *I'm* different."

"You're you, Ewan," she whispered. "There is no need for you to ever be different. If you accept yourself more, that's all I ever wanted."

He leaned in and kissed her briefly. When he pulled away, she cocked her head. "What's brought all this on?"

He shifted, and she sensed the deep discomfort in him. Her heartrate increased as he lifted his hands and signed, "Jonathon apparently overheard a conversation recently about..."

He reached out and covered her belly with one hand. With the other he slashed out four letters as his gaze held hers. "B-A-B-Y."

CHAPTER 4

The look of horror on Charlotte's face erased all of Ewan's remaining questions about whether what his son had heard was true. Charlotte was obviously pregnant and shocked that he had exposed the news she had withheld from him. Her shaking hands dropped down to cover his on her stomach as she stared at him in silent surprise.

He slid his hand away so he could sign, "I understand why you didn't tell me, Charlotte."

"I don't think you do," she whispered.

He shook his head. "I was so afraid the first two times. So worried the babies wouldn't be perfect. That they would be like…like me."

Her face crumpled and a tear escaped and slid down her cheek. "You *are* perfect."

"No, I'm not. But neither are they. No one is, are they?" he signed. "And if this baby—" He brushed her stomach a second time with his fingertips, in wonder that there was a son or daughter there, being protected and housed by his wife's body. "If this baby was born and couldn't speak, I want you know that I no longer feel like that's something to be mourned or feared."

She blinked and her lips parted in wonder. "I—you don't?"

"No. I was sitting with a not-quite-two-year-old and a three-year-old today, and they were signing without even thinking about it. Even better, they both understood everything I signed to them. The new baby will learn to speak with our language, Charlotte. Just as Jonny and Abby have. Our family language."

Her smile broadened. "Just ours, no one else's."

"And I'm certain if he couldn't speak, he would learn to write earlier so he could communicate with those in the outside world. I did just that, even though my father tried to deny me any education." A bitter taste filled his mouth. "I overcame what they tried to do to me."

"You did," she agreed, lifting her chin as if she would like to battle the long-dead man who had hurt him. Ewan had no doubt she would win.

"I realize now that if the baby inside of you was born mute, he wouldn't be held back that way. Or treated as broken or damaged. I would *know* he wasn't. My child would never be ousted like I was, abused like I was. His cousins and his friends would never even see his mutism as something different because they would be so accustomed to it."

"Your friends *are* used to it. When we were in London last, I watched Baldwin hand you a quill when your pencil broke without even seeming to notice he'd done it," Charlotte said with a laugh. "He didn't even miss a beat."

"I have been nothing but accepted by them my entire life," Ewan signed with a nod. "Sometimes it was hard for me to take that in, but the truth is, I was always part of a group who would protect and love me to the end. Not because they felt I was weak, but because we're a family. And you, you are the leader of that family. The most important member. I don't doubt for a second that if this baby couldn't speak, you would be his greatest champion."

"Or hers," she said.

He grinned. "Or hers. But Charlotte, I need you to know, really *know*, that I feel *no* fear in this news. Only joy. Because I am not afraid of what I am or what I'm not anymore. I would never say that being mute isn't a huge part of who I am. But it is not the only part. I have no fear of passing on any part of myself to my child."

She stared up at him, her smile wide and broad now. Filled with happiness and joy and love. He drowned in it. Charlotte's smile had always been his undoing. He knew it always would be.

"My love," she said softly. "To hear you say all that brings me such joy. Especially since I know how difficult it has been for you to overcome the feelings of inadequacy that your horrible father and mother and brothers put on you during your most formative years. But I want you to understand what my motives were in not telling you I was pregnant."

He shifted. He knew she deserved to be able to speak about her disappointment or worry. He wanted to be open to that, though he already felt enormous guilt in it. "Go ahead," he signed.

"I didn't keep the secret about the new baby out of fear. Certainly not out of some sense of frustration in how you reacted in the past."

"No?" he signed, relief flooding him.

"*This* was your Christmas gift," she said, touching her stomach with a laugh. "Or at least the most important one. I had every intention of telling you tomorrow, after the arrivals of our friends and family. It was to be part of our celebration, timed as a whisper as the clock struck midnight and Christmas Day was begun."

He blinked at that clarification. One he hadn't actually thought of with his mind turning on his own regrets over his past behavior.

"So I have made this great confession and ruined your Christmas surprise for nothing?" he signed with a smile and a shake of his head.

She touched his hand. "No, my love, not at all. We talked a great deal about your image of yourself and your worries about our future all those years ago when everything seemed so uncertain. But since our marriage, we haven't really taken the time, have we? To reevaluate where we stand, what we think."

He shrugged. "I suppose not."

"And yet we're in such a different place from where we began. So maybe this misunderstanding was the perfect opening for us to talk about a subject that has held less and less power over the years." She lifted his hand to her lips and kissed it. "I know how much our family means to you. And I would never hide something this important from you out of a fit of pique or worry. I pledge that to you today."

He nodded. "I think I knew that. I was just so surprised by what Jonathon said and then the realization that he was right. I thought back to how I reacted in the past and jumped to a conclusion. But I'm not sorry. After all, it helped me look at where I am, who I am. I accept myself."

Tears flowed down her cheeks, but they were happy tears. Ones that lit up her expression and warmed him all the way to his core. To the heart she had owned from the first moment he met her, all those decades ago.

"You could not have said that when we first shared a Christmas at this house five years ago," she said. "You couldn't have even thought it."

He shook his head. "No," he signed.

He thought of his life, which had begun so fearful, so lonely, so dangerous. He had been threatened with asylum, with death, with abandonment. Until he came to live with his aunt and uncle and Matthew, there had been no certainty.

And then...there was. And though it had taken many years, many instances where his faith in his friends or Charlotte was proven right, he had developed more confidence in himself as well. He knew his strengths, his intelligence, his foibles, all of which had nothing to do with his ability to speak.

He smiled at her, feeling the sting in his eyes, the tears that, like hers, were joyful.

"I'm so thrilled about the baby," he signed. "I cannot wait to meet him or her. To see this new child fold into our family and become their own person. I am so excited to see it all. And to fall in love with you even more because you are the mother any child would be lucky to have."

She smiled. "Thank you. And thank you for this gift. You telling me that you are finally able to accept yourself, your pleasure at this news…Ewan, it is the best gift you could ever give me for Christmas or any other day."

"So I should take this ring back?" he signed before he tugged the ring box he'd been carrying around all day from his pocket and popped it open.

She stared down at the sparkling square-cut sapphire, which was flanked by diamonds. He could see how much she liked it. Charlotte was not a vain woman, but she was stylish and liked pretty things.

She glanced up to his face and her smile was wide. "Oh, well, since you've already purchased it, it would be silly to take it back."

He grinned as he took the ring from the box and slid it on her finger. As it shone in the firelight, she leaned forward and kissed him.

And all was right with the world.

AUTHOR'S NOTE

If you enjoyed Silent Night, check out Ewan and Charlotte's original emotional romance, *The Silent Duke*. And enjoy all the books in the 1797 Club Series:

The Daring Duke
Her Favorite Duke
The Broken Duke
The Silent Duke
The Duke of Nothing
The Undercover Duke
The Duke of Hearts
The Duke Who Lied
The Duke of Desire
The Last Duke (Coming November 13)

EXCERPT: THE LAST DUKE

He got up but didn't back away. He came closer, settling back into a seat next to her. Now she could smell him. A soapy, clean, fresh and masculine smell.

"I pulled you out of the water," he continued. "And my world shattered when you weren't breathing."

She blinked. It was all she could do in the face of this unexpected confession, in the face of all the emotion in his voice and his dark eyes. She watched his hand lift, hesitate, and then he touched her cheek.

It was like someone set her body aflame. He slid his fingers along her cheekbone and tingles flared in their wake, making her aware, once more, of what a precarious position they were in. He ought not to be touching her while she lay in his bed.

But she wasn't about to stop him.

Nor did she stop him as he leaned in, closer, close enough that his breath stirred her lips. And then he kissed her. For a brief moment, it was the lightest of touches. A chaste brush of lips on lips. Then his fingers burrowed into her hair, cupping her scalp as he tilted her head, and the world exploded.

His mouth became insistent. She opened to him without understanding why and tasted his tongue as he breached her lips. She reached for him, trying to find an anchor as she lost all sense of time, of space, of propriety, of everything but the feel of him as he touched her.

She was alive. Back from the dead. And she understood it now, felt what she had nearly lost under that dark water. This. This pleasure, this wicked bliss, this dark desire that pulsed through her entire body and settled in the most private and inappropriate places.

But she didn't care about appropriateness anymore. Or whether he liked her or judged her. All she cared about was that she didn't want this heated, sparkling moment to end.

All she wanted was more.

End of Excerpt

CPSIA information can be obtained
at www.ICGtesting.com
Printed in the USA
LVHW041428301018
595356LV00004B/543/P